Blood
and
Bone

V. M. Giambanco was born in Italy. After her degree in English and Drama at Goldsmiths, she worked for a classical music retailer and as a bookseller in her local bookshop. She started in films as an editor's apprentice in a 35mm cutting room and since then has worked on many award-winning UK and US pictures, from small independent projects to large studio productions. V. M. Giambanco lives in London.

www.vmgiambanco.com
@vm_giambanco

Also by V. M. Giambanco

The Gift of Darkness
The Dark

V. M. GIAMBANCO

Blood and Bone

AN ALICE MADISON THRILLER

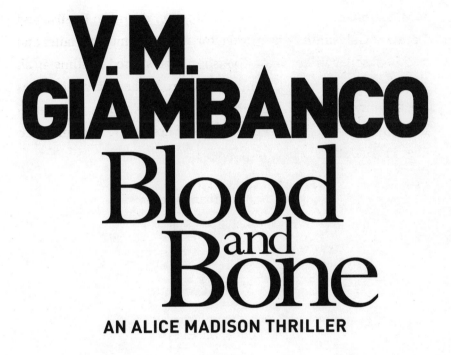

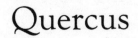

Quercus

First published in Great Britain in 2015 by

Quercus Publishing Ltd
Carmelite House
50 Victoria Embankment
London EC4Y 0DZ

An Hachette UK company

A CIP catalogue record for this book is available
from the British Library

HB ISBN 978 178429 139 6
TPB ISBN 978 178429 143 3
EBOOK ISBN 978 178429 141 9

This book is a work of fiction. Names, characters,
businesses, organizations, places and events are
either the product of the author's imagination
or used fictitiously. Any resemblance to
actual persons, living or dead, events or
locales is entirely coincidental.

10 9 8 7 6 5 4 3 2 1

Typeset by CC Book Production

Printed and bound in Great Britain by Clays Ltd, St Ives plc

For Gerald

Prologue

Alice Madison, twelve years of age, listened out for sounds beyond the hammering of her heart. All was quiet. The rain tapped over the trees outside and the road that led to Friday Harbor was blessedly empty this time of day. Mrs Quint from next door would get up any minute now and feed her chickens and Alice had to decide quickly whether to rush and be out of the house before that blabbermouth was in her yard or delay until she had gone back into her kitchen and out of sight. It was hardly a choice: Alice wanted – needed – to get out of there as fast as her feet would carry her.

She took stock of her bedroom: everything wrecked, broken, smashed. Alice took a deep breath and grabbed her rucksack. She crammed in a few essentials and one book she couldn't bear to leave behind – *Treasure Island*, which her mother used to read to her – and managed to tie her sleeping bag in a tight bundle at the bottom of the bag.

Her eyes moved over the familiar surfaces, the familiar objects. She couldn't stay and, one way or the other, she wouldn't come back: all her life up to that point would be held in that rucksack, and Alice had to travel light.

She stood on tiptoe and took down from a shelf a pink wooden box that had survived the onslaught. She emptied the beaded bracelets and the WWF badges with the mournful panda onto her unmade bed and lifted the fake bottom: three tight rolls of bank-notes had been flattened, held together by elastic hairbands. She shoved them into her jeans back pocket and placed the box on her bedside table. Her Mickey Mouse clock told her it was 7.03 a.m. She picked up her baseball bat and her mitt – the ball went into a pocket of the rucksack – and surveyed her room. Time to go.

Alice tiptoed down the hall, stopping only to listen to her father's breathing and snoring lightly in his room. She closed the front door behind her and started down the side of the house, long steps, almost but not quite running. She was pleased she didn't have to push the creaking garage door open: her red bicycle was leaning as usual against the work table. She walked it up to the road, got on and pushed off.

Alice pulled down her faded blue baseball cap and the raindrops drummed on the visor. It would stop soon. The mist hung low but the heat of the coming day would burn through it by mid-morning. The last thing she heard as she turned the corner was Mrs Quint stepping into her yard and calling out to her chickens.

Alice pedaled under the soft rain. She still couldn't believe what had happened in the last few hours and her heart was beating like it wanted to burst out of her chest and get clear away from her.

The mist was heavy on the San Juan Valley Road and Alice stuck close to the ditch in case an unlikely car was to speed past. At that time of the day the road was deserted – lush green fields and patches of trees on both sides – but you never know. San Juan Island was a tourist resort between Washington State and Vancouver Island; it was a stone's throw from Canadian waters and any traffic was probably guests of the bed and breakfasts scattered in the valley. The island counted roughly 10,000 permanent residents and in the summer months the number swelled to almost double. Alice had lived there for a little over a year – long enough to start making friends, camp out a lot in the mild evenings and watch her mother die only weeks after a late cancer diagnosis. Alice sped past the Turners' place. Her father was all she had left now. Except, that was not true either, not anymore.

There was a long stretch just before the Valley Road became Spring Street and Alice heard hooves in the paddock running alongside the bike; she stopped and whistled. The horse came out of the fog – a pale shape the same color as the sky – and it watched her, pawing the dirt a few feet away from the fence. The horse was curious and bored and had often trotted up to the edge of the enclosure to see who was walking past. Alice didn't ride but, as a child born in a big city – Los Angeles – and growing up in a variety of charmless urban zip codes, she was enchanted and delighted by horses. This one was as wary as they come but it recognized her as she cycled back and forth to school and always came to the fence; once it had let her pet the hard space between its dark eyes. It didn't come close today but regarded her cautiously. Suddenly, with hardly any sound on the damp grass, it twisted around and disappeared back into the mist.

Alice looked at the spot where it had stood then shook herself and got back on the bike: she seemed to remember that a ferry left Friday Harbor for Anacortes and the mainland a few minutes after 8 a.m. She would catch her breath, think and make a plan once she was on it, but all that mattered was getting to the harbor, buying a ticket, and making sure the smallest possible number of people saw her. She had to get away from this island, from the one-story bungalow with her destroyed bedroom, and from her father.

As she got close to the town Alice passed a couple of cars driving in the opposite direction; the fields and the trees were replaced by an old-fashioned main street with wooden houses on both sides and a few neighborhoods stretching behind them. Alice slowed right down as she hit Spring Street: some coffee houses and diners were open for the breakfast crowd – or as close to a crowd as it ever got – and she didn't want to be noticed. With perfect timing her stomach started to grumble and she ignored it.

On the left she passed the Palace Movie Theater and tried not to think about the last time she had sat on the wooden seats, eating popcorn from a paper bag. It had been days and it felt like years. Mr Burrows who sold tickets and snacks from the booth also read the ferry announcements during the holidays and during term time was the caretaker of the Friday Harbor Middle School, which meant he *knew* Alice, the kid with the Nevada accent who had joined the class the previous year.

Alice looked left and right and kept pedaling. If she was extremely lucky Mr Burrows wouldn't be anywhere near the ferries this morning. She noticed a few groups of tourists walking towards the harbor and some car traffic joining the ferry holding lanes on East Street. The rain had turned to drizzle and she felt warm in her sweatshirt and jeans, perspiration trickling between her shoulder blades. She turned the corner and the ferry was there – massive and lumbering in the still waters, the loading-bay door already open.

Alice looked over her shoulder, not sure of what she expected to see. Not her father – she knew he would sleep until midday, as he usually did after that kind of night. For everyone else she was just a little girl out for a bike ride.

Alice exhaled then and wiped her face with her hands. She was angry and scared, and even if the bicycle had stopped the ground felt unsteady under her feet. She saw the line of tourists waiting to buy walk-on tickets and watched them for a moment. An elderly couple, a single man, a family group of five with teenagers, a couple in their twenties. Alice watched and waited. She saw a young couple with bicycles and slipped into the queue right after them. When it was her turn she passed a ten-dollar bill under the glass partition and said: 'Anacortes.' The clerk – a man she didn't know – gave her her change and she quickly followed the young couple onto the pier, walked onto the ferry like they did, and locked her bicycle in a slot next to theirs. No one looked twice at the little girl. As the cars started to drive onto the ship Alice climbed the stairs to the passenger decks.

There was one more thing she needed to do before she could allow herself to sit down: she found a restroom, checked that no one was in the cubicles and locked the door. She had maybe a few minutes but hopefully it would be enough. She leant her rucksack on the sink and looked for the thing that had caught her eye as she had left her bedroom, and found it.

Alice stared in the mirror and she knew what she would see: a skinny twelve-year-old girl. Not a chance that she could pass for anyone older than that. Her father would wake up and see the switchblade knife buried two inches deep into his bedside table; he'd look at the destruction in her bedroom and he'd know that she had meant business. Nevertheless, he'd probably think she'd gone to one of her favorite hideouts and would not start looking for her until the afternoon, maybe even nightfall.

Alice took off her baseball cap, smoothed down her long straight hair and with her scissors she cut off everything below her ears. The fringe was easy and she cut it long – like Ronny Kopecki at school – the kind of fringe that falls almost past the eyes and teachers hate.

The locks fell into the sink, dark gold streaked by the sun; she scooped them up and threw them in the bin, then rinsed the sink for good measure. Alice looked into the mirror again. She was wearing a pale pink T-shirt under her hoodie. Well, shoot, that would have to go. She dug out her navy Mariners shirt and balled up the pink one at the bottom of her rucksack. Maybe, just maybe, if she kept her voice low and her answers short. The cut was not a bad job but no hairdressing prizes there. She didn't care about that: the important thing was to look different, perhaps to pass as a boy long enough to give her the slightest advantage over whoever was going to come after her. And somebody would, that she knew for sure.

Chapter 1

Present day

The nightclub sat a little off the main road, surrounded by trees on one side and a warehouse on the other. It was almost eleven and the parking lot was full. The music – a series of eighties classics – had found its way out of the squat building and low thumping pulsed in the chilly air.

Two men sat in a gray Mazda with the engine running and the heating turned up high. They had been parked for half an hour, waiting. They already knew when they drove there that the club would be closed for a private event – a bachelor party – and still they sat in their car, drinking and smoking in silence. The waiting felt almost as good as what was to come later; it gave their enterprise the guise of a hunt.

The club door opened, spilling orange light on the wet concrete with a blast of U2, and a woman walked out. One of the men wiped the condensation on the windshield with his sleeve to get a better look at her. His eyes tracked her long strides as she reached an SUV.

'Here we go,' he said and he pulled the handle to get out of the car.

Alice Madison felt the bite of the air, and it was a relief after the heavy warmth and the alcohol fumes inside. Her Land Rover Freelander was parked close by and she was rummaging in the back seat when she heard car doors opening and closing behind her and steps approaching.

'Hello there,' a man said.

Madison turned. 'Hello,' she replied. Two men stood a few yards away; she didn't recognize either of them.

'Club's closed,' the taller one said. 'Bachelor party.'

'Yes,' Madison replied, and knew instantly that they were not guests: they were two guys in their late twenties – only a handful of years younger than she was – who wanted to make conversation with a stranger in a parking lot and who would definitely blow a 0.1 if breathalyzed.

'Do you work in the club?' The man continued. 'I've been here before but I've never seen you, and I'd sure remember some-one as cute as you.' He grinned and it was neither friendly nor pretty.

His friend giggled and darted a look at the lot. No one else was about. Madison clocked him doing it.

'No, I don't work here,' she said, politely, but that was all the chat they were going to get from her, and she closed the car door. The plastic bag in her hand was wrapped around a DVD case; she had found what she wanted and it was time to go back inside. The men stood between her and the club door.

'If you're not a waitress then you must be the *entertainment*,' the taller man said, and he looked her up and down. There was a nasty slick behind the words and Madison smelled rank sweat and beer in the cold November air.

She took the measure of them: white, six feet tall or thereabouts, built and dressed like they did their running in gyms and their fighting on the Xbox. *Had they been drinking in their car, waiting for the right person to leave the club?*

'Gentlemen, I heartily recommend that you ask the staff inside to call you a taxi to take you back wherever you've come from,' she said and moved forward, but they blocked her path.

The shorter one opened his mouth and his voice was reedy and too high for someone his size. 'I don't think she likes you,' he told his friend.

Madison sighed. 'You're having a really bad night, you just don't know it yet. Go home, before you do something stupid.'

Their smiles went away. They were somewhere between tipsy and drunk and yet lucid enough to understand that for some reason the woman in front of them was neither charmed nor intimidated by their efforts.

This is going to go one of two ways. Madison squared up to them – hoping they were smarter than they looked but ready in case they were just as dumb as she thought.

'We only wanted to make friends, you prissy little bitch,' the tall one said quietly as he stepped forward.

Madison stood still. He had a few inches on her and clearly believed that it would be enough. *Enough for what?* Madison asked herself.

'You've just done a show for the party, I think you should do one for us too,' he continued.

Three people in a parking lot. Many cars but nobody else within earshot. Madison did not want to feel overconfident: there were two of them and only one of her, and *cocky* is what gets you into trouble. She was dimly aware of the familiar weight around her ankle. 'Have you done this before?' she asked the one who seemed to be the leader. The small pulse of her anger was like a ping on a radar.

He blinked. 'What?'

'This. Have you ever approached women and hit on them and been a complete asshole?'

'You have no idea—'

'Is this what you do on a Friday night? Is this where you come and look for your next meaningful relationship?'

'What?'

Madison tried to step on her temper, but it didn't work. 'I'll speak more slowly for you. Is this the first time you've approached a woman in a nightclub parking lot? It isn't, is it? Have you and Wonder Boy here ever managed to get one cornered? Have you ever actually managed to convince one to come back with you? What happened then?'

'All we wanted was to be friendly and offer you some extra work. Would have paid you for it too. Do you think you're too good for us?'

He was wide in the shoulders and the dark threat in his voice came easy to him. Madison could have ended it there and then; she could have told them her name and job title. All they had was bluster and the illusion of muscle and her words would have stopped them dead. She gazed from one to the other. She was not afraid, no. Next to her average work day they were merely an annoyance. Nevertheless, Madison considered, there they were, trying to chat her up and bully her at the same time. And so she did not speak; she breathed deeply, feeling a reckless calm that rested on her anger. She knew the taller one would move first.

'Do you think you're too good for us?' he repeated.

'You have a chance to do the smart thing and walk away now,' she replied.

'Why would I want to do that?'

'Because when you look back on this evening you will feel either very smart or very foolish, depending on what you're going to do next. Quite frankly, I don't care either way, but it would save us both a lot of time if you called for a taxi and went home.'

Watch their hands.

'Shut up,' the tall man hissed and his right hand went for Madison's arm.

Snake fast she took hold of his wrist and with a quick twist she had it in a lock. The DVD dropped onto the ground. Her other hand went to the back of the man's neck and she grabbed him and pushed him down. Now his arm was extended painfully high behind him and the slightest pressure from Madison made him yelp.

The friend moved forward and her voice snapped him out of it. 'You move an inch and I break your friend's arm.'

He stopped.

'Happy now?' she asked them.

The shorter man shifted his weight, raised his hands and leant forward. 'Hey,' he said.

Madison pushed his friend's arm a little higher.

'Stop moving!' The taller one shouted to his pal with a yelp. 'Just fucking stop moving.'

The man froze where he was. This was new, this was not some-thing they had planned for. His mouth hung open. Madison let them appreciate the situation for a moment then she let go of the man's neck and her hand went inside her blazer; her badge caught the light from the club's neon sign.

'Seattle Police Department. You, close your mouth and lie down on the ground, hands behind your head. You too,' she addressed the taller man. 'I'm letting your arm go, mind you don't fall forward on your face. There you go. Easy. My name is Detective Alice Madison, SPD Homicide.'

The taller man shuffled forward, almost slipped and caught himself. He looked up at her and somehow his world had tilted on its axis. Madison saw it in his eyes: two minutes ago he was about to take a woman home for some Friday-night fun and now he was sprawled on the concrete staring at a detective's badge. Life was not fair.

'It's a cop's bachelor party,' she said. 'Every single car in this lot belongs to a cop.'

She wanted to say something like *you crashed the wrong party, guys*, but it felt crass. There was the real possibility that these two morons had coerced women to go back to their place and do God-knows-what. Some might have followed them because it was easier than getting into a fight if all they wanted was a lap dance. Was it though?

Madison had to call dispatch, get a patrol car over and give a statement. She was pleased that she was stone-cold sober.

It started to rain and big fat drops smacked on the ground.

'Stay right where you are, fellas,' she said; one of the waiters had come out for a breath of fresh air and she waved him over.

'If it's a bachelor party,' the shorter one muttered under his breath, 'what the hell are you doing there anyway?'

At the far end of the club wall, invisible in the shadows under the low hanging roof, Detective Chris Kelly stomped his cigarette into the ground. For a moment there things had gotten interesting; for a moment it looked like Madison might have been in trouble. It hadn't lasted long but it had been the highlight of his evening.

*

The patrol officers bundled the two men in the back of their blue-and-white and told Madison to give their regards to the groom. Their charges had been breathalyzed and had indeed blown a 0.1. White powder in the tiny clear plastic bag in the front pocket of the shorter man's jeans turned out to be cocaine – a minute amount, for sure, but possession of a controlled dangerous substance in Washington State would ensure they received more than a slap on the wrist.

Madison walked back inside; she was calm and yet the levity of the evening had gone and been replaced by a dull anger that had nowhere to go. Early Springsteen boomed from the speakers, there was not a stripper in sight and a local stand-up comedian had just entertained the guests with a routine on the daily life of a cop. The audience had loved it. She looked around the room: the groom, Homicide Detective Andrew Dunne, stood by the bar with the best man – his partner, Detective Kyle Spencer – and nodded to Madison when he saw her. His red hair stuck out in all directions, as usual, and his color was high; he spoke fast and laughed easily. She nodded back. Kyle Spencer was second-generation Japanese and in every way the polar opposite of Dunne, who was finally getting married in his late thirties. They wore suits but the ties had been lost sometime after the second Scotch.

When Madison had joined the unit two years earlier they had treated her as if she had always been part of the team; it had meant a lot in those days when she had so much to prove. *Two years*. Madison could hardly believe it. Two years that in her mind split neatly into the first six months and the following year and a half. She stopped that train of thought and headed for a table in the corner.

Detective Sergeant Kevin Brown, Madison's partner, was in his early fifties, ginger going gray, and looked about done with the day and the party. Madison sat next to him on the banquette and he pointed at a fresh drink.

'Done?' he asked her.

She took a sip of the Coke he'd got for her and nodded. 'One of them had a little blow in his pocket he'd forgotten about.'

'What a shocker.'

'I know, what with them being such great guys and all.' Madison paused, feeling around the edges of her dark mood and not knowing what to do with it. 'They are going to be checked against local complaints in case they've done it before. Harassed women, I mean.'

'You okay?'

Brown had gone to her side the second he had heard. The two men stretched out on the concrete under the rain had seemed so very young to him. And Madison – who was standing over them – had looked angry enough to kick a bull on its birthday, like his father would say.

Madison shrugged.

'Why didn't you tell them?' he said.

'What?' she replied, but she knew what he'd meant.

'Why didn't you tell them who you were the second they approached you?'

Madison took another sip. 'Most women don't have a badge they can hide behind. The next time they think about doing that again I want them to remember that I didn't need the badge.'

Brown had seen Madison at full tilt in the best and the worst times of their last two years. He knew there was something more there, but he didn't press her; when she wanted to get it off her chest she would. She was not *most women*, he wanted to say, but instead he clinked her glass with his cream soda.

Lieutenant Fynn – their shift commander – slipped heavily into the banquette seat next to Brown.

'What time is it?' he asked, getting himself heard above 'Dancing in the Dark'. They had all been up since 3 a.m. for the arrest of a robbery/murder suspect and he was ready to go home.

As Fynn began a tale from Dunne's days on patrol, Madison's attention wandered. Andy knew so many people that his best man had to organize two different parties to fit everybody in. Madison had never met an officer in Seattle and King County who didn't know Andy one way or the other, and most of them had stories to tell.

Tonight the club would see most of the festivities, including the screening of the DVD Madison had brought in – a merciless digest of Dunne's life so far, cut by a pal in Public Affairs. In the early hours Spencer, Dunne and his brothers and cousins would travel east to a rented cabin to fish and quietly sleep off their massive hangovers. However, Madison was due at the precinct at 11 a.m. the following morning, which is why she had stuck to Coke. On Sunday, to complete the set, she would be at the bride's bachelorette party – Stacey Roberts from Traffic – who had opted for a spa day at the Four Seasons. Madison had never been to a spa and she was glad she had not been asked to be a bridesmaid. She had known Stacey for years and they were friends – not the kind of friend you call at 4 a.m. if your car breaks down, but a friend nevertheless. Madison was glad she wouldn't have to wear the heavy silk fuchsia dress; she was glad to be on the periphery of the celebration and not smack in the middle of it; glad to wish them all the future happiness they deserved and, most of all, glad to evade the questions about her own private life.

Fynn continued his tale and Madison's eye caught Detective Chris Kelly talking with someone from Vice. Kelly had been watching her and looked away when she'd turned. *Nothing new there*, she thought. There was something reassuring in the predictability of their relationship: they had detested each other from day one and the feeling had not slowly turned into a grudging respect for each other's skills and capabilities; in fact, over the months, it had hardened into a ball of loathing that colored each word and each exchange. The brief period they had partnered – while Brown was on medical leave – had only confirmed their opinions of each other.

The music cut off and Spencer took to a small stage with a mike. There were whoops and hollers as the film of Dunne's life started, and in the club's half-light Madison forgot all about Kelly and the men in the parking lot.

A little after 1 a.m. Madison left and drove home; she could still smell the club on her skin. It had stopped raining and she wound down the windows to let the cold air flow through. The evening had swung from joyous to nasty and back to a rowdy cheer that had left her wiped out and unsettled at the end of very long day. She drove automatically – for once without music – and every turn in the road was as familiar to her as if she had drawn it herself on the map.

Madison had lived in the same house since she was thirteen – except for the years in college in Chicago. It was her grandparents' home and it would always be her grandparents' home, even though they had both passed away. Three Oaks was a quiet, upper-middle-class suburb on the southwestern edge of Seattle, shaped by Puget Sound on one side and thickets of firs on the other; the crop of houses hid among the evergreens, and the backyards rolled into the water.

Madison let herself in and, tired as she was, she still could not go straight to bed. She crossed the living room and opened the

French doors to the deck. It was pitch black. She didn't need to see the landscape: the water at the end of the lawn was a whisper over the gravel beach and the trees to her right creaked and ticked in the breeze.

Madison was not looking forward to the meeting in the morning: she didn't want to think about it because she knew where her thoughts would run, where they always ran. She waited until she was chilled to her bones then turned away from the night and went inside.

In the darkness she unbuckled the ankle holster with her off-duty piece – a snub-nosed .38 – and slid it under the bed. She toed off her boots and stepped out of her jeans. Her clothes in a heap on the wooden floor, she slid under the comforter and felt the distant warmth of Aaron's body, stretched out on the other side of the bed. He slept soundly, peacefully, and Madison – awake and still under the heavy quilt – wished for some of the same.

Chapter 2

The following morning started with a pale gray wash over the lawn, the water and Vashon Island across the Sound. Technically it was Madison's day off but the meeting had been scheduled for the convenience of the other people attending and she had agreed – it would probably be the only concession they'd get from her.

She was making coffee in the kitchen when Aaron padded in. They had been seeing each other for just over six months and it still felt new when he stayed over and would stagger into her kitchen in the morning, thick with sleep and wearing only his sweat bottoms and a T-shirt.

'Morning,' he said.

'Morning.' She passed him a steaming mug.

'How was it?'

Madison had known Aaron Lever since she was thirteen and he was a couple of years older; he was a cousin of her best friend, Rachel, and they had met again when he had returned to Seattle after a divorce, two children and the sale of his software company in San Francisco. He had been a skinny, handsome blond boy who couldn't part from his video games and he had grown up to be a very tall, handsome man with fair hair and kind eyes.

It had taken some time to persuade Madison to go out on a date with him, but six months ago she had run out of excuses. Both were keenly aware that the lure of a relationship with a long-lost childhood friend was almost too strong to resist. Nevertheless, over the last months they had filled the empty hours in each other's life as if they had been together for years. It had been surprisingly easy.

'It was loud and funny and Andy had a great time, which was kind of the point of the whole thing.'

'Is he freaking out yet?'

'About the wedding? No, I don't think so. Well, maybe, quietly and on the inside.'

Madison broke five eggs into a saucepan as the butter melted and sizzled.

'The only girl at a bachelor party and you didn't even have one drink,' he said. 'That's very sad.'

'Just as well.' Madison stirred the eggs. 'A couple of guys confronted me in the parking lot, thought I was a stripper, tried to grab me and—'

'Are you all right?' Aaron had frozen with two plates halfway out of the cabinet. His eyes were wide with concern.

Madison was thrown out of her story and looked at herself through his eyes.

'What happened?' he said.

I got one in a wrist lock and almost broke his arm, his friend wanted to play silly games but he changed his mind.

'I persuaded them that it was a bad idea,' Madison said quickly, 'and they finished the night in a cell. One of them had a little coke too. A Friday-night special, I suppose.'

Aaron put the dishes on the table. 'And you're sure you're all right?'

'Last night I was angry, today . . .' She shrugged.

Aaron smiled a little. His ex-wife only used ATMs inside the banks and wouldn't even stop at petrol stations if she was driving alone at night.

They ate the eggs at the kitchen table then Madison got up to get ready. Aaron would find things to do around the house until she was done with her meeting and then they would go and do the things couples do. A movie, a restaurant, maybe meeting her friend Rachel – and Neal, her husband.

It was a different life from where she had been only a year ago.

It was what grown-ups did, Madison reflected under the shower. She hadn't told Aaron what the meeting was about – and in all probability wouldn't tell him later either.

Chapter 3

The conference room in the precinct was overheated. Madison walked in ten minutes early with a cup of coffee and the others were already there. Special Agents A. J. Parker and Curtis Guzman from the Los Angeles office of the Drug Enforcement Agency stopped talking and stood up when she came in. The suits were freshly pressed and so were the smiles. Madison saw they had already been there a while: half-empty cups and papers were scattered on the table.

'Detective Madison, thank you for meeting us on your day off. We took the earliest flight and we'll be heading back home when we're done.' Within the pair Parker was clearly the communication specialist; Guzman had said maybe seven words in their previous meetings.

'Agent Parker, Agent Guzman, good to see you back in town – but I'm not sure we couldn't have done this over the phone.'

Parker smiled again. 'Sometimes it's better to meet face to face, it's more personal, more direct.'

Madison took a sip of her coffee and sat down. This was the fourth time they had met, always at the request of the DEA. The first time she had briefed them on a kidnap and attempted murder by members of a cartel they were investigating. She had rescued the hostage in a field near the Canadian border and had been able to identify one of the cartel's men – even if he had escaped. Three men had died that day; one of them had been shot and killed by Madison. She had never pointed her piece at a person and squeezed the trigger before and she thought about it still from time to time, the way you run your finger over a scar to check it's still there. She had spoken about it with Stanley Robinson, the psychologist she had to meet as dictated by department policy after a firearm was discharged. They had spoken about many things and not spoken about just as many others.

'We have some news about Roberto Salvo,' Parker said.

Salvo was the cartel operative Madison had identified for them.

'We have him, so to speak,' he continued.

'You have arrested him?'

'We have found him, tucked away pretty much as he had been left a few months ago.'

Madison remembered him as clearly as if she had just spoken to him in the hallway – the smart suit and the horrors buried in his voice.

'What happened to him?' She suddenly knew what Parker would say and felt something icy cold between her shoulder blades.

'Knife wound to the neck, almost decapitated him. A right-handed person, about five feet eleven inches to six feet tall. Someone who was confident enough, strong enough and mad enough to take Salvo on by himself with a knife.' Parker leant forward. 'Not a firearm, no. A knife. A dangerous weapon to use if your target is armed, as Salvo most certainly would have been.'

Madison said nothing.

Parker opened a file and a close-up of the remains was clipped to the first page. It was beyond description. It was the result of a violent death, decomposition and possibly animal infestation. Madison had seen the bright sheen in Parker's eyes when he'd turned the page and she merely nodded.

'It takes a special kind of guy to do that,' he said. 'Do you know anyone who might fit that description?'

Madison had only one name: the man whose life she had saved that day, the man alleged to have killed nine and maimed two human beings.

'Cameron,' she said.

'John Cameron, the one and only. The pathologist estimated that Salvo was killed about nine months ago – that is to say, nine months after the kidnap you foiled – enough time for Cameron to get his health back, his blade sharpened and his ducks in a row.'

'Where was Salvo found? Did you recover any evidence?'

Parker snorted. Guzman's eyes rested peaceably on Madison; he kept his silence.

'No, of course there was no evidence; we're talking about John Cameron. But Salvo died like the five guys on the *Nostromo*, like Erroll Sanders, like the three dealers in LA two years ago. He was found in a cellar in a derelict building – what was left of him. The rats had not been kind.'

Madison thought about what Salvo had been planning to do to Cameron if he had managed to get him back to LA: at least the rats had had him *after* he'd died.

'So, here we are again,' Parker said.

'Nothing has changed since the last time we spoke.'

'Well, we now have Salvo's decomposed body in our morgue and we thought we'd make sure we have covered every base.'

'Go right ahead,' Madison said.

'Do you mind?' Parker pushed forward a little voice recorder.

'I don't mind.'

'When was the last time you saw John Cameron?'

'Eighteen months ago.'

'That would have been at the memorial service for Nathan Quinn's brother?' Parker said, and added for the benefit of the tape: 'Nathan Quinn is John Cameron's attorney and Detective Madison investigated the murder of his brother who had been killed when he was a child.'

'Yes.'

'Have you seen or heard from John Cameron in the last eighteen months?'

'No.'

'Has he contacted you in any way that might help us to determine his present location?'

'No.'

'You saved his life.'

Madison waited. No question was forthcoming. 'Yes,' she said.

'Is he the kind of person who would consider that a debt?'

'I have no idea what kind of person John Cameron is.'

'You are the only officer of the law he has spoken to. Ever.'

'We didn't share secret recipes.'

'I'm sure you didn't, but the fact remains that you're the only person who has ever gotten that close to him.'

'Everything I know is in the file.'

Parker paused; when his eye caught the spinning wheel of the tape in the recorder he spoke again.

'When was the last time you saw Nathan Quinn?'

'Eighteen months ago.'

'You haven't been in contact at all over the last year and a half?'

'No.'

'Did you ever talk about the kidnap with Cameron?'

'Not really. He was there. He knew what happened.'

'Did he say anything to you about going after the cartel?'

'What do you think?'

'Detective, Mr Salvo is not the first person from that particular cartel to have met an untimely death. In the last five months we have found three—'

'Four,' Guzman interjected.

'We have found *four* other men killed in similar fashion. And I'm not talking about soldiers: I mean people who had power, who gave orders. Cameron has devastated the organization.'

Madison thought back to the day of David Quinn's memorial service, sitting in the empty restaurant afterwards with Cameron, Quinn and O'Keefe, the chef.

'*I'm going to do some traveling,*' Cameron had said.

'*Business or pleasure?*'

'*Bit of both.*'

'He said he was going to do some traveling,' she said. 'That was all.'

Parker nodded.

'These other homicides: was any evidence recovered for those?' she asked.

'No,' Parker replied.

'Cameron has been in custody: there could be prints, DNA trace—'

'I'm aware that he was very briefly in custody and that he's in the system, but if there's nothing to match his records to . . .'

Madison sat back in her chair. They had flown all the way to Seattle to see her face when they told her Salvo was dead. A year and a half ago she had pointed without hesitation at his photograph in a heap of other mugshots on the table.

'What exactly did you hope I could tell you? He could be in Antarctica for all I know,' she said.

Parker pursed his lips and cocked his head to one side. He was debating with himself. Finally he shook his head. 'I'm going to level with you, Detective.' He leant forward again. 'I don't trust you. You did what you did to save the life of a serial killer. Because that's what he is – however you want to dress it up – and I don't know that he hasn't been calling you to keep you updated on his progress. That he didn't get right on the phone to you and say, "Hey, hon, I've just cut Salvo's throat." And his lawyer could be in it just as deep.'

'Are you insane?'

'You're the one who went out for dinner with them after the kid's funeral.'

Anger was batting at her chest. He was provoking her. Guzman sat serenely with his legs crossed. That's what they had planned for her from the start. Her partner, Brown, came to her then, his words a simple comfort and a straightforward instruction. *Don't let them yank your chain.*

'It wasn't a date, Agent Parker. It was the memorial service for a boy who had been murdered twenty-five years ago. We arrested his killer and I went to the funeral as a representative of the Seattle Police Department. And, for the record, Nathan Quinn is not Cameron's lawyer any longer. He's Senior Counsel to the US Attorney for the Western District of Washington.' Her voice was clear, her temper in check. 'You couldn't find Salvo in time and you're just pissed off Cameron got to him first. It's regrettable but there you have it. You want me to help you catch him? Give me something to work with. If you had anything worth my time you'd be knocking on his door with a warrant instead of talking to me. J.J.—'

'It's A.J.,' he said.

'Whatever. If you have any issues about my conduct with John Cameron or Nathan Quinn, feel free to call the Office of Professional Accountability – actually, since you're here, you can just take the elevator, go straight up and talk to them.' Madison gazed from one to the other. 'Are we done here? Yes? Good.' She stood up.

Madison left the room and the precinct. It was chilly as hell outside and she strode away, shaking off the men with their sharp suits and cheap words. Salvo's suit had been just as sharp – and look where it got him.

Alice Madison had been on a collision course with John Cameron from the first time their paths had crossed two years ago; she knew all too well that he had never been indicted for any of those nine deaths, and in her bones she was convinced that one day she would get to be the one who would go after him and hunt him down. Those men could not possibly fathom how much that simple notion had cost her.

Those names and memories needed time to settle back into their allotted space, into a drawer she usually kept shut.

Madison would walk and clear her mind; she would be in no mood for company for a while. The sky was low and heavy with rain and the clouds were blowing in from the sea in streaks of bluish gray like an old bruise.

Chapter 4

The rest of Saturday ticked on. Aaron met her for a late lunch at the Steelhead Diner by Pike Place Market. It was full of tourists but Madison didn't care: everything was a distraction and she badly wanted to be distracted. Aaron had not asked her about the meeting and they had spoken about other things – normal things, things that could be talked about while surrounded by strangers and eating margarita chicken sandwiches with a glass of Pinot Gris.

They spoke of Aaron's children: a girl and a boy, eight and six, whom Madison hadn't met yet but probably would at Christmas. She was looking forward to it and was anxious about it in equal measure. She had seen their pictures; they looked like miniature Aarons – same blue eyes, same easy smile.

Afterwards they had gone to the Seattle Art Museum to see the Peruvian art exhibit which had been even more crowded than the diner.

Later, at home, as they lay naked in each other's arms Aaron said softly, 'What happened at the meeting? Bad news?'

Madison pulled back – her head on the pillow next to his, side by side, facing each other. She didn't know how much to tell him. She didn't know how other cops brought some things home and left others in their patrol cars.

'Yes and no. Someone I met once was found murdered in LA, in all probability killed by someone whose life I saved, months ago. This man might have been involved in the deaths of other men too. I don't know for sure.' Her voice was quiet; the rain fell in sheets against the windows.

Aaron was computing all this. It was entirely outside the range of his life experience.

'Is he . . . ?' he ventured. 'Is he going to come after you?'

'No, he has no reason to.' She stroked his hair. 'I'm just a minor part of the story, but they wanted to tell me what had happened.'

He nodded and laid his hand against her cheek. 'You know, when I met you earlier, you didn't seem worried,' he said. 'You seemed sad, so sad. Like when I met you the other summer.'

Madison didn't know what to say; something inside welled up but she shook her head. 'I'm not sad,' she said finally.

'Good,' Aaron whispered and held her close.

His skin was warm and his hands smelled of rosemary.

'I'm not sad,' she repeated.

The light of a late spring day patterned the wooden floor of the empty restaurant on Alki Beach and seagulls called to each other as they glided above the waves. Donny O'Keefe, the chef, came back from the kitchen with drinks and coffee. 'Since we don't know when you gentlemen will be in the same neighborhood again, we should have our game now and let it see us through the long night.'

The memorial service for David Quinn had brought to the end a nightmare that had lasted twenty-five years and touched everybody who was present – one way or the other.

'I'm going to do some traveling,' John Cameron explained to Alice Madison.

'Business or pleasure?' she said.

'Bit of both.'

Late thirties, dark and dark. Madison was used to his presence like you are used to walking by the edge of a cliff: never too close because you shouldn't forget the ground could betray you anytime.

Nathan Quinn had studied his oldest friend and his black eyes had come to rest on Madison. It was the end of something, they all knew it. Madison's path had crossed theirs six months earlier and this was the day their lives would continue as they were meant to a long time ago.

O'Keefe had already prepared the table and brought out the deck of cards: poker.

'I don't play,' Madison said.

'You might not, but you sure can,' Cameron said.

'How do you know?'

'Does it matter?'

A silver dollar appeared between the chef's quick fingers. 'Heads, you play. Tails, you don't.'

'Stay and play, Detective,' Nathan Quinn said. 'Just this once.'

By the time they were done with the game the first hint of dawn was lining the sky.

Madison woke up with a start just after 4 a.m. Maybe it had been a nightmare, a tree branch brushing against the window – she couldn't tell, she couldn't remember any dreams except for a sense of being wrapped in deep unnatural silence, as heavy as a shroud.

Madison slid her feet out from under the comforter and into her bunny slippers – a present from Rachel three Christmases ago – and reached for her toweling robe. Aaron slept the sleep of the dead and she padded to the kitchen, gently pulling the door behind her.

She poured herself a glass of cold milk and curled up on the sofa in the living room.

Parker and Guzman had brought bad news, terrible news. It wasn't something she had dwelled on in the last eighteen months. Nevertheless, it had been there – like a storm over the hill that at some point is going to hit, whether you're ready or not. Alice Madison knew that John Cameron was a killer when she had saved his life. And even in that instant of fear, rage and sheer adrenaline she had been perfectly aware that he would kill again, because that's who he was.

Madison's religious beliefs had been shaped by a vaguely Episcopalian background and years on the streets as a police officer; it meant that she wasn't too sure or concerned about the details of heaven and hell but she definitely believed in karma. And if John Cameron would ever be judged by an authority higher than the law of the United States as administered by the courts, those last five lives he had taken since she had saved his might very well carry a small clause that read: 'See Alice Madison.' She hadn't pulled the trigger or held the knife to their throats and yet the murdered men were connected to her through Cameron because if he had died at the hands of Roberto Salvo they would all still be alive, doing whatever it was that they did with their days. Did they have families? Madison stopped herself. All the people Cameron was alleged to have killed had been 'in the business', just as he was: they had known the risks and all had been armed.

Madison stretched out on the sofa and pulled over her the blanket that had been folded on the armrest. How many lives would it take for her to be clean of those five deaths? And how many more would there be?

The DEA agents had missed one crucial point: although Nathan Quinn was not Cameron's lawyer any longer, and despite working within the parameters of the law, he was just as dangerous and ruthless as his former client. Criminal defense lawyers across the state had worn black the day Quinn had joined the office of the US Attorney. If Parker and Guzman wanted Cameron so badly that they were ready to jangle empty threats in order to unnerve her, they might try to go after Quinn too. It would be a mistake, probably the last they'd ever make on the force.

Most of the room was in shadow and some of those shadows seemed to quiver with the wind outside. Madison, wrapped in the blanket, gave herself a couple of minutes to get up and go back to bed. Her eyes closed and she fell instantly asleep.

Sunday was mostly about Stacey's bachelorette party and the spa day. What Madison gained from it was that she didn't like spas very much. It seemed a waste of time to just lie there while a masseuse worked on her stiff shoulders and someone else tidied up her nails – short with clear varnish. However, it seemed a social enterprise that the other women – all met for the first time – enjoyed and were thrilled by as they chit-chatted and dissected the forthcoming wedding.

They were impressed that Madison had been invited to the bachelor party and she realized then that she was the only cop at the spa day aside from the bride-to-be; Stacey took her aside for some shop talk while the others went into the hot tub.

At the end of the afternoon Madison was relieved when the co-ordinated pampering was over. She drove home with the windows rolled down and the Soul Rebels Brass Band blasting 'Sweet Dreams are Made of This'. She didn't think once about Agents Parker and Guzman.

By the time she got home Aaron had returned to the house he owned in Kirkland, forty minutes away across Lake Washington, and Madison changed into her sweats and went running for an hour around the neighborhood. She was used to the weight of her off-duty piece on her right ankle and felt unbalanced without it. Aaron, she had noted, looked away when she undressed and took off her weapons – as if it were a strangely intimate gesture he ought not to be a part of.

Chapter 5

The landing gear of the small charter plane hit the concrete runway and the Lear taxied slowly towards the two-room bungalow that passed for an airport. The short runway was surrounded by mountains which were surrounded by more mountains until the land dropped off into the sea and the next solid ground was Greenland.

One man stepped out of the Lear holding a rucksack and headed straight for the beaten-up SUV that was waiting near the weathered building. It was cold – the kind of cold that took your breath away and didn't give it back – but it didn't bother the man.

The driver of the SUV had not left the car to greet him because social niceties take a beating in sub-zero temperatures, but when the traveler yanked the door open and climbed into the car he pushed a beaker of hot chocolate into his gloved hand.

'Welcome. Here you go, take this.'

'Thanks, man. I sure need it.'

'Ready to go?' the driver asked, ramming the clutch into gear.

'You bet.'

The SUV left the airport by the only road available – a single track that led towards the only town for hundreds of miles. The sky was pure blue, untouched by big-city pollution, and the mid-morning light was so dazzling that each pine needle in the woods around them seemed to be standing out to be counted. The tops of the mountains were already white with snow; it showed in long stretches of the road too. Soon more would come and stay until spring, making flying into that region – and even driving on that road – a challenge.

The traveler drank the chocolate and watched the landscape.

'Pretty country, uh?' the driver said.

'Sure is,' he replied.

'Where were you flying in from today?'

'A place not as pretty as this, I'll tell you that much. You were born and raised here?'

'I'm from Quebec. Came here with my wife about ten years ago.'

The traveler nodded and looked interested as the driver recounted in detail the last ten years of the life of the small town. In truth, the traveler saw only the road and thought only of the job that he had to do; the talk was camouflage, no different from contact lenses that changed the color of the eyes or a prosthesis that altered the line of a jaw. It was just another layer. He nodded, listened and asked more questions.

After twenty-five minutes they pulled into the front yard of a one-story cabin on the outskirts of town.

'Some things still have to be done in person, right?' the driver said.

'Yes,' the traveler replied.

'Well, I'll wait here.'

'Sure?' The traveler did not want the man to come inside but it would have been strange if he hadn't asked. If the man had said yes he would have found a way to conduct his business in private.

'Go ahead, you're not going to be more than a few minutes, are you?'

'I don't think so, no.'

'Okay, then.'

The traveler walked up to the front door and knocked. He was expected and a woman let him in. She was in her sixties with a long braid of gray hair resting on her left shoulder.

'He's in here,' she said, eyeing him with open distrust.

John Cameron pulled down the hood of the parka and took his gloves off. 'Thank you,' he said.

She led him to the main room of the cabin. The place had been made comfortable without much money or design; it had been shaped by the life of the couple who lived there and that had been enough to give it warmth.

The man sat in an upholstered armchair and got up when Cameron came in. He was a little older than the woman and his hair and beard were completely white. His pale blue eyes met John Cameron's amber with resignation.

'I still don't know how you found me,' he said.

'Does it matter?'

There was no need for introductions: his visitor's name did not matter, only the fact that he was there. A deep scar ran from a corner of the man's mouth to his ear and Cameron knew that the man had not offered to shake hands because his right hand had been amputated below the wrist. It had happened in another place, at the other end of the country, and he had moved as far away from there as possible.

The man looked at Cameron and saw in him the very thing that he had fled; he had begged his wife not to be in the house when his visitor arrived, but she had refused to leave.

John Cameron unshouldered the rucksack and took from it a large padded envelope. In the middle of the room there was a dining table, the wood polished and honey-gold. From the envelope he took out fifty photographs and lined them up on the surface: black and white, color, Polaroids, new and old. Each picture was a close-up of a different man, as clear as a mugshot.

The old man looked at John Cameron. He didn't want him in this room and he didn't want him in his life – this new life he had fought for in the middle of nowhere – and the sooner he would leave the better. He approached the table cautiously as if the pictures were omens of an ill future instead of shapes from his past. When he was close enough to look he did, running his eyes over the faces of those strangers, all of them unknown to him. Except for one. He spotted him quickly and the watery eyes blinked once, twice. Then he lifted his left hand and pointed at that one picture.

John Cameron gathered all the photographs and returned them to the bag. In seconds he was out of the house and back in the SUV driving towards the airport. On the honey-gold wood he had left a black plastic zippered bag; inside it there were rolls of banknotes, neatly stacked and tied.

'All done?' the driver asked Cameron.

'All done,' he replied.

The Lear took off and John Cameron looked out of the window; for miles there would be nothing but sky above and woods below. He adjusted the snub-nosed revolver in his ankle holster and stretched his legs.

In the cabin the old man closed the door of the bedroom and sat down on the bed; he needed a few minutes by himself. He had not been this afraid for a very long time, not since the injuries to his body were new and he hadn't thought he would live. He'd rather the man had never found him, never turned up in his home, and all the money they had was what was in their checking account. He knew killers – he had spent a large chunk of his life in their proximity – and the man who had just left his house was one of them.

On Monday morning, Madison woke up alone in her bed and listened to the trees and the shrubs shift in the wind and rub against the house. She ambled into the kitchen and leant against the table as her Italian stove-top coffee percolator worked its magic, then took a cup by the French doors. It was too early for daylight; what glimmer there was looked like mist but was in fact a veil of rain shimmering between her and Vashon Island.

The day was about a robbery/murder coming to trial. Madison and her partner, Detective Sergeant Kevin Brown, worked on the interviews and the details of the investigation. They grabbed a quick lunch in a diner close to the precinct – one chicken salad, one tuna sandwich – and were about to go back when Brown spoke.

'What about Tweedledum and Tweedledee?' he said, balling up his napkin.

Madison sat back on the leather banquette and sighed: she had just about managed not to think about the five deaths for a couple of hours. 'Cameron is going through the cartel, picking them off one by one. Five killed including Salvo. Parker and his pal flew all the way up here to tell me in person, and to make sure I knew that they don't trust me. That was the cherry.'

Brown shook his head. 'They can choose how to waste their time, it's their birthright. But I'm sorry they ruined a perfectly good Saturday morning for you.'

'I don't think they're going to come back in a hurry. Somehow I sense our acquaintance has run its course.'

'I'm sure you're heartbroken.'

'How could I not be?' Madison stood up.

'They're only annoyed they didn't get to Salvo first.'

'That's what I told them.'

'And you were as cool and composed as the circumstances called for.'

'I was positively unperturbed.'

'Good. I'd expect no less. They're a lesser kind of dung beetle.'

They made their way back to the precinct in the drizzle. And although Brown didn't ask – or bring up the subject again – he read Madison's mood and what he saw concerned him.

The call came in at the end of the shift. Lieutenant Fynn strode into the detectives' room – an uneasy marriage of old and new with gray metal filing cabinets from the first Bush administration next to modern computers next to scarred desks and office chairs. Andy Dunne and Kyle Spencer were still away and would be back tomorrow, but everyone else was there.

'One DOA in a private residence off Fauntleroy Way SW. Who's up?' the lieutenant asked.

Madison grabbed her coat. 'It's mine.' It was her turn to be the primary on a case, with Brown as her backup.

It never went away, she thought as she looked around the room: that spike of adrenaline as she took charge of an investigation. Two years in Homicide and it was still there and, as they quickly made their way out, she could see it in Brown's eyes too. Each case was their own private little war against willful, sometimes random, evil.

Brown drove into the early-evening rush hour and towards south-west Seattle – no one ever drove Brown around – and crossing the

West Seattle Bridge their whole world became a line of flickering headlights, water above and water below.

Madison settled into the seat and focused on what was coming. It wasn't the first time that she was the primary and Brown the backup. She threaded the slim chain with her badge around her neck and straightened her shoulder holster. All that mattered was to do well by the victims, by Brown and by the shield she carried.

The road was parallel to Fauntleroy Way SW where Lincoln Park juts out into the waters of Puget Sound like a deep green triangle. The houses were large single family units – mostly clapboard with some brick – almost hidden behind the greenery.

Blue-and-whites were parked along the street with their lights flashing and the police tape flapped in the rain. Madison was glad to see the Crime Scene unit van pulling in at the same time and sent a brief prayer that Special Investigator Amy Sorensen would be on duty. Brown was waved in by one of the uniformed officers guarding the perimeter; the woman didn't greet them, just nodded as they drove past.

Outside the front door a young patrol officer was bending forward – hands on his knees, head low – and swaying slightly with his eyes closed. Another officer put a hand on his back, speaking words they could not hear. Both officers were pale.

Brown and Madison left their car and ducked quickly out of the weather and into the hall. As they stepped in a wail rose and fell somewhere nearby. In the lobby they slipped on the regulation full-body-protection paper suit and the disposable overshoes.

The foyer opened into a wide living room with a chimney set into a wall of exposed red brick. The opposite wall was glass; it looked onto a deck and a view of the trees rolling down towards

Lincoln Park and the Sound, but now it was just tall shadows and darkness.

'Detectives,' a man said behind them.

'Officer Giordano,' Madison replied. There was no need for introductions. 'What have you got? Were you the first to respond?'

'Yes, I was the first on the scene. And this . . .' he hesitated. 'This is what we have. Mind your feet. I wouldn't be telling you except it's everywhere.'

Giordano was an experienced officer who had known both Brown and Madison for years; he looked shaken and that was bad news. He picked his way towards one end of the room and they realized what he had meant: the dark wooden floor had been spattered with blood and droplets had hit the walls too. A sharp, ugly scent hit them and a brief thought about the quantity of blood loss barely had time to formulate itself before Madison turned the corner and everything else went away – except for what lay at her feet.

Giordano let them look for a few moments then started his report. He spoke clearly, simply, knowing that they needed to retain what information he was giving them while standing by something he didn't have a name for.

'His name is Matthew Duncan, thirty-seven years old. He was found by his wife, Kate Duncan, when she came back from her run in Lincoln Park. She left the house at 6.30 p.m. and he was fine, she came back at 7.25 p.m. and found him – she's pretty sure of the times because she runs every day. She came in, she saw him, she called us. The French doors to the deck – it's a wraparound deck – were open . . .'

He pointed, they looked, then their gaze came back inevitably to the body.

'Seems like that was the point of entry. Drawers have been

searched in the bedroom upstairs and the study. A real mess. The intruder might have grabbed some valuables but the wife was in no shape to check. I called Medic One too. She's very distressed.'

'Thanks, Giordano,' Madison said. 'Open doors say B&E – and the intruder would have been covered in blood when he left. For what it's worth we'd better put out a BOLO alert. The killer must have done something with his clothes: we need to check garbage cans and dumpsters as soon as possible. And ask about any unfamiliar cars in the road in the last two hours. Let's hit the neighbors quick before they forget what they've seen.'

The uniformed officer nodded and left them to it. A 'Be on the Lookout' alert without a physical description was worth very little but they needed to get it out there anyway.

This is what we do, Madison thought, this is what we deal with. She didn't need Brown's *tell me what you see*; she took a deep breath and started.

'Caucasian male,' she said, and she could be certain only because Matthew Duncan had been wearing a plaid cotton shirt with the sleeves rolled up; his arms were unmarked and untouched.

'No protective wounds, no tussle. He didn't have a chance to defend himself,' she continued. 'Extensive . . . extreme injuries to the head and the face caused by what seems to be a blunt object, something heavy, something that struck him many times over and over.'

His shirt was soaked in blood. Matthew Duncan lay on his back, his arms to his sides and his unblemished hands palms up. She didn't need to add what they both knew: sudden brain injury and decease had caused the victim's insides to let go and, mixed with the coppery scent of blood, there was the stench of every unlawful death.

Madison turned to Brown and saw in his eyes what she was feeling: someone didn't just want to get him out of the way of a burglary, someone had meant to erase Matthew Duncan from this world. His face had been destroyed – bone, cartilage, and tissue had caved in under the attack – and nothing was left except the horror of it. No other part of his body had been damaged. Madison looked over the walls, seeing shapes of red everywhere around them.

Brown followed her gaze. 'The attack continued after he was incapacitated,' he said.

She nodded. They were both staring at the blood spatter on the ceiling. The way the droplets had hit the wallpaper indicated that the killer had kept on hitting the victim when he was on the ground, unconscious and unable to protect himself.

'When the ME gets here we'll turn him,' Brown said.

'You're thinking first blow to the back of the head . . .'

'. . . and the rest to the front, yes. He was surprised. It makes no sense otherwise—'

Madison finished his thought. 'You don't just stand there while you're being . . .' She couldn't find the right word for what had happened to this man and let the sentence hang there.

Muffled steps and the rustle of the protective suits told them they were not alone any longer. Dr Ernie Fellman and Special Investigator Amy Sorensen rounded the corner. The former was the Medical Examiner for King County and the latter a Crime Scene unit investigator whose skills Madison had come to rely on heavily ever since she had made plainclothes.

Normally they would have greeted each other warmly, but today their reactions were the same as Brown's and Madison's: silence, the struggle to comprehend and, finally, the ingrained habits of years kicking in.

'I'm going to create a safe path so we don't tread all over the evidence. We'll work the other end of the room while you're here with the body.'

Madison nodded. 'This seems to be the primary scene,' she said to no one in particular.

The Crime Scene unit photographer who had followed Sorensen started to take pictures of the victim's body from every angle, the flash searing into their eyes the red and the white on the body.

Dr Fellman stood to one side patiently, waiting for the photographer to finish before he could move or even touch the victim. His eyes scanned the injuries and the position of the limbs. When the photographer had finished he knelt next to the body and tested the mobility of the hands and wrists, the feet and the knees. He took the liver temperature and examined the victim's clothing.

'Rigor hasn't started yet,' he said.

Madison knew only too well that death is a process which follows its rules like any other process in nature: rigor mortis would steal over a dead body between three and four hours after the last heartbeat; it hadn't visited Matthew Duncan yet.

'It confirms what the wife said,' Brown commented.

'Can we turn him over?' Madison crouched next to the medical examiner.

'Yes,' the doctor said, and very gently they lifted one shoulder off the ground. 'There, that's your first blow. I'll know for sure after the autopsy.' It was a sticky dark patch on the back of the victim's head. 'It doesn't seem bad enough to kill him outright but he was most probably concussed. Likely he would have dropped down on his knees and never managed to get up again.'

'He was a tall fella,' Brown said.

The implications were clear: whoever had taken him on had to be sure he could stop him with a single blow.

The doctor continued with his assessment while Brown and Madison took notes. Around them the small, organized army of Crime Scene unit officers had gone to work: sifting, identifying and preserving evidence. Somewhere behind her Madison heard voices and police radio crackle and out of the blue she realized that she didn't know what Matthew Duncan had looked like. It seemed obscene to stand over his dead body and not know that. Almost like not caring what his name had been.

Her gaze traveled over the room and the furnishings while the doctor continued his checks until she found what she was looking for above the mantelpiece: a wedding picture. A blonde woman in a slim, elegant silk gown and a tall, wide-shouldered man in black tie. His hair was light brown and his eyes pale blue. Boyish features with an impish grin, and a deep sky behind them.

'I'm going to bag the hands before I take him, but it doesn't look like there was much of a scuffle between them. I don't know what we'll find but I'll try anyway.'

'Thanks, Doc.'

The body of the victim had sucked all the energy out of the room; now they needed to concentrate on their surroundings, see what the attacker had seen and begin to follow the trail left for them.

As the ME started to place plastic bags over the hands of the victim, one of his assistants unrolled a body bag and another snapped open a gurney.

The sound found Madison suddenly and unexpectedly – the low rattle of a helicopter engine swooping above the house. She exchanged a look with Brown. The press had found them and the only thing they could be grateful for was that the crime had happened inside.

Madison didn't want to think how they always knew so quickly. A beam of light swept over the tops of the trees and she hoped the pilot and the cameraman weren't bold enough to try to get a shot inside the living room. It wouldn't have been the first time.

She turned to Brown. 'The wife,' she said.

He nodded and they followed the thin path that Sorensen had cordoned off for them.

They found Kate Duncan shaking uncontrollably in the red and white Medic One van; she was wrapped in a blanket and her cheeks were streaked with mascara. Her eyes shone, glazed and unfocused; she had been mildly sedated. The wedding photograph had not revealed just how tiny she was – and how nature had taken its time to draw her features with a very fine pencil.

'I'm Detective Madison and this is Detective Sergeant Brown. I'm very sorry for your loss, Mrs Duncan. May we speak with you for a moment?'

She nodded.

'A girlfriend is on her way,' the paramedic said.

'Where's Matt?' Kate Duncan asked. Her accent was delicately Southern with a few years of Pacific Northwest thrown in for color. Her wide blue eyes found Madison through the haze of shock and grief. 'Where's Matt?'

'Mrs Duncan, your husband is with the medical examiner.'

The woman nodded. 'When can I see him?'

'I'm terribly sorry but—'

'I understand he's . . .' she said. 'I'm asking you when will I be able to see my husband?' Her gaze was steady now and she demanded an answer.

'We can take you to him later,' Madison replied softly. 'Would you be able to tell us what happened?'

Brown stood quietly to one side. People who didn't know him well missed that about him: where other cops pecked at witnesses and gained little, his attention was a gentle instrument that missed nothing. Madison was a note-taker, while Brown often wrote things down a few minutes after a conversation. But he could have recounted how many times the witness blinked, and whether he had blinked at the wrong time.

Kate Duncan spoke. And what she said was surprisingly clear and to the point.

'It was a completely normal day. I work in a pharmaceutical company and I got home at 6 p.m., changed to go for my run and said goodbye to Matt – he was in the kitchen, he's a very good cook . . .' She gathered herself for a moment, then continued. 'I did my usual route around Lincoln Park and then I came back.' She paused.

The memory of the moment she arrived at the house was all there – Brown and Madison could see that – and it unspooled behind her eyes as she spoke.

'I unlocked the door and called out to Matt, he didn't answer, I called again and by then I saw . . . I saw the blood on the floor. And then I saw him, and I knew that he was dead.'

In the street outside Sorensen's army clattered about doing their job and the uniformed officers guarding the perimeter fought the good fight against the gathering crowd with their cell-phone cameras. However, inside the ambulance no one moved, spoke or even seemed to breathe as Kate Duncan spoke.

'I couldn't understand what had happened to him, what . . . had done that. I dialed 911 from my cell phone and sat down next to him. I don't know how long it took for the officers to arrive. They were suddenly there and they saw Matt too and searched around. It hadn't even occurred to me that someone might still be in the house.' She wiped her cheeks; fresh tears were spilling out and wouldn't stop. 'And now we're here . . .'

The paramedic – a Japanese-American man in his early twenties – passed her some tissues. She thanked him with a small nod. She wasn't sobbing but the tears kept coming.

'When you went for your run, did you see anything or anyone unusual in the street?' Madison asked her.

'No, there wasn't anybody else in the street.'

'Do you run every day, even in this weather?'

'Every day. I don't mind the rain.'

'When you first walked into the house . . . you said you unlocked the door. So the front door was definitely closed and locked.'

She nodded.

'Did you pick up on anything odd just before or just after? A sound, footsteps, car engine starting?'

'No.'

'Did you see a car driving away as you were coming close to the house? Maybe a person on foot?'

'No.'

'Mrs Duncan, do you know of anyone who might want to harm your husband?'

The woman squeezed her eyes shut and shook her head. Madison felt the inadequacy of her words under the circumstances. They were not dealing with *harm* here, they were dealing with the malevolent destruction of a human being, and these were the bullet points of the investigation.

'Do you think you would be able to come inside and tell us if the intruder has taken any valuables?'

For a moment it seemed as if Kate Duncan wouldn't answer, then she straightened up on the seat. 'Let's do it now.'

They trailed her from room to room as time after time she repeated that nothing had been taken, nothing had been touched. It was a neat, carefully decorated upper-middle-class home where even the flowers in the vases matched the fabric of the sofas, the curtains and the rugs.

The bedroom door was open, the drawer in the dresser ajar. The woman looked inside and picked up a red leather box lined with chamois. The clasp was undone.

'My jewelry is missing. A pearl necklace, some earrings, some rings.' Kate Duncan didn't care: she was bewildered and puzzled, as if she had expected to find something that would explain everything.

She gave them a list of every item the intruder had taken and then they led her back downstairs. Her friend was waiting by the front door.

'Kate?' The woman stood there, rooted to the spot, uncertain of what to do next.

'Annie . . .' Kate Duncan opened her arms and walked into her friend's embrace.

They left after it was agreed that Madison would take her to see her husband the following day. No, Mrs Duncan did not need a doctor. Yes, she would be staying with her friend. They exchanged phone numbers and a uniformed officer sheltered them under an umbrella as they made their way to the friend's SUV.

Vans from local television stations had already positioned themselves and the lights from their cameras tracked every movement. Even the helicopter swooped low and took its fill before it disappeared back into the rain.

Chapter 6

The portable lights of the Crime Scene unit burned dazzling white in the living room and the temperature had already become uncomfortably warm; Madison wished she could take off the protection suit.

'Let's have a look at the entry point,' she said to Brown.

Amy Sorensen was busy making a chart of blood spatter patterns, but one of her best and brightest was working on the French doors.

'Hey, Lauren,' Madison said. 'What do we have?'

'Standard glass panels,' Frank Lauren replied. 'Easy enough to break with something hard and sharp. They were unlocked and open. Here and here,' he pointed, 'I have some blood transfer, probably from when the killer left. Rest of the door? No prints so far.'

'Was there any water or dirt next to the door when you arrived? Any marks at all?' Brown said.

Lauren knew what Brown was driving at and didn't even turn around. He continued to work with his swabs. 'No water marks, no dirt, no footprints, no trace evidence brought in from the deck. This section of the wooden flooring was as immaculate as the day it was laid.'

Madison found herself drawn back to where the body of Matthew Duncan had been found. Her mind was beginning to sift through all the information they had gathered. 'The victim must not have heard the intruder coming in,' she said to Brown. 'If he had seen the intruder the first blow would have been a frontal one and he wouldn't have let him get that close.'

'Have you seen the deck?' he replied.

'I know. Anyone walking in from outside in the last few hours would have left some kind of footprints.'

'And . . . ?'

Madison suppressed a smile: sometimes Brown could still be the benevolent if exacting teacher. It was either mildly annoying or very useful, depending on Madison's mood. Tonight she decided it was useful.

'And anyone walking about would have most likely worn some kind of wet-weather gear, but . . . no marks on the floor from the water dripping either.'

'Could have dried before we got here.'

'Possibly. But the footprints?' Madison looked around. 'Maybe he took his shoes off as he came in. I'm not being flippant. If the victim was in the kitchen he wouldn't have seen him sliding the French doors open and coming in.'

Madison's gaze found the body shape on the floor by their feet.

'Here's the thing though,' she said. 'We have a missing pearl necklace, some earrings and other jewelry. Is that what the intruder was hoping to find? If it was, why didn't he just incapacitate the victim and move on to do his business? This was a horrific release of violence for a pretty mundane B&E.'

'Whatever it was he wanted, he wanted it very badly.'

Beyond the glass wall there was nothing now except for a pitch-black night and a human being who had done an awful thing.

'There is another option,' Madison continued. 'And time of death is going to help us only up to a point because it all happened in minutes.'

'Go on.'

'The intruder breaks in. At some point, for some reason, Matthew Duncan comes to check what's going on – maybe he was still in the kitchen fixing dinner – and the intruder attacks him, leaves him on the floor unconscious. Then he goes upstairs, takes everything he can find of any value, comes back downstairs and *then* he finishes off Matthew Duncan.'

'After he picked up the jewels?'

'After. So no blood transfer from the killer except on his way out.'

'Mrs Duncan said the jewels were worth maybe $12,000. The rest was in the safe and the safe was not touched. That's not a bad haul for a few minutes' work and wouldn't leave a trail as hot as murder in the first degree.'

'I know.' Madison thought about the small transactions of daily life that happen in the street without us even noticing. 'I hope somebody saw him,' she said. And if somebody did, would they have noticed the dark stains on the clothing? Would the rain have washed clean the killer's face?

They spent another hour on the scene and one more canvassing the neighborhood. The first forty-eight hours after a murder were the most valuable time – when witnesses might remember what they would have forgotten days later, for sure.

Now was also the time when most people were at home after a long day at work: they were eating dinner, their attention was dulled and their minds ready to switch off. The detectives' quest was made worse by the crops of thick vegetation around the houses: it wouldn't have been difficult for someone to slip into the backyards unnoticed from the street.

The call came as Brown and Madison were retracing their steps to the crime scene – damp, exhausted and with very little to show for their efforts.

It was Frank Lauren.

'Got your murder weapon,' he said.

An object that reminded Madison quite inappropriately of an Academy Award had been placed inside a clear plastic bag which had already been signed and countersigned by Lauren and another Crime Scene unit officer. It was covered in something that Madison would rather not examine too closely.

'What is it?' she asked Lauren.

'Bronze, I'd say. Some kind of sporting trophy. I'll tell you more but we'll have to wipe off the blood and everything else first.'

'Where was it?'

'Under the sofa. Rolled or kicked under it.'

Madison felt the weight of the object and passed it to Brown. It carried enough heft to turn a single blow into a lethal hit.

'Are you going to fast-track this?' she asked Lauren.

'We'll do what we can but we're going to be here a while . . .' he said and gestured to the rest of the room.

It would take days to process the house – days spent fastidiously covering each place where the intruder had been.

Again Madison went back to the spot where they had found Matthew Duncan. 'If you're a burglar . . .' she said to Brown.

'Let's say I am.'

'You know enough not to leave immediately obvious fingerprints or footprints by the point of entry. And none of the neighbors has come forward yet with a description.'

'Let's agree I am adequately competent at my job.'

'Well,' Madison continued, 'if that's the case, what are you doing getting into a house at 6.30 p.m. with all the lights on and a person – a big, footballer-player-type guy – clearly visible from the garden and the deck? Why on earth would someone try to rob a house with the owner right there? And if you are going in for anything other than a robbery, why are you not armed instead of using something you just find lying around? And why wait for the small window of time when the husband is alone in the house and the wife is on her run – when you had all day for the burglary as they were both out at work?'

'All good questions.'

'Questions, Sarge, is all I've got right now,' Madison said.

In the empty detectives' room, late into the night, after the hot lights at the scene and the rain as they canvassed the neighbors, Brown and Madison sat in silence at their desk, picked at takeout from the Hurricane Café and finished their paperwork.

Madison sipped from her beaker of coffee; her eyes had been on the same line of the report for a few minutes.

'I've never seen anything like it,' she said finally.

Brown looked up.

There was much he wanted to tell her: about his first homicide case and the crevice it had left somewhere in his soul, about the fierce light and the warmth he had seen in her the first day she had joined the unit, and how he had learnt in the decades on the job that those things had to be protected at all costs. For a moment he looked for the words he needed but they were not there for him to catch.

'I know,' he replied.

A couple of hours later, Madison twisted and turned in her bed but sleep would not come. Her mind never quite stopped, never quite left the room with the pretty wood flooring and the sweeps of red high on the walls. A while later she found her way in the dark to the sofa in the living room and lying there, wrapped in her duvet, she fell asleep.

The dream came as it always did – as a comfort and a sharp, sudden ache. In it she sat curled up on the armchair watching someone sleeping on the sofa. The morning light crept into the room and moved towards the recumbent figure. Madison didn't have much time. There was never enough time. And still she watched.

She woke up hours later, still feeling the dream on her skin.

Chapter 7

By the time Madison was drinking her second cup of coffee and attempting to finish her oatmeal, the day was bright – brighter than it had felt for days – and the wind had swept up what was left of the night's rain and left in its place a hard blue sky and gusts that bent the trees and disheveled the lawn with dry leaves. So much light. It reached into Madison on some subatomic level and scrubbed off the half-formed thoughts of the previous night. There had been doubts, there had been uncertainties, and they had left traces like words in chalk on a blackboard after the class is done. Madison felt the balm of the unexpected light on a cold, clear morning and took it for what it was: a gift. There was going to be an autopsy, there were going to be more devastating questions and worthless answers, but there was also this, and Madison gave herself a few minutes by the windows, sipping her coffee and watching the seagulls gliding, utterly still, in the northeastern wind.

In the car, traveling as fast as the boundaries of civic rule and street courtesy would allow, Madison turned on the radio. When the news came on she knew what the first item would be: after a brief, vague description of Matthew Duncan's murder, the local pundit went on to talk about the young, relatively inexperienced Homicide detective in charge of the investigation and speculated whether, for the good of the community, it wouldn't be more effective to have a senior officer in charge.

It wasn't Madison's first homicide but without a doubt it was the most brutal and senseless. She swore under her breath and turned off the radio: she wouldn't let herself feel undermined by someone who had never walked a crime scene, never smelled it in her hair after the shift was done.

Brown met Madison at the front door of the Duncans' residence; he was wearing the protective suit and an expression that said he'd heard the same news item. His silent message was simple: ignore the idiots and get on with the job at hand. Madison slipped into her own paper suit – message received.

Morning light flooded the room and Crime Scene unit Investigator Amy Sorensen straightened up and looked over her domain. She was a tall, striking redhead in her early forties and the bane of defense lawyers across the state. Sorensen worshipped at the altar of Edmond Locard whose exchange principle – every contact leaves a trace – informed every second of the life she had devoted to finding the truth through the interpretation of collected evidence; she liked Madison because they both believed that the evidence would tell them the story if only they asked the right questions. And this was going to be one nasty piece of storytelling.

Sorensen had examined, photographed, studied and collated, and she had a rather good idea of how the action had played out. Of course, she thought, *good* had had nothing to do with it.

*

Madison stepped into the bright room: through the glass windows the deep green below rolled down towards Fauntleroy Way and Lincoln Park, and beyond it the waters of Puget Sound. She put away her doubts and the echoes of the broadcaster's voice and let the room speak to her. The Duncans had led a comfortable life and someone had killed for a paltry slice of it. The question was, as always, who were they really looking for?

Sorensen turned when she heard them approach and smiled. 'My favorite Homicide detectives,' she said. 'Welcome to my humble crime scene.'

'Amy,' Madison said, 'you are the shining center of our universe.'

'And so I should be.' She took a deep breath and her joviality went away. 'Ready for it?'

'As ready as we'll ever be,' Brown replied.

Sorensen launched into it and ran through her findings. They were grim.

'The first blow,' she concluded, 'would have been struck with limited force – there was hardly any blood loss – but we also have high-speed droplets cast off from the murder weapon. They struck the ceiling as the attacker lowered and raised the object repeatedly while the victim was splayed out on the ground. The cast-off pattern is clear . . .' She pointed.

Sorensen let them absorb the facts. 'I'd say there were well over six or seven blows. This here is where he fell on his knees, then a blow pushed him onto his back – see the cast-off on the sofa . . . there . . . and there. I doubt he had a chance to defend himself at all. And here is where the wife slipped and crouched when she found him. See the transfer from her hand when she touched him and then steadied herself on the floor? The only footprints with blood transfer in the room are hers.'

Madison nodded.

So much violence, so much inexplicable violence.

She turned to Brown. 'Drugs?' she said.

'Possibly,' he replied.

It wouldn't have been the first time that a burglar high on something or other had turned a perfectly straightforward job into something altogether different.

'Except,' he continued, 'if the intruder was high I'd have expected a messier scene and prints everywhere. Maybe not fingerprints but definitely transfers.'

'No transfers upstairs, just the ones on the French doors,' Sorensen confirmed.

'If he killed Matthew Duncan first he would have been covered in blood,' Madison said. 'He would have left a trail this wide when he went upstairs and searched the bedroom.'

'Unless he found a way not to,' Brown replied.

'How?'

'I don't know. Maybe I just don't want to entertain the idea that he would have gone back to kill the man *after* he found the jewelry, that he killed him out of spite or just because he could.'

'He only had fifty-five minutes from when Mrs Duncan left to when she came back,' Madison said. 'He could very well have seen her leave and must have known that she would be back soon.'

Brown nodded.

What they knew of the killer made him vicious and reckless: if the former made him dangerous maybe the latter would get him caught.

Madison walked the perimeter around one side of the house, Brown walked the other. The air was surprisingly soft and under the firs it smelled of mulch. The thicket had grown between the houses as if they and their well-tended gardens had merely borrowed the land for a brief moment in time and nature was determined that sooner or later it would get it back.

Madison kept her eyes on the ground, still damp, and sought the small disturbances that betrayed the passage of the intruder and maybe a quiet, hidden place from which he had been able to observe the inside of the house. Low branches brushed against her shoulders and raindrops found their way under her collar. It was pleasantly shaded there and after a minute Madison was level with the deck at the back of the house. A small ridge in the ground had created a kind of trench next to a fir. She crouched under the tree. It was a natural shelter, Madison thought, and then revised that notion: it was a hunting blind.

Madison had a perfect line of vision to the living room of the Duncans' home and Amy Sorensen inside it, busy with her kit, directing her team. Sorensen's cell must have rung because the investigator picked it up from her open kit box. It was a personal call – Madison had no doubt even though she couldn't hear her. Sorensen had stepped closer to the glass and was talking to some-one. One of her kids maybe. Madison looked away. How easy it was to pry, to eavesdrop on the life of the house and those within it. A memory came and went before she had time to pluck it out of the stream and she returned to the intruder: it would have been even easier to burrow into the trench in the dark, when the back of the house shone out and the trees lay in darkness. He could have watched them, learnt their habits, their routine. Did Matthew Duncan use a glass for his beer or did he drink from the bottle? Where did Mrs Duncan sit to watch television?

Madison examined the damp ground and the knots on the tree roots: someone could have made a nest for himself there. She looked across to the house, pulled out her cell and dialed.

Sorensen picked up. 'Madison?' she said.

'Hey, Amy. I'm running a little experiment. I've found a good place where the killer could have kept an eye on the house. I need you to walk up and down the room and see if you can spot me.'

'Haven't played hide-and-seek with my kids for a while . . .' she replied and ran her gaze over the line of trees on both sides of the house, first from the living room then from outside on the deck.

After the third time her eyes had passed over Madison without seeing her, the detective called her back.

'I think it's safe to say you can't see me,' she said.

'But you can see me?'

'Yes, perfectly.'

'How many fingers am I holding up?' She smiled and lifted her left middle finger.

'Thought you was brung up better than that,' Madison commented.

'Never mind my manners. Take yourself out without doing damage. We should process that area. Ways in and out, the lot.'

Sorensen didn't press Madison to be careful not to spoil or contaminate the spot. Madison knew better than to mess with her crime scenes.

Brown had found nothing of interest on the other side of the house. The view had not been as clear and, most importantly, the intruder would have been more exposed.

Sorensen's team was starting to work on Madison's discovery when Brown turned to her. 'We have a date with Dr Fellman,' he said. 'Before or after lunch?'

Madison checked her watch. The morning had disappeared as they had walked every inch of the house.

'Before?' she replied.

Two years into their partnership there was no pretense that what they saw in the morgue did not affect her, and Brown rewarded her honesty with his own.

'Good,' he said.

Just because they had made their peace with it, it didn't mean it wasn't something they had to force themselves to endure each and every time.

Brown and Madison slid into a couple of window seats in Kafe Berlin on 9th Avenue with their lunch – two turkey-and-apple salads, one Coke, one ginger ale. They ate in silence, watching the passing traffic and the shadows getting longer so early on a winter's day.

Brown pushed away his empty plate. 'Andy's back from the bachelor party today,' he said.

'Is he? You spoke to him?'

'Yes.' Brown smiled a little. 'He's in one piece. A little frail perhaps.'

The wedding was going to be on Sunday: a massive Irish affair with relatives flying in from all over, without mentioning the contingent from the department in full dress uniform – Brown and Madison included.

'Aaron coming?' Brown asked.

'Yup, I thought I'd get him to meet everybody all at once, while we're all dressed up and armed, so he won't feel at all awkward and intimidated, you know.'

Brown chuckled. 'Had to happen at some point.'

Madison didn't ask him if he was bringing a plus one. In spite of all they had gone through together – including gunfire and near death – Brown's romantic life was still uncharted territory in their conversations. Madison was too shy to ask and Brown was happy not to share.

Just over a year ago their shift commander, Lieutenant Fynn, had beckoned her into his office one morning when Brown was in court giving evidence. Fynn had closed the door and Madison's alarm bells had chimed quietly.

'How is he?' he asked her, getting to the point without preamble.

Madison's brain had caught up fast: Brown had been injured the year before and his return to active duty had not been without issues.

'He's fine,' she had replied without hesitation.

'That's what I think,' Fynn had replied, 'but I need to hear it from you, and I need you to be frank – loyal, sure, as I know you are – but frank most of all. For his sake.'

Madison had stood there, feeling disloyal just by contemplating the notion of Brown's fitness for duty. *For his sake*. She had been watching him closely from the day he had come back – she couldn't deny that, not to herself. She pondered the question.

'He's fine,' she repeated. And she couldn't begin to tell Fynn how glad she was deep in her heart that she didn't have to lie.

A couple of weeks later, as they were leaving the precinct at the end of the shift, Brown had caught her off guard. 'Fynn checked in with you about me yet?'

She had felt about ten years old then and she had blushed. *You don't lie to Brown. Not ever.*

'Yeah, he did, couple of weeks ago.'

'What did you say?'

She thought it over. 'That you are a danger to yourself and the public, and they should take back your badge and your weapon lickety-split.'

'That's what I thought.'

Brown and Madison left the café and drove to the Harborview Medical Center and Dr Fellman's home-from-home, where Matthew Duncan had been patiently awaiting their visit.

Madison had tried not to think about it too much – whether the medical examiner would have finished the autopsy and the sheet would have been pulled up over the body's head or whether they'd find the pathologist still in the middle of things. Madison was not squeamish and she did not get queasy. She had seen much – a lot of it in the last two years in Homicide – and certainly more than most people had ever seen. And yet there was something about what had been done to this one victim that spoke to her of an insidious evil, something twisted and murky whose pleasure had been to leave a man's body intact and yet destroy his face so completely that none of it was left. In order to find that person, to catch that person, Madison had to stand close and breathe air from the same world as that person, and she knew herself enough to know that such ugliness was hard to shake off and impossible to completely forget.

She had heard the saying enough times and knew it to be true: cops and doctors and nurses and firemen marry each other because no one else has seen up close what they've seen and they can't go through life alone and in silence.

The doors swished open and Brown and Madison walked into the autopsy room in their coveralls. It was chilly – it was always chilly there. The scent hit them at the same time and they both breathed in deeply: the sooner they deadened their sense of smell, the better. Dr Fellman was still working on the body with one of his assistants.

Under the heavy lights everything was open, revealed and exposed: outside, inside and everything in between.

The assistant – Sam or Glenn, Madison couldn't remember; they all wore masks and never spoke – lifted the victim's liver out of the thoracic cavity and placed it on a set of scales on a metal side table.

Dr Fellman spoke in a soft monotone into a hanging microphone, dictating the notes that would become his final report. In his position as the King County Medical Examiner Ernie Fellman would perform or oversee well over one thousand autopsies a year; he had stopped keeping a personal tally a long time ago.

Madison kept her eyes on the doctor's back and away from the table. When he realized Brown and Madison were standing behind him, leaning against the bare wall, he turned to them.

'Aside from a couple of old fractures he was in good – no, excellent – health,' he said. 'I've taken X-rays of every nook and cranny and aside from two broken fingers and a broken ulna from years ago he was in great shape. He was an athlete, right?'

'Yes,' Brown replied. 'There were some trophies around the house. He played college football, which might explain the fractures – we'll ask his wife.'

'Doc, what can you tell us about the sequence of injuries?' Madison said.

Fellman continued his procedure as he spoke. 'First blow was to the back of the head – enough to give him a concussion, possibly enough to render him unconscious. If that was all he'd had he would have survived this. From the neck down the body was untouched. From the angle of that first blow I'd say the killer was right-handed.'

'Height?' Madison said.

'Difficult to say. It depends on how the killer wielded the statuette.'

Brown and Madison waited for his next words. The doctor's hands worked quickly; the steel instruments dinged against the table.

'You can look at the X-rays on the viewer,' Dr Fellman continued. 'I'll have to study them myself quite carefully when I'm finished here. But from what I can see I'd say between ten and twenty blows. Sorensen emailed me a picture of the murder weapon.' The doctor turned. 'This is the worst maxillofacial trauma I have ever examined. The bones were crushed, the soft tissue destroyed.'

Madison's eyes traveled over the X-rays.

Dr Fellman looked ghostly pale in his scrubs. 'Do you understand what you're dealing with here?' he said.

By the time they walked out into the dusk the street lights were on and the sky was streaked red with thin, harmless clouds. It would turn pitch black in minutes.

'She can't see him as he is,' Madison said as they got to their car. 'There's nowhere for her to look.'

'It's her choice.'

Madison nodded. She didn't want to think about what she would have done in that situation; she didn't want to think about that at all.

Brown and Madison met Kate Duncan at the precinct. She had come with her friend and seemed drowned in the dark coat she was wearing. She gave them a sworn statement and answered all their questions about the house, the neighborhood, where and when she had last worn the stolen jewelry. She was ashen and yet answered each question painstakingly as if each insignificant detail about their life was the most important clue to the insanity that had taken place in her home.

Afterwards, they took her to the Harborview Medical Center.

'I need to see him,' she had said simply.

Dr Fellman had covered the body of Matthew Duncan with a sheet. His hand and forearm on the side of the viewing window were exposed: they were smooth and flawless and a thin white band showed where his wedding ring had been.

Kate Duncan was shivering. She leant her forehead against the glass partition and stood there until her friend put her arm around her.

Back at her desk, Madison uploaded pictures of the pearl necklace and the other items that the insurers had been able to provide. The killer would want to sell his spoils as quickly as possible and she would be ready to follow the trail straight back to the hellhole from which he had crawled out.

Brown had only just left and Madison found herself standing by the open door of the barren office fridge as Aaron's text arrived; it was after 10 p.m. 'Still in the office? Wld you lk takeout?'

Madison smiled. Aaron texted like a teenager. In many ways he was just as he had been when she first met him as a kid – except now he had kids of his own.

Not just cops, doctors, nurses and firemen, Madison mused. She texted back. 'Yes, please.'

He brought pizza which they ate out of the carton on her sofa as they watched television. He didn't ask her about her day: she had told him what case she was working and he'd rather she forgot about her day altogether. As they were about to fall asleep, she stood and took his hand and led him to bed. They were too exhausted for anything more than a long, soft kiss and Madison drifted off with Aaron's heavy arm around her.

In her dreams she saw a house surrounded by the woods on the side of a hill. The house was made of glass and every room shone impossibly bright against the pressing night. As she watched the house and the tiny, distant people moving inside it, Madison realized – aware, as she was, that she was dreaming and with neither fear nor surprise – that her body was gone and that she herself was the night.

Madison slept through and when she woke up, just before dawn, she turned to Aaron's warm shape next to her. He had long blond eyelashes, like a boy's, and a small nick on his cheek where he had cut himself shaving. Madison felt blindingly grateful that he was there and he was whole, and that they had met again.

Chapter 8

Over thirty-six hours had passed from the murder of Matthew Duncan. Thirty-six hours. Madison drove towards the precinct in the early-morning light thinking about how little progress they had made in those hours. The neighborhood had been canvassed twice already and no one had seen anything unusual. In fact, no one had seen anything at all. No strangers' cars, no deliveries from unmarked trucks, no strangers of any kind. The Fauntleroy commuters had driven home from work with their eyes on the road and stepped inside their lovely homes without lifting their gaze once.

All of which left Madison without witnesses. The family who lived next door to the Duncans – the Andersons: father, mother and a little boy, eight years old – had come back home from dinner at their relations just before 9 p.m. and could testify to nothing. Every single one of the people who lived in the street and had known the Duncans by name or by sight had been left in various degrees of shock and, without fail, everyone had attested that they were a nice couple and wasn't it awful. Madison had got to the point where she knew within twenty seconds of talking to someone whether they had anything to contribute to the investigation. So far she had a pile – yea high – of statements but no useful facts.

Waiting at the traffic lights on 4th Avenue Madison checked her cell which she had thrown on the passenger seat.

No messages.

At some point a trickle of results from the Crime Scene unit would begin to flow her way and she couldn't afford to miss it.

Thirty-six hours.

Madison walked into the detectives' room with two cups of coffee in a cardboard holder and the *Seattle Times* under her arm. She put one beaker on Brown's desk and scanned the headlines while sipping her coffee. Something was trying to get her attention from way back in the last couple of days but she couldn't quite grasp it. Something to do with the media. There had been nothing striking in the reporting in the *Times*. And yet . . .

Madison went online. It took her three minutes to find it. It had been downloaded late the previous night. The helicopter – she had forgotten about the helicopter. The footage from the news helicopter had been downloaded and it was outrageous: in one of the low swoops at the back of the house the cameraperson had managed to get a shot of the body with Madison and Brown standing next to it. There had been a frantic zoom and they had caught a few frames of the victim's ruined face. Only a few frames – nevertheless, it would be enough to feed the grubby appetite of a certain section of the population. Could they get it taken offline? And if they did, where did the First Amendment stand on lurid reporting?

She closed the webpage. The Forefathers had not established a clear and undisputed defense of the freedom of speech to allow the last shreds of dignity of a murdered man to be bartered online.

Madison finished her coffee and slam-dunked the empty cup in the recycling bin. The Forefathers, in all their wisdom, might have had to create a whole New World but at least they had not had to deal with it online.

When Brown arrived he let Madison rant about the news helicopter for a few minutes, until her frustrations and her worries had played out and she had ran out of expletives. He knew what she knew: thirty-six hours.

Brown and Madison spoke to Matthew Duncan's colleagues at the architecture firm where he had worked, to get a fuller picture of the man. He had been very well liked and no one had a bad word to say about him. In fact, they had very few words to say about him because he had been a quiet, gentle man whom everybody had been fond of without knowing him very deeply. His family in Oregon were devastated; a brother was traveling to Seattle to see his wife.

No one, either at work or in his family, could imagine anyone wanting to hurt Matthew Duncan or any reasons for anybody to want to end his life.

'Something is bothering me,' Madison said to Brown as she was going over the records of recent burglaries to find similarities.

'Just one thing?'

'Let me rephrase that . . . A multitude of things bother me but this one is right at the front. Are we looking for a burglar who gets his kicks out of extreme violence, or a killer who decided to round off his evening with a robbery?'

Brown pushed his glasses up on his nose.

'Because I'm telling you,' Madison continued, 'I'm going through the records of southwest Seattle – what with burglars being territorial and all – and I'm not finding anything remotely like this.

And city-wide it's the same story. The occasional violent burglary, but the violence is always a means to an end. And every single homicide we've had on the roster so far this year has been drugs, money, drugs, sex crimes, gang violence, drugs, what have you. This,' Madison tapped the file, 'is something else.'

'I should speak with Kamen,' Brown said.

'Definitely,' Madison replied.

Fred Kamen worked at the FBI's National Center for the Analysis of Violent Crime. He headed the Behavioral Analysis unit 4 (crimes against adults) and worked with VICAP, the Violent Criminal Apprehension Program, a database of cases that covered the full spectrum of human awfulness over the fifty-one states. He was a friend of Brown, who was the Seattle Police Department contact person for VICAP. The last time Madison had spoken to Kamen it had been to hunt down a sadistic killer who worked for the mob.

Brown picked up the phone – he wouldn't email unless he had to – and Madison went back to check the list of jewelers and pawn-brokers who had been given pictures of the stolen items.

There were no messages from Sorensen in her in-box.

The call came through a while later.

'Am I speaking with the detective who's working the murder case, the robbery/murder in Fauntleroy?'

'Yes, this is Detective Madison. Who am I speaking to?'

'This is Ryan from the Seattle Pawn Company, downtown branch.'

Madison lifted a hand to stop Brown who was about to walk out of the detectives' room.

'What's your surname, Ryan, and how can I help you?'

'Clifford, name's Ryan Clifford, and I have one of the rings you're looking for. Gold ring with a ruby. A dude just came in with it.'

Madison stood up. 'Mr Clifford, Ryan, I need you to give me a physical description. Height, hair, eyes – everything you can remember.'

She scribbled on her notebook and passed it to Brown who got on the phone to dispatch.

Madison wrote down the details and spoke them out loud so that Brown could pass them on to patrol. 'Male, Caucasian, six feet tall, thirty years old or so, dark hair, blue eyes, about one hundred and fifty pounds. Wearing blue jeans and a red and black coat. What kind of coat, Ryan?'

Ryan Clifford sounded like a very agitated young man. 'A lumber-jack hooded jacket, I think.'

'You're doing great, Ryan. How long ago did he leave the shop?'

''Bout three minutes ago.'

'Hood up or down?'

'Up. He walked off in the direction of the ferries. I wanted to make sure he wasn't coming back before I called you guys.'

'We're on our way. Patrol officers will be with you very shortly.'

Madison replaced the receiver and grabbed her jacket. 'Can you believe this?' she said to Brown.

'We'll see,' he replied.

The pawn shop was only minutes away by car. The radio crackled with the communications from the uniformed officers who had arrived there and were searching for the suspect.

'If he's got transport, we've already lost him,' Madison said.

'We're not going to lose him,' Brown muttered with grim determination.

Blue jeans and a red and black lumberjack jacket didn't exactly make him stand out from the crowd, but it was what they had.

The traffic was moving too slowly. Brown and Madison were three blocks from the pawn shop and their eyes scanned the sidewalks. Men in suits, men in jeans with leather jackets, men in heavy sweaters and fleeces.

The radio came back: 'Possible suspect on foot on Pine Street, crossing 1st Avenue, headed southwest. Approach with caution.'

Brown and Madison were stuck behind a school bus. Every driver in the downtown area seemed to have decelerated to a painful crawl.

'Suspect has seen us and is running. Be advised the suspect is running southwest on Pine.'

'He's going for the market crowd,' Brown said.

At the end of Pine Street, the Pike Place Market would be busy with tourists. There were fresh-food stalls at street level and a multi-level warren of shops and restaurants inside that led down towards the water. They could not afford to let him get anywhere near it.

'I see him,' Madison said and she opened the door and was gone, darting quickly between the slow cars.

'Shit,' Brown cursed under his breath.

Madison had been faster than the patrol cars. She was about two hundred feet behind the suspect and pounding the concrete. Sirens howled somewhere nearby. She ran with all she had. *Was he armed? Would he take somebody hostage?* She should have had a plan but she didn't have one – except to get to the man and stop him where he was.

The man took a sharp left and continued on Pike Place, avoiding shoppers and tourists and never looking back. He dashed under the market's roof and down a stairway.

Damn, he's inside. He's gone in. Madison followed him twenty seconds later, aware that a couple of uniformed officers were also in pursuit behind her. Madison took the steps two at a time. The stairway was empty and as they reached the first level, crumpled at the bottom, she recognized the red and black lumberjack jacket. Out of the stairway the landing opened into a wide avenue of shops.

Madison turned to one of the patrol officers. 'We need to know what he was wearing *under* his coat, if the clerk saw it. Suspect's not wearing a coat now.'

The officer, a woman Madison had never met – her tag said M. Richards – started on her radio. Madison looked around; all she could see were placid shoppers going about their business. The hallways were teeming: a holiday group from England – their guide narrating the history of the market – seemed to have filled every available space. She reminded herself of the description. *Dark hair, blue eyes, about one hundred and fifty pounds.* How many men wore blue jeans? How many were shopping alone? She looked at the red and black jacket. She looked at the crowd of tourists. Within a few steps of the stairway there was a handful of shops: collectibles, magic tricks, prints and stamps, a barber. More uniformed officers had arrived and were making their way through the throng. Madison let them go past. What she had seen when she first arrived was stillness, people looking at the shop windows. It didn't look as if a man had just come tearing through, running for his life.

'He could be close,' Brown said, suddenly by her side.

'Look at the man in the barber's chair,' she replied.

A dark-haired man kept his eyes on the cops, coming and going, in the mirror while the barber was chatting away. The man had a wide black gown that covered his clothing and Madison could not see what kind of trousers he was wearing. The man's eyes shifted back and forth.

The British group was beginning to move to another area, dutifully following their guide.

Officer Richards was back. 'The clerk says a white T-shirt. Maybe. Couldn't swear on it. And we've got officers on all the exits now.'

'Thank you,' Madison said. Her eyes were focused on heads and shirts.

The man had had enough of an advantage on them to be able to reach the first level, get rid of his jacket – nothing in the pockets, Madison had checked – and mix with the tourists without the smallest ripple of unease in the crowd. He wasn't going to stick around if he could help it; he would want to get out of there as quickly and smoothly as he could. And there were cops waiting for him at each exit. Madison didn't want him to get that far: she wanted him isolated and alone. *He can see us, wherever he is, he can see us.* If he hadn't visited the Duncans with a firearm in his pocket maybe he wouldn't be carrying one now – or a knife.

Brown and Madison followed the British group at a distance; their chatter bounced around the shops and the wide hallways. As she passed, Madison looked at the guy in the barber's chair – he wore white sneakers and the strip of trousers visible under the gown was pale gray.

'He knows we're close enough to touch him,' Brown whispered. 'My bet is he won't be able to keep himself from checking us out.'

Madison nodded.

A handful of teenage boys – loud, giggly and loaded with bags from the collectibles shop – came running past and Madison was startled.

'There,' Brown said.

The British group had parted as the boys ran through, revealing a couple who had been in middle of it: a slim brunette with a deep red mountain jacket and a rucksack, and a man. He was speaking to her and she laughed. He had dark hair, blue jeans and a long-sleeved white T-shirt, and on that sunny November day he was most definitely not wearing a coat.

He saw them observing him and stopped talking, his eyes traveled around the hall and Madison knew he was weighing his chances with that many cops around. Their eyes met. She shook her head. A tiny movement that said: *Don't do it, whatever you're thinking of doing. Don't.* He seemed to be thinking about it. He could have easily grasped the woman by the arm and things would have gone sideways very rapidly from there. The memory of Matthew Duncan lying in his own blood came and went, but a cold, clammy feeling nestled in Madison's gut.

Brown was next to her; Madison felt his proximity like steady ground when you've been swimming hard. He was utterly still.

The man's features were plain, with a straight nose and high cheekbones. His smile to the woman had been pleasant and now she was looking at him curiously.

His decision was a heartbeat away. Madison sensed it and feared it and was about to move, and yet Brown's stillness was like gravity and it kept her where she was.

'Wait,' he said softly.

The man's pale blue eyes did another circle around the market. Maybe he was seeing all the futures that he might be allowed, all the possibilities that twisted away from this single moment: if he ran and made it outside, if he stayed and seized the woman by the neck, if he gave himself up.

He blinked. His face went blank and, very slowly, keeping his hands away from his pockets, he raised his arms, laced his fingers over his head, and dropped to his knees.

They were on him, cuffed him, read him his rights and marched him out so quickly that most of the tourists didn't even realize what was happening. The woman who had been chatting with him was left slightly bewildered as a uniformed officer took her to one side and explained.

By the time the British group spilled out of the market onto the bright waterfront, the man was in the back of a patrol car on his way to the precinct.

The man's name was Mark Tyler Jefferies and one hour later he sat in the empty interrogation room; his legs were stretched long under the table and one arm was draped behind the back of the chair. He had been there before; maybe not in that particular room, but certainly in a similar one, with a lock on the door and people with badges asking the questions. Madison watched him from behind the mirrored glass. He was calm and he hadn't asked for a lawyer yet. The way he had dealt with his arrest was as if it was a question of ill luck on an already bad day – inevitable, sure, but nothing to get too worked up about.

Madison had called Sorensen and left a message on her voicemail: she had a suspect in the box and no evidence except for the ring. She felt underprepared. If this man was a ruthless killer she was the one who had to put him away with almost nothing – any lawyer would be able to talk away the ring. He could have found it, a friend of a friend could have given it to him in payment for something, a UFO could have landed in the middle of Pioneer Square and a little green man could have given it to him before flying off. And yet, if he was the man who had done what the killer had done to the victim . . .

The door opened and Brown came in; his face was a mask of disbelief. 'It's not the ring,' he said.

'What?'

'It is *a* ring, obviously. Just not our ring.'

Brown held up a small plastic bag; a small gold band caught the light. 'This has a ruby with two diamonds on each side. Ours has three. Three diamonds. This is not our ring.'

Madison turned her gaze back on the man in the box.

His eyes were closed and his head leant back against the chair.

Mark Tyler Jefferies had run when he saw the uniformed officers were following him because there was an Idaho arrest warrant on his head for assault in the second degree and larceny. He knew he was running a risk with the ring he had stolen from his girlfriend's mother but he had run out of money.

It was Brown's pleasure to tell him that in all probability no one would have noticed the ring if he had pawned it three days earlier.

He would be remanded to the King County jail until the marshals had the time and the inclination to pick him up and ferry him home to Boise.

Chapter 9

Madison was as disappointed as she was relieved, and felt guilty about both. Andy Dunne had teased her once that she would make a great Catholic. *Just let guilt run pretty much everything you do*, he'd said, *and after six days of agonizing soul-searching and self-doubt you'll be ready for church on Sunday.*

Brown brought her a cup of coffee from the rec room.

'Do I look that bad?' Madison said.

'You look like you need a cup of coffee.'

'That I do.'

They both knew that it tasted like thin mud. *But it's the thought that counts.*

'Did you get through to Kamen?' Madison asked. As Brown was about to answer her cell started vibrating. 'Madison,' she said.

'This is Annie Collins, Kate Duncan's friend.'

'Yes, of course.' Madison remembered the hug between the two women.

'We were followed,' the woman said.

The words had rushed out in a panicked flow.

'What do you—?'

'I took Kate for a short walk around the Botanical Gardens and we were followed. A man followed us.'

'Was he from the press? Did he take pictures?'

'No, no pictures.'

'Look, we'll be right over. How's Mrs Duncan?'

'She's terrified. Wouldn't you be?'

Annie Collins was pale when she opened the door but otherwise she looked composed and her voice had lost the edge of fear that Madison had heard on the phone. The house was in Montlake which, Madison automatically estimated, fell in the Seattle PD East Precinct territory; she briefly considered who she knew in the East Precinct patrol who could keep an eye on the house as they went about their shift.

Annie Collins led Brown and Madison into the living room and went to get Kate Duncan. It was a large, comfortable room with a matching set of flowery sofas and armchairs. Nothing in it was more than three years old and the kitchen, glimpsed as they walked past, was a shining expanse of white.

Kate Duncan came through. Her blonde hair had been tied back and there were livid shadows under her eyes. She sat on an armchair and pulled her legs under her like a young girl. Her friend stood by with a protective hand on her shoulder.

'Thank you for coming,' she said, her voice shaking. 'I haven't been sleeping, we haven't been sleeping.' She gave her friend a wan smile. 'And today it was all too much.'

'Please tell us what happened,' Madison said.

The woman gathered herself and her friend squeezed her shoulder. 'We decided to take a little walk because the gardens are close by and the sun was shining and everything in the last two days has been so . . .' She couldn't find a word to describe the enormity of what had happened so she continued. 'We had been walking our usual paths and I noticed that a man who had been behind us when we first walked into the gardens was walking behind us again. I didn't think too much of it but as we went on he followed exactly . . . I mean he was always there . . . he took the same . . . he was watching us.'

Her eyes were wide.

Madison turned to Annie Collins.

'I saw him too,' the woman nodded.

'What happened then?' Madison said.

'I was sure that he was following us so I turned and looked at him. I thought he might have been a photographer . . .' The word hung in the air; photographers had chased her out of the house that first horrendous night. Kate Duncan shook her head. 'But he just stood there. He stopped and he stood there and he stared at me.'

'How far away from you was he?'

'About twenty yards,' Kate Duncan said.

'What did he look like?' Madison said.

'Tall, thin, I don't know . . . he was wearing dark clothes. A black windbreaker with a hood. The light was behind him and I couldn't see his face clearly.'

'How tall?'

'Over six feet tall.'

'Did he do anything, say anything?'

'No, he just stared for a really long time and then turned around and left.'

'Did he try to speak with you at any time?' Madison asked her.

'No.'

'And are you sure this is someone you have never met before?'

'I've never seen him before in my life.'

'And you?' Madison asked her friend.

'No, I've never seen him before.'

'Were there other people around?'

'A few, not many. He stood out,' Kate Duncan said, and she forced a small laugh. 'You're going to tell us this has nothing to do with what happened, right? That this was some weirdo in a park?'

'We're going to look into it, Mrs Duncan. Chances are that, yes, that's exactly what it was. You've been in the papers and there are many people out there who are curious and inappropriate.'

'Did you get a sense of whether he was looking at either one of you in particular?' Brown said. 'Or perhaps he was looking at both of you?'

'He was looking at me,' Kate Duncan said. 'He was looking straight at me.'

The traffic was slow as they made their way back downtown. They had jotted down their notes and after a few more questions they had left the two women sitting next to each other on the plush sofa. Mrs Collins's husband would be home soon from work and her young children were expected back any minute.

Kate Duncan had asked Madison whether they had any leads or maybe a suspect for her husband's murder and Madison had to tell her that, no, they didn't, they were still working on it.

'She looked petrified,' Brown said, almost to himself.

Madison had noticed that he had hardly spoken – nevertheless, his focus had been absolute.

'We can't rush in and assume that this stalker-type person is linked to the murder,' he said. 'But we can't rule it out either.'

'What we have is a tall, thin guy in dark clothes driving a car they did not see and not attempting to make any contact with them – that is, with her,' Madison said. She was trying very hard not to look for zebras where there might only be horses.

'He did exactly what he was supposed to do and then he left.'

Madison shifted in her seat and turned to Brown. 'What was he supposed to do?'

'He wanted her to see him,' Brown said simply. 'He wanted to make sure that she saw him and that she knew he had seen her.'

'To what purpose?'

'We'll ask him when we get to meet him.'

'I see.'

'Well, either he's your garden-variety creep who saw Kate Duncan, recognized her and wanted a closer look. Or he's something else altogether but did not want to harm her, in which case he might turn up again and we'll get to ask him.'

'You don't sound too worried.'

'The only thing that matters is that he could have gotten a hell of a lot closer and he chose not to.'

'True. Then again, what if he didn't spot them for the first time in the parking lot? What if he followed them from the house to the gardens and then decided to let himself be seen?'

Brown did not answer. Whether he had gone back to the flow of his own thoughts as a preferable way to pass the time, or the act of driving through the early-evening rush hour was absorbing all of his attention, Madison could not say. Nevertheless, she was glad that, on leaving the Collins house, she had reached out to a colleague in the East Precinct and let her know that Mrs Duncan was staying there and that she might have a stalker. The colleague had commented that at present they had seventeen stalking-type situations they were aware of in the precinct and one more wouldn't break the bank.

Madison's cell vibrated and when she saw the caller's ID she let out a sigh. 'Sorensen,' she said. 'Please tell me you have something for us.'

'Who's the Deputy Prosecutor on the case?' Sorensen said, and her voice told Madison that she bore no gifts for them that night.

'It's Sarah Klein, I spoke to her earlier.'

'Good, that's what I was hoping. Brown with you?'

'Yes, we're driving back from Montlake. We were with the victim's wife.'

'Okay, I need the two of you and Klein as soon as you can make it to the lab.'

'What's going on?'

'It's easier to explain face to face.'

'I'm calling Klein now.'

Brown gave her a questioning look.

'Sorensen has something and it doesn't sound like good news,' Madison said and speed-dialed Sarah Klein.

Madison was puzzled. Evidence *was*. It existed as a neutral tool to help find the truth: if Sorensen had found something, whichever way they looked at it, it should turn out to be useful. Still, Sorensen had been less than happy about it, that much had been clear.

Sarah Klein was on her cell in the lobby when they arrived. Madison had worked with her enough times to have a healthy regard for her skills: she was the only prosecutor she knew to have ever challenged attorney–client privilege in a criminal prosecution and got the judge on her side. As always, Klein was impeccably turned out in a shiny dark bob and a slate-gray skirt suit. She finished her call and turned to the detectives.

'Lucky you caught me before I went into a hearing,' she said by way of greeting. 'I have fifteen minutes.'

She wasn't being churlish: her minutes were measured by the court calendar and the judges' dockets. Madison was glad that she was on board for whatever Sorensen needed to share with them.

'I'll get to it in a moment,' Sorensen said as they stood around one of the work benches in her lab. 'But first I'll quickly run through some bullet points.'

Madison loved the lab and Sorensen had more than once suggested that she should come to work for her 'where the real investigating is done' instead of all that foolish gun-waving that cops were apt to do. It was a joke – sort of.

The room was dim except for a wide pool of light over the table. Sorensen's files had been scattered over it together with a number of evidence bags – including the murder weapon's, which shone under the overhead lamp.

'No surprises in terms of how the action had played out. The blood spatter pattern confirms the victim was bludgeoned with this,' she pointed. 'And the only prints we recovered from it were the wife's and the victim's himself. These were "handling" prints and not over the part the killer would have held. That part had been wiped clean. Aside from the victim's and his wife's we did not recover any other prints at the scene except for the cleaner's – she came in this afternoon to be printed for exclusion purposes.'

Madison made a mental note to speak with her as soon as possible; the woman had been out of town from the previous Friday.

'As you know,' Sorensen continued, 'we didn't find any footprints either – except for the wife's, after she came back from running. All the movements and transfers around the victim's body match her statement.'

Madison could see that Klein was keen for Sorensen to get to the point but was respectfully and uncharacteristically biting her tongue.

'What we have found,' Sorensen said finally, 'is a drop of blood – less than a drop, in fact – and epithelials in the drawer which contained the wife's jewelry box. It's consistent with someone putting his hand deep in the drawer and then pulling it out quickly and getting caught by a splinter on the underside. A scratch, in essence.'

She certainly had their attention now.

'The blood – Caucasian, male – was a match to a hair found on a crime scene seven years ago. It was found on the victim's body at the time of death. It was never identified and it had remained unmatched and nameless in the system.'

'What crime scene?' Brown said quietly. 'What victim?'

The air in the room had suddenly changed.

'It was the Mitchell case; the body in the closet,' Sorensen said. 'You investigated it,' she said to Brown. 'And you prosecuted it,' she said to Klein.

It was before Madison's time in Homicide but she saw that both Brown and Klein had instantly remembered.

'The neighbor was charged,' Brown told Madison. 'He pleaded not guilty, he had no alibi and the murder weapon – a hammer – was found buried in his garden. There was a history of bad blood between them and there had been threats flying both ways. We even had the victim's blood on a rag in the suspect's house.'

'How did he explain it?'

'He didn't. He said he was passed out, stoned and drunk, on his sofa at the time, alone. Toxicology confirmed he had enough in his system to set up his own Walgreens.'

'What about the hair?'

Klein came in on that. 'We explained it away because the victim had been on a busy bus on his way home from work: the hair could have been transferred through contact with another passenger and when he scuffled with the suspect it ended up on one of the injuries.'

'This could still be valid,' Madison said. 'There might be reasons why someone else might have been handling the drawer—'

'Peter Mitchell was beaten to death with a hammer,' Brown interrupted her. 'His injuries – if you account for the difference in weapon – are very similar to Matthew Duncan's. Not as extreme but definitely in the same neighborhood.'

'The suspect never pleaded,' Klein said. 'He rejected all pleas we sent his way. He kept saying he had been framed and somebody had buried the hammer and hidden the rag so that we would find it. No one was going to benefit from his going to jail, there was no money involved and so the jury put it down to one final quarrel that got out of hand and too much alcohol. They returned a guilty verdict in record speed. He had brought a weapon to the scene with the intent to cause harm. He had meant to kill but he didn't have any previous strikes so . . . twenty years.'

'Twenty-three,' Brown corrected her softly.

Klein looked at Brown. 'The minute they hear about this, his appeal team is going to—'

'He committed suicide two years ago,' Brown said. 'Four years into the sentence they found him hanged in his cell. He had never stopped saying that he was innocent.'

'I hadn't heard that he'd died,' Klein said and, for once, she seemed shocked. 'Even when it was looking terrible for the defense and it was clear the jury was going to convict, we wanted to close the case and offered him murder in the second degree. But he wouldn't take it. His lawyer was practically in tears.'

There was a moment of silence around the bench. Sorensen knew full well what kind of grenade she had just pitched in their midst and Brown and Klein contemplated the possibility – however remote at that stage – that they might have put the wrong person in jail, and there was absolutely nothing that they could do to fix that mistake.

Madison was the only one who had not been involved in the Mitchell case and her mind was catching up and lurching forward.

'Amy,' she said to Sorensen, 'forgive me for even asking you this, but—'

'Yes,' Sorensen replied without animosity. 'I'm sure it's the same person. I've tested the blood twice to make sure.'

'Okay. Sarge, were you the primary on the Mitchell case?'

Brown nodded. This was the noose every cop feels against their own throat when a suspect's life is in the balance.

'We're going to have to look at the whole case again,' Madison said. 'We don't know one way or the other yet for sure.' However, as Madison looked around the table, it seemed to her that conclusions had already been drawn.

'I'm going to have to get my boss in on this,' Klein said without any joy.

Her boss was Ben McReady, the King County Prosecuting Attorney, and he was not going to be happy to hear from her that night.

Klein left and the three of them examined blood-spatter charts and photographs of the Duncan house, wondering about exit and entry points.

'I have something from that possible observation site you found under the trees,' Sorensen said to Madison, and smiled. 'We found a small tin, well buried under the roots of the tree.'

'A tin?'

'Yup, it was full of Hershey Kisses wrappers and, judging by the size of the fingerprints on the tin, it belongs to a young child with a taste for chocolate who hides in there when he wants a quiet snack.'

Madison sagged. 'The kid next door. Eight-year-old boy. The family wasn't at home the night of the murder.'

'Eight-year-old boy sounds about right. There's a thin trail behind the tree that leads to the house next door, and small sneaker footprints coming and going. However, there was nothing at all that would indicate that an adult has spent any time there.'

'There might not be any trace evidence but it doesn't mean he hadn't been there. It is the perfect place to observe the Duncans without being seen.'

'I tells it like I sees it,' Sorensen said.

Sorensen was right and Madison felt they were now fighting not one but two ghostly figures. Her usual reliance on physical evidence today had bestowed on them more questions than answers.

It was a relief to leave the building. Brown had been very quiet since the revelation about the Mitchell case and Madison didn't want to intrude. At some point it would happen to her too – she was sure of that – she would be one, two, ten years down the line and someone she had put in jail might be discovered to be innocent.

She didn't know how she would cope with it. Watching Brown silhouetted against the dusk and the headlights she hoped that she'd have the kind of record he had – that, by then, she'd have become the kind of cop he was.

She approached him. 'Sarge, the cleaner just texted me back,' she said. 'She's still nearby and is going to come in to give us a statement.'

'Good,' he replied. 'If you can talk to her yourself, I'm going to go to Records to get the file.'

Madison didn't need to ask what file. Soon she would see with her own eyes how Peter Mitchell had met his end.

Chapter 10

Lisa Waters sat at the rec room table, weeping. She was in her early fifties, a fit and good-looking brunette with a Florida tan.

'I hadn't even seen Mr Duncan for the last two years,' she said. 'They're never home when I'm there.' She wiped her eyes with a sheet of kitchen roll Madison had found by the sink. 'And before then I must have seen him no more than three times,' she continued, and the tears were not drying up.

Madison let her gather herself at her own pace.

'Okay,' the woman said, wiping her face energetically. 'Okay, let's do this, let's do this now. I'm sorry.'

'You don't need to apologize,' Madison said. Lisa Waters' response to the Duncan murder was in fact the correct human reaction, she thought.

Empathy, distress, sorrow. Even if you didn't know the victim personally. Except Lisa Waters knew Matthew Duncan: their lives had somehow intersected and she had been intimately connected to the daily workings of his life without actually meeting him.

They spoke of her work in the house – four hours, twice a week – and her impressions of the couple – regular people, polite, tidy –

and then Madison came to ask about the last weeks because that's what mattered the most to her.

'We had the usual deliveries of groceries – they always ordered a box of organic vegetables that would arrive when I was there to receive it. And then there were the utilities companies.'

'Go on,' Madison said.

'In the last month we had fellas from Seattle City Light, Puget Sound Energy and also the air-con company coming in to do maintenance and checks.'

'Were you expecting their visits?'

'I knew about City Light but not the others.'

'Do you remember what these fellas looked like and exactly what they did in the house?'

Lisa Waters told Madison. She was a good witness with a sharp memory and when she got up to leave after a few more questions she grasped Madison's hand in hers. For a moment it looked as if she might start weeping again, but she didn't.

The minute she had left Madison put in calls to the utilities companies to check the engineers' logs. Maybe, just maybe, she thought, *their* fella had wanted to do a quick recce before the main event.

It would be a while before they'd come back with the answers she needed. And even if it turned up that the killer had visited the house before, what would have stopped him from stealing the jewelry then? On the living-room table, the night of the murder, the expensive, latest model Apple laptop had sat in plain view and there it still was – untouched – when the police had arrived, as was the Nikon camera in the study.

Through the open door Madison saw Lieutenant Fynn talking on his phone, and she hoped she'd find some answers sooner rather than later.

Brown returned with a thick file. 'I'm going to tell Fynn about what Sorensen found unless you want to do it,' he said – it was her case, after all.

'No, you go ahead,' Madison replied. Telling Fynn felt too much like telling on Brown.

'This is the file.' He placed his palm flat on the card cover. 'Before we talk about it, before I say anything about anything, you should read it and draw your own conclusions.'

Madison nodded.

Their shift had been over for a while but there was no way that she'd leave without reading it cover to cover. She opened the file, started reading and barely looked up when Brown came back from talking to Fynn. Sometime later she realized he was asking her a question.

'What?' she said.

'Are you going to finish it tonight?'

Madison looked at the clock: it read 9.37 p.m.

'Yes, I am. What are you still doing here?'

The next time she looked up there was a toasted chicken sandwich from Jimmy's Bar with a cup of coffee on her desk and Brown was gone.

Madison made it home just before midnight. She had texted Aaron earlier and went straight for a hot shower. Her mind was full of the details of the Mitchell case and she didn't want to start analyzing and evaluating any part of it now. She needed to sleep and let the facts simmer for a night.

Her last thought was for Brown: his kindness for bringing her food she had not asked for, and his dread that he'd made a terrible, lethal mistake.

What Madison had discovered in the files was that seven years earlier Peter Mitchell had not turned up for work in two days and there was no answer on his cell phone. One of his colleagues at the warehouse – his best friend there – had driven over to his house near Westcrest Park and arrived to find the car parked in the driveway and the door unlocked. He called out and when he received no reply he walked into the house. It was January and the weather was bitterly cold with a scrubby daylight that was of little use to raise spirits or illuminate the day. However, it was enough for the man to realize that he had walked into something – he just didn't know exactly what. In the living room the table had been upturned, a couple of plates had been knocked over and smashed, and the radio was murmuring in the kitchen.

What stopped the man though, what nailed him where he stood, was the scent: heavy, metallic, mixed with something rotten that came through in spite of the cold draft that had followed him into the room. He knew what it was because when he was a teenager he had worked in a slaughterhouse – not for long, just long enough to turn him into a vegetarian. And as his eyes adjusted to the gloom he noticed the dark streaks and splashes that seemed to reach everywhere in the room. He called his friend once more, his voice failing a little, and then stepped backwards and called the police from his car.

They found the body of Peter Mitchell in a closet. It had been easy to find because a drag mark in blood from the living room had shown them the way. The Medical Examiner, Dr Fellman, estimated that Mitchell had died almost forty-eight hours earlier, instantly, when a hammer had struck his parietal bone, crushing his skull. After three more blows, the killer had gone to work on his hands.

Early canvassing of the neighborhood and interviews with friends and colleagues had revealed that Mitchell had had a long-standing grudge with his next-door neighbor, Henry Karasick. When interviewed about it Karasick had joked that Mitchell had got himself killed just for the pleasure of getting him into trouble. Karasick did not see the clouds coming – not until Detective Sergeant Kevin Brown, who was in charge of the investigation, had read him his rights. A crime scene officer had found the rag under a chair and they were about to dig up an area of the garden which looked recently disturbed.

After that, it was textbook. Karasick denied everything. He would have denied ever having met Mitchell if he could. His non-existent alibi had been that he'd spent the evening alone at home, partaking of large quantities of weed that an acquaintance had given him, together with alcohol and a few other illegal drugs that were slowly but surely working their way out of his system.

The prosecuting attorney, Sarah Klein, suggested that he might very well have blacked out and therefore could not be sure about what he did or did not do. Karasick denied it. He never wavered, not for a second. His story never changed, even after they found the hammer buried in his backyard. There was a restraining order taken against him by his ex-wife and a long list of people he had argued with and fought with – and some of those times had landed him briefly in jail. And yet Karasick had kept denying being anywhere near Mitchell the night of the murder.

No one in the street had heard a thing because doors and windows were shut against the cold and only the pathologist could confirm the time of death, which was when the prime suspect was alone and a few meters away, with opportunity and intent. Karasick told them he had a drug and alcohol problem, that he was going to an anger management support group, that he had had a horrendous childhood that had made him what he was. He told them every last dark and twisted thing he had ever done in his life but he denied taking a hammer from the toolbox in his garage and going to Mitchell's home with the intent to kill him.

Without a guilty plea they went to trial and there were witnesses for both sides; Karasick's public defender even managed to rustle up the priest who had led the anger management group. However, he could not testify to the whereabouts of the defendant on the night of the murder, and Sarah Klein, with respect for the cloth and derision for the attempt, took the defense to the cleaners.

Karasick had listened in shock to the verdict. His mother was in court with his younger brother. They had cried. He started his sentence at the King County Justice Complex and lasted just over four years. His death did not surprise the authorities even if he had not been on suicide watch. He had proclaimed his innocence of the crime he had been sent to jail for until that last day, while he'd been happy to admit to everything else – the priest had called it a step in the right direction. In the end, the jail counsellor had said to the family, after his latest appeal had been turned down he had decided that enough was enough.

Madison had waded through evidence lists and witness testimonies. She had pored over Dr Fellman's autopsy report and Brown's interview notes and she was sure of one thing: if she had been in Brown's place she'd have reached the same conclusions and gone the same way he had. They had never found the clothes Karasick had worn at the scene – and that bothered Madison – but aside from that it seemed as straightforward as they come. In fact, she reflected, it was more straightforward than most: the line joining Mitchell and Karasick had been sharp and clear from day one.

Madison slept badly and only skimmed the surface of deep sleep. That line, she thought, was what troubled her now. Had it been too clear? The autopsy report had not been easy reading – they never are – but Madison had discovered in the turn of Dr Fellman's words a killer who seemed capable of a degree of cruelty and savagery that reminded her too closely of Matthew Duncan's death.

When Madison woke from a fitful sleep it was too early to go to work so she changed into her sweats. She needed to think, which meant that she needed to run. Her nose stung and her lungs burned in a matter of seconds. Nevertheless, she found an easy rhythm that allowed her mind to wander as she pounded the damp concrete.

The sky was inky blue and the stars still visible. Some windows were lit but most were not, and she didn't meet a single car on her route around the neighborhood. She passed Rachel's house – her best friend since they were both thirteen years old – and thought of Rachel, Neal and their boy, Tommy, who would be nine soon.

Their windows were dark.

By the time Madison got home forty minutes later she was both warmed up and freezing.

She drank some coffee, made herself scrambled eggs and was out of the door by the time the sky was turning from indigo to cerulean.

Brown had said he wanted to know what she thought and she would tell him. Hand on her heart, she would tell him that he had done – they all had done – a good job with what they had, and if she had been with them Madison would have put the cuffs on Karasick herself. Yet she did not believe in coincidences: for the same DNA to turn up in two different crime scenes with similar – unusually brutal – murders, well, the odds were against them. And they had never found Karasick's bloody clothes and, with everything in the world against him, when a plea might have shaved some time off his sentence, he had maintained his innocence.

Madison arrived at the precinct and found Brown already at his desk.

He took one look at her face and he knew.

Chapter 11

Alice Madison, fifteen years old in 1995, slid her bicycle to a stop and leant it against the garage that stood next to Rachel's home. It was an early-summer evening and it was warm. She knocked on the front door and waited.

Alice loved coming to Rachel's, always had. From the first time Rachel had brought her home – two years earlier – her mother had made her feel more than welcome. Rachel had told her mum that Alice lived with her grandparents because her mother had died and her father was somewhere else. Her mum had made it her mission to include Alice in all kinds of family celebrations and anniversaries with the result that Alice had had more Shabbat dinners than she could count and could recite the prayer together with everyone else. The fact that she hadn't had a bat mitzvah was neither here nor there: Alice was part of the family in all the ways that mattered.

The door was yanked open from the inside; Rachel was in a strop. 'Mickey's staying in,' she hissed.

Mickey was her older brother – three years older and already living in a different universe.

'Or I should say *Michael*,' she continued. 'Since he got the letter from Yale, Mickey is not good enough for him anymore.'

Alice shrugged. 'I don't mind.'

'I do. Mum and Dad are out and we were going to have the house to ourselves. But no, *Michael* is playing poker with his friends, drinking beer and pretending to be all grown-up. And the Leech is there too. Joy.'

The Leech, whose legal name was Lori, was Michael's girlfriend.

They reached the living room and, sitting around a table, five boys were busy dealing cards and looking cool. Alice knew them all: Michael, his two goofy friends from Burien High, and his cousins Aaron and Josh. Lori was draped over an armchair reading a magazine. She looked up when Rachel and Alice came in and then went back to her reading. Aaron's attention flitted towards Alice for a second and then went back to his cards before any of the other boys could notice.

Alice glanced at the table: they were playing Five Card Draw. In the world of poker it's the equivalent of using stabilizers; her father had taught her when her hands had been big enough to hold five cards. She didn't say anything. It would probably hurt their feelings if she told them.

Michael took a swig off a long neck. 'Hey, Alice.'

'Hey, Mickey.'

'Rach, you're going to watch TV or whatever in your room, right?'

'I'm going to watch TV wherever I want,' Rachel replied.

'We're playing here. Just go someplace else.'

'I don't know. It seems to me a fine evening to put on some of my favorite music while you boys play cards and I lounge with my dear friend Alice right here on the sofa.'

Alice knew full well that Rachel would have been happy to decamp to her room but it was a question of principle.

'You can stay, but no music and no TV,' Michael said.

His friends sniggered, though Aaron didn't. He was checking his cards and looking glum.

'Says who?' Rachel replied and started riffling through a stack of CDs. She turned to Alice. 'I think Michael Bolton, don't you?'

Alice was watching the game.

'That's Mum's, it's not yours,' Michael said.

'Still, let's see how loud I can get it to go . . .'

'Jeez, Rach,' Lori said, 'you're such a child.' And she looked them up and down.

Something about Lori irked Alice and she was not sure what. Lori was a senior, she had long, straight dark hair and perfectly applied eyeliner. Alice had never seen her do more than simper and paint her nails. For some reason they had always disliked each other and Alice and Rachel often wondered about her, about the silly writing on her T-shirts – 'Beautiful by birth, Bitchy by choice' – and her eyelashes. Were they fake, were they real or were they spiders that had crawled up her face and died there?

Michael giggled. 'You're such a child,' he repeated from the maturity of his freshly minted eighteen years.

He was not bad – as older brothers go – but here's the mystery, thought Alice. You can talk to a guy by himself and he's all right – no moronic tone and mostly okay manners – but you get more than three together in a group and they instantly turn into numbnuts.

Rachel was about to open her mouth to reply, but Alice cut in. 'Why don't we play for it?'

'What?'

'We play – that is, I play you – and if I win we can stay and listen to—'

'Michael Bolton,' Rachel said.

'Michael Bolton,' Alice continued. 'And if you win we go to Rachel's room and you won't hear a peep from us for the rest of the night.'

'You want to play poker?'

'Sure, why not? How hard can it be?'

Alice looked at Rachel who knew Alice's father played in Las Vegas.

'You can play?' Michael said as if Alice had just told him she could pilot jets.

'Yes.'

Lori snorted; it was a delicate mouse-like snort that she probably practiced in mirrors to get just right.

'Okay, we're going to finish our hand and then you're on,' Michael said.

'Not much to finish,' Alice said.

'Meaning?'

Alice had kept an eye on their hands and now she looked around the table, at the cards that had been discarded and who had bet what. She could only see Aaron's – a pair of kings. He was watching her, his long blond hair framing his face, and he didn't seem to mind too much if Alice and Rachel decided to stick around a while.

'Well,' Alice said, 'Josh here is going for a flush or a full house but you didn't give him what he needed and he's sulking. Goofball Number One has a good hand and cannot wait to get you betting but he can't bluff to save his life. Goofball Number Two has a two pair – one could be kings or queens – he wanted a full house but you gave Josh the card he needed. Aaron should fold while he can. And you, Mickey,' Alice smiled, 'you tried for a straight flush but you didn't get it. You eyed the cards Josh discarded but luck is a bitch and tonight she ain't on your side. What's going to happen next is that Aaron will fold, Goofball Number One is going to bet way too much 'cause he can't help himself, and the rest of you will keep playing single-dollar bets just to see what he's holding – which, by the way, is three of a kind. Jacks.'

They gaped at her.

Aaron grinned. 'Come sit next to me,' he said as he folded his hand.

The other boys looked at each other and at their cards.

'How did you do that?' Goofball Number One said when he could find his voice – his three jacks were on the table.

Alice shrugged. The boys threw down their cards. Alice picked them up and shuffled – not just a Sunday-night-at-home shuffle but a proper Vegas shuffle.

'Freak,' Lori said softly behind her.

Ten minutes later Michael Bolton blared through the speakers. Rachel and Alice allowed themselves a one-song victory and then turned it off.

They all ended up watching *Texas Chainsaw Massacre* together for the nth time and eating pizzas.

'Are you going to tell us how you did it?' Aaron asked Alice.

'Nope.'

'Why not?'

'It's a secret. I mean, sure, I could tell you, but then I'd have to kill you.'

Aaron had laughed. The French doors to the garden were open and the air was sweet.

Chapter 12

'Are you happy here?' Judy Campbell, the US Attorney for the Western District of Washington, asked her Senior Executive Counsel. She had sent an email to Nathan Quinn to pop into her office before the scheduled staff meeting to have a private word with him. Her eyes were crinkled with a smile but the question had not been asked lightly.

'What an interesting question,' Nathan Quinn replied. 'What brought this on?'

Judy Campbell had known him since their early days in the King County Prosecutor's Office when they had both been young, driven, idealistic attorneys who wanted to change the world one trial at a time. Now, twenty-odd years later, they sat in the smart office to which the President of the United States had appointed her and talked about happiness.

Nathan Quinn sat in the armchair opposite her desk. He crossed his long legs and straightened his shirt cuff as he pondered her question. The thin scars left on his fine features by an encounter with a madman two years earlier were almost invisible and he certainly looked better than he had done when he started to work for her.

'Nathan, how long have you worked here?'

'About eighteen months.'

'In these eighteen months as Senior Counsel would you say your workload has been light, heavy, or about what you expected?'

'I'm not sure I follow . . .'

'Let me put it another way. Do you realize that you have taken on the workload of three attorneys and your staff is mutinous?'

'I see.'

'They can't complain because you're here before them and leave after they do. However, you have taken half the cases of the Senior Litigation Counsel and I know for a fact that the Criminal Division is relying very heavily on you. You seem intent on making up for having spent twenty years in private practice and would be quite happy if we all scooted off home and left you to do all our jobs. Mine included.'

'I think you're exaggerating a little.'

'Am I?'

'Do you have any worries regarding the standard of my work?'

Judy Campbell sat back in her chair and let out a bark of a laugh. 'Do you know what your staff calls you behind your back?'

'Do I want to know?'

'Probably not.'

'What's wrong, Judy?'

She studied him for a moment. She was glad that she had known him a long time. Long enough that they had talked about the good times and the bad – and his bad times had been very bad indeed. Long enough that she knew his strengths and the keen edge of his skills.

'You are a litigator, Nathan,' she said after a moment. 'A wartime *consigliere*. And I don't know how long I'll be able to keep you here

– after all the years it took me to persuade you – because we are not at war. And war is what you need.'

There were thoughts behind his black eyes that she could not and would not fathom.

'I'll make sure my staff know they can go home for a couple of hours at night, if they absolutely need to,' he said.

'You do that,' she replied as he stood.

He left and her eyes fell on the picture on her desk of her husband and three children. Nathan Quinn was a cool, tall drink of trouble and she was suddenly thankful that she was a happily married woman.

As the meeting with senior staff was winding to an end, Jessica Decker, the Criminal Chief, turned to Judy Campbell. 'I had breakfast with Ben McReady,' she said. 'Something came up in the Duncan murder. One of his prosecutors called him last night. It might be something, it might be nothing, but they have some trace evidence that links it to a seven-year-old homicide. A homicide we have already tried and sentenced somebody for – somebody who committed suicide in KCJC two years ago.'

'Was it a solid case?'

'Solid as can be. The prosecutor was Sarah Klein and the primary was Detective Sergeant Kevin Brown.'

Nathan Quinn looked up from the file he was reading.

'I don't even want to think about the kind of mess this could turn into,' the Criminal Chief continued. 'We need to make sure t's are crossed and i's are dotted because the potential for screwing up is endless and the Duncan murder is media catnip.'

'I could keep an eye on it, if your plate is full,' Nathan Quinn said, as if it didn't matter one way or the other. 'I know Sarah Klein. I've worked with her before. If a mistake was made I'm willing to bet it wasn't hers.'

Decker nodded. 'It's yours if you want it.'

'Good,' Quinn said, and went back to the document he was reading.

Chapter 13

John Cameron adjusted the gum prosthesis in the restroom mirror and checked how it subtly altered the shape of his cheeks and jaw. He blinked. His eyes, normally a color close to amber, were blue – a natural-looking gray-blue – and his dark hair was a few shades lighter than usual.

The empty restroom was on the third floor of the Holy Pilgrim Hospital in Los Angeles. He sighed. He had enjoyed the trip to Newfoundland – brief as it was – more than he had expected and would have stayed longer if previous engagements had not called him back to Los Angeles. Then again, the point of the trip was to acquire – no, to confirm – information to round things up in LA, to conclude a project that had taken almost eighteen months to come to fruition, and then he would have all the time in the world to wander those vast, empty forests and the jagged coastline.

The air in Newfoundland had been deliciously cold and shockingly clean, such a complete contrast to the tepid, sticky warmth of the city and its sluggish traffic. There was something extreme in that landscape that appealed to him immensely even though the place could easily kill you if you forgot what you were dealing with. Maybe that's why he liked it so much.

John Cameron had been thinking about today's work for many months: ever since he had been kidnapped on the orders of people who meant to do him unthinkable harm. It had taken him a while to regain his balance, to metabolize that single day when death had been so close he'd felt it brushing against his skin like a cat. If not for Detective Madison the cat would have got him. He knew now that what he had felt was not fear but a sense of frustration that his life should end in such an untidy manner at the hands of men he despised. As his wounds had healed he had decided to make sure the men would not have the chance to try their luck again.

In the moments when he thought he might die, it had been a comfort to him that Nathan Quinn had been safe. Nathan was a brother in all but blood and John Cameron had killed for him – for him and for the memory of a boy who had been good and brave. That first murder – a fledgling killer's attempt at justice – was only one of the many things they did not talk about. And now that Nathan worked for the State Attorney it made it even less likely that they would ever talk about it. It didn't matter. Their friendship was layers of shared memories from when they were kids, from when their fathers worked together in the restaurant they owned. It was a lifetime of joy and sorrow and, most of all, secrets.

Cameron straightened the white coat that he had procured himself from the doctors' locker room. He cocked his head like a bird and studied the small fake pregnancy bump that gave him a belly and changed his body shape. He looked like a man who didn't do much more than hit a golf ball once a month. He did miss the familiar weight of the Smith & Wesson .40 he usually wore in a shoulder holster but it would have been too visible under the coat.

Still, the snub-nosed .38 was by his ankle and a six-inch knife had disappeared under his shirtsleeve. He hooked a pair of glasses he didn't need on the breast pocket of the coat. All he wanted was a cup of coffee and he was ready to go. His heartbeat – although some acquaintances might be surprised that he had one at all – was slow and it wouldn't rise much even during battle. He gave himself one last check in the mirror.

When John Cameron had killed his first human being he was indeed seeking a sense of justice that could not have been achieved in any other way. Since then, however, he knew himself well enough to know that he did what he did because he enjoyed it – and had survived this long because he was good at it.

On his way into the hospital he had passed the chapel and in a sudden impulse he'd gone inside. His ancestry was Scottish – Catholic – and he had no doubts about the kind of fate that his parents' faith predicted for a man who'd done the things he'd done. The chapel was bland and he wished for a touch of glorious over-the-top Catholic flair – a Madonna wrapped in heavenly blue or possibly a Christ with eyes raised to the next world. From somewhere he had remembered that in the fourteenth century the Vatican had passed laws to restrict the use of the very expensive and magnificent color blue so that the Virgin Mary would be the only blue mortal eyes would ever glimpse. This chapel had no blue at all but only a sense of polite, dutiful belief and Cameron had left.

He was not afraid of the next world, he considered. All in all, he had already used up his share of fear a long time ago in this one.

Half an hour later John Cameron, holding a metal clipboard with fake patients' notes, traveled to the fifth floor in an elevator with visitors, patients and other staff. The hospital was so large and busy that a new face in a white coat went completely unnoticed. Sharp chemical scents rose as the doors slid open, together with the regular hospital fixture of equal parts hope and despair.

He knew where he was going and headed for a corridor on the left. It was late morning and the life of the modern hospital was in full flow. He stopped by the vending machine and patted his pockets for change. He inserted the necessary amount and pressed the keys for a black coffee. It poured out into a plastic beaker and he picked it up gingerly and took a sip. It was horrendous. He walked on and then his feet tripped over something; it was only a tiny little jolt but the coffee went all over his coat and the floor.

'Darn it,' he swore under his breath and then looked at the two men standing by a patient's room and smiled an apology. There was a paper cloth dispenser within reach and he grabbed a few and started to wipe the spill on the tiled floor.

The two men standing by the closed door watched him because there was nothing else to look at in the corridor. They were tall, broad and looked Latino.

'Aside from anything else,' Cameron said pleasantly as he balled up the paper towels, 'it's possibly the worst coffee in the world. Have you tried it?'

One of the men snorted. Clearly the vending machine coffee was way below their standards.

Cameron straightened up and wiped at the stain on his coat. 'Are you visiting Mrs Rojas?'

'Yes,' the older one said with a heavy Hispanic accent.

They both wore leather jackets on a warm day because, Cameron knew, they both had semi-automatic weapons tucked into the back of their trousers. Had they known who he was his life expectancy would have been measured in nanoseconds.

'A nice lady,' Cameron said, his smile respectful and sad because they would know, as he did, that Mrs Rojas was terminal.

He threw the paper in a bin and, as he turned to leave, he nodded goodbye to the men. They nodded back.

John Cameron went back into the elevator. The coffee really was terrible. However, other than that, the day was swell.

Chapter 14

There was a lot of naval imagery and turns of phrases going around in the Gleneagle Heating Ventilating and Air Conditioning Company and, sure, it was a bit of a joke between the guys – and one woman – who worked in the field because the boss was ex-navy and still had the attitude and the slang. The result though was that when a call came in from the Seattle Police Department with regard to whether one of their engineers had visited a specific address in the Fauntleroy area, they were able to find out quickly when he had last been there to check the air-con system, how the devices had performed in the maintenance test – *checks-5-0's*, all of them – and how long he had spent in the Duncan home.

Tony, who booked all the engineers' visits, picked up the phone and dialed. 'Hey, Bobo,' he said when Robert Miller picked up. 'I have to double-check something. You're in the middle of a test?'

'No,' Bobo replied with his usual grace. 'I'm picking wild flowers. Yes, I'm in the middle of a test. What do you want?'

'Seattle PD is asking me the last time we checked the systems at a residential address in Fauntleroy. That's the place the guy was murdered in the burglary.'

Bobo Miller took a moment for an attitude shift. 'I saw it on the news, I recognized the house.'

'Right, I've got here you were there last Thursday. Can you confirm that?'

'No, I haven't been there for months. Not since last spring.'

'The previous appointment I have down was in March.'

'Sounds about right.'

'Are you sure?'

'Yes, last Thursday morning I did two houses near Alki Beach and then I had a dentist appointment.'

'But the log—'

There was a rustling of clothes and Miller's voice came back. He read out two addresses on Alki beach. 'This is where I was last Thursday, it's on my PDA. You can call them up and check.'

'That's not what I've got here. My records show that you haven't been in the Alki Beach addresses since last November.'

'Well, your records are wrong. Call them up and check.'

Tony ended the call and did just that – because if you can't trust a log, what can you trust?

One call went to voicemail but the second one did not.

Yes, the man replied, a Gleneagle HVAC engineer had come around the previous Thursday.

'The HVAC engineer hasn't been around since last March,' Madison said to Brown with the receiver cradled against her shoulder. 'But the log in the server says he's been there last week.'

'He hacked the company computer?'

'Looks like it. He changed the record to show he'd been there and cancelled the real appointments. If the booker hadn't checked with the engineer we wouldn't have known.'

'He's gone to a lot of trouble for a burglary,' Brown said quietly.

'Sorensen's computer people are going to want to look at that server.'

He nodded.

They were both slightly in shock: this was horrible news. A little reconnaissance from the killer might be expected – especially in the case of a burglary – but nevertheless, hacking into a company server to wipe any trace of that recce was more than a regular burglar would have, and could have, accomplished.

Neither said anything and yet both realized that the investigation had just turned a corner.

Seattle City Light and Puget Sound Energy had already confirmed a visit to the house just as the cleaner had told Madison. The Gleneagle HVAC engineers wore navy-blue trousers and white shirts with the company name emblazoned on a pocket: the uniform wouldn't have been difficult to reproduce, Madison thought. It would have been easy for a man to gain entry into the Duncan home and walk around, from room to room, scoping out the place without hurrying as the cleaner gave him a guided tour.

Madison called Lisa Waters. 'We need you to come back to the precinct, Mrs Waters. We need you back now to work with a sketch artist.'

The woman didn't need Madison to explain. One of those men she had let into the house . . . one of those men she had made coffee for and chatted with pleasantly, as a welcome interruption to her day. *One of those men.*

She replied that she'd be right over and Madison heard in her voice the shadow of guilt and shame. She would have to tell her that there was nothing she could have done and no way she could have known. And yet a part of Madison worried only that Lisa Waters might not have twenty-twenty vision and flawless memory.

There was also another issue, and Madison did not need to bring it up with Brown. If they had a half-decent composite drawing of the man who had lied his way into the Duncan home, they could also use it to jog the memories of anybody who had lived around the Mitchell house seven years earlier.

Brown had not tried to rehash the details of the Mitchell case or in any way rationalize and justify what had happened. He had taken on board Madison's single comment: 'We need to take a look at this.' And he'd gotten down to work. There would be time for recriminations later; today they had to hunt a vicious killer who might have killed more than once. The Mitchell case had been seven years earlier and Brown did not want to think how the killer had entertained himself during those long winters and summers and what he'd done to relieve his boredom.

The forensic artist sat with Lisa Waters as Madison stood, paced and spoke on her cell in the corridor.

She had tried to sit in with them, but forensic art was craft and patience, and a look from the artist had told Madison that if she couldn't show a measure of the latter she should remove herself from the room.

Amy Sorensen stood in her protection suit by the front of the Duncan home. The pallid sun had blessed them again and the air was soft with an underlying chill. Good weather for hunting evidence, she said to herself. Dry and bright and still. She didn't have all day but she had some time to go over ground that had already been covered. She had found the time because of Madison's words. *There might not be any trace evidence but it doesn't mean he hadn't been there.* Sorensen wasn't going to let it go: if there was a chance they could find the place from which the killer had kept an eye on the house – and with the wide glass side there was no way he hadn't – then she'd sieve every bit of ground like a prospector before she'd consider it properly covered.

The left side was a mess of shrubs and too exposed – exactly what Brown and her own officer had said. Sorensen struggled through the bushes for a few minutes then returned to the top and started back on the other side. She walked the dense, wooded area in a grid with her eyes first at normal level – to pick up on alterations and breakages in the branches – and then with her eyes on the ground.

It came down to the same result: the spot under the tree in the ditch was the best place to hunker down and play spy – even the little kid next door had worked that one out. Sorensen did just that. She squatted and rested with her back against the roots and looked up. The light slanted through the limbs of the fir and filtered in patches onto the ground. It bounced off the small rocks covered in moss that were scattered about. Some rocks were slightly bigger than the others and her eyes fell on one roughly the size of a football. She noticed it because she was sitting there as sunlight fell on the rock and she could see that the pattern of moss didn't match the ones next to it.

Sorensen leant forward and her hand closed on the stone.

They had a likeness. They had the face of a man on a piece of paper. He had worn a navy-blue baseball cap and Lisa Waters could not swear about the hair but she wanted to say dark and short, certainly above the ears. Dark hair and blue eyes. He was tall – just over six feet – with slim, high cheekbones and a straight nose.

'Are you sure you're not mistaking him for any of the other guys who'd come over? I don't want to doubt you, Mrs Waters, I just need to make sure.'

'I know what you mean and I don't mind you asking. I remember him best because he was the one who spoke the most to me.' Her voice faded a little there.

I just bet he did, Madison reflected.

They drove back to the house in a two-car convoy – Lisa Waters first, followed by Brown and Madison in their unmarked car. They pulled in on the driveway behind a single Crime Scene unit van, which stood locked up and deserted. Someone, thought Madison, was still in pursuit.

Brown paused before they filed in. 'What you're doing, Mrs Waters – Lisa – is of great help to us. Never forget that. And I know it's going to be hard and what you'll see will be things that are very hard to see for anybody. So just do your best to remember, that's all we can ask. We are with you.'

The woman nodded.

Madison wished that she had thought about comforting the witness herself. Brown had said the right thing at the right time and Lisa Waters, however pale, took her first step inside.

The impact was immediate and Madison saw it in the woman's face: the house even *smelled* wrong.

She took a big breath and started. 'I answered the doorbell and there he was,' she said and closed her eyes. She saw the white shirt, the hat; he wasn't wearing a coat.

'What time of day was this?' Madison asked her.

'Morning . . . it was morning, because I usually get here at nine. I couldn't tell you more than that.' The woman looked around: she needed to see and she didn't want to look.

She told them about his easy patter and how he had asked her to show him into each room so that he could check each unit in turn. She turned and walked to the living room, following the path cleared by the Crime Scene unit crew. She wanted to deal with the worst first.

The sunlight through the glass reached into every corner. She stopped and stared; her eyes took in everything. It was the strangest thing: violence and evil revealed through all the blood spatter and yet each splash had been tidied up by a number on a card.

After a moment she nodded and turned to the detectives. 'He wanted to see the bedroom first. He definitely asked me to show him in there first because he said there had been a problem in the past,' she said. 'And I took him.'

The man had been very thorough, probably making a mental map of the place as they went along.

'Did you ever leave him alone?'

She nodded. 'Yes, the telephone rang and I went to answer it. He must have been alone for a minute or so.'

'Who was it?' Brown asked. 'On the phone. If you remember.'

The woman blinked a couple of times, her eyes fixed on a spot on the wall as she went back to the day.

'No one. There was nobody on the line when I got there. I remember now that I made a joke when I went back to him – something about call centers.'

'Where were you when the phone rang?'

'In the bedroom. He was standing by the thermostat over the bedside table and I was by the door.'

'When you came back to the room, where was he?'

'He was over by the window. Made a comment on the view.'

The dresser, Brown and Madison noted, was next to the wide window.

*

It took them half an hour to trail Mrs Waters around the Duncan house. Being there had helped her and more memories had floated up to the surface. It gave Brown and Madison a good picture of the man who had been so at ease with her, so calm and collected as he took the measure of his prey.

They said goodbye to her and, as much as she had been glad to help, it was obvious that she was even happier to leave.

Sorensen found them on the doorstep. She had come out of the side of the house and looked like the terrier who'd got the rat. She held up a clear plastic evidence bag inside which there seemed to be another smaller plastic bag. And inside that . . .

Madison screwed up her eyes to see.

'It's a stainless-steel cigar case,' Sorensen said. 'It was buried close to the spot and deliberately hidden under a rock. And I'm ready to bet the kid didn't put it there.'

'Can we—?'

'No, Detective, shame on you. We're not going to open it here for all the contents to blow away and/or get contaminated. You want to see what's inside, you come to my lab and ask nicely.'

'How long had it been there?' Brown asked.

'Difficult to say, but probably a few weeks, judging by how grimy the bag is. Not a long time though. The kid's tin had seen more weather, and it wasn't wrapped in plastic either.'

'We need to show the neighbors the artist's sketch first, then we'll come over to the lab,' Madison said. She couldn't begin to imagine why anyone would bury a cigar case.

A picture began to form in Madison's mind: it was the angle of the eyes from the artist's drawing and the memory of the man's voice – local, educated, lower register – from the cleaner's testimony. It was the fact that he was right-handed and tall and unafraid to go in without a mask, to show his face to a potentially devastating witness, and capable of hacking into a protected server.

'He's confident,' Madison said to Brown as they watched Sorensen's van drive away.

'Yes,' he replied. 'He is an extremely capable man.'

'He risked going to the house with practically no disguise except for a baseball hat. Why do that when it was likely we'd interview the cleaner?'

Brown shook his head. He wasn't going to give Madison a wild guess when they had so little to aid their guessing. She didn't push him.

They each took one side of the street and started knocking on doors. Many people were out at work but some were at home. Most were keen to discuss the murder even if none had anything to contribute. No one had seen the man in the picture or noticed him that morning. Apparently, Madison thought, he had simply materialized on the Duncans' doorstep and vanished after his visit.

After a couple of hours anyone who could be interviewed had been spoken to and the composite had been shown. Madison nodded to the people carrier parked in the driveway of the house next to the Duncans.

'They're back,' she said.

Brown rang the doorbell and a tall, dark-eyed woman opened it a few moments later. She smiled, then recognized them from earlier in the week and the smile faded a little.

'Mrs Anderson, I was wondering if we could talk very briefly with your boy.'

'Paul?' She unconsciously looked towards the living room. 'Sure, but why? I already explained we were not here when . . . it happened.'

'I understand, but your son plays in the yard from time to time and if someone was being nosey around the Duncans' home he might have seen this person in the last few weeks.'

'He doesn't know it was a murder,' she said, her voice low. 'We told him it was a robbery and it's dreadful enough for him to consider that someone could get into our home.'

Privately Madison thought that if the boy had been anywhere near the news or a paper he would know. However, she didn't remember watching the news when she was that age and so just nodded. 'We're not going to tell him.'

Mrs Anderson mulled it over: the idea of Homicide detectives having anything to do with her little boy was not pleasant.

Madison smiled reassuringly. 'It will only take a moment.'

She led them into the living room where Paul was watching television curled up on the sofa. He was little and skinny, with his mother's dark eyes. On an ottoman by his feet there was a plate of chopped-up carrot and celery. It was untouched.

'Paul, sweetheart,' his mother said, 'this lady and this gentleman are police detectives and would like to ask you a question. It's about the robbery in Kate and Matthew's house next door.'

'Hi, Paul, may I speak with you?' Madison said.

The boy nodded and sat up straight.

'Do you play in the yard sometimes?'

He nodded again.

Brown leant towards the mother and said quietly, 'May I show you the picture of a potential suspect?'

She turned to him and Brown reached for the composite in his pocket.

Madison perched on the edge of the sofa as the sound from cartoons the boy was watching washed over the room. She dropped her voice. 'Paul, have you ever buried anything in the yard, in the space between your home and the Duncans?'

The kid's eyes flew to his mother's back.

'It's okay, I know about the tin with the chocolate wrappers. I love Hershey Kisses too.'

He gaped at her.

'I mean something else. Have you ever buried anything else around there?'

Paul looked at his mother again but she was talking with Brown, looking at something.

'No,' he whispered. 'Just my tin. Am I in trouble?'

'No,' Madison smiled. 'You're absolutely not in trouble.' And she took out the picture. 'Have you ever seen this man anywhere near here?'

His mother had turned back to them. He looked at her and he looked at the picture. He shook his head.

'When you were playing in the yard have you ever seen anybody hanging around outside the Duncans' home who didn't look quite right to you?'

There was a copy of the *Seattle Times* on the dining table and the boy's gaze went to it. The kid knew it wasn't a robbery, Madison thought.

'Anything at all that seemed out of the ordinary?' Madison repeated gently.

'No,' the boy said and he looked very small then and afraid.

Madison stood up and said, 'Thank you very much, Paul, we really appreciate your help.' She put out her hand formally and he shook it, a shadow of a smile crossing his features.

Brown and Madison returned to their car.

'Carrots and celery?' Brown raised his eyebrows.

'Kid's smart, he's made sure he's got his own stash of goodies squirreled away.'

'Did you?'

'No, but I had a tree house with a pantry.'

'A pantry?'

'Well, a cooler box.'

At thirteen Madison and her friend Rachel had been too old for little kid's games and yet the tree house had been perfect for those conversations that needed the absence of grown-ups.

'Talking about food . . .' Brown said.

Chapter 15

Fauntleroy was mercifully close to California Avenue SW, and Brown and Madison were pulling up in front of the Husky Deli in minutes on their way downtown. They sat at the old-fashioned counter while the sandwiches were being prepared and watched the shoppers and diners around them.

'I used to come here with my grandfather,' Madison said out of the blue.

Brown turned to her. 'Really?'

'Yes, it was a Saturday treat. Ice cream cone. Maple walnut, mostly, with occasional ventures into mocha.'

Brown knew that her mother had died when she was twelve and five months later Madison had run away and spent seven days alone on the road. Then she had moved to Seattle to be brought up by her grandparents. They hadn't spoken about her father much.

'Chocolate,' said Brown, who was Seattle born and bred. 'Mine was chocolate and strawberry.'

'Together?'

'Yes.'

'Really?' Madison frowned.

'The heart wants what it wants,' he said, and picked up the sandwiches – chicken cashew for Madison and his own Italiano.

The heart wants what it wants. Emily Dickinson was right, Madison considered as she ate her food and for a few minutes tried to think of nothing at all.

Sorensen was waiting for them. She was pacing in her office and looked relieved when they stepped out of the elevator.

'Did you interview every single man, woman and child in Fauntleroy?' she said.

'As many as we could find, yes,' Brown replied.

'Well, good for you. Come with me and don't dilly-dally. I have already sent Lauren and Joyce back to the house with metal detectors.'

Sorensen was walking fast, headed to the main lab, and they followed her.

'What was it?' Madison asked her.

'Easier to show you,' Sorensen said over her shoulder and led them to a bench in the corner.

It rested on a clean white sheet under a powerful lamp: a short metal tube whose lid had been unscrewed and placed next to it.

'This is a stainless-steel cigar case. The dimensions are eight inches with a sixty-ring gage. It had been wrapped in this plastic bag. As you can see, it's your basic resealable bag – you'll find a box of these in every pantry.'

Brown and Madison stood and watched: it was Sorensen's show.

'Whoever put this inside the plastic wanted to make sure the contents would be dry and preserved for as long as possible. And this is what I found inside the cigar case.'

Sorensen picked up a tray from a nearby shelf and placed it under the lamp. Brown and Madison leant forward.

'No touching, please. It's going to be hard enough to get anything off them and I'm trying to handle them as little as possible myself.'

Seventeen strips of paper rested on the tray. They were all about half an inch wide but varied in length. Some were dense with typing and others had snatches of color; some were almost blank and others were nothing but a plain strip of paper. Sorensen had extracted them carefully with her tweezers and they lay in parallel lines, more or less crumpled, waiting to go through an onslaught of tests.

Brown pushed his glasses up on his nose and Madison swiped a magnifying lens from a table nearby and bent closer.

'I can tell you this much,' Sorensen continued. 'This is not the kind of thing that a shredder does. Shredders produce a much thinner strip of paper. From what I can gather after a first superficial examination, the strips have been cut by a very sharp razor blade and intentionally made this width – see, there's a tiny pencil mark on the top of the page there. It's almost invisible.'

'Page,' Madison repeated. 'They're pages cut from somewhere and short ends of something we haven't identified yet.'

'That's what I think,' Sorensen said. 'Books, magazines, leaflets, receipts – I don't know yet. What we know is that they were purposefully sliced off, placed in the tube and buried in the Duncans' garden in a place that was not immediately obvious but would have been at hand if someone was watching the house from that spot.'

'Prints?'

'Nothing on the bag and nothing on the cigar case.'

That was it. Lack of prints on a surface that by all accounts should have been covered in them could only be explained if someone had deliberately wiped them – and the cigar case positively gleamed under the lamp.

'Before you get too excited about tracing the case, you can buy them on Amazon at fifteen dollars a pop. Unless there is something markedly unusual about it – and I don't think there is because everything about it says *plain* – it won't be much use to you.'

'We need to know exactly what books or magazines – or whatever – these came from,' Madison said. 'And it's a priority. In fact, could we have copies made so we can—'

Sorensen whipped up a sheaf of papers from a table and offered them to Madison. 'Here you go. Knock yourself out.'

Each one had a magnified copy of a single strip.

Frank Lauren and Mary Kay Joyce had worked in much worse places than the Duncans' garden on a cold, sunny November day.

They were suited and booted and their headphones were plugged in and ready.

'Grid?' Joyce said.

'Grid,' Lauren replied.

They switched on their metal detectors and each started to work on their section of the imaginary grid, the detector swaying like a cumbersome, unsightly extension of the human arm.

Later, after more canvassing – which caught the people who had been at work earlier but held the same meagre result – Madison briefed Lieutenant Fynn on what they had so far, including Sorensen's discovery and the hacking of the Gleneagle HVAC company server.

The detectives' room was still busy. Spencer and Dunne were huddled by their desks, going over a case, and Kelly and Rosario were both on the phone. Brown took Madison to one side. She had been turning things over in her mind since they had visited the lab. There was something they needed to do, but she needed Brown to bring it up, and as he approached her she allowed herself to hope.

'I don't know what you think, but maybe Sorensen should send some metal detectors over to the Mitchell house tomorrow. See if we find anything buried there too.'

Madison nodded. *Thank you, Sarge.*

'Yes,' she said. 'I'll call her now.'

Sorensen confirmed that Lauren and Joyce had not found anything more of any interest to the investigation in the Duncans' garden and told Madison that she had just been waiting for the go-ahead from her before going to the Mitchell place.

'Did he bring it up?' she asked Madison.

'Yes, he did.'

'Good man.'

The last job of the day was a quick visit to Kate Duncan.

She held the picture the artist had sketched in both hands and stared at it. A mixture of dread and incomprehension played on her face. She gazed at it for a full minute and then, almost disappointed with herself, shook her head.

And no, she said, neither she nor her husband had ever buried anything in the yard.

Brown and Madison had not really expected a different result.

Madison parked her Freelander in the usual spot by Alki Beach. It was dark and she couldn't see the water of Puget Sound; she could only see the points of light suspended in the distance – Bainbridge Island, Elliott Bay – and before them thick, black nothing.

She had changed in the precinct's locker room and the fresh salt air felt good. She leant on the car with one hand and with the other she pulled one foot high behind her. She repeated the stretch on the other side.

Madison started running and tried to empty her mind of every single thought except for the sound of the tide on the pebbles. She kept going back to the briefing, to Fynn's face as she charted their progress – *her* progress – with the case. Did he trust her to bring it home? Yes, he did, otherwise he would have hauled her off the case faster than a whip crack, so fast there would have been a small sonic boom.

That's what Madison told herself as she ran, and she smiled a little, but she did not want to think about it too deeply. Instead, her thoughts went to chocolate and strawberry and Emily Dickinson's heart.

Detective Sergeant Kevin Brown lived alone in a house in the neighborhood of Ballard. He had always lived alone in the house and was used to it – the way a person is used to the sound of one's own voice. He had recovered from small injuries and serious injuries there. In that house he had recovered from injuries he could not see but which had threatened his future in the only thing that had real meaning in his life – being a Homicide detective.

Brown poured himself a measure of the Isle of Jura Prophecy his sister had brought him back from Scotland the previous summer. Tomorrow, by the time he came back to the house at the end of the day, he might know for sure if a man was dead and a killer was still breathing free air as a consequence of his actions seven years earlier.

Brown sipped the Prophecy and went back to the book he was reading – even though, for all he tried, he could not remember the last paragraph he'd read. It was *Bleak House*, an old favorite and often reread in times of trouble.

Brown went back to the first page.

Madison rested on the sofa with her eyes closed, listening to Hitchcock's *Notorious* on a DVD, slowly falling asleep and thinking about Ingrid Bergman being poisoned by a bunch of Nazis. The real killer there was Claude Rains' mother, Hitchcock's masterpiece of evil.

Madison wrapped herself tightly in the tartan blanket. Her thoughts seemed to disperse as sleep took hold and the fabric of the blanket brushed against her cheek.

Black Watch. Madison's last thought drifted past. The name of the tartan fabric was Black Watch. Wasn't it what they did all day in Homicide?

They *were* the Black Watch.

She fell asleep.

Chapter 16

Jerry Lindquist's eyes snapped open. For the last two years of his life there had been no mellow awakenings and that day wasn't any different. He took a deep breath: he knew his heart would start racing, and it did. He closed his eyes and waited for it to slow down as sounds began to filter through and the memory of his dream ebbed away. He had dreamt of the house he used to live in; he had walked barefoot on the pier out onto Lake Washington and felt the warm wood under his feet.

Twenty years ago he had graduated from college, ten years ago he'd got married, eight years ago he'd started his accountancy firm and three years ago he had woken up in his garage after an alcoholic blackout and found his wife dead in their bedroom.

His neighbor yelled out a man's name and from somewhere down the corridor that man responded with a holler. The King County Justice Complex had been Jerry Lindquist's home for the last two years and there was nothing mellow about it. He had been woken up by a man's bellow and in all probability he would fall asleep to the sound of another man's shout. He had become used to it – or so he told himself every day. In fact, what had happened was more akin to walking deeper and deeper into a cavern. And the only real living and thinking that he did was now far away from the mouth of the cavern, where the calls of his companions in C Wing rang out.

Jerry Lindquist got up and stretched and, as he often did, he asked himself why hadn't he spent all the time of his life outside running and being outdoors and throwing things and hitting things – or whatever it was people called sports. He had not anticipated that he would miss physical activity so much. But there it was, right there on the list of unexpected things he missed the most.

On the outside he was by trade an accountant who had never so much as kicked a football, inside he was a wife-killing accountant who had notched up another kill the second week of his sentence. An inmate had lunged at him with a shiv at yard time and, with a mixture of luck and intent, he had dodged him. There had been a scuffle and the guy had tripped and fallen; the shiv had cut an artery and that, the prison doctor had said, had been that. Now Jerry Lindquist carried a two-inch scar on his cheek and a reputation that no one had as yet attempted to challenge. His real luck had been that the whole episode had been caught on the yard CCTV and his attorney had been able to prove self-defense. He was still inside, of course. *But it's the thought that counts*, he had joked to himself darkly.

Jerry got himself ready for his breakfast of powdered eggs and the bagged lunch that he would receive on his way out of the mess room. He was not tall or wide but his fellow inmates knew what he was there for and what he had done since, and they let him be. He nodded hello to a couple of fellas he occasionally chatted with – Eduardo (murder in the first) and William (robbery/homicide) – and went to his usual table.

It was Friday, and the previous day – and for as long as his good behavior continued – he had helped out in the bookkeeping class that a volunteer held in a room off the central C Wing hall. Some of the guys who came to the class could hardly count let alone deal with the double-entry system. Still, it was a change from the routine and any change was welcome.

He was working on his eggs when William sat down next to him. If Lindquist was average size William was minute: he was wiry and pale with a thin face and tattoos all the way up his arms – not gang tattoos, just ugly prison art born out of boredom.

William did not belong to a gang or a specific faction; he spoke to everyone and disseminated information. His nickname was 'Western Union'. If there was money or intelligence – or both – to circulate he was the man for the job.

'I have something for you and I'm giving it to you for free,' he said quietly.

'Is it my birthday?' Lindquist replied.

'Maybe,' William said. 'Though all I want you to do is keep eating your chow and look cool.'

Lindquist ate his eggs; they tasted like cardboard.

'Right, I'm telling you this,' William continued, 'because there's going to be money flying around and I'm betting on you, brother, and I don't want you to be standing with your pants down and a smile on your face when it happens.'

'What are you talking about?'

'Your self-defense shiv from two years ago? The guy's brother just got through reception in C Wing. He's got a different surname from your man but it was his brother all right. Now the powers that be don't know or don't care about it but he's going to be mighty interested in you, and money's already changing hands.'

Jerry Lindquist kept eating his eggs. 'What's his name? What does he look like?' he said finally.

'C'mon, man . . . I can't tell you everything, otherwise where's the fun?'

'You don't know his name.'

'I know everything there is to know about everyone.'

No, Lindquist thought, *you don't*. 'You're all heart,' he said.

'I'm what the world made me, brother,' William said with a crooked smile.

Lindquist looked around: the canteen was the usual combination of inmates and guards, concrete, bars and cameras. Sounds bounced hard on the walls and the noise was suddenly harsher and nastier.

William was eyeballing him and he couldn't look scared. He straightened up. 'Is that it? Is that all you wanted to say to me?'

'Yeah, just wanted to say don't get yourself shivved. Watch out and earn me some money.'

William left and Lindquist finished his eggs, stood up and picked up his bagged lunch on the way back to his cell.

He wasn't feeling cool. He was feeling terrified. The guy two years ago had been pure luck. And he had never laid a finger on his wife. He was a double-murderer who in fact had killed no one at all and he felt as vulnerable and exposed as he had the first week in KCJC.

His thoughts scurried like mice. He needed to call his lawyer. He needed to call him and get them to move the guy to another wing – or get him moved. Except that, in that case, surrounded by cons he didn't know and who didn't know him, he would lose whatever cred he had managed to build in the last two years.

How had he got here? How in the name of Sweet Jesus, Mary and Joseph had he got here?

He was an accountant. He was – had been – a husband. But if there was one thing he had been on the outside more than anything else, he had been a drunk. And chances were he would be again, if he ever got out – which, that day, seemed increasingly less likely.

He hardly ever allowed himself to think of her and yet there she was now. Jennifer. And the only comfort he had in the black pit of his desperation and his sorrow was that he knew he had never harmed her and the case the cops and the prosecution had built was nothing but circumstantial evidence, the absence of an alibi and one single spot of her blood on his shirt in the basket.

When it came to it he had been a good accountant and a terrible husband. But he wasn't a killer.

Jerry Lindquist's grief was an abyss of anger and helplessness – and yet in that moment, alone in his cell, he slipped her picture out of the Bible he had been given and gazed at her and wondered when it was all going to end.

Chapter 17

Kate Duncan rolled over to one side and noticed the strips of light shifting on the wallpaper – tiny rosebuds and green leaves. The feeling of drowning that had started on Monday evening had not let her go and she wondered if you could drown in air, if you could gasp and not be able to breathe, your chest frozen in panic. Everything was all right, she said to herself, she was safe at Annie's and the detectives were looking for the man in the picture. God bless Lisa and her memory.

Her mind went back to the man in the Botanical Gardens. He had stared; he had looked at her with such intensity that she could still feel her skin crawling under his scrutiny. Annie and the detectives could say what they wanted but in her heart of hearts she knew that he wasn't just a curious passer-by, he was something else. And she had to be ready, she had to be ready for anything if he came again. Her whole life was a cursed game of *ifs*.

She got up and looked at herself in the mirror. She had to keep it together. She had to be strong. The sounds from the house reached her and comforted her – the voices of the children, Annie calling out to them. She had met with Matthew's brother the previous day and would see him again today. It was almost too much to bear and she squeezed her eyes shut.

She had to keep it together. She had to be strong.

Kate Duncan pulled on a toweling robe and went downstairs to join the others.

Madison woke up early and a sense of dread seemed to find her straightaway, even before she'd had a chance to make herself a cup of coffee. This was not going to be a good day.

She pulled on jeans and boots, wondering how long it would take to search the Mitchell garden. Suddenly, for a brief surreal moment, she remembered that her dress uniform had to be ready for the wedding on Sunday. Her eyes scanned the hanging clothes in her closet and found the dry cleaner's bag with the navy-blue trousers, the jacket with the gold buttons and the white shirt. For her sins, she had a hat to go with it too. Madison did not enjoy wearing the dress uniform but, for once, it was nice to be able to wear it at a joyous occasion and not a funeral.

Aaron was meeting the guys for the first time and she hoped they'd be on their best behavior – although, knowing Dunne, it was doubtful. Then again, she wasn't exactly sure what *best behavior* meant. There would be shop talk, there was always shop talk. And Aaron, who seemed slightly uncomfortable at the sight of her firearm, would be surrounded by them.

She closed the closet door and her thoughts turned again to Brown, to Sorensen – and to Peter Mitchell's garden.

Amy Sorensen beckoned Frank Lauren and Mary Kay Joyce into her office and sat them down. She went through with them how they were planning to walk the grid in the garden with their metal detectors. She did not need to tell them what was at stake.

It had been Amy Sorensen who had matched the prints on the hammer to Henry Karasick's; it had been Amy Sorensen who had matched the blood on the hammer and on the rag to Peter Mitchell's. Her test results had been correct and, even though no one was questioning them, Sorensen knew that if another metal tube was found, it meant that she had played a part in somebody's game and that she had been used.

One of the other officers had the bad idea of interrupting them during the briefing and Sorensen asked him briskly to come back for her later.

Madison showed the artist's composite to Matthew Duncan's colleague Dean.

He shook his head. 'No, I've never seen him before,' he said.

The architectural practice was based in Kirkland, across Lake Washington, and it was housed in a beautiful early-twentieth-century building that had once been a firehouse.

On the other side of the hall, through a glass wall, Madison could see Brown asking the same questions of another colleague. Brown looked grim and had been quiet when they'd met at the precinct.

'How long did you know Mr Duncan?' she said.

'Four, five years at least,' Dean replied. He was about the same age as Matthew Duncan.

'Did you socialize outside of work?'

'Not really. I mean, sure, we might have gone out for the firm's dinners and we sometimes ate lunch together at the café opposite but we've never met after work.'

'You've known him a few years: did he look worried or concerned about something in the last weeks?'

The man hesitated. 'Matthew worried about everything. He was a really nice guy, the clients loved him. If anything he was too soft, too kind, and he always worried about every little detail. Everything had to be perfect all the time. But no, nothing specific, nothing big. Just the usual – where do we put the windows, where do the kitchen cabinets go?' He shrugged.

Madison nodded but her eyes kept wandering back to the round clock in the hall.

Frank Lauren and Mary Kay Joyce's arms moved in perfect synchrony. They traveled right to left and back just ahead of them as they walked the grid of what used to be Peter Mitchell's garden. The house had changed hands twice in the previous seven years and the present owner – a woman who worked for the County – had been a little baffled but accommodating when the two Crime Scene unit investigators had turned up on the doorstep of her clapboard house as she was leaving for work.

They told her that they needed to check her yard for evidence left by a fleeing felon. Sorensen had been clear: do not get caught in a lie but do not mention the Mitchell case. The last thing they needed was for the media to sniff a connection between the two investigations.

As the sallow sun progressed along its path Lauren and Joyce worked Sorensen's brief to the letter: first an overall, thorough sweep of the ground then a second one, paying particular attention to all the spots where it might have been easy for a person to conceal what they were doing from the neighbors.

Lauren and Joyce had worked together for five years; each knew where the other was without needing to look up from the barren grass. Through their earphones the beeps and squeaks of the detectors mapped the world around them. Some of neighbors noticed them, most didn't. They worked all morning and their time was measured not in minutes but in steps as they searched for something they hoped they would not find.

Brown and Madison had just left the firehouse and were comparing notes when her cell started vibrating. Sorensen's name flashed on the small screen.

'They found something,' she said.

'What? Where?' Madison replied and she felt dizzy with the implications. She had known that it was a possibility. However, this was Sorensen holding the evidence in her hands.

Madison turned to Brown. He exhaled as if he'd been holding his breath for days.

'It was buried at the back of the house, behind some bushes. About a foot deep,' Sorensen continued.

'What is it, Amy?'

'A *container*.'

'We're on our way.'

They climbed into the car and Madison was about to say something but Brown cut in.

'We're going to go through the case again and I need you to call it like you see it. Do you understand? If I see you showing any kind of regard because it was my case, if you hold back anything on my account . . .'

'I won't,' Madison said as Brown accelerated between two cars and beat the traffic light.

'I mean it. You can't—'

'I won't,' Madison repeated with finality.

Going across the floating bridge was the usual traffic nightmare and they kept to their own thoughts.

'I must tell Klein,' Madison said and picked up her cell.

Chapter 18

The part of the building that housed the Crime Scene unit worked within its own atmosphere of rarefied industriousness – Madison had noticed this on various occasions. They were the evidence gate-keepers and yet there was a calm and purposefulness to the mood of the place that was quite different from the detectives' room on a bad day. The Crime Scene investigators were neutral in their findings: they pursued and analyzed, but science and technology worked as a filter while cops on the street dealt with the outcome of their discoveries.

When Brown and Madison walked into the lab there was no hush – and no sense that something ominous had happened. Investigators and technicians went about their business, stopping to chat and to exchange pleasantries. Madison, however, felt like a screw had tightened her chest by one turn.

They found Amy Sorensen standing by her work bench examining an object they could not see under a powerful lamp. She turned and they caught a glimpse of bright red. It was not a cigar case.

Madison leant forward.

A red vintage tobacco tin sat on the clean white paper sheet that covered the bench. There was an American eagle in the oval in the center, on the front, and 'Union Leader' was spelled in gold above it. It was small and a little rusty in patches with a couple of tiny bends. Next to it a grimy, soil-encrusted plastic bag had been laid flat. The lid of the tin had been removed and so had its contents, which were balled up and crushed on a tray nearby. The detectives did not need to be told what they were: thin strips of paper of various lengths waited patiently for Sorensen to begin separating and analyzing them.

'It's four and a quarter inches long by three inches, with a depth of seven-eighths. Your regular Union Leader smoking tobacco tin,' Sorensen started without a greeting. 'It was buried a long time ago – don't know when yet, hopefully the contents will tell us – in a resealable plastic bag. Someone wanted to keep things inside clean and dry and actually wrapped this around the lip of the lid to make sure.' She pointed at a thin strip of white camera tape that was curled up by the lid. The edges of the tape were caked in specs of dirt and anything that had managed to find the adhesive surface and stick to it.

'It's going to take us some time to separate the strips of paper. But judging from these four slivers here you can see that they've been sliced with a sharp razor and the width matches the strips recovered at the Duncans' house.'

Sorensen concluded her description, leant on the edge of the bench and crossed her arms.

'I have no reason to believe – at this stage – that the cigar case and the tobacco tin were put in the ground by two different people,' she said. 'There are no fingerprints on the tin. When it went into the plastic bag it was spotless.'

Brown nodded. 'All your Mitchell case evidence safe and ac-counted for?'

'Everything. I went to pick it up myself this morning.'

'Good. I don't want you to get caught up in the shit storm,' Brown said.

'Never mind the shit storm,' Sorensen said. 'By every little bit of evidence recovered it was a solid case – concrete solid.'

'We didn't have eyewitness testimony and we didn't have the clothes Karasick wore when he killed Mitchell.'

'We had a murder weapon with the victim's blood and his prints on it.'

'It was his hammer. His prints were always going to be on it—'

'What else could you have done?' Madison interjected. 'You had two guys known to be arguing all the time and one with the murder weapon with prints and blood and no alibi.'

'And a rag he had cleaned himself with, stained with the victim's blood,' Sorensen added for good measure.

Brown did not reply.

Sorensen nodded at the white camera tape. 'I like tape. In fact, I love tape. Tape brings us all that's good and true in this world because the douche-bags don't know what they're giving us is a present. I'll work that tape and I'll work those paper strips and if there is anything to find – if there is one micron worth of epithelials – I will find it. Now, let me tell you about the strips from the cigar case and what we know so far.'

Chapter 19

The offices of the Release Project Northwest could not be described as stylish or well designed. They could, at best, be considered tasteful – if one had a taste for spartan furnishings and eighties wallpaper. This, Saul Garner reflected as he walked in, was because all their money went towards getting their innocent clients out of jail and therefore – usually here a mild sense of smugness crept in – smart tables and art on the walls took a second place to justice. He had the same thoughts every time he visited some law school friend in his classy office downtown but the thoughts evaporated as soon as he sat at his desk and got busy.

He held his briefcase in one hand and a cardboard holder with two coffees in the other. So he pushed the door open with his shoulder, trying not to lose the paperwork he'd stuck under his arm.

His secretary, who also held the title of receptionist and office paralegal, was on the phone. He placed one of the coffees on the edge of her desk.

She smiled a thank-you and mouthed, 'D-o-C.'

They spent hours of their already hectic lives on the phone with the Department of Corrections. He nodded and went into his office.

The Release Project Northwest, or RPN, took on cases where a defendant had been convicted on DNA evidence, false confessions, or perhaps a shaky and inadequate defense counsel. They tried to get a retrial – if not a complete dismissal of the charges – and worked mostly with volunteers from law school supervised by certified attorneys. Their caseload was spectacular because, sooner or later, every innocent inmate would come knocking.

Saul Garner dropped into his leather chair – a present from his father who'd said that, in the long run, a good chair was more important than an elegant satchel – and turned on his computer.

His secretary put her head around the door. 'I have Jerry Lindquist on the line.'

Saul frowned as his mental Rolodex flipped to the name 'Lindquist': the case, the sentence and the state of the appeal. He was not expecting a call from Jerry and, in his experience, a sudden call from a jail was never good news.

This would be the fifth in the last two weeks: everybody wanted out and they all had someone about to shiv them in the back.

'Put him through.'

The red light flashed and he picked up.

'Jerry, what's wrong?'

After a few minutes of quiet conversation Jerry Lindquist returned to his cell.

Saul had to give it to him: he was keeping it together in the best way he knew how for an accountant who'd never so much as run a red light.

And yet, much was wrong.

If the brother of the man who had attempted to kill Jerry had his way, the state of Jerry's appeal would not make a blind bit of difference.

Chapter 20

The elevator doors opened on the fifth floor of the Holy Pilgrim Hospital and John Cameron stepped out. It was late morning – the same time as the previous day – and he wore the same white coat and carried the same clipboard. By the door of Mrs Rojas's room stood the same two men wearing leather jackets and – Cameron assumed – carrying the same weapons.

Mrs Rojas was the mother of Jaime Rojas, the last surviving member of the drug cartel who had organized Cameron's kidnapping. Rojas was a cautious man who kept to his estate and rarely went out – that's why he had lived to the ripe old age of fifty-one in a business where longevity is notoriously difficult. The cartel was just one of many, all warring with each other and measuring their rewards in body bags and gold. The empty space left by the Rojas cartel would be taken by a new one who would continue their business without pausing for a moment to think about John Cameron.

The issue was not how to kill Rojas but how to kill the man and walk away. Cameron had already dealt with seven members of the same cartel – five bodies had been found and two were still undiscovered. Jaime Rojas he had kept until last because he was the most important and Cameron wanted him to see his world fall apart. While Jaime was a good son who visited his dying mother every day, he was also the man responsible for ordering the disposal of at least forty business rivals, informants, associates and probably a couple of east Los Angeles cops too. Cameron considered it a preemptive strike more than revenge.

Two men stood by the door and four paced in the underground parking lot. Cameron was calm because this was the game and this was where he lived. He put on the glasses that he'd placed in his pocket – the gold frames altered his features another notch and added to the layer of deception.

He headed straight for the door as he slipped on regular latex gloves. 'Hello,' he said.

The men had already clocked him and remembered the clumsy doctor with the spilled coffee from the previous day. Both nodded hello.

Cameron's hand was on the handle and he walked inside, closing the door behind him. It was a comfortable room that ensured a comfortably private death. The monitors attached to the patient ticked and beeped in their approximation of life.

Jaime Rojas looked up. He was sitting facing the door on the far side of the bed where his mother lay; she had been unconscious for the last week but her white hair had been combed out on the pillow. Rojas was an unremarkable man with dark features shaped by malice and grief. He could have been any businessman on a particularly bad day. They had never met in person before and he saw only a slightly overweight doctor with light brown hair and blue eyes.

'I'm Dr Ryan,' Cameron said. 'I've just come to check on Mrs Rojas.'

Cameron had timed it so that it would be long enough after doctors' rounds not to raise suspicions.

Rojas nodded.

The IV stand was on the near side unfortunately. Cameron flicked the bag and examined its contents, then walked around to the side where Rojas sat. The man seemed lost in his sorrow, barely noticing the doctor. So many nurses, assistants and medics buzzed around his mother all day that he had lost track.

Cameron wanted to finish the job without delay to minimize the possibility of exposure and yet he found it strangely intriguing to stand in this room where one person was already dying and another was about to be killed. He cleared his mind and with one smooth movement he extracted a syringe from his pocket and plunged the needle into Jaime Rojas's neck. The man flayed, but Cameron's left hand had closed on his mouth and barely a whimper came out. Cameron dropped the syringe and his arm went around Rojas, holding him tight as he thrashed. It took maybe five seconds before the man's body flopped in his arms – so heavy that he had to arrange it half on the bed and half sitting on the chair. Gently he placed one of Rojas's hands over his mother's and cradled the man's head in the crook of one arm – as if, in his vigil, he had fallen asleep. He picked up the empty syringe and slipped it back into his pocket.

Cameron leant forward and whispered into the man's ear, 'Enjoy the ride.'

The muscle relaxant was known to act almost instantly and Cameron remembered very well when it had been used on him by Rojas's man – the feeling of drowning in darkness as each cell struggled for air and yet the lungs would not inflate. Rojas was perfectly aware of everything that was going on around him as he sat slumped in the chair and slowly suffocating. The drug was used

as an aid to intubate unconscious patients and help them breathe
and its effects lasted only a few minutes. However, if the patient
was not helped to breathe, the consequences were lethal. And the
good doctor had just given him a massive dose.

John Cameron studied the scene: Rojas looked as if he had been
overtaken by emotion at his mother's deathbed and was quietly
sobbing his heart out. It was time to leave. He started to move away
from the bed.

'*Papi* . . .'

Cameron turned, his hand flying to the knife against his
underarm.

The boy, five maybe six years old with huge black eyes, stood by
the bathroom door. His gaze swept over his father and the man in
the white coat.

Cameron's mind staggered. He had staked out the room for days
and Rojas had never brought anybody before. The boy stared at
him. How much had he seen and heard? Cameron wondered if the
child had seen him inject his father and considered idly whether
he'd make a good witness on the stand. He was so small. His body
could fit under the bed or in the closet and they wouldn't find him
for hours. So small.

'*Papi* . . .' the kid repeated and Cameron realized the boy was
about to touch his father.

He trusted that the kid's first language would be Spanish. He
needed him to understand.

'*Tu Papá necesita un momento solo con tu abuela. Pórtate bien y ven afuera
conmigo por un ratito.*'

The boy looked at his father. Cameron could only imagine what
Rojas was feeling at that point – if he could still think and feel.

Cameron crouched and extended his hand. '*Ven conmigo, hombre-*

cito. Quieres una soda?' (Come with me, little man, would you like a soda?)

Say yes, little boy, because I do not want to leave you here with your father, Cameron thought, and he didn't ask himself whether it was out of compassion or the certainty that the kid would find out something was wrong and call the men outside.

The boy looked at his father again, but the man's silence seemed to indicate consent. He took Cameron's hand and followed him out of the room.

The bodyguards turned as Cameron and the boy came out and he closed the door behind him.

'Mr Rojas is very distressed, his mother is close to the end. He doesn't want the boy to see him like that. Please keep him out of the room for ten minutes or so. Give him a chance to get himself together, you know?'

One of the bodyguards nodded. He understood. No man wants his boy to see him upset.

'Would you like a soda?' Cameron asked the boy.

'I'll get it for him,' the bodyguard said and the boy followed him like a puppy to the vending machine.

Cameron nodded goodbye to them and walked off to catch the elevator.

His child. The man had brought his child to his own execution. Cameron did not turn back; he stood by the elevator and waited until the doors opened and then he stepped inside. As the doors slid shut he saw the boy pick out a can from the vending machine.

John Cameron went into exit strategy mode. He needed to get out of the hospital as quickly as possible. He would be very surprised if the bodyguards waited for ten minutes before checking in with their employer.

Cameron got out on the third floor and took the emergency stairs but not before he had retrieved a small black rucksack that he had stashed inconspicuously behind a bench. As he hit the stairs two at a time he took off the white coat, the glasses, the gloves, the belly and the gum prosthesis and shoved everything that carried traces of his DNA – including the clipboard and the contact lenses – into the pack.

By the time he stepped out of the stairs into the lobby he wore the workman's coverall that had been under the doctor's white coat together with a navy baseball cap and sunglasses; the pack hung on his shoulder. His car was parked one block away and he reached it easily. He hadn't run or looked back even once at the hospital entrance.

'*Papi está durmiendo*,' the boy said, sipping his Coke and swinging his legs as he sat on the bench by the closed door.

The bodyguards looked at each other. One – the older and more experienced one – checked his watch. They'd given their boss nine minutes.

'*Durmiendo*?' he repeated.

The boy nodded.

The man knocked lightly on the door and walked in.

His boss lay half on the bed, his slack hand over his mother's, his face still hidden in the crook of his arm.

'Jefe?' the man said softly.

As it was, Mrs Rojas would outlive her son by eleven days.

Chapter 21

Alice Madison splashed water on her face in the restroom. She was used to briefings but this was going to be a bigger deal than usual. She wiped her hands on the paper towel. She had to get it right. She could not afford to screw it up. Other detectives were going to be involved now but she was on point and what was at stake was more than they could possibly have imagined when they had walked into Matthew Duncan's home that first night and seen his body.

The case had started morphing and changing from that moment. It was like shifting smoke that choked and tainted everything it touched. Madison's fears went unspoken – she hadn't really been able to talk about her thoughts to Brown when so much rested on the implication that he might have got it wrong seven years ago. Nevertheless, she reflected, she needed to be completely honest if they were going to work through it.

Madison walked up and down the restroom – it was the only place where she could be alone for a few minutes and it would have to do. She had to get the ball rolling on something that would change the game plan entirely and could be crushing for Brown. He had not made a mistake but they were only now beginning to understand the consequences of his deductions.

Brown was the one whose judgment she had trusted from the very first day in the Homicide unit and she was not happy being forced to second-guess his decisions. Then again, *happy* had nothing to do with this – whatever *this* would turn out to be.

There was no good way to talk about it; the only way was to just do it. Madison left the restroom and went searching for Brown. She found him getting his notes together.

'We need to talk before we go in,' she said to him urgently.

'I know,' he replied.

'Let's just find a—'

'I mean I think I know what you're going to say. I've been thinking about it since we left Sorensen . . . and I agree.'

'Sarge, I wouldn't have done anything different from what you did back then, but—'

'I know. This is what we have to deal with today. Let's get into the briefing and we'll take it from there.'

They stood around the long table: Lieutenant Fynn, Detectives Spencer, Dunne, Rosario and Kelly. Brown and Madison had put the files in the middle and the crime scene photographs were passed around. None of the other detectives had been part of the Duncan investigation; none had been part of the Mitchell case. They had listened to the facts and studied the pictures and now they had come to the questions. Questions are always the most important part of an investigation: you ask the wrong ones and – whatever else you might get right – nothing else much matters.

'Murder weapons?' Dunne asked Madison. He'd had a fresh haircut in honor of his imminent wedding on Sunday and his red hair looked uncharacteristically tidy.

'For Duncan it was the little trophy – a bronze statuette – for Mitchell it was a hammer. In both cases the killer would have had those at hand. No firearms, no knives. Nothing that we wouldn't find lying around in any house.'

'The implication being . . .' Fynn said.

'Spur-of-the-moment situations,' Madison replied. 'A quarrel between Mitchell and Karasick; Karasick grabbed his hammer and things went south from there. For Duncan, a burglar gets caught out by the victim and attacks him with the first thing he can find.'

Madison felt Chris Kelly's eyes on her – small blue eyes lost in a wide face with dainty features. He managed to radiate hostility just standing there.

'The killer broke into the Duncan home while the wife was out for a run, the husband was fixing dinner and all the lights were on?' Kelly said.

'Yes,' Madison replied.

'Not a particularly good burglar,' Kelly commented.

'I can't explain why he would do that, why he would choose that time of day. Except that he must have had a very good reason since he had taken the trouble to check out the house the previous week. And in order to cover his tracks he had hacked into the server of the HVAC company – Sorensen's people are looking for any trail he might have left behind.'

Kyle Spencer held a close-up of the victim's body still at the crime scene and gazed at it. 'It doesn't make any sense that he would put so much preparation into knowing about the house and yet when he gets there he's unarmed and has to improvise.'

'It doesn't,' Madison agreed; she hated the feeling that the more facts they had, the less they seemed to know. 'This was always going to be more than a burglary,' she said, and looked at Brown who gave her the tiniest nod. 'The containers we found buried in the garden told us that. Sorensen is still working on the contents from the tin but we have the ones from the cigar case in the Duncans' garden right here.' She spread the magnified copies on the table. 'Some have already been identified.'

Madison gave them a moment to look over the strips of paper.

'This was not something the killer accidentally left behind; this was not a mistake. He found a safe place and buried the case, making sure it was protected from the weather. Making sure it would last.'

'As it did in Mitchell's garden,' Brown said.

Their eyes met for a moment and then Madison continued. 'This slice of paper is taken from a ferry ticket, this from a petrol receipt, this from a grocery shop, this long one here comes from a page of the *Seattle Times* from three weeks ago.'

The men around the table looked stunned and she could read on their faces the worst of her own fears.

'This,' she continued, 'is from *Time* magazine, this one is from a map of Seattle and this is from a Ferris wheel ticket. The other ones are still being worked on but we do know that none of them had any fingerprints and, as you can see, none of the receipts gives us any clue in terms of date and time. Nothing that could lead us back to him.'

'This is . . .' Dunne struggled with putting the notion into words. 'This is *a day in the life* of the killer.'

'Is there any chance at all that these . . . whatever we want to call them . . . the tin and the cigar case . . . is there any chance that they have nothing to do with the killings?' Spencer asked.

Brown stepped forward. 'They had both been wiped clean,

meticulously so. And the killings are tragically similar: both victims were beaten to death with an excess of violence. As if the violence itself was the point of the whole exercise. A hair found on Mitchell's body and a drop of blood in Duncan's dresser are a DNA match. The same person was present at both crime scenes.'

Brown looked at Madison: he was asking her to say it and say it now in front of everybody. She'd rather have spoken quietly to him first – to clear the air – and yet this was where they were. The storm was about to hit.

Madison took a deep breath. 'I don't think it was a quarrel and I don't think it was a burglary. We were meant to think they were a quarrel and a burglary. The killer staged the crime scenes so that we'd have ready-made suspects.' She paused to let them get their heads around it. 'This was about killing, in the most violent way possible, and getting away with it. The killer targeted Mitchell and Duncan and created false paths for us to follow: Henry Karasick could not give us an alibi, he was drunk, stoned and passed out at home all night. Plenty of time for someone to plant the evidence that would lead us to him.'

'Someone made sure he was high?' Fynn said.

'Might very well have. We need to go back to the file and find out who he was buying from,' Brown said.

'And Duncan?' Spencer asked.

'The Duncan murder was meant to look like a burglary – that's why the jewelry was missing – but he didn't bother to take the laptop or the camera. It was a quick in and out before the wife came back. However, he had spent God knows how long recceing the place and knew exactly where everything was by the time he broke in.'

The photographs in the middle of the table bore witness to

unspeakable cruelty. Madison took a sip from a bottle of water. *Here we go*, she thought.

'And I think we should look for more,' she said.

'More what?' Fynn replied.

'More of the same kind of murders. They would be, in all probability, closed cases. Like Mitchell's.' She looked around the table. 'What if Mitchell was only the first? The violence was bad, but clearly we can see how it escalated to what he did to Duncan. What happened during the last seven years? Can we honestly think that he would have stayed at home quietly just biding his time? There might be more . . . and we have to look. We *must* look.'

She didn't need to say it. There could be people in jail – people any of the men standing around the table could have put there – who were innocent. And if Detective Sergeant Kevin Brown had been taken in, anybody could have been.

Fynn looked like a man who had to give his boss impossibly bad news.

'What do we have on this man, Madison? Give me something because I can't go to the Chief with a serial killer and a bunch of paper strips.'

'We have a likeness from the cleaner. It's a pretty good sketch, good enough for witnesses to identify him. And we have his DNA.'

'That's a starting point. We need to release the likeness to Public Affairs and put it out there.'

'Definitely. But let's keep it connected only to the Duncan investigation. The killer should not know that we're working backwards as well. The least he knows, the better. Let's just let him think that we're still looking at it as a horrific burglary. And be ready for the jewels to turn up somewhere – anywhere – where he might have found a scapegoat.'

'Do you have any ideas about how to look for other possible murders by the same subject?'

'I'm working on something,' Madison said, and she was glad she had thought of it three seconds before the meeting had started.

'And we need to find out how and why he picked these victims.'

Madison nodded.

The meeting broke up. The lines of investigation would be divided up between the detectives and the hunt would start for real.

Chris Kelly sidled up to Madison just as he was leaving the room. 'Funny how the serial killers seem to find *you* every time, isn't it? Going to make friends with this one too?'

His partner, Tony Rosario, who had not spoken a word in the meeting, opened his mouth, but Kelly nodded to him that they should just go.

Madison wanted to give him a dry, quick-witted reply. She wanted to give him Dorothy Parker at her sharpest, but he was already walking away from her.

'Fuck off, Kelly,' she murmured to herself.

Coffee was needed. Coffee was needed very badly indeed. And if all they had was percolated mud, then that would have to suffice.

Spencer stood by the machine, mesmerized by the thick trickle that was slowly filling the pot.

'Have you written your speech yet?' Madison asked him.

It was a little surreal to be worrying about table settings, flower arrangements and the best man's speech.

'Yes and no. I'm hoping on some last-minute inspiration to put in the funny.'

'How was the fishing weekend?'

Spencer grinned. 'I'm afraid not a lot of fishing was achieved.'

'Andy looked a little peaky when you got him back to town.'

'I never thought it would happen.'

'What?'

'I've known Andy since the academy, we've been partners as long as I've been married to Cristina and I've always thought I'd end up building a shed in my backyard so that Andy wouldn't have to grow old alone.'

'Your boy is growing up.' When Rachel and Neal had got together and then got married, the ground had shifted a little under Madison's feet.

Andy Dunne had always embraced the role of wild bachelor brother; their working partnership had been shaped by Spencer's quiet, steady ways and Dunne's reckless energy. And now Andy was settling down and buying a house and even talking about starting to invest in a micro-brewery, and Spencer looked a little lost.

Madison and Spencer stared at the full pot. It smelled like a fire in a barn after a rainstorm.

'Maybe, just maybe, cream and sugar will help,' Spencer said, and they each grabbed some mugs.

Lieutenant Fynn replaced the receiver. The conversation with the Chief had gone as predicted: he was expected to call him with updates pretty much every hour on the hour, but that was nothing compared to the censuring the department would take if innocent people had been convicted for crimes they had not committed.

Washington State had recently passed a law whereby a wrongfully convicted person could file a claim against the state and, if successful, would receive $50,000 for each year spent in jail and a further $50,000 for each year on death row. It was a step forward in terms of compensation. Nevertheless, it did not begin to soften the impact of being incarcerated, of time lost that could never be reclaimed, of families broken up and children grown.

Fynn looked up the number of the Public Affairs office and picked up the receiver.

How many lives had really been taken by the killer?

Chapter 22

The best way to follow someone when they are on a run is to match their speed exactly, and it would be even better if you could run on the other side of the street. Better still, the man thought, to skip a block and meet the target at the other end and pick up the trail again.

He enjoyed watching her run. In fact, the project had almost been delayed because of it. Still, he was working on a deadline – amusing how odd words worked when you stuck them together – and in the end he had done what he must. He couldn't have predicted the world of possibilities that she would open for him and while, yes, there was the inconvenience of improvisation, there was also the thrill of invention and it had been a long time, such a long time, since he had felt challenged in the only way that mattered.

The man looked ahead and watched Kate Duncan wind in and out of the crowd as she ran along the Alaskan Way. She wore dark colors as usual and her gait was light and strong. He could have picked her out among dozens of runners. Light and strong. The man followed at a distance. He also wore dark clothes and ran easily, his long strides keeping up with hers.

The sun had set and the embankment was a jewel of colors and lights. Against the dusk the Ferris wheel was like a giant toy dropped and forgotten. He had so enjoyed getting to know her. In the empty evenings, in the silence of his house where the only footsteps were his and no one ever moved his things or called out to him, thinking about her was like a spot glowing warm in the middle of his chest.

Kate Duncan ran and felt the joy of running, moving, stretching after days of being cooped up in Annie's house. She was so used to running in all weather conditions that the enforced stillness had been torture. Annie had dropped her off and would pick her up at the other end.

Wrapped as she was in her neck warmer and hat, her face was almost completely covered. She felt invisible, moving among the people and yet not one of them. She was safe and unseen. A number of runners used the Alaskan Way and no one was paying any attention to her.

Kate Duncan needed this time alone. She had hardly begun to process what had happened and when she was with Annie and her family – grateful as she was for their support – she could not be fully herself. The tiniest details of her day were examined as indicators of her state of mind. Did she eat anything for breakfast? Did she watch TV? Did she cry at all today? Her tears had dried up completely, as it happens. And even though she went to bed early, she wouldn't fall asleep until very late. Her mind went back over and over again to Monday night and tried to make sense of what had happened. The pain in her chest was like an acid spill. Except for these moments when she was running, it felt as if she'd been holding her breath for days.

She reached the Ferris wheel and saw Annie, waiting by the car, and gave her a little wave.

Two hundred yards behind her a man clocked the two women getting into the car and continued his run right past and beyond them into the darkness under the viaduct.

Chapter 23

Madison was at her desk when her cell started vibrating. She recognized the ID and picked up.

'Madison,' she said.

'It's Stanley Robinson.'

'Stanley, are you all right?'

During their acquaintance Dr Stanley F. Robinson PhD had never once called Madison on her cell; changes in appointment times were dealt with via text messages. Such a change in the routine – however trivial – seemed ominous.

'I am, but my office has been burglarized.'

'When was this?'

'Last night. The day was spent between police officers, carpenters and insurance advisors.'

Madison flipped through her mental Rolodex of felonies. The sign in the hall did read Dr Stanley F. Robinson PhD and it was likely that the culprits thought they might find drugs and prescription pads.

'Madison, there was a prescription pad right there on my desk and they didn't touch it but they took my hard drive,' he said.

'That's . . . unusual.'

'Yes, it is.'

He did not sound shaken and yet there was an unfamiliar edge to his voice. He made a living listening to other people's issues and helping them resolve their problems. Madison had rarely met anyone calmer and more relaxed. Stanley could have talked a pack of hyenas out of their lunch. And yet today he sounded *angry*.

'I could be right over,' Madison said.

'Thank you,' he replied.

Madison told Brown she'd be gone for half an hour or so and left the precinct. The dusk was clear and cold and it felt good to be outside. Beyond the orange city glow the stars were invisible but she knew they were there. A brisk walk downtown and she arrived at the familiar building.

Madison had first met Stanley Robinson after a disturbing case when he was assessing whether she was fit to return to regular duties. She told him as little as possible about how she felt and nothing at all about the nightmares that she had lived with since childhood. In return, the doctor had given her a surprisingly correct assessment of her state of mind, wished her a good life and signed off on her psych evaluation.

After Madison had shot and killed a man – one of the cartel men who had kidnapped John Cameron – she needed to speak to someone about it, about what it felt like in her bones to have killed a human being, and she had found her way back to Stanley. It had been months since they had last met.

The elevator doors slid open. Madison was suddenly back eighteen months earlier and felt the dull pain that had seemingly nested in her chest. She heard her own words, spoken to Stanley, and realized they were still as sharp, still as painful to hold.

The door to the office was open and the small waiting room seemed untouched.

'Stanley?' she called.

'Come in,' he replied from inside.

The main door, she noticed as she went in, had been artfully jimmied.

Madison stood by the door and looked around: Stanley's office was a mess. The burglars had taken out their fury on the soft furnishings and the books – and his computer was noticeably missing from his desk.

'Thank you for coming, Alice,' he said.

Few people called her Alice anymore. It was a touch of intimacy that she didn't mind from this man who was so quick and kind and good.

'I'm sorry, Stanley. This looks horrendous.'

'Well, mostly the mess . . . it's the filling from the sofa and the chair cushions. To be honest, it's . . .' He hesitated. 'Can I run something by you? Use your finely honed detective skills?'

'Go ahead.' Madison smiled.

'The men – or man – came in from the front door, obviously, as we can see. What happened here is this: they broke into one of my filing cabinets, they took my hard drive, they destroyed my sofa and chairs. The prescription pad I found under the desk must have been kicked there in all the commotion.'

Madison knew he was getting at something.

'See,' he continued. 'This is the filing cabinet they forced open – except there's nothing there, because I keep all my notes in digital form. And there was nothing on the hard drive either, by the way, because I keep my notes on a portable drive that I always carry with me.'

Stanley slid shut the metal filing cabinet drawer so that Madison could see it. The small tag in the slot read 'K–O'.

'I have four patients with names that begin with those letters and I'm not breaking any confidentiality agreement if I tell you that one is a housewife, one a surgeon, one runs a company . . . and then,' his brown eyes searched her face, 'there's you.'

'None of the other drawers were forced?' Madison crouched to look.

'No.'

'And there was nothing in the drawer?'

'Nothing, the whole cabinet is empty, I was going to have it carted out next week.'

'And when they realized there was nothing there they took your computer.'

'Fat lot of good it is going to do them too. I'm careful, Alice,' he said. 'Because people tell me private things and I have a duty of care, which I take very seriously.'

'I know you do.'

'If they were looking for incriminating material from my patients it doesn't make sense that they would just ignore the first two drawers, which are closer to the door, and start on this one instead.'

'No, it doesn't.'

Stanley was mid-fifties with salt-and-pepper hair in a short cut; he was the uncle you tell your troubles to because he's not going to bullshit you or condescend to you and his advice is invariably solid.

'Do you have enemies, Alice?' he said.

Madison was wrong-footed: she had never considered things from that angle. She worked cases and reached conclusions and sometimes some of those conclusions had consequences.

'I don't know,' she replied honestly. 'Maybe.'

'None of the other people whose confidences might have lived in that drawer has anything at all to do with people who might want to use them against them.'

'God, Stanley, if that's true I'm so sorry, I mean . . . look at this place.'

'I don't give a hoot about the chairs and the computer, that's not why I wanted to see you.'

She nodded. This had been a safe place, a place where she could deal with things that had nowhere else to go.

'I wanted to see you,' he continued, 'to make sure you knew there might be – I'm saying *might* here, because we can't know for sure – there might be someone who is after you, after something that could be used against you. They forgot the pad, which would have been valuable. And the mess was make-believe anger.'

'You should have been a cop,' she said.

'I wouldn't have passed the psych screening,' he replied and as he watched her his smile was a little sad. 'Watch out,' he said and then added quickly, 'just in case.'

Madison walked back to the precinct. Her feet found their way back while she was lost in the memories of all that she had told Stanley during their sessions.

He knew that she had struggled with the notion that she had killed a person, that she felt keenly the moat between what she, as a cop, did every day and how other people lived their lives. He knew that after chasing Salinger in the forest her nightmares had been more horrifying than anything that had ever been done to her.

Stanley knew that Alice Madison had run away from home when she was twelve because her father – a professional poker player – had stolen all that was left of her mother's things to play a losing hand. And he knew that Alice had destroyed her room with a baseball bat before she'd gone and caught a ferry to the mainland, before she'd cut her hair off to look like a boy and then lived completely alone for a week. He knew that Alice, before she'd left, had stuck the blade of her father's switchblade knife two inches deep into his bedside table so that he'd know that she knew what he'd done and how she felt about it. And for a brief, shocking moment she had considered whether her father should live at all; then a dog barking had brought her back to reality and she had run.

The only other person who knew was Rachel: Alice had felt that she needed to tell her if they were going to be best friends – a kind of full disclosure clause that works when you're fourteen.

Yes, there were definitely things there that could be used against her. And yet she had no idea who might want to do that – and why.

Madison took one last big lungful of the chill air and walked into the precinct.

'Point is,' Brown said, watching her above his glasses. 'How did they know that Robinson was the one who did the psych assessment?'

'True,' Madison replied. 'If that's the case, it means there really was a degree of preparation involved and someone got into police records.'

'Was he okay?'

'He was fine. Just sort of worried for me, I guess. And hacked off that they trashed his office for nothing.'

'Does he keep the portable drive at home?'

'Yes, in a safe, inside a house that is alarmed anytime he's not there. I asked him to be careful for the next few weeks because they will work out there's nothing on the hard drive and he carries the notes on his person.'

'He agreed?'

'Yes, reluctantly.'

Brown checked his watch. They had arranged a late meeting with Prosecutor Sarah Klein to update her on the case and, since she had been in court all day, this would be their first chance to get together and consider the potential legal onslaught the case could become.

'It's time,' Brown said.

Chapter 24

Brown and Madison walked to the building that housed the offices of the King County Prosecuting Attorney. One of the many reasons Madison loved Seattle was that it had been built on hills and you were never far from water. As they crossed the road briskly she spotted a glint of Puget Sound between two buildings reflecting the city lights and throwing them back for anyone who might be watching.

There had been a tacit agreement with Brown since they had left the briefing earlier in the day: they would work the hell out of the case – wherever it might lead them – and any other consideration that had to do with guilt, blame or what those things meant for their relationship would be shoved onto the back burner while they tried to catch a killer.

After the day's rush the building was hushed. Most of the staff had gone for the weekend and the great marble hall was empty.

'Did Fynn say when Public Affairs are going to put out the likeness?' Madison asked while they were in the elevator.

'Evening news and again on the morning news. They're going to try for breakfast TV as well. Spread it as wide as they can.'

Madison was glad they were alone in the car. 'He let the cleaner see his face,' she said. 'That's risky – and it's so arrogant that it's dangerous.'

'You know what that means, right?'

'That he's going to trip over his ego and fall on his face?'

'That too, but mostly it means he thought we wouldn't even get to the cleaner because the company would confirm an engineer had indeed visited the Duncans' house last Thursday. Something must have gone wrong: by now we should have already got to the scapegoat, but we haven't.'

Madison took it in and asked the question. 'How long before you found the trail that led you to Karasick?'

'Less than twenty-four hours,' Brown replied. 'The neighbors told us about their feud, we asked for his alibi – he didn't have one – we searched the house and found the rag. We even had the hammer within two days of the murder.'

'Then something definitely went wrong this time. If I were him I'd want the whole thing wrapped up as neatly and as swiftly as possible.'

They knocked on the open door of Sarah Klein's office. It was a small room that managed to be smart while being crammed with files and documents and legal reference books.

'We're in the conference room,' Klein said as a greeting. 'We'll be more comfortable there.'

Their steps clicked on the tiled floor. Only a few lights were still burning in the offices along the corridor. She showed them into a long, narrow room and someone was already there.

Madison froze for a beat.

'My boss told the Criminal Chief,' Klein said, 'and she told the State Attorney, who asked Quinn to keep an eye on the case. Nathan called me earlier to talk about it and it made sense that he should be here since he was in the neighborhood.'

'Mr Quinn,' Brown said.

The last time they had met they had been on different sides of the courtroom.

'Detective Brown.'

Both men carried the scars of a case that had changed their lives: meeting like this seemed oddly polite after the ugly war in which they had fought, even if ultimately they'd been on the same side.

'Detective Madison,' Nathan Quinn said as his gaze briefly met hers.

'Counsellor,' she replied.

Civility was promptly dispatched before they sat around the table and Madison began to relate the briefing and their conclusions. Klein didn't interrupt but scribbled notes on her pad. Nathan Quinn's attention, though, was a subtle instrument and it felt uncomfortable against Madison's skin.

'Are you going to contact Karasick's attorney?' Quinn asked Klein after Madison had finished.

'Yes, I think I should. We need to head off any implication that we're doing this under the radar. It will be confidential, of course. The last thing we want is for him to run to the press.'

'Are you ready for this to be completely transparent?' Quinn asked Brown.

Madison remembered that, among cops, when Quinn was still a criminal defense attorney a moderate to serious bout of torture would have been far preferable to having to go on the witness stand and be cross-examined by him.

'Absolutely,' Brown replied without hesitation.

'We don't want to find anything that is going to discredit the original investigation.'

'You mean, aside from the fact that we got it spectacularly wrong?'

'You were working with what you had – and what you had was a solid case that secured a conviction. I'm talking about anything from a missed search warrant to a dubious confession or an unreliable witness that the prosecution found a way to work into its case.'

'It was by the book,' Klein said without animosity. 'No one is going to find police or prosecutorial misconduct.'

Madison had not seen or spoken to Nathan Quinn for over a year and unconsciously found herself searching for those eighteen months in his features. She caught herself and looked away.

'Is the Duncans' cleaner a good witness?' Quinn asked her. 'She's the only one who can put him on the scene, though not at the time of the murder.' His black eyes regarded her coolly.

'She is,' she replied. 'She worked very well with the forensic artist. But I'd rather have a photo, of course.'

It was true. Having a sketch was great: however, a lot of people had trouble matching it to a real-life person.

'Wouldn't we all,' Klein commented.

'And Karasick had not pleaded?' Quinn turned to Brown.

The detective shook his head. There had been no plea bargaining in Karasick's case: even in the face of a certain conviction he had stuck to his 'not guilty' plea.

'That might work in our favor,' Quinn said.

'How so?' Brown asked.

'You said you had an idea about how to find other potential murders that the killer might have been involved in,' Quinn said to Madison.

'Yes, I'd filter out any homicide where the murder weapon was a firearm or a blade and concentrate on those where the killer could have picked up something owned by the scapegoat, something that carried prints, or something that would have already been on the crime scene.'

'Sure, we can do it that way. But we can also search through pleas – or, better still, the absence of guilty pleas,' Quinn said.

Madison saw exactly where he was going. 'Because Karasick never wavered.'

'Exactly,' Quinn continued. 'We should look into any cases which looked strong in court and still the defendant pursued appeals through the Release Project in spite of the evidence against them. What does the FBI say?'

'Fred Kamen will get back to me as soon as he can,' Brown replied. 'He's using different filters, including the burying of the tin and the cigar case.'

'Will he give us a profile?' Klein asked him.

'If he can. He's reluctant to come up with one if he doesn't have enough to go on. I have given him all the details of both murders, though, and he should be able to triangulate something out of that.'

'Any connection between Peter Mitchell and Matthew Duncan?' Quinn asked Madison.

'Not that we know of.'

'How does he choose his victims?'

'We don't know yet.'

'Is he on a cycle, time-wise? Monthly, yearly, whatever?'

'We don't know yet.'

'You don't know very much, do you?'

Madison bristled. 'We know he exists – which is a hell of a lot more than we did twenty-four hours ago.'

'Well, it only took us seven years to work it out. So, you know, good for us.' Quinn's voice was low and sharp.

Seven years ago Nathan Quinn was still heading the most successful criminal defense firm in the Northwest and, if anything, at the time he would have been defending Karasick.

'Not even you could have got Karasick off, Nathan,' Klein said.

Quinn ignored her. 'When are the Mitchell witnesses going to be re-interviewed?'

'We're starting tomorrow,' Madison said, and suddenly remembered, quite clearly, how her early meetings with Quinn had been less than warm and fuzzy.

'Will you show them the picture?'

'No, I think I'll describe the killer through the medium of music,' she replied.

Something flitted across Quinn's face. 'I'm glad we had a chance to go over things,' he said as he stood to leave and flicked invisible lint off the sleeve of his suit. 'Sarah, if there's anything I can help with to speed things up, please let me know. Detective Brown, good to see you again . . .' Quinn extended his hand across the table and Brown shook it. 'Detective Madison,' Quinn said and he offered his hand.

She took it automatically and the next moment he was gone. His steps echoed in the corridor.

'Kind of makes you wish for the good old days when we were *not* on the same side, doesn't he?' Klein said, after a moment.

Outside the cold found Madison and she breathed it in and let it wash over her. They were walking back to the precinct and her thoughts stumbled and staggered in circles.

'What's wrong?' Brown said.

'Nothing. Just thinking,' she replied and her voice was so unconvincing that she felt she had to add something. 'I'm going to look into the Release Project tomorrow.'

'Tomorrow is Saturday. Most people have days off, occasionally.'

'I'm sure I can find a number to call in case of emergencies.'

'Well, it will be good news for us and bad news for anybody else.'

It was true: any case they might find would give them more details to add to the picture of the killer – more potential ways to seek him and find him – and one person behind bars who shouldn't be there.

'Do you want to grab something to eat?' Brown said.

'No, thank you. I'm just going to go home and heat up some week-old leftovers.'

'Sounds delightful.'

Madison smiled, but Brown watched the smile fade when she thought he didn't notice. He had seen that look before.

Chapter 25

Eighteen months earlier

Four people were playing Texas hold 'em through the night in an empty restaurant on Alki Beach and it was not a kids' game. What Madison had learnt from her father looked like a magic trick to her teenage friends, but these men were not so easily impressed.

Hold 'em is war and strategy, guts and inspiration. They each held two hole cards, face down on the table, and five community cards had been dealt face up for all to see. The first three were 'the flop', followed by 'the turn' and 'the river'.

Madison had watched them play and, she had to admit, it had been a pleasure. Quinn and Cameron were skilled and unsurprisingly lethal but the chef, Donny O'Keefe, he was world class. He was Johnny Chan in 1988 to their Eric Seidel. They had bet on the flop, on the turn and on the river. Madison knew by then that she ought to fold because her hole cards were the five of diamonds and the eight of spades – and nothing in this universe could prevent her from losing to either Quinn or O'Keefe who, she thought, were holding a flush and a full house. So she folded. Cameron folded too.

Quinn won with a full house – kings and fours – over O'Keefe's ace-high flush.

The chef, short and wiry, stood up. 'More coffee, I think,' he said and he went into the kitchen.

Cameron decided to get a breath of fresh air out on the deck, leaving Quinn and Madison alone. If, five months earlier, someone had told her that one day there she would be, in the company of these men, playing as she had not played for two decades, she would have thought it madness. Still, too much had happened: lives had been saved, secrets – some secrets, at least – had been unraveled. And when all was said and done Nathan Quinn had been able to put his brother to rest. Madison had been part of it; she had been one of those who had managed to bring his body truly home after the child had been lost in the woods for longer than he had ever been alive.

She watched Quinn. Once, before the night in the forest and before the blood, she had called him 'a cheap used-car salesman in a good suit'. She still cringed at that. What did she see now? Why had she stayed and played? Quinn shuffled the deck. His hands moved easily on the cards and, out of the blue, she wondered what he had been like as a young man. She had seen him fleetingly in some old photograph and remembered the curly dark hair, the black eyes and the beginning of what might someday become a beard.

There he was, she thought, as he shuffled the cards quietly, enjoying the fact that she was watching him and not speaking because it might be the last time they'd ever be in the same room. And that silence was too precious to break.

There he was, that boy.

Then the others came back and they played on until dawn.

*

There were only four cars in the parking lot. Cameron and O'Keefe left first. Madison approached hers – the old Honda Civic that would be sold in a few weeks – and in the half-light something caught her eye.

She crouched. 'Damn,' she said.

Nathan Quinn stepped out of the misty gloom. 'What is it?'

'Flat tyre.'

'Do you have a spare?'

Madison thought about it for a moment. 'No,' she replied. 'I used it a month ago and didn't replace it.' She could barely see his face.

'I'll drive you home. It's late,' he said.

It was so late that it was early and, after a long night of cards and food and drink, Madison was glad for the quiet as Quinn drove towards Three Oaks. The world was precariously balanced between night and day and she knew why she had stayed and played.

The drive, with neither traffic nor anything else that might delay them, was all too quick and before long Quinn was pulling into her driveway.

The late spring air still held the chill of the night as they stood by her front door.

'It's been a long day, Detective,' he said, and he smiled. 'And now it's done.'

She nodded.

For them the day had been measured in weeks and years. Madison could barely remember a time when work had not meant this case – this man – even if it had been only five months, even if they'd fought more than they'd agreed, and concealed more than they'd revealed. Still, they had never lied to each other.

Madison raised her hand and laid it against his cheek. Quinn was frozen. She caressed the dark hair by his temple. There was the tiniest amount of gray and she hadn't noticed it before; she sighed and her fingers trailed through it. In the faint light he was pale and utterly still, and as she leant in he did not move.

His voice was close to her ear. 'Don't . . . toy with me.' His eyelashes brushed her cheekbone.

Madison shook her head and kissed him, and for the longest time there was nothing but the kiss. Her arms reached around him and the sudden warmth of his skin through the shirt was almost too much. He slowly bent forward and now they were leaning against the door, pressed against it, and his mouth tasted so very sweet. At some point in the far and distant future they might have to breathe but for now, Madison thought briefly, all she needed was this kiss.

'Maybe we could . . .' Quinn whispered after a while.

'Yes, definitely,' Madison replied and fumbled to find her keys and open the door.

They walked in together. Quinn closed the door behind them and they were in the cool semi-darkness of the house. She reached for his hand and he followed her into her bedroom. For a split second Madison considered the unmade bed and the clothes on the floor that she hadn't had a chance to put in her hamper and she stopped, grateful that the lights were still off.

She turned to him. 'I wasn't exactly expecting guests.'

Quinn chuckled, a low rumbling sound that she had never heard before. 'I didn't think you'd be the messy type.'

'I'm not. Usually.'

'I couldn't care less if we had to burrow our way through laundry to get to your bed,' he said.

'I'm glad.'

Quinn dropped his jacket on the floor on top of her running things from the previous day.

'You're going to feel right at home here,' Madison said, looking at the small pile, and she wanted to giggle because all of a sudden she had realized that she really was in her bedroom with tall, dark Nathan Quinn and the reality of it was unreservedly bizarre and yet completely fitting.

He stepped closer and took her hand. 'I have scars,' he said. It wasn't an apology, it was more of a warning in case she'd forgotten. How could she? The ones on his fine face were healing but his body had been through hell.

'I know,' she replied quietly.

He unbuttoned his shirt and gently placed her hand against his bare chest. His skin was soft and she felt his heart pounding. He guided her hand and there it was: the long, thin scar that snaked around his flat belly. Her hands trailed under his shirt, helped him to take it off and her eyes welled up. She had never felt as fiercely protective of another human being as she did in that moment.

She kissed his chest lightly and reached for his belt but he suddenly pulled back, holding her hands away from him.

'I don't have any condoms,' he said in dismay.

Madison blinked. 'Neither do I.' And of all the moments to think back to her grandmother's 'talk' when she was fifteen this was surely the least and the most appropriate. 'I don't care,' she said.

He hesitated and then his hands were on her clothes and he helped Madison yank her top off as she toed off first one boot then the other, lost her balance, and only then remembered the familiar weight on her right ankle.

'My piece.' She bent down and unstrapped the holster with the snub-nosed .38.

Quinn watched her wrap it in the leather straps and shove it under the bed. 'You are a strange creature, Detective Madison.'

'You have no idea, Counsellor.'

He smiled and there was wickedness there that her grandmother would have most definitely disapproved of.

'Show me,' Nathan Quinn said.

Hours later the shapes of light on the ceiling told Madison that it was late morning or even early afternoon. It felt like a dream after a long night that had been a kind of dream anyway.

Quinn's arm around her tightened.

She realized that he was awake too and turned to him. His hair was mussed up and he looked like a man who had had two hours' sleep. He cupped her cheek and kissed her brow. There was awkward, crooked happiness there. He was not handsome – no, he was so much more than that – and Madison fought the need to speak. Because all the words could wait when holding him in her arms, in her bed, surrounded by unruly laundry, was sweeter than she could ever have imagined.

Chapter 26

After the meeting at the King County Prosecuting Attorney's Office Madison drove straight home. She had so much to think about, so much work that they needed to get through to have at least half a chance against the killer.

Yet all she could think about was that, in all the time she had known him, she couldn't remember Nathan Quinn ever shaking hands with people. Nevertheless, in the conference room he had leant across the table and shaken Brown's. And when he'd turned towards her it had been a reflex she couldn't help: before she knew it he had clasped her hand for a moment, and then he was gone.

Nathan Quinn arrived home in Seward Park and saw the lights blazing in the windows. It had to happen, he considered, sooner or later, and offering to keep an eye on Brown's old case had ensured that he would meet Detective Madison again. After eighteen months it had been just as difficult as he had predicted. How had she looked? He didn't want to think about that.

He had been sitting in the car for a couple of minutes, staring into nothingness, when he grabbed his briefcase and got out. Inside, he knew, Erica Lowell, the woman he was going to marry next spring, was waiting for him to have dinner.

The joys of a clear, cold night in late autumn are never as obvious as when one is standing in open ground with a telescope on a tripod looking up at the heavens. The man loved autumn and winter more than any other time of the year, and a night like this was reason enough to be alive. He was aware of the chill but it was on the periphery of things, distant enough not to intrude on his most immediate concerns. And his most pressing concern was, without a doubt, Jupiter.

It would have been hard to explain to someone who had never looked at the skies without anything other than the naked eye the shock, the delight and the reverence the man had felt the first time he had seen Jupiter when he was a boy. The thing was, his grandfather had said, planets were so far away that we only saw them as tiny points of light – privately the boy had thought that even being a tiny point of light in the sky was pretty impressive – but Jupiter was another story. Jupiter was so vast that even with the plainest kind of binoculars you would be able to see more than a point: you would see a surface like the smallest, brightest coin you could imagine, suspended in the black. And what was best, the grandfather had continued – like a conspirator sharing secrets – was that Jupiter had moons, many moons, and the four larger ones you could see right there and then.

The boy had looked through the binoculars, struggling at first, and then there it was: not a nondescript speck but a reddish smudge – an actual smudge! – and four dots aligned around it. A different world with mountains and valleys and moons, out there in the infinite, fathomless universe.

The man had never really gotten used to it, however many times he had observed Jupiter, and he had done so with increasingly sophisticated technology. Other planets and constellations had been customarily examined and tracked but none had touched him in quite the same way because Jupiter was the one that had first revealed its secret to him: the universe was a fabric of visible and invisible matter held together by gravity and trajectory. He wouldn't have used those words when he was a boy, but even then he would have understood the sentiment. Something that was too far away for us to see – maybe even something hidden behind something else – was still an integral part of the fabric because it affected everything else and the celestial harmony wouldn't have been the same without it.

The man looked into his telescope and adjusted the focus: he too was part of the celestial harmony, he reflected, even if he was for the most part invisible to all others. A night like this could not be wasted indoors. It was as good an opportunity as any to mingle with the rest of humankind – such as it was.

The park was not as free of light pollution as other spots further away from the city, but for the time being it was enough. A number of others had thought along the same lines and odd groups of star-gazers were busy with their kits and portable tables, with Thermos flasks and travel mugs. Some of those people he had noticed on other occasions. There was the couple in their late fifties with the latest Meade telescope and the smart camping gear. There was the noisy, scrabbling astronomy class of teenagers who were more interested in each other than in the heavens. Somewhere to the man's left there was a couple and he watched them as he pretended to adjust his Autostar hand controller. The boyfriend was stocky and the girlfriend taller and willowy and – how very interesting

– tonight they had been arguing. It was obvious in the way they moved around each other – a sort of rigid dance around the tripod, where every movement was spiked with conflict. Their voices, he noted with pleasure, were muted and their exchanges curt.

The man did not study them because he was attracted to either: his attention was on the cloud of tension and strain that appeared to emanate from them. That, he liked very much. And he was extremely adept at reading the story of their disagreement: whatever had happened, the girlfriend had started it and the boyfriend was sulking.

The man looked away and returned to his eyepiece. He had only so much of his time to give them if all they were doing was stomping about like sullen adolescents. His eyes feasted on Jupiter – tonight he could see all four moons – for as long as he could and then he began to pack things up and head back to the car.

He noticed the dog barking as he was walking across the long stretch of grass towards the parking lot. It was a yappy, annoying bark and no doubt it belonged to some small, impossibly aggravating beast that had been left in the car while the owners stargazed. What he should do, he thought, is let the dog out and let it run away. With any luck, the shrill sound the creature created would be lost with him.

As the man approached the lot he saw why the dog was barking. A boy – no older than four – was standing one foot away from the car window, watching it with curiosity and no fear. The dog – the man couldn't tell what breed it was – was launching itself at the window as if the continued existence of humanity depended on its defending the car. There was slobber on the inside of the glass and the small paws clawed hard against the door.

The man looked back towards the field: someone must have

lost this child, someone must be looking for him. For the briefest moment he considered whether he should take him, just lift him clear off the concrete and put him in his trunk. Then again, what would he do with a child? And wouldn't people have seen him on the field anyway?

The boy placed his little hand against the window and at that point the dog really lost it.

The man crouched next to the boy. 'Not a very nice dog, is it?'

The boy looked up and shook his head.

The man could see that the car was unlocked. *Sweet Jesus, who leaves the car unlocked these days?* He could open the door and let the dog out, see what would happen with the kid. See if the silly dog was all bark and no bite. The man was wearing gloves and it would just be a dreadful incident and a combination of bad luck and neglect. Or even better . . .

He looked at the boy and then at the snarling dog. 'Would you like me to kill it?' he said. His voice was so calm he could have been asking for the boy's name.

If the child was surprised by his question he did not show it, and the man was pleased by the intense regard with which he seemed to be pondering the issue. The dog continued his barking and, way back in the field, the man heard raised voices and someone calling out.

'We don't have that much time, my friend. Would you like me to kill the dog?'

The boy gave it another moment of consideration then shook his head.

'As you wish,' the man said and he left.

By the time he reached his car a few rows away he heard a woman calling out to the boy and his whiny reply to her. He waited for the mother to scoop the boy up and take him back to the field and only then did he turn the key and make the engine come to life. What would he have done if the boy had said yes? No question about it: breaking the dog's neck would hardly have been tougher than breaking the child's.

The man had lived in the Queen Anne neighborhood in Seattle for the last five years and, as always, when he drove home his eyes found any windows that were lit, with curtains open, and whatever scraps of life he could glimpse. People honestly believed that locking their doors at night meant that they were safe and secure, that what they owned and who they were was protected, when in fact their whole existence was open for scrutiny anytime someone with motivation and the right skills came along. And the man had both.

He would never be so silly as to do that in his own neighborhood, but in other areas of the city – and southwest Seattle was perfect, with its green yards that sloped into the water and the thickets of trees between the houses – the man loved to go *prospecting*.

It had started one summer day when he was eleven and playing – alone – in his tree house. It was a rickety thing that his father had built for him in the spring, hoping that it would entice him to invite some school friends over to play. What it did for the boy, though, was give him leave to be happily entrenched in his very own command post, examining the neighbors' backyards and gazing unseen into their homes. It was a hot summer, windows were open and he saw much more of the couple next door than he would have expected, or hoped.

The sex wasn't particularly interesting – though he knew that there were kids in school who would have courted his friendship for a chance to come up to his tree house just at the right time. What took his interest, what drew him back there evening after evening between dinner and bedtime, was that Mr Hendricks had slapped his wife. His parents were a quiet, contented couple who never even raised their voices to each other but Mr Hendricks, who worked for the county and washed his car in his driveway on Sunday, had slapped his wife hard across the face one evening – out of the blue – when she had said something that had been too faint for the boy to hear. It had been an ugly, jagged movement that had caught both the woman and the boy by surprise and, while she had held her hand to her cheek, the boy had looked on, mesmerized and greedy, drinking in the foul gleam in the husband's eyes and the shock and hurt in the wife's.

It happened four times in all that summer – at least, those were the times he had been able to watch them hidden in the tree house. When his mother announced at the beginning of October that she had seen the wife leave in a small U-Haul van driven by another man and packed with her belongings, his parents had commented on how the neighbors had seemed so happy only one week earlier, as they had exchanged jokes from their respective stoops. But the boy knew then that people's lives are mysteries and no one knows what goes on in another person's heart even if they live three feet away from you.

The husband moved away four months later and, to the boy's disappointment, a boring if cheerful family moved in – two dull, unimaginative parents and one pathetic little girl who tried to make friends with him.

As an adult, what his life lacked in personal relationships he more than made up for with the collection of information, insights and private affairs that he had gleaned through what he liked to call 'craft' and 'art'. He had learnt early the techniques which helped him achieve the results he wanted. However, the fact that the fall-outs had a kind of particular beauty, that was art.

His home was a smallish, pretty house in a residential street lined by similar houses and it would have attracted no undue attention – he had made sure of that. *Keep things nice, but not ostentatiously so; never buy a big flashy car, only something that may be instantly forgotten.* And so it was with his neighbors: he was careful to be polite and friendly but he never got personal. He doubted that they could have picked him out of a line-up – he loved that phrase.

By the time he got home the street was quiet. He unloaded the telescope and the rest of his gear from the trunk and let himself in. He turned on the light in the spotless kitchen and made himself a chicken and ham sandwich with French mustard, which he had with a beer while watching Letterman. Not a particularly good night, he thought – then again, a middling night with Letterman was still better than most other stuff.

After he ran hot water over the plate he had used, he washed his hands with the special moisturizing soap that he bought at the chemist and dried them carefully with a clean dish-towel. His second bedroom looked like a guest room, though no guest had ever stayed, nor indeed would ever do so. His third bedroom, looking out onto the backyard and the tall trees, was his office, and there his heart truly lived.

It was the largest room and the one where he spent most of his hours. During the day it was bright and airy and at night he could occasionally see clumps of stars above the treeline, clearly enough to engage his interest. It was his office, his playroom and the place where all his dreams began.

The man went to a small table on the side and switched on the anglepoise lamp. There had been much work to do but he was almost ready and this was his reward. He slipped on a double layer of latex gloves, stood by the floor-to-ceiling bookcase and chose a tome.

Under the pool of light from the lamp he found the page he needed, picked up his box cutter and sliced a thin strip off the page. A cigar case inside a clear plastic bag sat on the corner of the table and inside it other priceless fragments of his life waited to be delivered to the next home.

Chapter 27

Alice Madison woke up early that Saturday morning after a night of broken sleep and unsettling dreams that she could not remember. She dragged herself under the shower and made coffee strong enough to keep her awake until the new year. She was not surprised, she had known it would happen sooner or later, but meeting Nathan Quinn again unexpectedly after all that time was disorienting and she still felt caught out.

She could not afford to think about it, though: decisions had been made, they had both moved on. And that, she said to herself with a finality she wished she felt, was that.

She rummaged in her closet and found the boots she would need for the wedding the following day. They looked clean enough for regular use but for that kind of event she'd have to spend some time tonight brushing and polishing. Madison sighed. *Beware of all enterprises that require clean boots.*

She forced down some breakfast – oatmeal – just for the sake of the ritual of making it before leaving the house. Her mind was on the picture of the fake HVAC man that had been released to the public. After the car engine started she switched on the radio and waited for the breakfast news. She was ready for anything that might be thrown in about her lack of experience, or any smears on her capabilities. They wouldn't make her day any better, but – what the heck – she had bigger fish to fry.

The neighborhood was quiet as she drove off, her thoughts on murder and desire.

Madison had never personally investigated a serial killer case – whatever Detective Chris Kelly might say. They are rare, though not as rare as people would like them to be. The idea of murder is repulsive to most human beings; nevertheless, some few individuals find their twisted joy in it and Madison had seen their work. She had studied it like others had scrutinized the Riemann hypothesis in mathematics. And she knew that the hardest part was going to be finding the connection between the different murders: the victims had been chosen by the killer and, as yet, they did not know whether the killings were random or not, and how the man had insinuated himself into their lives. The why was clear enough: his pleasure lay in the damaged bodies of Matthew Duncan and Peter Mitchell.

Pale shimmers of sun were caught in the skyscrapers downtown as Madison drove on the West Seattle Bridge and then onto I-5. Unwittingly her thoughts went back to the previous evening's meeting. Quinn's idea had been spot on: they needed to find all of the killer's handiwork and the best way was to go through the list of murderers who had appealed their convictions and maintained their innocence. Madison felt a tiny bit better; there were things they could do, avenues they could pursue. Unless they had a sense of what kind of man they were hunting, they would only be stumbling around in the dark.

The news came on the radio and Madison turned up the volume. It was the first item: the broadcaster spoke about the recent development in the Duncan case and said that there was now a sketch by a forensic artist that pictured a man the police were eager to contact. Madison was glad that her name had not been mentioned even once – although she was sure that, if they didn't come up soon with something more tangible than a sketch, it'd be out there every time right after the words *gruesome murder*.

Brown walked in with two coffees as per their ritual and put one on her desk.

'Thank you,' Madison said and went straight to the point. 'You know about the correlation and escalation between voyeurism, breaking and entering and violent sexual crimes?'

'Good morning and yes, I do,' Brown replied.

'Our man is a *watcher* but there isn't any sexual element to his murders.'

'How do you know he is a watcher?' Brown took off his coat and sat down.

'He must be. He knew when the cleaner would be in the house, the name of the HVAC company and the color of their uniforms. He knew when the wife went out for her run every day. The cigar case was found buried near the spot that's perfect for observing the house and – and this is the most important part – it takes time to do all this. He must have invested a lot of time and energy in the collecting of all this information. That's his turn-on. He enjoys it.'

Brown sat back in his chair and considered that angle. 'You're saying that he has all the characteristics of a voyeur but without the sexual element.'

'Exactly.'

'And his pay-off . . .'

'. . . is the violence,' Madison said. 'Knowing how far he can go and getting away with it. It's power, control and an unmistakable F.O. to the rest of us. Well, especially *us*.'

'He must have gotten pretty close to Mitchell and Karasick too, to know what he knew about them,' Brown said.

Madison nodded. *How close did he get to them? How close did he need to get to them?*

She picked up the phone, dialed the number she had found online earlier and hoped someone would pick up at the other end.

'Hello,' a man's voice replied just as she thought it would go to message.

In the background Madison could hear the sound of at least three children squabbling over what might have been breakfast. 'This is Detective Madison from Seattle Homicide,' she said.

'Yes,' the man said, and there was hesitation there, the kind that is born out of the expectation of bad news.

'Is this Mr Saul Garner, from the Release Project Northwest?'

'It is.'

'I need to speak with you with a degree of urgency regarding an open case. Could you meet me in your office later?'

'What is this about? Is it one of the appeals? I don't understand.'

'No, it's not, and I appreciate that it is Saturday. But I really need to speak with you and I'd rather not do it on the telephone.'

The noise from the children in the background had reached rock stadium level and Madison heard Garner move away to another room.

'What is this about?' he repeated, and she could tell that he was not upset about the intrusion into his weekend but was genuinely concerned.

'We need to talk about Henry Karasick,' she said. 'To begin with.'

'Henry's dead,' the man said after a beat.

'When can you meet me, Counsellor?'

'Okay, okay, let me just think about it . . .'

They agreed a time and Madison terminated the call.

By now the detectives' room was busy around them – chatter, phones ringing – and Lieutenant Fynn watching them all, his eyes sharp and somber.

Madison looked around Saul Garner's office: whatever it was that got him there and working every morning it certainly was not gold or glory. Garner had listened intently as she had explained the situation and then had gone next door to find the Karasick file. His eyes had met Brown's when they were introduced and Madison was surprised to find something there akin to regret.

Garner came back with a large box, which he dropped on top of his already crowded desk. He measured Brown with a quick glance and said, 'We haven't met before today, Detective, and I say this in all honesty: we never stood a chance with Karasick's case. We had zero and the only reason I took it on was that – perversely, perhaps – there was something about Henry that I could not shake off. I mean, the guy would not give up. He would not plead when everybody in the world was telling him to. Did you know his own mother begged him to plead and get a lesser sentence?'

'No, I did not.'

'He wasn't stupid, he wasn't mentally incapable of understanding the kind of pickle he was in and yet he hung on in there.'

Madison didn't need to look at Brown to know that each word would have been painful for him.

'He was a stoner and a drunk with anger management issues,

that's for sure, but before that night he had never done anything remotely like it. And today, seven years later, you're telling me he really hadn't done it.'

'That's what it looks like,' Madison said.

'There will be a time for publicity,' Brown interjected, 'but this is not it. When we are done, when we have the man we are looking for, then you can talk to the family or whoever needs to know. However, should this get out now, it would compromise our investigation. And we have every reason to believe that, if the killer has got this far, he will continue unless he's stopped.'

Garner gazed from one to the other. 'I'm not interested in publicity but I have clients in KCJC, I have clients upstate, and if there is the smallest chance that they might be innocent, that their cases are related to yours, then I need your cooperation to make sure they are going to be given special consideration, that they are kept *safe* inside – wherever they are – until the time when they're released. That is my priority.'

'We cannot talk for the King County Prosecuting Attorney but you should get in touch with Sarah Klein. She will be able to work things at that end.'

Garner nodded. 'Seven years?' he said.

It was a lot of time to fill for someone whose taste was what lay in Dr Fellman's morgue.

He grabbed his notebook. 'I need an exact series of parameters that you want me to use.'

'Murders with a particular degree of violence,' Madison said. 'And the weapon is not a firearm – possibly, but unlikely, it could be a blade. More probably a hammer or something that could be used to batter the victim.'

'No alibis,' Brown said. 'And no plea bargaining.'

'What else?' Garner said.

They went back and forth for a while. When Brown and Madison left him he had a long list and looked like someone who was going to war with it.

Good, Madison thought. It was what they had wished for and what they needed. Most of Saul Garner's life was lived among the hopes of desperate men in horrendous places; the notion that he might be able to lift even a few of them from their private hells must have been irresistible.

Sarah Klein would get a call within the hour to get things rolling just in case – no question about that.

Saul Garner called his wife and told her that something of an emergency had come up and he had to spend some time in the office. She was a doctor and was used to those; in the background the kids howled.

He debated whether to call his secretary and try to rope her into the search or not. It was true that time was a factor, but he paused. He knew the cases inside out and he would be faster than she could possibly be in his digging, and – deep down in a place he didn't particularly want to admit to himself – he doubted whether he would have been able to trust her complete silence about it, whether this was not something too good, too juicy not to share with a friend, a colleague from another office in the building. The same reason ruled out the volunteers from Law School. This was his, and his alone. Everyone else could come on board once they were in the open and there was a case to answer.

Where was the number of the Prosecuting Attorney the detective had left? Garner dialed and left a message for Sarah Klein. She was another name in many of the files he had labored on all these years and now they were all finally meeting, courtesy of this man – this crazy, violent nutjob.

Saul Garner called up on his computer screen all the cases that he had worked on in the last seven years. The list was overwhelming: he would start from the oldest and work his way towards the present. He might think it – he might even say it in the privacy of his own deserted office – however, if what the detectives had said was true, the man wasn't crazy.

He was just plain old-fashioned evil.

The face of the fake HVAC engineer had made the prime-time news the previous evening and the breakfast news on local and national channels. There had been twenty-seven calls so far: most from within Washington State, three from Texas, two from California, one from Maine.

A man picked up a copy of the *Seattle Times* from a vending machine and read it as he walked back to his car. The police sketch was on the front page. The man looked at it and then caught his reflection briefly in the window of a shop. The reflection showed a bald man with a perfectly naked, hairless face and piercing tawny eyes, nothing at all like the dark-haired face in the picture.

The man looked up at the sky: so much light that hid all the secrets and the beauty held by the heavens. He wondered where Jupiter was when he wasn't looking at it. Some philosophers would have wondered if it even existed at all. The man smiled. His life was made by small pleasures.

Chapter 28

Madison was on the phone speaking to a caller about the sketch in the papers and slowly losing her will to live.

'He definitely looks like my brother-in-law,' the man was saying.

'That's very useful, sir. May I have your brother-in-law's details.'

'I can give you his name but not his address. Sonofabitch works on one of the big fishing boats that sail to Alaska and back. Doesn't have an address; we get his mail and keep it here when he's away.'

'I see. And is the boat in the harbor now?'

'No, they left one month ago. He called my wife from Juneau last weekend.'

'Thank you very much, sir.'

Madison replaced the receiver, ran a black line through a name on a list and looked up. For a moment her brain could not quite compute what she was seeing. Right there, standing six feet away from her, Matthew Duncan met her eyes. It was him – and yet, as Madison gazed at him, she noticed small but definite differences. This man was a little younger and his hair was darker.

He stepped forward.

'I'm Casey Duncan,' the man said, and then added, as if she hadn't realized, 'I'm Matt's brother.'

Madison led him to the rec room, where they could sit away from the bustle, and made him some hot chocolate from a sachet she managed to find in a drawer. Casey Duncan was apologetic; being in the place where they were investigating his brother's murder seemed to have poked at the open wound. He knew he didn't have an appointment but he'd hoped to meet her anyway.

'You don't need an appointment, Mr Duncan,' she said. 'I'm glad you came.'

He nodded. His eyes were red-rimmed and he looked pale under the freckles. Casey Duncan chose his words carefully and his grief was barely kept in check.

'Matt was eleven months older than me and, when we were young, we did everything together. Everything. This has been . . . this has been hell for all of us and I don't know how Kate has managed to keep it together.'

Madison let him speak. If he was there, he wanted to get something off his chest.

'Matt was very kind. He was a good, kind, gentle person. You saw him and you'd have thought he was a typical jock but he wasn't. He was not loud or aggressive or . . . I don't know. I just wanted to tell you that and give you this.' He slid a DVD across the table. 'So that you'd see how he was. So that you would see him alive and think of him as a real person not . . . not . . .'

'I see him as a real person,' Madison said gently.

'I mean, you couldn't even see his face,' he said.

And Madison understood: the killer had destroyed something the brothers had shared. 'The injuries were terrible – it's true – but we spoke to his wife, to his colleagues and his friends. We tried to create a picture of your brother from all who knew him. He is very real to me.'

Casey Duncan nodded without looking at her. His eyes were welling up.

'I just thought you should see him in life,' he said.

Madison placed her hand over the DVD. 'Thank you,' she said. 'I will watch this.'

'Is there any news?' he asked.

They had decided that the family should not be told of the link to Mitchell's murder and Madison heard herself say, 'We're going through the calls from the public at the moment. The response was good.'

She wanted to tell him that they would hunt the bastard down to the ends of the earth, but that was not what she was trained to say.

Madison watched the man gulp the last of his chocolate because he couldn't sit still and words were failing him. She sat on the edge of the chair and leant forward. She had been in that room, she had seen Matthew Duncan on the wooden floor in a sea of red and nothing left to tell them that he had looked like his brother.

'We will find him,' she said softly.

The man looked up.

'We will,' she repeated.

He nodded. 'I have your word?'

'Yes,' she replied.

Casey Duncan left and Madison felt like a complete idiot. She had just given her word. It might have been the right thing to say but she didn't even want to consider the story five years down the line with Casey Duncan saying *you gave me your word* while she was trying to explain that they'd done all they could. It didn't bear thinking about.

Madison looked out of the window where the light was beginning to dim and realized only then just how smart Casey Duncan had been because, as they spoke, she had looked into his dead brother's eyes too. And it was to him that she had made her promise.

Brian Baines, the friend who had found Peter Mitchell's body seven years earlier, didn't work in the warehouse any longer: he had moved up to a management job in the harbor and a house in Ballard. He met Brown and Madison in his driveway – a man in his early forties who wore a knitted tie over a denim shirt.

'I remember you,' he said to Brown as he led them inside. 'I thought the case was closed . . .' he continued once they were sitting around his dining table.

Sounds from the life in the rest of the house were muted by the closed door.

'It was,' Brown replied. 'But some new evidence has come to light and we want to look into it.'

'But the guy who did it went to prison for it.'

'Henry Karasick was convicted, yes.'

'Well, I don't know, everything I knew I said at the time,'

'Mr Baines, have you ever seen this man?'

Brown pulled out a number of sketches which, essentially, were the Duncan killer's composite but had been altered to account for the suspect being seven years younger. The artist had also done a couple of variations with different hairstyles and a beard.

'This man might have been around at the time of the murder. He might have known Peter Mitchell from the warehouse.'

Baines's eyes traveled across the pictures spread out in front of him. 'You're saying he could have been involved? There could have been *two* of them?'

'We're looking at all the possibilities,' Brown replied.

He was about one hair's breadth away from lying outright, Madison thought.

Baines frowned. 'Seven years ago we had many temporary workers who would just stay for a few weeks, a few months, and then move on. Just before the recession, you know.'

'Do you remember Peter Mitchell ever talking to anyone about his neighbor troubles with Karasick? Do you remember anyone ever taking particular interest in that subject?'

Baines let out a wheezy laugh. 'You're going to have trouble finding people who *didn't* know about it. Peter – God rest his soul – never shut up about it. It was always the Ruski did this, the Ruski did that.'

'Karasick was from Tacoma,' Brown said.

Baines shrugged. 'It was a Russian-sounding name and it was enough for Pete.'

'Look at these pictures again, please.'

A teenage boy burst into the room – all skinny legs and floppy hair.

'Not now,' Baines said, not unkindly.

The boy gaped at the detectives – Madison received a long, lingering glance that took in her sidearm – and then he backed out, closing the door.

'Maybe,' Baines said, eyes still on the sketches, his mind traveling back to snatches of conversations, to moments half glimpsed through stacks and loaders. 'There was a guy, he was stuck to Peter like white on rice. He was with us for two to three months max, then he left.'

'Did he leave before or after Peter Mitchell died?' Brown said.

'Before, but I remember someone must have let him know and he came to the funeral. That's right,' Baines slapped his hand on the table. 'He was always around Peter and couldn't get enough of all the stuff that Peter would come up with. Don't get me wrong: he was my best friend but he was talking crap half of the time—' He stopped with a smile half formed on his face. The sudden memory had unfolded itself and it was ragged and searing.

'Do you remember his name?'

'No. He had a thin face. Dark hair. Couldn't tell you about the eyes.'

'Did he look like the picture?'

'Sort of. But I don't really remember him very well, you know. More like his presence around us.'

'Do you think we could get the records from the warehouse?'

'Company went bust two years after Pete died. I'd left just in time.'

'Who else might remember?' Madison asked him.

They left the house and the sky was already inky violet. Baines had given them the names and numbers of his former colleagues. Someone had to remember the man who had been Peter Mitchell's shadow during the last months of his life.

'I didn't ask the right questions,' Brown said, as he turned the key and the engine started. 'Seven years ago, I didn't ask the right questions.'

Madison didn't want to offer platitudes. In her experience they cheapen the giver and irritate the taker.

'It was an aberration, Sarge,' she said finally. 'How many cases do you know where the most pressing issue is to find out who really *liked* the victim?'

It didn't seem that Brown had heard her, or maybe he just didn't bother to reply.

Madison leant her head against the window and let him be.

Chapter 29

Detective Kyle Spencer ran the palm of his hand over his tie to flatten it. He was a tie-and-sports-coat man and, after many years, some of his style had rubbed off on his partner, Andrew Dunne, who had started out as a detective in a T-shirt and a leather jacket, graduated to button-downs and finally attained tweed.

They had parked their car a few yards away and the walk to the imposing house at the end of the driveway was pleasant in the early dusk as the gravel crunched under their feet. There was woodsmoke in the air and the scent of fresh damp earth mixed with something like pot roast from the kitchens at the back of the building.

Spencer rang the doorbell of the Cedar Grove Home for the Elderly in north Seattle.

'I still think it's a waste of time,' Dunne whispered.

'Indulge me,' Spencer replied.

Dunne rolled his eyes. He was a ball of energy, barely contained by his badge and his partner – and best friend – and he felt that interviewing seniors whose memories and recall were notoriously dicky was not the best use of their already limited time.

'Just tell me something: didn't the person who called say that this is someone with the early stages of dementia?' Dunne said.

'Yes.'

'Then what are we doing here?'

'Don't be a smart-ass. If your grandmother told you she'd seen Joe DiMaggio walking down the street you'd be tripping over your feet to get your bat for an autograph.'

'That's different.'

'How?'

'I know my Nanou. She's brighter than both of us put together.'

'She called me Anthony three days ago.'

'Anthony was her brother.'

'I'm saying she didn't notice I'm half Japanese. And fifty years younger than her dead brother.'

'Details,' Dunne replied as the front door opened.

They were shown into a comfortable sitting room at the back of the house, overlooking a garden. Most of the residents were slowly making their way to dinner but some were still chatting or reading. Clearly this was the upper end of senior care and yet it was still a different world: a place where adult human beings were shepherded like kindergartners through their day by other people, and the notion – however lovely the surroundings, however kind the shepherds – was terrifying.

Spencer and Dunne had grown up close to their grandparents – Spencer could even briefly remember a great-grandparent – as part of their Japanese and Irish heritage and they were used to a multi-generational family. They watched as the residents filed away until the nurse returned with a white-haired lady who barely came up to their chest.

'Mrs Walker,' the nurse said, 'these are Detectives Spencer and Dunne from the Seattle Police Department.'

They sat down and the nurse left them.

'Took your own sweet time, didn't you?' Mrs Walker said.

'Excuse me?' Spencer replied as his automatic courtesy kicked in.

'Call me Edith. All this Mrs Walker stuff makes me feel like people are talking to my corpse – which, considering I'm eighty-seven, they probably are.'

'You look pretty damn good for eighty-seven, Edith,' Dunne said.

The old lady's eyes – pale blue and clear – crinkled with her smile. 'I have good days and bad days and this is a good one. Lucky you.'

'How can we help you?' Dunne continued, and Spencer could see he had gone straight into his Nanou-mode.

Her smile went away. 'Will he know that I've spoken with you?'

'Who?'

'The man. The man in the picture. Will he know?'

'No, he won't. And if you need to be protected, we will protect you. Do you know who this man is?' Dunne took out a copy of the sketch and smoothed it out for her.

Edith Walker's eyes gazed at the picture. Her mind chased after a memory and a name from another life. 'I think it's my neighbor's son,' she said.

'Your neighbor here? Or where you used to live?'

'Where I used to live. In Bellevue.'

'Do you know his name?'

'The family was called Burrows or Bryant or Burns – something with the letter B.'

'And his name?'

'I can't remember his name. It was twenty years ago.'

'Twenty years ago?' Dunne's voice was gentle but he couldn't hide his disappointment.

'He was a boy then.'

'A boy?'

'Yes, and the boy had fox's eyes. He was always watching everything that was going on in the street. Nobody noticed but I did,' she looked from one to the other. 'Because I was watching too.'

'How long were you neighbors?'

'I was staying with my daughter and her family for maybe six months.'

'Six months, twenty years ago?' Dunne said.

'I had broken my foot. All I did was sit by that window. I can't tell you the day of the week or who the President is but I can tell you that the neighbor's kid could be this man.'

'How old was he then?'

'I don't know. A teenager, I guess. A tall, gangly thing.'

After a few more cursory questions they took down her daughter's details and stood up.

'Thank you very much, Edith. It was a pleasure to meet you,' Dunne said and shook her hand.

'Thank you for your help,' Spencer said.

'*Siete due bravi ragazzi*,' the old lady said, gazing at both.

'You speak Italian, Edith?' Dunne smiled.

'Apparently,' she replied with a mischievous smile.

The nurse was already coming back to help the old lady to her dinner.

'It was worth a try,' Dunne said as they walked back to the car.

Spencer looked at him. 'What's wrong?'

'Well, Edith is a nice lady, but—'

'I mean with you. What's wrong?'

'Nothing,' Dunne shrugged.

'Are you worried about tomorrow?'

'No, it's going to be a great party. Everything's ready. It'll be great.'

For the first time since Dunne had asked him to be best man Spencer wondered if his friend was nervous about the wedding. In the last months he had seemed to embrace his new life. And yet, somehow, in the last few days – as the fog of the bachelor party had cleared – a restless gloom had settled in.

'Maybe we should have stayed for the pot roast,' Dunne said, but his eyes were serious and did not meet Spencer's.

Chapter 30

Madison drove home late after a long round of calls trying to put a name on the guy that Brian Baines had remembered. There was a man out there who looked exactly like any other man and yet was capable of such evil that words could barely contain it.

What was Saul Garner going to find? She tried not to imagine the list of names, of victims, of defendants, of injuries and autopsy photographs. She saw for a moment Casey Duncan's eyes – his brother's eyes – and again was grateful that he'd come to meet her. She had watched some of the home movie and seen the person who had been destroyed in death very much alive, and the thought of spending the following day at a wedding seemed absurd when there was so much to do, when people needed to be protected, when even as she drove home to polish her boots the killer might be getting ready to harvest more sorrow, more grief, more indescribable pain.

Madison pulled into her driveway and was glad that Aaron would be coming for her in the morning. Tonight she needed the space to be alone with ugly thoughts and, under all that horror, the single notion – like a short, poisoned dagger – that others might be right and she would fail both the living and the dead.

She had barely turned on the lights in the living room when her cell vibrated. It was an unknown number.

'I understand it's late, but would you mind taking a walk down to your pier?'

The voice was certainly not unknown. *Quinn.*

'I'm not alone,' he added.

Madison kept her voice neutral. 'Right now?'

'No, Detective, at some indeterminate point in the future,' Quinn sighed. 'Yes, right now, if you please.'

She let him hang there waiting for a long, quiet moment. 'Okay,' she said finally.

Madison slid open the French doors and walked onto the deck. The salty chill was raw and it became sharper as she made her way down to the water. Her steps were soft on the hard ground and she trod lightly, her hands deep into her pockets.

As the lawn began to slope she cut to the rickety stairs that led to the narrow cobbled beach. A glimmer of silver from the sky illuminated two dark silhouettes by the pier.

I'm not alone. She approached the men. There was something terribly familiar about this and it was equally welcome and worrying.

'Mr Quinn, Mr Cameron,' she said pleasantly. 'I thought we were past the tricksy entrances.'

'Be that as it may,' the tall shadow that was Nathan Quinn replied. 'This was necessary.'

'Good evening, Detective,' John Cameron said.

Madison's instincts kicked in: they might have played Texas hold 'em together until the sweet light of dawn but Cameron's voice still carried something that curled up like a knot of ice at the pit of her stomach.

For a moment there was just a murmur where the water met the beach, then John Cameron spoke: 'You are under investigation. The Office of Professional Accountability has been investigating you for the last four months.'

Madison's brain staggered, caught itself and started racing. 'I'm . . . what?'

Later, when she thought back to that moment, she realized that not even for a second had she entertained the idea that Cameron might be wrong.

'OPA is investigating *me*? Why? What in the sweet name of—?'

'I'm afraid it is because of our acquaintance. The push came from the DEA in Los Angeles. They suggested it.'

'I joked about it with those two bozos I met with a week ago and they took me seriously? This is a joke.' Madison started to pace the thin beach.

'No, it isn't, and they have been keeping an eye on you for months, not since last Saturday.'

'How do you know for sure?'

'I have contacts.'

'Inside OPA?'

Cameron did not reply. He didn't need to. Madison figured he probably had contacts who could tell him what each OPA officer had for breakfast if he cared to know.

'There's worse,' Quinn said.

For a bizarre moment he sounded to Madison like a doctor about to give a patient the shittiest news. 'OPA investigating me is not the worst you've got?'

'No . . .' Quinn took a deep breath. 'Someone close to you is talking to them.'

He was right. He knew her well enough to know that this was worse. 'Someone I work with?'

Quinn nodded.

'This comes from your contact too?' she asked Cameron.

'Yes. They are very skittish about this informant and it's kept under about five different code names. But it's definitely someone close to you and they want to protect this person from you – and, quite reasonably, from me – ever finding out.'

Madison could have paced the hell out of the small beach. She understood now why they had to meet there and why they wouldn't drive up to her door.

'This is nuts. What do they think I've done? How can they possibly justify an investigation?'

'They think you might be feeding me inside details about the cartel deaths.'

'How? I don't know anything at all about the cartel – except for what Agent Parker himself told me.'

'You have gone to great lengths to save my life when others might not have done.'

'Yeah, well, I knew that one would come back to bite me.' Madison felt anger and adrenaline taking over and stomped on both. She needed to think – and think clearly.

'Tell her,' Nathan Quinn said, and his voice was low, his fury neatly contained.

'Tell me what?'

'Two years ago the cartel put a wire tap on Nathan's home phone to monitor our calls. They were after me, but without much success, and they hoped they'd get some valuable information that would lead them to my safe house. Two years ago,' Cameron repeated.

Madison followed the trail of his words. *Two years ago.* She remembered a frantic drive in foul weather, a madman stalking the city, a last-minute phone call to Quinn's home to save the lives of a SWAT team about to storm Cameron's boat.

'They have my call?' she said. Her voice came out all right even if her heart was thundering.

'Yes,' Quinn replied.

It had been one crazy moment in a long series of crazy moments, but Madison had warned Quinn that the police were about to break into Cameron's boat and told him that he should give himself up, and she had assured him that she could prove his innocence of a hideous crime. She could not bear the thought of innocent lives being lost and knew that Cameron would not let himself be taken down easily. If that tape were made public, her life as a police officer would effectively be over. OPA would rule the day; the King County Prosecuting Attorney would have plenty of grounds to charge her with anything and everything they wanted – except maybe jaywalking – but all that didn't really matter anyway because no cop would ever serve by her side again.

Cameron continued, and his voice reached her through a fog of anguish.

'The DEA has dozens of agents working against the cartel. But the cartel, as I do, has its own contacts inside the DEA. For a long time the cartel didn't know there was anything useful in the wire-tap recordings because Nathan and I were always careful.'

Madison snorted: at the time they'd had to subpoena Quinn to break attorney–client privilege and all they'd come away with was the color of Cameron's trousers.

'However,' Cameron continued, 'someone who knew what they were doing listened to the recordings properly and realized they had an SPD detective on record warning a fugitive's attorney of a raid.'

'Why have I not been arrested?'

'Because OPA doesn't know about the call.'

'But—'

'It's leverage, Detective,' Quinn interrupted her. 'The cartel is not interested in the legalities of it. They want to make sure you are put under stress – and when the investigation becomes public, you will be. And at the right time they will come to you with the tape and ask you for a favor in return for its disappearance.'

'And the favor will be to help them to get to you,' she said to Cameron.

'Most likely,' he replied.

Something clicked and resettled in her mind. 'The office of the therapist I visited after the Salinger case and after the shooting in Whatcom County was burglarized a few days ago and it looked like the thief was particularly interested in my file.'

'Did they find it?' Quinn said.

'No, it wasn't there to find.'

'That's not how OPA works,' Cameron said.

The ice in her gut turned into corrosive acid. 'I don't . . . I don't . . . I don't have time for this,' she managed to spit out. 'I have a serial killer who beats his victims to death and a list of fatalities that could stretch back years. I don't have time to worry about some OPA investigation, your damn cartel *and* an informant who—' Madison stopped abruptly. There was one thing she knew. One thing in that horrid mess that had just spilled out on the pebbles that she was sure of without any doubt.

'I know who's talking to OPA. I know exactly who in my unit is talking to them.' She looked at Nathan Quinn and John Cameron through the darkness. 'Chris Kelly,' she said. And it really wasn't a surprise, come to think of it – not after the many arguments and the deep, mutual loathing. 'It's Chris Kelly,' she repeated.

'Are you sure?' Cameron's voice was silk-wrapped danger.

'Yes, I am.'

The moon came out from behind a scrap of clouds, then hid again. The breeze picked up and, somewhere out on the water, invisible in the gloom, something leaped and splashed.

'Well,' Madison said after a while with a levity she did not feel. 'At least I won't be losing any friends over this. Kelly and I already hate each other's guts.'

'What are you going to do?' Quinn said.

'About what? About OPA? About the tape? Nothing. I'm going to do absolutely nothing because there's nothing I can do and my energies are better employed elsewhere. Once we have Matthew Duncan's killer I'm going to have what will no doubt be a short, sharp conversation with my boss and tell him about the tape myself. Because I'm not going to hang around while a bunch of vicious, subhuman, sadistic drug dealers in their landscaped gardens decide my future.'

'You will do nothing of the kind,' Quinn said.

'Really?'

'Really. Because you care about your job, about being able to do your job. We've already talked about this, remember?'

Madison flashed back to an argument between them two years earlier on exactly the same subject. 'I told you to shove it, Counsellor. They would get the same answer.'

'We're looking for the recordings,' Cameron said quietly as he picked up a small pebble and skipped it into the dark water.

'What?'

Cameron turned to Madison and she caught a sparkle from his eyes.

'We're looking for the recordings and we'll shut down that part of their organization. Tonight's conversation was just a courtesy visit so you'd be prepared in case anyone approaches you, so you'd know you might be under surveillance. We have work to do and, by the sound of it, so do you. Have fun with your murderer, Detective, and let me know how it turns out. Goodnight.'

There was hardly a whisper on the stones as Cameron moved away and disappeared, and Madison was suddenly alone with Quinn.

'*Shut down* the cartel?' she said.

'By any and all legal means,' Quinn replied, and he moved closer to her. 'Watch your back, Detective, and I beg you not to do anything foolishly noble that we would all deeply regret.'

Just then he was near enough that she could feel his body warmth. Madison started to speak but the moon came out and she realized that she was alone on the beach.

Madison went inside and lit the fire. She was cold and her hands trembled as she struck the match. They might be quivering out of cold or anger or frustration. She couldn't tell which was which, and she poked the logs in the hearth as they hissed and crackled.

Sitting cross-legged in front of the fire she brushed and polished her black boots with an energy bordering on ferocity. By the time she was done her mind had reached a plain truth that she couldn't shake off: OPA, directly or not, was investigating her for something she had indeed done.

And Chris Kelly – obtuse, brutal, and a bully – was right about her: her mistakes would be measured in body bags.

*

Nathan Quinn had not yet said a word but John Cameron knew him too well to try to crowbar any conversation out of him. Cameron drove fast in the latest of a long line of black Ford Explorers he had owned and waited for his oldest friend to return from wherever he was.

Quinn stared into the darkness ahead.

In the last two years there had been a shift between them: not so much because Quinn was no longer Cameron's attorney but because, for the first time, Quinn had seen with his own eyes his best friend's handiwork – the pictures of a man Cameron had maimed. Did it matter that the victim was a homicidal maniac? That he had slaughtered innocent people? It did and it didn't. There are things that cannot be unknown and they change you in ways you cannot predict. John Cameron was grateful that his bond with Quinn had not been severed over the long years of their acquaintance. Nevertheless, he was careful about how much of his life he would share. His friend had not turned away from the worst of him but there was a subtle edge to their friendship. Sometimes it felt like the cold blade of a knife resting casually against his skin.

'We shouldn't have told her about the recordings,' Quinn said.

'She needed to know.'

'She's not going to wait around for someone to blackmail her. She's going to blow this thing wide open as soon as—'

'She's not going to jeopardize her case. You agree with that, right?'

'Yes.'

'Then we have some time. And I hope Detective Madison has a shred of self-preservation left under all that fire.'

'I wouldn't bet on it. She was ready to give up her badge to hunt down the man who had shot her partner.'

The road was a blur of orange street lights punctuated by black patches of vegetation.

'I think it would be quite something to be on the hunt with Detective Madison,' Cameron said after a while. 'Don't you?'

Quinn did not reply.

The car pulled into his driveway in Seward Park. The house was dark and still – wood and stone weathered by the Pacific Northwest looking over the waters of Lake Washington.

For a moment there was just the sound of the engine ticking over. The sky was nothing but heavy clouds: the moon long gone, the stars extinguished.

'Drink?' Quinn said. He felt edgy and tired and he was not entirely sure that his friend's company was what he needed. But there was no one else he could talk to about this. If they didn't have their secrets, what was left between them?

'Thank you but not tonight,' Cameron replied, and then added, 'I guess that means Erica's not staying.'

'That's correct.'

'When am I going to meet her?'

'Soon,' Quinn replied and got out. 'Goodnight, Jack.'

Nathan Quinn let himself inside – past the locks and the alarm with biometrics access. On the living-room table that day's copy of the *Los Angeles Times* had been left open to the page that reported the death of a Jaime Rojas while visiting his mother in hospital. The post-mortem had not been performed yet. However, LAPD was treating the death as suspicious. How perspicacious, Quinn thought. The article was sparse on facts and generous with speculation. Quinn did not need to speculate.

Almost six months earlier, John Cameron had appeared on his porch. They had not seen each other for a while and, although Quinn had some ideas about what his friend had been doing, he had not been prepared to hear what Cameron wanted to tell him and the details of the deal he wanted to strike. But he had agreed in the end – as Cameron had known he would – and he'd got to work on his side of things. Now the whole mess was moving faster than they wanted and in directions they had not expected.

Nathan Quinn poured himself a measure of bourbon and stood by the French doors looking up at the overcast sky. He took a sip. How far was he capable of going in order to protect the ones he loved? He hoped he'd never have to find out because the answer was quite simply terrifying. He was an officer of the court, sworn to uphold the law – it was almost funny, when he thought of it in those plain terms. But most of all – and it stung that the State Attorney had been right on the money about it – he was a wartime *consigliere*. He had looked for his own war and found it, not the other way around.

Quinn knocked back the rest of the bourbon. He would not allow himself to think of Detective Alice Madison and their awkward proximity in the darkness of the beach. He would not allow himself to think of her.

Nathan Quinn went to bed and the sheets were cool on his skin. He would not allow himself to think of her at all.

Chapter 31

The church was a sea of blue. The first notes of Schubert's *Ave Maria* trembled high in the chilly air, sung by one of Dunne's young cousins, and rain lined the stained-glass windows. Dozens of police officers in dress uniform crammed both sides of the aisle in the Blessed Sacrament Church in the University District. Every bench and every pew had been taken and Madison stood between Aaron and Brown, behind a group of Andy Dunne's Irish relatives.

The bride and the groom stood by the altar – one with a train that had required three bridesmaids and the other looking as pale as the freshly dead. Stillness had been tipped into the church and held every person in their place. It wasn't Madison's first Catholic wedding but it certainly *felt* the most Catholic – if that were possible.

Aaron had arrived good and early that morning, wearing a charcoal suit with a dark purple tie, and found her already in her smart blues, sidearm in place and boots shining. Her eyes, though, told him about a bad night with little sleep, so he had offered to make breakfast.

In the end Madison had made pancakes for both because she needed to be distracted by something, anything, and cooking might just do – at least for a few minutes.

'Is it the case?' Aaron had asked her.

'Yes,' she had replied since it was certainly part of the truth.

'Maybe you can take a few hours off,' he had said. 'From everything. Just enjoy the day.'

He had meant well and she had put her arms around him and hugged him without speaking. Chris Kelly would be at the wedding and enjoying the day might be a tad beyond Madison's capabilities.

They had run into Brown on the church steps and introductions were made. For a brief, bizarre moment Madison had felt like a teenager bringing home her first boyfriend. Of course, that had never happened in the reality of her life. Brown, who had come by himself, had shaken Aaron's hand with warmth and they had joined the crowd. Aaron had looked around with something akin to bewilderment. She had warned him that there would be *a lot* of cops. Nevertheless, the experience was something else and she had noticed his eyes taking in the uniforms, the decorations, the weapons worn with the familiarity of everyday objects. She was used to it, he was not. She had slipped her hand into his and squeezed it.

Now Schubert held them all and the boy's voice rose above the carved crucifix, above the high altar and the wood-paneled sanctuary. And Madison felt raw, as if the music had somehow peeled off a layer of skin, of protection, and left her vulnerable to everything and to everyone, and to those vows that promised a life. There was such hope in those words and they shot straight through Madison's core.

'Do you take this man . . . ?' the priest said.

A wave of emotion swelled and caught Madison's breath; she was glad that most of Dunne's family seemed to be struggling with handkerchiefs. She blinked and lifted her gaze up to the west window above the altar: there were six panels of stained glass and, in the leftmost pane, the top symbol was a scale to represent the virtues of justice. *Justice.* Madison looked away. She turned to her side and noticed Chris Kelly, who must have been pushed into the bride's side of the church and was shifting in his seat. She was out of herself and so preoccupied that she didn't even realize he had turned until their eyes met.

He was a blank. He could have been standing in the middle of a parking lot or maybe a particularly disappointing department store. His gaze slid over Madison and returned to the front, devoid of expression.

A pinprick of anger pierced her and she hung on to it. Anger was better than that blinding sorrow. Anger she could handle – with or without Schubert.

Then the groom kissed the bride and they were done. Madison exhaled and wiped her cheek where a tear had dried. They had witnessed something, they had been part of something.

The guests came out under the rain and the wind whipped their coats. The photographer attempted to take some pictures on the steps but no one really expected the happy couple to come out. Madison spotted Dunne's red hair as he climbed into a limo among cheers and hollers, surrounded by other red-haired people under black umbrellas.

The inside of Aaron's car was steamed up as he leaned over and kissed her softly. 'I like weddings,' he said.

A small part of Madison was still in the church, trying to make sense of the ragged pain in her chest.

They drove in convoy to Ray's Boathouse in Ballard for the reception. Aaron looked Madison up and down as he steered through the traffic.

'I like you in your dress blues,' he said. 'A little stern perhaps, but we could make it work.'

'I hadn't realized you had a thing for uniforms,' Madison said.

'That's because I'd never seen you in one before.'

'Stop smiling already.'

'I can't.'

They parked in the restaurant lot just in time for a frail sun to come out and shine wanly on the slick piers around it. Madison remembered that it was lucky for the bride to have rain on her wedding day. Good for Stacey, she thought. The water, like a bright sheet of metal, caught every shard of light and bounced it back.

Hours later – after canapés and champagne followed by more food than Madison thought possible – Aaron nipped outside for a quick call to his children and she found herself alone, sitting next to Brown.

'Sarge,' she said, aware that she'd had a couple of drinks and her thinking might not be as straight as it should be. 'What would you do if you couldn't do this?'

'What do you mean?'

'If something prevented you from being a cop.'

They both knew that he had come dangerously close to it in the past – when he'd had trouble passing the firearm test after being shot, nearly two years earlier. Brown looked at Madison: this was about something else.

'I didn't want to think about it at the time. I suppose I didn't want to believe that it could happen for real. So I guess the answer to your question is that I don't know what I would do if I couldn't do this.'

Madison nodded; she had thought as much. The notion of Brown not being a cop was inconceivable.

'What has brought this on?' he said.

Madison wanted so very badly to tell him. *See, OPA is investigating me for something that – however I want to dress it up – I have done. And Chris Kelly, right there at the table in the corner having a slice of wedding cake, is keeping an eye on me for them.* She wanted to tell him because he already knew about the call to Quinn – she had told him at the time – and the idea of keeping something like this from him went against everything they had built during their relationship.

'What is it?' he asked her.

If she told him, she would be dragging him into the chaos that she had created for herself. And one day – under oath, as he was likely to be – he would have to admit that yes, she had known she was under investigation and yes, they had talked about it. If she told him, she would be taking away his deniability – and that, Madison reflected through the blurry focus given by two glasses of champagne, would not do. She would not have Brown interrogated by some grasping punk about every exchange they'd ever had and all that she'd told him about John Cameron. When a cop is under investigation, his or her partner more often than not has to weather the shit storm. If they're clean, why had they not noticed the rot taking hold right next to them? And if they're not clean, well, it just goes to show that it's never only the one bad apple, is it?

'I think about it sometimes, that's all,' Madison lied. 'What I would do if I couldn't do this.'

Brown saw the lie – even if she had kept her tone light enough for the question not to really matter, and her eyes on something happening with the bride at the other end of the room – but he didn't challenge her. He didn't know anyone less likely than Madison to leave the force and get into something else.

'If you had to,' he said carefully. 'If, for whatever reasons, you could not do this any longer, what would you do?'

'I don't know,' she admitted.

Her eyes traveled around the room. Lieutenant Fynn was talking to Kyle Spencer, their wives deep in conversation themselves. Dunne was considerably less pale, though still surrounded by family; he saw Madison and winked at her. Tony Rosario, Kelly's partner, was chatting to the father of the bride and – for once in his life – not looking as if he were about to succumb to a slow and painful illness. Madison knew most of the people wearing blue in the large room – she knew them the way you know someone when you stand with them on the street, doing a job that often meant danger, even death. It was not the way other people might know each other from the office. Like it or not, these were *her* people.

'I don't know,' she repeated.

Kyle Spencer joined them. His best-man speech had been appropriately funny and touching, more so because he didn't have any brothers himself and Andy had applied for and got that job many years earlier.

Spencer drained his beer and leant in. 'Any news from the Release Project lawyer?' he said.

'He's going through his files,' Madison replied. It was just the three of them at the table and she felt free to talk. 'We gave him some parameters yesterday and he's going to do some digging for us.'

'And he's not going to the media with it?'

'I don't think so. Looks like he really wants to help.'

Spencer dropped his voice. 'I've read the Duncan autopsy report. Eighteen blows to the face. Some of the bones almost pulverized.' He shook his head.

Spencer was an experienced Homicide detective and didn't spook easily. Brown and Madison had seen the pictures and the real thing. They had felt the presence in that room of the man who had done this to Matthew Duncan; they had seen him standing over his victim.

'He's going to do it again,' Madison said. 'He thinks we have no idea about how he works and he's going to do it again. And somehow it'll be even more horrific, because he's not going backwards. Eighteen blows will become twenty-five. One victim at a time will become two. It's a game and he's going to push it as far as he can go.'

'We do have a very limited understanding of how he works,' Spencer conceded.

'We know what turns him on: extreme violence, blood and manipulation,' Madison said. 'And that—'

'Aaron, come join us,' Brown said suddenly.

Madison realized that he had been standing behind them and, judging from his face, he had unwittingly heard quite a chunk of their conversation.

'I'm . . . I'm going to get a fresh drink,' Aaron said. 'Alice?'

'No, thank you. I'm fine.'

He left for the bar and Spencer stood up to return to his own table.

'Do you talk much to Aaron about what we do?' Brown said to Madison.

'Surprisingly, not a lot, no,' she replied. 'Would you?'

She found Aaron at the bar drinking a Coke as some young children played tag around the room and bumped into the grown-ups.

They both cheered when Andy and Stacey left in the limo – with a crooked *Just Married* stencil stuck on the trunk – and Madison said, 'Let's go home, let's light a fire and forget about everything for a little while.'

They did light a fire once they got home, but didn't do more than collapse on the sofa – Aaron's long legs stretched out towards the hearth and Madison's head leaning on his shoulder. They watched the flames and soon they were asleep in the glow of the coals.

The drive back had been quiet. Madison hadn't asked him about what he'd heard and he hadn't brought it up. They woke up around midnight and made it to bed, shedding clothing on the way and wrapping themselves in the cold duvet. They held each other for warmth and went back to sleep.

Madison's last thought was stained-glass windows high above her and a memory of music.

Saul Garner's Sunday had not been one of his best. He had spent the morning with his family and then had returned to work – his shirt still sporting the trace evidence of a cooked breakfast. A paper bomb had exploded in his office and files covered every surface. A paperless world was all very well, but that was not the world he lived in.

His meeting with the detectives on Saturday had been a shock to the system: by the time he got involved in a case the victim had often been in the ground for years. Today he was in the office because the case was still open and the victim might be the last in a long daisy chain of the dead.

The software that could do what he needed to do did not exist yet; it was a matter of patience, thoroughness and determination. Garner slumped into his chair and picked up the first file of the day – a six-year-old homicide. His eyes scanned the preliminary investigation report, the detectives' notes and then the autopsy report.

There were pictures too. He looked quickly and then covered them with a sheet. He was not squeamish – he had spoken to vicious, brutal human beings in detail about their crimes – but even Saul Garner had a finite capacity for cruelty and these last twenty-four hours had severely tested it.

He went back to the report and then skipped to his own notes to decide whether the man might fit the criteria. Had he pleaded not guilty?

The lawyer sighed and went back to the photographs and the description of the murder weapon – a crowbar. Yes, the defendant had pleaded not guilty.

Saul Garner was alone in the empty building with his reports and his pictures. The egg stains and orange juice on his shirt – discovered once he was already in the car and driving – were a comfort and a talisman of normality.

Chapter 32

Monday morning dawned in all its gray splendor. Madison woke up with a headache without actually having had the pleasure of being even remotely drunk the night before. The rest of the day was a perfect match for her headache: they talked to as many witnesses from the Mitchell case as they could find; they studied the strips in the tins left by the killer; and all the while they received no news of any kind from Amy Sorensen at the lab, Saul Garner at the Release Project or Fred Kamen at the FBI. The identity of the man Brian Baines had remembered was, after sifting through the company records with the Inland Revenue Service, still unknown.

Sipping her first coffee of the day Madison had decided that she would simply not think at all about Chris Kelly, the OPA investigation or the drug cartel. She just couldn't. Her brain could not compute all the different variations of dung about to hit the fan. And any time spent trying to consider all the faces of that particular Rubik's Cube was time spent not thinking about Peter Mitchell and Matthew Duncan – two men whose paths had crossed someone who'd been ready to lay waste to their lives.

How had their paths crossed? Had she missed something?

Aaron had said goodbye with a hug and a kiss and he'd wished her a good day, like couples do, and yet Madison could not shake the feeling that now that he knew a bit more of what her day comprised, something in Aaron had recoiled a little. And if so, wasn't that the normal reaction? In fact, the *right* reaction?

Madison picked up her cell.

'Stanley? It's Madison. I just wanted to check in.'

'Everything's all right here, Alice. All back to normal. Are you all right?'

'Sure. Yes, of course. I just wanted to make sure that you hadn't noticed anything odd around your home. No strangers in places they shouldn't be, no people who looked wrong to you.'

'No, nothing of the kind.'

'Good, great. Just call me if anything worries you – anything at all.'

'Now, *you're* worrying me. Would you like to come in for a chat?'

'Thanks, Stanley. I might when I'm done with the case.'

She had been thinking about the break-in at her therapist's office since her conversation with Nathan Quinn and John Cameron. The notion that Stanley might have been targeted by the cartel because of her was too hideous to contemplate.

Madison turned off the lamp on her desk and picked up her coat – Brown had left five minutes earlier and everyone else was long gone. *The job prospects are what they are but, man, at least the hours are great.*

Kate Duncan rolled down her window and peeked. She was not familiar with the Bremerton Ferry Terminal holding lanes and wanted to make sure that she was getting into the right one.

She had spent the day with Matthew's cousins and his brother, Casey, who was staying with them, and she was exhausted. It had been a necessary day, a day of emotion and memories and hugs from relatives who could not begin to grasp her pain and her fretfulness. Nevertheless, it had been a guilty relief to be away from Annie. This short hour on the ferry – a stolen time between the homes of people who wanted nothing but the opportunity to help her and support her – was a balm.

Nobody truly understood what she was going through. And seeing Casey was like seeing Matthew alive again, hearing Matthew's voice. Her heart beat like a rabbit's caught in a snare. *The blood, so much blood.*

Madison let herself in and turned on the lights. She toed off her boots and padded to the kitchen holding a paper bag of shopping she had bought in less than ten minutes during her twenty-minute lunch break while Brown did whatever it was that Brown needed to do.

Dinner would not win any Michelin stars but eggs were her go-to comfort food and that's what was on the menu tonight. She poured herself some milk from the carton, fresh out of the bag, and reached for her frying pan. Her cell started vibrating and the number on the small display was unknown. Was it Quinn again from another disposable device?

'Madison,' she said picking up.

Nobody spoke. A thrumming vibration filled the open line.

'Hello?'

It was like metal clashing against metal. A deep grinding that held no human sound.

'Hello?'

Madison held the cell phone to her ear for a moment and then terminated the call. Clearly the connection had not worked properly and whoever had called would call again if they had anything to say.

She grabbed the butter out of the fridge and sliced off a portion which slid into the pan over the low gas. She dug into the bag for the box of eggs and took three out. She was about to break the first on the edge of the pan when her cell started vibrating again.

'Madison,' she said.

The shuddering sound was even louder now.

'Hello?' Madison repeated, trying to raise her voice against the noise.

'Help me . . .' the voice was less than a whisper. A woman? A child?

'Who is this?'

'Help me, please . . .'

Madison automatically reached for the stove and turned off the gas under the pan – the butter had begun to melt and even the soft sizzle was louder than the voice on the line.

'Who is this?' she repeated.

A sudden flash told her who it was before the woman spoke again and a spike of adrenaline pierced Madison in the chest.

'It's Kate Duncan. The man has come back. He followed me. Oh God, help me. Help me, please.'

'Kate, where are you? What's going on?'

A beat with nothing on the line but the deep, low pulse. Madison closed her eyes as if it might help her to hear better, to reach through and pluck the woman out of wherever the hell she was.

'I'm on a ferry.'

'Which one? Where from?'

Madison sprinted to the living room and booted up her laptop. A quick scan around the room told her where her landline telephone was and she grabbed the receiver.

'I'm on the Bremerton–Seattle ferry. It left Bremerton five minutes ago. He's here. He followed me.'

Madison thought fast. 'I'm going to ask you some questions now, Kate, just say yes or no.'

Another beat of deafening engine noise.

'Can you see him from where you are?'

'Yes.'

'Are you on the car deck?'

'Yes.'

Madison tried to remember what the ferries on that line looked like.

'Can you get up onto the passenger decks?' Madison wanted her to get to a member of the crew as soon as possible.

A pause.

What was she doing? Madison closed her eyes. If she remembered well some of the ferries on that line had two car decks and two passenger decks. They could carry about 150 cars or so and at least 2,000 travelers. How many people was the ferry carrying now? How many cars were parked between Kate and the man?

'Kate . . .' Madison said. 'Kate . . .'

'I can't,' came back a whisper. 'I can't get up to the passenger decks, he would see me. He's walking between the cars. He's looking for me . . .'

The voice fell away.

Shit. Madison held her cell to her ear and with the other hand she dialed 911 for the US Coastguard. She stuck the receiver between her chin and her shoulder and keyed in the webpage on her laptop. It went to the Washington State Ferries Vessel Watch: the ferry Kate Duncan was on was a tiny green triangle traveling towards Seattle and still well outside the city limits.

Damn. Harbor Patrol would be her next call.

'Kate . . . Kate, can you hear me?'

If she couldn't get up to the passenger deck and the crew, Madison had to get her to a safe place. *Her car. Get her back into her car. Locked doors and windows and sound the horn like doomsday is coming.*

'Kate, can you get back to your car?'

How could she call the ferry directly? How could she get someone to go and help her? Madison wanted to pace but she was rooted to the spot – one telephone in each hand now – watching the tiny green triangle crawling across the screen.

'I don't know. I can't see him.'

Madison had seen the Duncans' car: a heavy-duty SUV which probably had not seen a day of off-road driving but looked solid enough to delay the stalker for a few minutes – long enough to attract somebody's attention. Madison's mind was leaping ahead and trying to find patterns and meanings. *What the hell is he doing? Why is he going after Kate Duncan? Is he armed? Does he have a firearm that will shoot through glass?*

'Kate, talk to me, what's going on?'

The engine of the MV *Kaleetan* rumbled in the background – in a splinter of thought it seemed quaint to Madison that she could see all the details of the ferry online, including where it was and its speed in knots, and yet she was not able to do one darn thing about this.

Suddenly a voice from the US Coastguard was on the line. Madison identified herself with her unit and badge number. She spoke quickly and clearly. They must contact the ferry, they must send someone, they must not leave her alone to deal with a maniac.

'Kate, what's going on?'

'He's walking between the cars, up and down the deck.'

'Where are you?'

'I'm . . . I'm in a corner, behind a pick-up truck.'

Kate Duncan sounded terrified; her breath rushed out in great shudders. And she must be cold too, Madison realized – it would be freezing on the car deck, the harsh wind blowing hard from the water. Her body temperature would be dropping, her thinking might become sluggish, her reactions slower, her muscles cramped as she crouched. *Keep her talking, keep her thinking. He will not hear her above the din.*

'What does he look like?'

'Tall, dark clothes, hooded top. He's the man from the gardens. I'm sure he is.'

Madison exhaled. In that instant she really hoped that Kate Duncan was wrong, that this was just a guy, that the imagination and the fear and the shock of the last week had been too much and that she was seeing monsters where there were none.

'Kate, is he armed? Is he carrying any weapon that you can see?'

The green triangle inched forward on the screen. The water was calm and the vessel would be cutting through it, a slender white crest in the inky black. It was the same water Madison could see outside her French doors. In the distance, the ferry would be a small bundle of lights slowly sidling closer to Elliott Bay.

'I don't know. I can't see him.'

Madison's priority was still to get her to a safe place.

'Where's your car, Kate?'

'It's a couple of rows away from me.'

Madison wondered if the woman had alarmed the car as she had left it. She probably had. Would it be worth the risk of the alarm beeps? Would he hear them and turn?

'Where is he?'

Madison heard the woman's breath catching. 'He's at the other end of the deck.'

'Can you make a dash for the stairs?'

'I . . . I . . .'

'Can you dash for the stairs right now and get up to the crew?'

Madison could not see them. She could not see how far away he was, or how far the metal door to the passenger stairs was from Kate Duncan. Nevertheless, she had traveled dozens of times on that ferry and her memories of it were clear: the tall, cavernous space with all the cars, trucks and pick-ups tightly packed next to each other in rows. And a man stalking one end with Kate Duncan stealing a look through the window of the vehicle she was hiding behind.

Madison felt stuck. She couldn't really give Kate any instructions if she couldn't see what was going on. Maybe the safest place for the woman was to stay exactly where she was, maybe moving her anyplace else was too big a risk. And, sweet Jesus, that engine noise washed over everything and made it hard to even think straight. Where was the Coastguard? Where the hell was the Coastguard?

Madison pressed her ear to the receiver and she realized that she had been cut off by the Coastguard – whatever else they were doing they were not wasting time speaking to her. She dialed 911 again – this time for Seattle Harbor Patrol – while one half of her listened out for Kate Duncan, for any changes in the solid clatter from the car deck of the *Kaleetan*. What would happen if the woman made a run for it and he caught her?

'Kate,' Madison whispered. 'I'm here. I've called the Coastguard. Just hang on in there, okay?'

There was a muffled whimper at the other end of the line – or perhaps Madison had only imagined it. Harbor Patrol came on and Madison went through the same question-and-answer routine. And on the computer screen the green triangle sailed ever closer to Seattle.

A fleeting thought popped into her head and vanished: why had the man cornered her on that ferry? A place where anyone could walk in on them at any time, where he could not control the circumstances of the pursuit.

Harbor Patrol came back to her and confirmed they would contact the ferry. Madison left them all her numbers and they rang off. She wanted to get into her car and drive straight to the harbor. But she was afraid to move – afraid that, between the noise from the car deck and the rattle of her own car engine, Kate Duncan's voice would be lost when she needed Madison the most.

There was a subtle change in the pitch of the vibration. Footsteps clanged on metal.

Madison held her breath. *Let her get away. Let her get away. Let her get away.* She didn't want to think about how tiny and slight Kate Duncan was, how easy it would be for someone to take her, bundle her in the trunk of a car and simply drive away. And what next? What next?

The sounds had definitely changed. *She's running. She's making a run for it.* A rustle of clothes close to the telephone microphone, the swish of a coat, a thud and a soft cry. Madison leant on the table with her eyes closed and her left hand clamped tightly over her mouth. Something thumped and she didn't know whether it was inside or outside her. More rustling, more steps, more thuds.

Madison felt sick, suspended in darkness, hanging on to every scrap of sound.

The bang was so loud that it knocked her off her chair.

Madison was on her feet, back in her living room, eyes wide, not daring to speak.

'I'm in the restroom. I've locked myself in the restroom.' Kate Duncan's voice came in gasps. 'I don't know if he saw me. I just ran . . . I just ran for it . . .'

Madison let out her breath. 'Make sure the lock is full on, Kate, make sure it's engaged.'

Madison heard hands scrabbling at something, pushing, shoving hard.

'It is. It's locked.'

'Where are you?'

'I'm in the restroom off the main cabin.'

'The Coastguard and Harbor Patrol are on their way. They're on their way, you hear?'

'Yes.'

'He's not going to come after you in the main cabin.' Madison wanted very badly to believe that. 'Just hang on for a little while longer. Okay?'

'Yes.'

Keep her talking. She can't go to pieces now. Keep her thinking. 'Good, you're doing great. Talk to me, Kate. What do you see? Is it a single restroom?'

'It's a restroom with sinks and three cubicles on one side. I've locked the main door.'

Madison wondered what kind of lock a public restroom would have on the inside and whether it would hold. Her landline phone rang and Madison nearly dropped it. It was the Coastguard.

Madison drove like an arrow through the night. Drizzle hit the windshield and blurred the rest of the world, but for Madison there was only the road. She had to get to the pier before the ferry docked. The *Kaleetan* had left Bremerton at 9.05 p.m. and the crossing time was sixty minutes. If she absolutely floored it she would get to Pier 52 in time to meet the people coming off, in time to seek him out.

The Coastguard had warned the ferry captain and they had called Madison when the car deck had proved to be deserted. Madison had given them Kate Duncan's location and they had managed to coax her out of the locked restroom – it had been a woman from the crew who had finally got her to unlock the door as their own key had been temporarily misplaced. Kate Duncan was spending the rest of the journey in the captain's cabin, wrapped in a blanket and drinking hot chocolate from a vending machine that the female crew member had insisted she took with trembling hands.

Madison had called Brown and he was on his way too. The SWAT team had been alerted and was ready to engage. And utterly unaware of what was happening on the various decks, the travelers on board the *Kaleetan* were having a pleasant and uneventful journey, marred only by the closure of the galley and the inconvenience of using the vending machine in its place.

Brown had called Lieutenant Fynn and a welcome party for the ferry had been organized. It would delay the return crossing but it could not be helped. The crew of the ferry was not equipped or trained to deal with the stalker and there was nowhere for him to go unless he fancied a dip into the icy waters of Puget Sound.

Madison drove on.

They were about to meet him. They were about to look into his eyes.

Pier 52 was unusually crowded for a Monday night at 10.05 p.m. The operation had to be executed carefully to make sure it would work, because Kate Duncan could only be in one place at a time. They needed to get the car plates of every single vehicle on the *Kaleetan* while making sure that Kate could observe the foot traffic on the off chance the stalker had not driven on board. Then again, if he had not driven, how had he followed her? And how had he known she would be on that ferry – that she was coming back from Bremerton?

Madison adjusted the Glock in her shoulder holster. She stood – edgy and restless – next to Brown, waiting for the gangway doors to open and let them on board. *Tall, dark clothes, hooded top.* As a description it was on the scant side, but at least they had their witness. Brown – in his suit and raincoat – was somber and impossibly neat for the end of such a long day. He looked ready for war, for a subtle war that had to happen without anyone noticing.

The passengers had been told that they needed to stay where they were for a few minutes while a security procedure was implemented. Nothing to worry about, just a short delay and then they would be on their way.

The doors opened and Kate Duncan was suddenly in front of them, flanked by crew members in their yellow high-visibility jackets. Her skin was translucent and black mascara streaks had been hastily wiped from under her eyes. She saw Madison and walked to her with her arms open like a child. Madison hugged her tight. It felt like holding a bundle of twigs.

'Kate, you were brilliant,' she said. 'Can you do this? Can you do this one last thing?'

Kate Duncan looked around. The hall was swarming with police officers in uniform; a dozen had already stepped on board to look through the travelers. The same numbers – though she could not see them – were scouring the car decks.

The woman nodded and they stood to one side as people started to file through: families with little children carrying sleeping toddlers on their shoulders, single men and single women, commuters, small groups of tourists. Kate Duncan stood slightly behind Brown and Madison and her gaze swept over the curious, the bored, the tired and the uninterested. So far none of the men looked like possible candidates. The single men were either the wrong body shape or too old or too young. Kate Duncan had only seen one person on the car deck searching for her between the parked cars. Their stalker had not come with friends.

There had been about 200 people on the Kaleetan and Madison was keen to meet only one of them – unfortunately, though, *he* did not seem to feel the same way.

The flow of people began to ebb. After a few minutes there was only a trickle of teenagers, laughing as they crossed the gangway and went past the line of police officers and detectives. Madison focused on the artist's sketch of the fake engineer who had visited the Duncan home. She held it in her mind against each face. *Regular features, dark hair, blue eyes, tall, confident, comfortable around people. Might be talking to other travelers he has just met.* No one came even close.

The radio crackle from the police radios filled the hall and it became clear, after no one had come through the passage for a minute or so, that there were no other travelers waiting to disembark.

Madison edged towards the windows. The orange lights glowed through the thin rain over the shiny concrete below and the parallel lines of the lanes ran straight up, leading all the way into the wide, gaping mouth of the ship. They were deserted except for the police cars. Inside the half-gloom of the car deck the torch beams of the Harbor Patrol officers and the Seattle PD patrols searched, explored and probed the empty darkness. They could only hold the ship for a few more minutes.

Madison left Kate Duncan with Brown and rushed across the gangway and onto the ferry. If the man had been on board, he would need to get off. There was no way around that simple point.

Madison found herself on the passenger deck: the *Kaleetan* was vast and the rows after rows of tables and benches stood eerily deserted. The engine noise was merely a low grumble as the ferry idled at the dock. She started down the first row, knowing that the patrols had already been there but not able to help herself. Her steps clacked as she hurried through, looking left and right, her eyes running over the nooks and crannies and seeking out corners where someone might be quietly waiting for the next lot of passengers to board so that he could conceal himself among them.

The outer decks were deep and long – the passengers who crossed during the day would be looking at the views of the distant Olympic Peninsula mountains on one side and Mount Rainier on the other. No one was admiring the view now as Madison burst through the doors and raced from one end to the other, then crossed and checked the deck on the opposite side.

Inside she ran into a crew member. Her eyes clocked the ID badge on a chain around the man's neck and the picture matched his face. He went past with a look that said *hurry up, we've got a job to do*. Madison knocked and walked into each of the deserted restroom facilities and then found her way out through the double-level car deck. The cold wind was harsh and cutting on the dock.

Kate Duncan sat on the chair, her arms tightly crossed over her chest. The passenger boarding hall was empty, except for the police officers, and the concessions were closed for the day.

Madison sat close yet far enough away to give her some space. The woman looked not only scared but bewildered.

'So, you had spent the day with your husband's relatives, you had said goodbye in time to catch the 9.05 from Bremerton and you drove to the harbor. What happened next?'

The woman frowned slightly, eyes narrowed, reaching out for the memory of anything that might have been out of the ordinary. 'Nothing happened until we were all on board, until the cars were parked and the ferry was moving.' Kate Duncan's gaze was fixed on a spot of worn fabric on the armrest of her chair. 'People started to go up to the passenger decks and I stayed behind a little because I was looking for a book that Matthew's cousin had given me and I thought . . . I thought she was so kind . . . and if I'd left the book at her place it would have been rude, you know?'

Madison nodded. Brown watched them from a few feet away.

'I found the book, got out of the car and locked it. Then, as some people who had stood between us moved to go up the stairs, I saw him. He didn't see me, but I saw him. He was way back on the deck.'

'What was he doing?'

'He was just standing there, waiting.'

'Waiting?'

'Waiting for me to leave the car, for the others to leave. I don't know. He was just standing there.'

'Tell me again what he looked like.'

'Tall, dark clothes, a hooded top. He looked exactly the same as he did when he followed me in the gardens the other day.'

'But he was further away from you this time.'

Kate Duncan blinked, coming back momentarily from her reverie. 'Yes, he was.'

'How far?'

'About one hundred and fifty or two hundred feet away.'

'That's quite a way away from you. Much further away than before.'

'I guess so.'

'What happened then?'

'I rushed behind the pick-up and I hid and he started to walk towards me, well, towards my car. He must know my car because how could he have followed me otherwise?'

Madison nodded.

'And then he just looked inside the car – as if, as if he was making sure I wasn't still inside it – and he went all around it and that's when I called you.'

'Right,' Madison said.

'And the man, he saw that I wasn't there and began to walk up and down the rows, looking into each car, looking up to see if there was anyone else about. All the time getting closer.' Kate Duncan closed her eyes.

'Did you see his face this time?' Madison asked her.

The woman shook her head. 'The hood was up. I didn't see his face.'

Madison knew she had to ask. 'And yet you're sure it was the same man?'

'Yes, I'm sure. Same height, same body shape, same everything. And he was looking for me.'

Madison held her eyes. Kate Duncan had seen a man wearing dark clothes walking through a car deck. That was all she could testify to.

'Wasn't he?' the woman repeated.

'That's what we need to work out,' Madison said.

'You don't believe me?'

'Of course I believe you,' Madison said, and she wasn't lying. She believed that Kate Duncan was utterly convinced that a man was stalking her.

'Could have been a thief,' Brown said. 'Checking out the cars for any valuables left in sight, ready for a quick bit of late-evening retailing if any car had been left unlocked.'

Brown and Madison stood under the shelter of the Ferry Terminal. Kate Duncan had been put in a patrol car which would drive her to the Collins home, where she was still staying. An officer was following in her SUV.

Madison looked at the place where the ferry had stood. The *Kaleetan* was on its way back to Bremerton. Lieutenant Fynn had joined them after the search of the ferry had revealed nothing more than occasional littering and a forgotten child's glove. She had given him the gist of the woman's testimony.

'Basically, she just saw a guy walking with his hood up on a cold night,' he'd said.

'Yes.'

'Wonderful.'

Fynn had left.

Madison felt a twinge of guilt – as if the whole operation had been a colossal waste of time and it had been her own fault. It was her case, her witness, her squandered resources.

She turned to Brown. 'Do you think she's cracking up?'

'She saw what she thought she would see.'

'We'll have CCTV tomorrow morning.'

'What do you think it'll show you?'

Madison thought about it for a moment. 'A guy walking with his hood up on a cold night,' she said.

'You had to call it in as you did.'

Madison didn't reply. She was about to shrug, but it felt juvenile and she stopped mid-shrug and turned away instead.

'You had to call it in because, if you didn't, Kate Duncan might have been killed and thrown overboard. And all that would have been left of her was her car blocking the deck.'

They parted and both dashed off under the drizzle.

When she got back home Madison peeled off her damp clothes and padded back into the kitchen in her pajamas. The eggs were still on the counter and the butter was a congealed pool in the pan. She turned on the gas and soon it began to sizzle.

Kate Duncan lay on her bed in Annie's home. Her cell was on her bedside table; its screen glowed for a moment then it switched off. The blankets felt heavy on her frame and one lock of hair was still wet from the hot shower. She knew what she had seen, she knew what had happened. Her mind was clear and her brain was working as well as it had ever done. A man *had* been following her – whatever the detectives said.

Her eyes were wide open and her fists balled up tightly at her sides. It came before she knew it: a wave of anger that blotted out everything else. She twisted the T-shirt she was wearing; she grabbed at the collar and pulled it as if she couldn't breathe. A couple of seams stretched and tore and the sound felt good. She pulled it off and tore at it, ripping the fabric in strips. When her breathing slowed down Kate Duncan placed what remained of the shirt carefully at the bottom of her bag and found a fresh one.

Sleep did not come for a long time that night – and when it did, it brought the scent of copper.

*

The man stepped into the hot shower. The chill on the car deck had reached deep into his bones and the heat brought his skin back to life with the sting of a whip.

What a night it had been. And yet, however much he wanted to mull over every moment of it, there was a decision to make and it could not wait. In what he considered a long and fruitful career he had always been careful not to rush and he had been especially watchful against being arrogant or presumptuous – the sins of the poor craftsman. He would not have been as successful as he had if he had not been wary of moving too fast, too early or too much in the open. *Be wary, be ready, be safe.*

This latest project had been, well, it had been the most fun he'd had in a very long time and he didn't want to spoil everything by rushing to the next one. Then again, the new one was good to go – and there was the issue of timing. If he didn't do it now, he'd have to wait another twelve months and the whole notion of cause and effect would somehow deflate.

The hot water worked its wonders and even his thinking seemed to warm, stretch and expand. He had never before started the next project when the old one was still *in play* but these were extraordinary circumstances. If he didn't do it now, he might as well scrap it completely and look for a new one. Finding a project would not be a problem when people seemed to be almost begging him to take them on. How could he resist them, how could he say no? And while he was prepared to ditch an operation, if necessary – even if it meant the waste of months of work – there was something so juicy about this next one that he found it hard to let go.

Maybe this was his own test: could he let go? Could he move on and let it be?

Not for the first time he went back to what he trusted most to help him make up his mind: it was a kind of celestial navigation, after all. He closed his eyes and imagined all his past and future projects like the heavenly bodies of a solar system with their trajectories, their orbits and their own moons. It was a complex, shockingly beautiful system that comprised death and rebirth, the arbitrary and the inevitable. He was there too – invisible – the force that changed their paths because his gravity was so much stronger than theirs and would affect their course, whether they liked it or not, whether they saw him or not. And there was his answer: he was invisible and had to remain so.

There was a pang of regret he did not expect – cutting and almost sweet. He had so looked forward to the next one; his hunger had already tasted the moment and played with it over and over. The man exhaled and reached for the disposable razor. He ran it over his chest and his forearms as he had done every day since just before he had moved into the house, five years earlier. His scalp and his brows would have to wait for the mirror. Although shaving had started as a useful precaution as his work had progressed, in time he had begun to see it for what it truly was: the shedding of a life that was beneath him.

He tried to distract himself from the bitter disappointment and wished he could find solace in his old friend, in the constellations around it, but tonight Jupiter was behind the clouds and the man felt completely alone. Rain without and within.

Chapter 33

Jerry Lindquist woke up and, as every morning, his first shock was realizing that he was in a cell of the King County Justice Complex. The second, as it had been since the previous Friday, was remembering that the brother of the man he had inadvertently killed in self-defense was in a cell on the same wing, waiting for the appropriate moment to strike.

Jerry craved sleep and yet every awakening brought a jab of pain: he dreamt like a free man dreams – walking, swimming, breathing free air under the warm sun – but he woke up as a lifer. And it seemed to matter not at all that he was innocent of the murder of his wife and that he should not be there, in prison, about to eat his powdered eggs, trying to look dangerous.

The only time he had been this afraid was when he had first arrived at KCJC. Those early weeks had been so terrifying that he had not expected to survive at all. Somehow, he had – and he had found in his days a faltering rhythm of abject fear and boredom – and here he was, two years later.

Saul Garner, his appeal attorney, had been supportive when he'd told him that the cons on his wing were taking bets on his imminent death. But there was only so much that he could do. It wasn't a hotel: you couldn't move to a different floor because your neighbor partied late or you didn't like the view.

Jerry Lindquist ran his hands over his face: on top of all the daily humiliations, the lacerating grief for his wife and the loss of everything that had been important to him, it was the fact that he didn't matter a jot that stayed with him every second of every day. What he thought, what he felt, who he was simply did not matter. If his life were swept away with the garbage, this week or the next, no one would notice.

He swung his feet off his cot and wondered idly whether the bookkeeping class on Thursday would be cancelled for Thanksgiving – and whether he'd still be alive for it, anyway.

At breakfast William (robbery/homicide) came to sit next to him. Jerry worked hard to finish his food and look normal.

The correction officers paced the gangway above the canteen and, as he did every day, Jerry hoped that they'd stay close. And that their aim was sharp.

Saul Garner looked like he hadn't slept in the previous twenty-four hours because in fact he had not. After he found the first one – and it had been with a sickening jolt in his gut – he had not been able to stop. He had gone home for a quick shower and breakfast with the children and then he had returned to the office.

The files had been lined up on his desk and with each came the memory of the defendant who had appealed his conviction. He knew each one personally – in some cases, he knew their families as well.

Saul made himself Earl Grey tea with the bags his mother had given him and took the mug back to his desk. The detectives would arrive soon and he had nothing for them. Nothing but the worst news.

Chapter 34

Madison arrived in the office early and found Brown already there. The coffee that he'd brought for her was cooling on her desk. He had been reading the previous day's interviews and when she arrived he barely looked up.

They checked the CCTV tapes from the ferry and their eyes tracked fuzzy gray silhouettes on the screen. However, nothing confirmed or denied Kate Duncan's statement. The CCTV on the car deck had not picked up the stalker. Whoever the woman had seen had known to keep well away from the range of the camera. At some point a figure dashed across and disappeared up the passenger stairs. After that there was no further movement until a crew member came to check the deck after the Coastguard call and then the travelers returned to get ready to disembark.

Madison froze the blurred image. Someone had been there, even if he had not been Kate Duncan's stalker. If it was just an opportunistic thief, he had certainly bothered to work out the range of the camera. Twenty-three male drivers had traveled alone, including four cyclists. Madison ran through the pictures of their driver's license but none of them resembled the sketch of the fake engineer who had visited the Duncans' home.

Madison checked the round clock on the wall and saw that it was time to go. One way or the other the meeting with Saul Garner was going to reshape her future and Brown's past.

They sat in his office with the door closed. Madison had steeled herself for whatever number the lawyer might come up with. There were still checks to be done, evidence to be accounted for and testimonies to look over; there was still a chance that he might have got it wrong somehow.

'Eleven,' Saul Garner said. 'I went back seven years and I've run the cases through the parameters we talked about and I have found eleven that present similar profiles.'

'Eleven?' Brown repeated.

Madison, who thought that she had been ready for it, realized that in fact she was not.

'Eleven,' Garner said. 'And one of the reasons why I believe the cases are related is an escalation in violence that follows the chronology.'

'He got worse as he got a taste for it,' Madison said.

'You could say that,' Garner smiled without mirth. 'He got worse as he got better at it.'

'*Better?*' Brown was not in the mood for droll.

'In the sense that the cases he built against his scapegoats were more complex just as the violence became worse. If, and I'm still saying *if* until we know for sure, he is responsible for all these deaths, for all these innocent people going to prison, then he has created evidence and manipulated it in a way that was practically impossible to detect. The Mitchell case is a perfect example and he's had no slip-ups since.'

Madison blew out some air from her cheeks. 'Okay, eleven. Are they all King County?'

'No, they're spread throughout Washington State. I've counted only seven in King County. The others are all over the place. Mostly cities. Some rural.'

'What's the strike rate?'

Garner consulted his notes. 'Eleven cases in seven years: if you include the Duncan case it works out at a murder every seven to eight months.'

He let the numbers sink in. 'I don't do the profiling thing the FBI does. But looking at what I've got here I'd say the time between the murders is not getting shorter but the crimes themselves are becoming more complex.'

'Great,' Madison said. 'He wants to challenge himself.'

'So it seems,' Garner replied.

A flicker of sunlight illuminated a shaft of dust in the room. Madison's mind kept latching onto one word. *Eleven.*

'How are you going to be sure?' Garner said. 'How will you know?'

'The crime scenes,' Brown said quietly. 'Do the houses have gardens?'

Things had to happen in a certain order: the right people needed to be briefed and the system for checking had to be put in place. Brown and Madison agreed that the priority was to verify the cases Garner had given them.

There was one sure way to do it.

'Tell me this is not a wild goose chase I'm sending them on,' Sorensen said to Madison on the phone. 'I don't have enough warm bodies to send on non-essential trips.'

'Actually, I'd love to tell you that it is. But I don't think so. I think they'll find exactly what we're looking for.'

'Eleven?' Sorensen said.

'Yes.'

'What are you going to do about the ones that are not King County?'

'We'll work with the local jurisdiction. I'm sure everyone will be thrilled to be told they screwed up.'

'Looks like we screwed up more often – and worse – than anyone else.'

'That's the angle I'm going to give them, if they'll take my call.'

'How's Brown?'

'I don't know . . . angry, upset, impatient, frustrated, distressed. Take your pick. It doesn't matter that they were not all his cases – his was the first.'

'So it seems. Are you mailing me the names?'

'I'm about to send you the lot. When can Lauren and Joyce start?'

'The earliest I can send them out is tomorrow morning.'

'Thank you, Sorensen.'

'Some of those cases were mine, you know.'

'I know.'

When Madison looked up Brown was still on the phone with Fred Kamen from the FBI. The sandwiches they had bought on the way back from Garner's office lay untouched on the edge of her desk.

Madison unfolded a page of the map of Washington State and pinned one corner to the top of the board. When it was secured she spread out the rest of the map and pinned the other corners too. It was the largest that she had been able to find and she had pushed and slid the board so that it rested near her desk and Brown's.

She looked at the map and then picked up a bunch of colored pins from a plastic container on her desk. She needed thirteen pins. She had typed out a chronological list and had stuck it to the board and now, in the same order that *he* had followed, she began to chart his work.

The first, Peter Mitchell, had been in Seattle. Madison stuck in a pin. The second, provisionary until confirmed by Lauren and Joyce, had also been in Seattle – a man called Steve Gruber. Another pin. The third was in Spokane and the fourth – and the first woman – was in Olympia. Another two pins. The fifth was back in Seattle. Madison continued with each name on the list until she reached Matthew Duncan's name – the thirteenth pin – and then she stood back. Thirteen names, thirteen horrific deaths.

Something occurred to her and she went back to her desk. She typed out a second list, checking Saul Garner's notes, and when she was done she pinned it next to the first. The initial name on the second list was Henry Karasick, the neighbor convicted of Peter Mitchell's murder. Each name on the first list had a matching name on the second, except for Matthew Duncan. The scapegoat for his murder was still an unknown quantity. Madison had no doubt that it wouldn't stay unknown for long. A fall guy would have been prepared for them to find and, Lord Almighty, he'd better be ready for the storm about to hit.

Why, Madison reflected, hadn't it yet?

Her gaze stayed on the lists.

Lieutenant Fynn was an expert at handling detectives. He had spent his working life getting the best out of people who dealt with the worst humanity had to offer. But he also had a boss to answer to and, since citizens of his city had become notches on a bedpost, he had a compelling need to see his team achieve something more at the end of each day than getting a day older. And Madison had had little to show so far. In fact, she seemed to be able to generate questions where they badly needed answers. In a near future when each decision he took was going to be significant, when it might mean the life or death of the next victim, nothing was more important than deciding whether to keep Madison on point or not.

Fynn respected her – he liked her and he thought she was an asset for the team – but, if this was going to be a multi-jurisdictional nightmare with a maniac plying his trade state-wide, he needed the best person for the job. And it just might not be her.

They were alone in his office now. The door was closed and Fynn was standing behind his desk.

'Madison, tell me something I don't already know.'

Briefing the lieutenant on Saul Garner's report had not been one of Madison's happiest moments in the unit. None of the new King County murders had happened on his watch, but that was of little comfort.

Madison knew what he'd meant was: *Tell me why I should keep you as the primary of this gosh-darned mess.* Fynn was talking to her alone because he was about to replace her.

She saw the map with the pins and the columns of names. She saw the pages of Saul Garner's notes and the Homicide reports they had recovered from the archives. Those pages held patterns and shapes and forms. They even held the killer's shape – as if each fact in the hundreds of pages contributed a single dot to his profile, like forensic pointillism.

Maybe Fynn would take her off the case, maybe he wouldn't. In the end it didn't matter. All that mattered was the hunt.

'Madison?'

'He started in his late twenties or maybe early thirties,' she began, 'which makes him in his late thirties now. He is mature enough to be incredibly thorough and organized but has the physical strength to take on someone like Matthew Duncan. He's a Seattle man who feels most comfortable in the city but has pushed himself to *perform* out of town as well. Sorensen's people just got back to me about the hacking of the server of the HVAC company. Do you remember? He hid the visit of the fake engineer by hacking into their booking system. Well, they found nothing except for what they call a "clean scar". That is to say, he got in, did his business and got out without leaving them a trail to follow. This man is good with computers, he's very good. He wasn't working a menial job at Peter Mitchell's warehouse. If he had been there at all he would have been doing something in IT and he would have been slumming it.

'This rules out the guy Brian Baines remembered who used to hang around Mitchell. The person we are looking for is someone exceptionally sophisticated, not a laborer, not someone who stumbled on all these situations and took advantage. He sought out the victims and built a . . . a story around the crimes. A story we have believed in each and every case. It started with Mitchell – I think – because it was the one where we found the hair in the victim's wound and we have not found any other DNA evidence since. Except for the blood in the drawer in the Duncans' bedroom, which was well away from the victim's body and entirely accidental.

'And he made a mistake. Something went wrong with setting up the scapegoat for Matthew Duncan's killing because in every other case we had the fall guy within forty-eight hours of the murder and it's been more than a week since Matthew Duncan was beaten to death.'

Madison took a deep breath. 'And a mistake makes him vulnerable because, I guarantee you, he's going to try to fix it somehow.

He's not just going to let it go. He knows we won't. And he must produce a fall guy, and soon. Last night . . . I don't know about last night on the ferry. But I tell you this, the CCTV is pretty fuzzy. It shows figures and silhouettes but it wouldn't have been enough to identify someone who was wearing a hood and dark clothes. There was simply no way it would stand up in court if someone was charged with stealing from any of the cars there, and a thief would know that. And yet, whoever was on that deck stayed the hell away from the camera, which means he did not want to be seen at all. As if he was not there.'

'Are you sure someone *was* there?'

'I think that's exactly the question he wanted us to ask, sir.'

Fynn measured Madison's words.

'If he started with Mitchell,' she continued, 'if his pleasure is . . . is what you saw on the autopsy pictures, then things were already pretty bad in this man's life. He would have had issues; he might have escalated to murder, just like his violence escalated once he started killing. He might have got himself into trouble with the law before Mitchell. I'm thinking court-ordered anger management courses, maybe temporary restraining orders from his nearest and dearest. And then, when he found out what he could do to let out steam, he just got on with it and no more trouble. I'd bet he lives a very quiet, neat life and manages his own working hours.'

'Why do you say that?'

'He visited the Duncans in the middle of the day, on a weekday. What he does takes time, effort and attention. He needs to be able to take off and do his thing whenever necessary and a nine-to-five job would mess around with his schedule.'

Madison had been pacing around the office, incapable of being still as her thoughts tumbled out. In the silence after her last words she stopped. Somewhere in the outer office a telephone was ringing and no one was picking up.

'What would your next step be?' Fynn said.

'Patterns,' Madison replied. 'We need to verify the cases as soon as possible and then we start building patterns of behavior.'

'Meaning?'

'Have you looked at the map, sir?'

'Yes.'

'Then the question has to be how does he find his victims? How did their paths cross? How did he meet them?'

'They could be random.'

'I don't think so.'

'Why?'

'Mitchell wasn't random. He had an ongoing quarrel with his neighbor, which made him a perfect target, and apparently Mitchell never shut up about it. Lots of people heard him talk about Karasick, and one of them had to be our man.'

'Patterns?'

'Patterns.'

'I'll think about it.'

Madison turned to leave. 'Lieutenant, the longer we can keep this away from the press the longer we keep the advantage. The minute he understands that—'

'I know, Madison. The minute he understands that we are after him for Mitchell, the whole game changes. What about the public, though, have you thought of that? How are we going to protect the public if they don't know what's going on?'

Madison did not have an answer. So far the only vaguely promising lead had been the sketch of the fake engineer – and that had not exactly brought starry results.

'Look,' Fynn said, 'the second we involve other jurisdictions we have to consider that something might get leaked. It happens. It's practically inevitable.'

'How long do we have?' Madison said.

'I'm already in touch with Spokane and Thurston County.'

Madison nodded. The best way to make sure something ended up on the evening news was to ask fifty people to keep it a secret.

Madison emailed Sarah Klein in the King County Prosecuting Attorney's office the list of new cases – her mind knew that they were still waiting for final confirmation but her gut told her Garner was right – and Klein emailed back a single word: an expletive that perfectly encapsulated her feelings on the subject. It was Klein's job to tell Ben McReady, the Prosecuting Attorney, and in this particular case it also involved telling Nathan Quinn – since the investigation had officially gone state-wide. Seven minutes later, Madison's cell pinged.

'You were right about going through the appeals,' she said as she picked up.

'Eleven?' Nathan Quinn replied.

'No, it's thirteen in total. That's the number we should remember.'

'How long can you keep it out of the papers?'

'Not long. Too many people involved and the hacks will sniff after it like hounds.'

'Are you . . . ?'

'Am I still on point? So far, yes. But Fynn is watching me closely.'

'How about Public Affairs?'

'No press conferences, no new releases about the Duncan case, not a peep until we have recovered what we can from the crime scenes.'

'Years-old crime scenes?'

'Absolutely. How much do you want to bet that if we went public some bright spark would go digging up whatever the killer has left for us?'

Quinn sighed and Madison wished the conversation would stop right then. She wished it would stop and she wished it would continue.

'Klein is on top of things for King County,' Quinn said. 'But if you need anything else for Thurston or the others you call me and I'll get it done. Quickly.'

'Good, thanks. I appreciate it.'

'Klein only sent me names and case numbers. I haven't seen—'

'You don't want to see the pictures,' Madison replied, and her eyes traveled unconsciously to the pile on her desk. There was a small private nightmare contained in each one.

'How bad?'

'As bad as you can imagine. He's been turning them out like clockwork. Each one worse than the one before.'

'Remember that you were the one who found Salinger.'

'That was different.'

'No, Detective, it wasn't.'

It was too easy to be honest with Quinn.

'I'm afraid of what will happen if I don't stop him,' she said.

'You do realize that you are not the only person looking for him in the whole of Washington State?'

'I know, I know . . . but if you saw what he'd done to Matthew Duncan. The rage, the evil.'

'That kind of destruction is usually associated with something personal.'

'I agree, but not for this guy. I really don't think he knew all thirteen victims personally. He only wanted them for what he could do to them, for the thrill of the violence.'

'What happens if Fynn puts someone else on point?'

Trust Quinn to beat around the bush.

'Well, anyone could read it as proof that he doesn't trust me to lead.'

'And are you okay with that?'

Madison mulled it over for a moment. 'Frankly, I don't care. Hey, sure, it would sting. But I'm looking to catch a guy, not to raise my profile. Say that Brown or Spencer were put in charge of the unit, I'd still go after him with all I've got.'

'I don't doubt that you would,' Quinn said, and there was something there that neither acknowledged. 'The unit,' he continued pleasantly. 'How is the unit? Are you watching your back?'

Madison's eyes found Chris Kelly at the other end of the room, talking with Rosario. His color was high and his tie undone. She looked away before he turned.

'I am,' she replied.

'Good,' Quinn said. 'Keep watch, Detective.'

He was gone and Madison realized that, without noticing, she had left her desk at the beginning of the conversation and had gone to stand by the window, where it was quieter and more private. Annoyed with herself, she returned, picked up the second file in chronological order and dove back into the killer's life's work.

What would happen if Chris Kelly was put in charge? How would she feel if he was given Matthew Duncan's case – her case?

Shit. If it has to happen, let it not be Kelly. Anyone but Kelly.

It was past nine o'clock in the evening and most of the shift had left for the day. Brown had been immersed in the files for hours. Madison was in the middle of her usual routine of standing in front of the open fridge and wondering why she hadn't brought anything more useful than a carton of chocolate milk. Spencer joined her and picked up a neatly wrapped bundle of carrot and celery sticks from a shelf.

'Spence,' Madison said. 'Can I ask you something?' The thought had just occurred to her.

'No good thing ever follows that question but, sure, go ahead.'

'When you're home, do you ever talk about all this? About what happens here?'

It was not the question he had been expecting. He regarded Madison as if to take the measure of her.

'Let me see,' he replied. 'A fairly new relationship – I remember him at the wedding on Sunday, a tall, blond, handsome fella – here we are up to our elbows in cases and you're wondering how much you can tell him without freaking him out.'

'You're the only one who's married and Dunne just married a cop, so he doesn't count. I'm assuming your wife knows what you do for a living.'

'Kelly and Rosario are married,' Spencer said.

'Well, good for them, but it's you I'm asking.'

Spencer wasn't going to give her a joke answer, which was why she had asked him. Patrol was different, plain clothes was different. All they had in Homicide was death.

'Nothing,' Spencer said.

'*Nothing?*'

'Nothing. We talk about her work, we talk about the kids, we talk about – I don't know – Peruvian agriculture. But if I want to talk about the job, I talk to Andy. I don't take it home.'

'Isn't that . . . ?' Madison couldn't find the word for it and didn't want to use the wrong one.

'It is what we made it, and it works for us. Took my wife five years to get used to having guns in the house.'

'Thank you,' Madison said, and she meant it.

She went back to her desk with her chocolate milk. She and Aaron didn't have kids and his work was interesting but wouldn't sustain the scrutiny of constant conversation. Peruvian agriculture was a possibility. But when it came down to it, she wasn't sure five years would be long enough for Aaron.

Detective Sergeant Kevin Brown had once been shot in the line of duty. When he was lying bleeding to death, all he had wanted was to survive. When he had woken up in hospital weeks later, his only focus had been getting better and getting back to work. When he had stumbled, when it had seemed likely that he would never get back to the shield, he had turned to Alice Madison and she had helped him to come back to the job that had been the spinal column of his life.

Since then, since that glimpse of his own mortality – everybody else's he contemplated every day – he had concentrated on one thing: training Madison to make sure that, when his moment came, she would be in the best shape possible and ready to pass on whatever he had given her to the next generation.

Maybe it had been arrogance on his part, maybe a long unbroken stint of safe convictions had lulled him into a false sense of his own worth. How could he have let it happen? Twelve people were dead because he had got it wrong seven years ago. If he counted the innocent defendants in prison and the families shattered, the count rose to an unthinkable level.

If Brown had been a drinking man, it would have been a grand time to get properly drunk – the kind of drunk that takes everything away except for maybe his name. Ever since that number had fallen from Saul Garner's lips he had felt the knot getting tighter in his chest. When Madison had put up the lists next to the map, he had made one small addition in his own tidy handwriting: next to Henry Karasick, accused of Peter Mitchell's murder, he had written *deceased (suicide)*. Not thirteen fatalities, then, but fourteen.

He wanted to cry like children do, with neither self-awareness nor restraint, but that's not how it works for adults. A thin, scrappy voice pricked his bubble of emotion. *Yes, that was arrogant, very arrogant indeed. As if you had been the only person who had put Karasick in jail. As if the whole of the justice system of King County and – why not? – Washington State and the universe rested only on your shoulders. A little humility would not go amiss right about now.*

He had not known about the real killer then, but he sure did today. And wounded pride and self-pity had no place in the investigation. There was too much he had to make up for. Briefly, before the voice told him to get over himself, he hoped that he had not lost Madison's good opinion forever.

Not Fynn's, not anyone else's, just Madison's.

Tonight, he thought, he did not have the heart for Dickens but, sitting in his chair, the mere gesture of holding the book was a comfort.

Chapter 35

Homicides are allocated on a rota basis. When the call came on Wednesday morning, Detective Chris Kelly was up. He signaled to his partner, Tony Rosario, who downed a chewable tablet of vitamin C as he grabbed his coat, and they left the detectives' room together. Vitamin C in November in Seattle was a sign of reckless optimism: outside it was raining hard, the temperature had dropped like a stone and they were on their way to a double homicide.

The house was in northeast Seattle and Kelly assessed the road and the neighborhood as they drew near. The wide yard around the property was a stretch of mud marked by scraps of grass. Trees lined the two-story building on three sides and the closest neighbor was not close at all, Kelly noted. It was a starter home which had been well maintained and freshly painted.

Blue-and-whites were parked by the curb and uniformed officers were already setting up a perimeter. The first officer on the scene – an experienced man both Kelly and Rosario knew well – saw them pulling in and hurried to meet them.

'Detectives, I don't say this to be disrespectful but I hope you haven't had your lunch yet. I've got a probie there who took one look and nearly lost it.'

'We're good,' Kelly replied in his usual clipped tone and threw a glance at Rosario.

They donned their protective clothing and walked in.

The first officer took them upstairs to the bedroom, entered and stood aside to let them see. If at all possible he'd never look inside that room again and that night, at home after the shift, he knew he'd hug his kids longer and harder.

Kelly and Rosario stood on the threshold: blood had reached into every corner. One body lay on the bed and the other was half hanging over the edge. Only the clothing told them which one was male and which was female.

'Beaten to death?' Rosario said.

'Looks like it,' the officer replied. 'But God only knows what the ME is going to find under all that.'

It was going to be impossible to establish cause of death until the victims' bodies had been cleaned, until the necessary rituals prescribed by respect and forensic medicine had been performed.

The man and the woman had been found by the man's brother, who was sitting in shock in a patrol car. Their names were Gary Nolin and Eva Rudnyk. Nothing but their names could identify them now since the killer had taken everything else.

Kelly's small, bright eyes searched the room and what he saw pleased him. No sign of drug paraphernalia, no weapons, nothing that wouldn't be found in any bedroom in any house.

He thought about the map in the detectives' room and how they were going to need another pin.

*

One hour later the Medical Examiner vans stood idling outside. The cordoned-off area had become much wider and uniformed officers in their rain gear paced the perimeter and answered questions in short sentences that held as little detail as possible.

Brown and Madison stepped into the bedroom. It had been a pretty room twenty-four hours earlier. They had received the call and Madison had dialed Sorensen's cell as they rushed out of the precinct. They had to make sure the Crime Scene unit officers going to the scene had metal detectors. This was the first time they knew what to expect right from the start. Everything Madison had dreaded seemed to have come to pass.

'It's him,' Madison whispered.

The temperature in the room was cool and she was glad that the powerful lights had not been set up yet. Once they had, the scent would become unbearable: copper mixed with a rotten sweetness and human waste.

'We don't know for sure,' Brown replied.

She knew it didn't mean that he disagreed with her – in fact, the carnage she was looking at seemed intimately related to Matthew Duncan's murder – rather that they had to look at the scene objectively and not make it fit the scenario they wanted. What would be worse, anyway? That it *was* him or that it was not?

Kelly was briefing Fynn in the hallway.

Madison had not missed the greedy sparkle in his eyes because he had bagged himself the latest on the list. She trod carefully around the pools that darkened the floor and started her examination.

'Two victims. One man, one woman. The brother said they've been living together for eight months. The back door was jimmied – and it wasn't a particularly good job. Could be someone wanted to make it look like an amateur did it. The intruder came in and found them already in bed. From their positions I'd say they were asleep and did not have a chance to react. I'm betting he went for the man first because he would have posed the greatest threat, and his body is lying as he would have been while he slept. The woman woke up – probably from the noise – and he . . .' Madison's gaze followed the line of the body of the woman as she had clearly tried to flee. 'He incapacitated her as well.'

'And then?'

'And then he destroyed as much of their bodies as he could with what looks like a blunt object.'

'Do you think the point of this was the destruction?'

There and then it was difficult to think clearly and stay focused and Madison wanted very much to leave and go where there was only the sea, fresh air and the sound of gulls screeching.

'Was this about destroying the bodies?' Brown asked her. His voice was kind, and the fact that kindness could even exist in that room was the tether that brought her back.

'I don't know,' she replied. 'Look at the walls. We have cast-off patterns from the weapon here . . . and here . . . and there are impact patterns on the headboard too. He must have been standing in this spot for several minutes. This . . . this took time.'

Brown nodded. 'What do the injuries tell you? Only a quick preliminary assessment before Dr Fellman's examination.'

Madison made herself look. *Shards of white bone breaking through the skin like broken sea shells.* She saw what he had meant.

'The weapon had to be a certain length in order to reach both victims from one side of the bed. And he had to be able to exercise enough force with it to do lethal damage with just one blow. He couldn't risk one or the other running off.'

'Yes,' Brown said. 'And he needed width as well as length for maximum damage. A crowbar would have made a different kind of injury.'

'I see it. A baseball bat?'

'That's what I'm thinking.'

'Time of death?'

'The brother says they spoke yesterday evening. I'd say it happened in the early hours of this morning.'

The floor was a pattern of clear wood and congealed blood. There hardly seemed to be any place to stand.

Madison shifted her feet cautiously. 'This breaks his cycle,' she said. 'It's the first time the victims are so close together. Matthew Duncan was just over a week ago.'

'He must have had a good reason,' Brown replied. 'He doesn't do anything without a good reason.'

No, he doesn't.

In the window, under the steady rain, two Crime Scene unit officers walked the yard in a grid pattern, their metal detectors hidden by the comings and goings around them. It would take them fifty-three minutes to find what they were looking for – a cigar case wrapped in a sealed, clear plastic bag. Roughly at the same time as across town Frank Lauren and Mary Kay Joyce found a tobacco tin buried in Steve Gruber's garden, now officially the killer's second victim.

Once the victim's brother could talk, the first thing he told Detective Kyle Spencer was that Eva Rudnyk's estranged husband had made threats and had been generally harassing the couple for weeks. He didn't know his name, but it wasn't hard to find. And the same quick search also told them that yesterday would have been their wedding anniversary.

The man was picked up at his place of work – a school where he was an administrator – and taken to the precinct. Chris Kelly interviewed him and it was obvious from the first second in the box that the man had absolutely no idea what the detective was talking about. He had been home alone the previous evening and no, there were no witnesses. Yes, he had been troubled after his wife had left but he had sought counselling and things were slowly getting better. Yes, weeks earlier he had left a string of abusive voicemail messages on his wife's cell phone but, he said, he had been drunk at the time and he was much more careful now and wouldn't let himself get out of control in the same way. No, he had not made or received any calls last night. In fact, he had gone to bed early and alone with a sleeping pill to make sure he'd sleep through.

In short, Kelly thought, he had no alibi.

When the detective told him why he was there, the man panicked and went into an anxiety attack that made him hyperventilate. At the same time as Kelly gave him a paper bag to breathe into, a patrol officer spotted the black plastic bag in a skip by a building site five minutes away from the suspect's home.

The bag was wrapped around a baseball bat.

Madison felt out of herself after leaving the crime scene, as if she was watching the great police department machine at work from a great distance. Kelly was interviewing the man but they all knew he hadn't done it; Sorensen was personally processing the baseball bat as a rush job and had been able to tell them in minutes that the bat carried the fingerprints of the estranged husband and so did the plastic bag. But they all knew he was not the man who had been wielding it over the victims' bodies. It was a process which had to be followed. The trail they walked was paper-thin: they had to be seen to do exactly what the killer wanted them to do.

'How did he get the bat?' Spencer said.

'It was in a closet, behind a whole load of clothes. It's November and he knew the guy wasn't going to use it anytime soon,' Madison said. 'All he needed was to get in and grab it. Then he'd just walk into the kitchen, find the roll of bin liners and tear off the last one, which would carry the guy's prints.'

'No alarm?'

'No alarm,' Brown replied.

'Is Sorensen going to work on the cigar case?' Spencer said.

'It's not a cigar case.' Brown picked up a printed sheet and passed it to him. 'I've just received some notes from the Investigative Support unit at the FBI.'

Fred Kamen, Madison thought.

'They think it's a time capsule,' Brown said.

The man watched the news as he sliced tomatoes for a salad. When the item about the double homicide came up he stopped what he was doing and gave it his full attention. The anchor concluded the segment by saying that a man who was known to the couple was already in custody.

'The wheels of justice . . .' he said out loud, and instantly regretted it because it had cheapened what was altogether a very pleasant moment and he deserved to enjoy it.

In spite of his decision not to go ahead with it the other night, when he had woken up yesterday he had felt a tingle in all the right places. He had put so much of himself into this – and it was their wedding anniversary, for Pete's sake. How could he pass up the chance? The husband had been going on about it for weeks. How much he hated her, how much he loved her, how much he hated the new man, what he would say to her if he could, what he would do to them if he had the opportunity. On and on and on and on.

It was a real pity that the news cameraman could not get inside the crime scene, stand close by while the cops talked about it. He would have loved to hear.

The man had no regrets. It had been a marvel, and when he thought back to it he visualized the lines that connected the couple to the husband and to him like the little model of the planets and the sun in the solar system he kept near his desk.

Those treasured minutes he had spent alone with them were embedded into his memory as if carved into it. He felt calm and at peace with the world: those minutes were already part of his DNA. When he had left the house under the rain – the bat already in the bag – he had briefly felt as if he himself were one of the elements. And he liked that notion very much indeed. After all, he didn't really exist as a person; he was only what they made him.

Chapter 36

John Cameron laced up his boots and checked that he had everything he needed: while most people stopped at key, wallet, cell phone, he continued the list to cover two firearms – a .40 in his belt, tucked in the small of his back, and a .38 in an ankle holster – extra ammunition for both, and a knife. The weather was sunny and it looked as if it were going to be a glorious day, yet *another* glorious day in Los Angeles. Again, he couldn't help thinking back to his brief visit to Newfoundland and was surprised by the piercing ache for that vast silence and the miles of nothing that separated forests and cities. It wasn't really nothing, of course, it was merely a different kind of death chasing you: no cartel there, only the stark realities of a world without helplines and twenty-four-hour convenience stores. He would do well there.

The drive to his destination went smoothly; he had done the route a number of times as he had prepared for this day. Sometimes it's the simplest operations that need the most work.

The house was in Brentwood and it had taken weeks for John Cameron to find it. The target had bought it under an assumed name for the sole purpose of having a safe place to hide all the things whose presence he could not quite justify in his regular life. It was certainly a problem having more money than could be explained to the Inland Revenue Service or having a whole load of weapons and ammunitions that were neither licensed nor legal in that country. A small but very high-quality amount of cocaine was also something that the authorities frowned upon and needed to be safely stashed somewhere private.

The two-bedroom stucco house surrounded by the overgrown garden with the palm trees had been the ideal solution. It had also meant a good investment for the owner, who would probably sell it in a couple of years and buy a bigger place in the same road. There was a primary school at the end of the block and cafés where young mothers bought their juices after the morning run. It was – in the realtor's words – a delightful place to live. The owner had bought it, installed a walk-in safe in the second bedroom and never once slept in the house. He had not been around to the cafés to taste the juice yet – and he was not planning to anytime soon.

John Cameron parked in an alley behind the house. He wore jeans and a light jacket over a black long-sleeved T-shirt that covered the .40 in his belt. Most people did not know how to protect things: they shared secrets with the wrong people, they used guns where they should have used brains, and they built a safe in a house without walls. This house had walls, but barely – that is, they were there to keep out the weather, not someone with Cameron's skills and motivation.

He checked his watch and looked left and right – the alley was empty and the trees from the gardens of the residences on both sides hung over the narrow stretch. He lifted himself easily over the six-foot wall and landed on the other side in a crouch. The bottom of the garden was thick with shrubs and tall grass. No one had mowed the lawn for a very long time and wild flowers had taken over.

The back of the house had a paved patio and a jacuzzi that seemed rather forlorn. Cameron scanned the windows for signs of life: they were dark and the only life was the hum of the insects. In three steps he was standing by the French doors. A guttering pipe ran the height of the house along the thick trunk of a mature wisteria which reached up to the roof. Cameron grabbed hold and in seconds he had reached the second floor and a Juliet balcony. From there he kicked up to the small attic window, pushed hard against it and it gave way. It had taken him only seconds and the view from the alley had been shaded by the thick vegetation.

The attic was a rectangular room and in the half-gloom he could see the bare wooden floor and his own footprints in the dust from the last time he had been here. Turns out dust was smarter than the top-of-the-range alarm system the owner had installed.

Nathan Quinn did not like Los Angeles very much. He liked four seasons and proper winters and the summers would have driven him crazy. The private charter landed in Van Nuys Airport at 10.37 a.m. and his car was ready for him. He knew where he was going and he was traveling light: the single file in his leather briefcase was all he needed.

For what he was about to do there was no exam in law school and no qualifications for the bar. For what he was about to do he called upon the steely chill that he had felt from the moment he had woken up, long before dawn. He had to use it to freeze everything else. Aristotle said that the law was reason, free from passion. Nathan Quinn did not have a name for what he was about to do but it sure as hell had little to do with the law – at least the written kind.

Nathan Quinn drove to Woodley Park and parked by Lake Balboa. A Wednesday in late November was not a popular time for picnics, but at the weekend the place would come alive again. His black eyes tracked the runners and the dog walkers – sparse human presence and no CCTV. He saw the solitary figure standing under the trellis pergola, where the ground curved by the side of lake, and he left the car.

The path led him directly to the pergola, but the man was lost in thought and did not look up until Quinn was ten feet away from him. When he saw Quinn, his chin went up and his shoulders stiffened.

'Special Agent A. J. Parker,' Nathan Quinn said. 'Good to put a face to a name, don't you think?'

Parker looked around.

'No, you're not meeting your contact,' Quinn said. 'You are meeting me.'

Special Agent A. J. Parker of the Drug Enforcement Agency knew exactly who Nathan Quinn was. 'What do you want?' he said.

'I want to help you,' Quinn replied, and saw something flitting across the eyes of the other man. 'You have come to Seattle a number of times in the last year or so and have met with Detective Madison of the Seattle PD, but you have never met with me. I'm here to correct that oversight and make sure you know precisely where you are and what is going on.'

'I know where I am,' Parker replied.

'I don't think you do,' Nathan Quinn said. 'But it's something we can easily remedy.'

He opened his briefcase and took out the thick file. He didn't offer it to Parker and saw the agent's eyes locking onto it.

'You joined the DEA ten years ago and for the last eight you have worked for a number of drug cartels. Here I have bank account numbers, payments, dates and details of the information you passed on to them. I have pictures of your meetings with a Rojas man and corresponding payments into your secret account. I have reports on all the work you have done playing different cartels against each other and against the DEA: two undercover agents, lost in the line of duty because of you; five seriously injured, one on permanent disability. Shall I go on?'

Parker's hand had moved unconsciously to his sidearm and now rested on the grip. Nathan Quinn was unarmed. He looked at the semi-automatic in the other man's holster.

'Put it away, Agent Parker,' he said. 'This is not going to get sorted with ammunition.'

Parker's face had slowly flushed pink like a bad sunburn. His hand stayed on the pistol grip. Quinn offered the file. Parker took it with one hand, flipped it open, glanced at the first page and returned it.

Quinn continued. 'You were the one who listened to the wire-tap recordings and recognized the potential of a little blackmail that might get you John Cameron – what's the price on his head today? And you pushed the Office of Professional Accountability to start an investigation into Detective Madison.'

Parker bristled. 'What do you want?'

'You mean money, don't you? That's what your kind always mean.'

'My *kind*?'

'Your kind, yes. Petty, sadistic, greedy, opportunistic little shits.'

Parker's mouth was a thin line. He flipped the safety latch on the holster, cleared leather and held his piece close to his leg. Around them the park was empty, the closest dog walker only a speck on a distant hill. Quinn was three inches taller and a whole world scarier than Parker could ever be – even with the threat of gunmetal.

'I've told you to put it away, Agent Parker.' Quinn's gaze did not waver. 'I'm here to help you.'

'What do you want?'

'I'm going to tell you in a second, but first you should know two things. The first is that if I don't contact my associate in a few minutes – and you don't need to guess who that associate might be – all these documents will be released within the hour to the relevant authorities. Which means you *will* be arrested – don't even think about running – and your options will shrink to two: to go to prison and wait to be killed to make sure you don't tell tales; or to turn informant, go into witness protection, and *then* wait to be killed for actually telling tales. Also, you're more than aware that these people are not dainty: your family – a wife and three children under fifteen – will be target practice just to make sure you get the message. The second thing,' Quinn said, checking his watch, 'is that the little house in Brentwood with the jacuzzi in the garden and the pretty flowers was perhaps not the best place to hide the recordings and everything else you wanted to keep safe. We already have them – the recordings, that is – the rest I don't care about.'

Quinn made sure his words had sunk in before continuing. 'This is what I want . . .' he began. 'I want you to help your family – the people you have dragged into this mess – by letting them have the good fortune of a future without you, and without the implications of a cartel revenge.'

Parker frowned, trying to get his head around this novel interpretation of his life.

'You cannot run far enough – with or without your family – and you don't want to be caught by your enemies. Which you will be.'

'What . . . ?'

'I suggest fire,' Nathan Quinn said.

'What?'

'You need to die, Agent Parker, or in twenty-four hours these documents will be made public and, instead of mourning the death of a law enforcement officer who had dedicated his life to the pursuit of justice, your family will be left with the tragic understanding of who you really are, without the support of a police pension – and with many questions to answer from people they should never have the disgrace to meet.'

'I need more time. I want three days.'

'You have twenty-four hours.'

'What difference does it make to you? I'll be dead either way.'

'It would be two extra days of potentially catastrophic ideas and plans you might try to carry out in order to save your neck. Twenty-four hours is a kindness, Agent Parker. Put your affairs in order and be done with it.'

'You sonofabitch.'

'I'm offering you the chance to do the right thing. Cover your tracks and make sure your death looks sufficiently accidental that no one is going to look into it. By the way, they will need to be able to recover a body for identification purposes.'

Parker returned the gun to his holster.

Quinn met his eyes.

There was nothing more to say.

Special Agent A. J. Parker drove to Brentwood. He had to salvage what he could from the safe, place a reasonable amount in his own home safe for his wife to find, and get rid of the weapons and the drugs. He was not exactly thinking straight; it was more like watching himself thinking and driving. *I suggest fire.* He went over ten different scenarios which started with going on the run and invariably finished with a slow and painful death at the hands of the men he had brought into his own life. He thought only briefly about his family – it seemed surreal that they could be a part of this in any way. His wife worked in an optometrist's and his kids played in little league.

Parker pulled in by the curb, unlocked the wrought-iron gate and drove in. The alarm was still on – the bastards had been able to reset it without tripping it, or it would have sent him an alert. He disarmed it and walked into the house. The air was warm and stuffy; he couldn't remember the last time he had been there – definitely a few weeks. His steps echoed in the empty house as he rushed upstairs to the second bedroom.

The safe had been constructed where the walk-in wardrobe would have been. Parker dashed across the room and placed his thumb on the biometric pad and, after the beep, punched in the eight-digit combination. The safe lock clicked and released just as the point of a knife pressed lightly against the soft spot between Parker's jaw and his neck.

'I'd ask you not to do anything foolish,' John Cameron said as he patted the man down, 'but we're way past *foolish* here.'

Before Agent Parker knew it he was on the floor, his wrists bound by plastic cuffs, and his weapons – the sidearm and the back-up – were on the other side of the room, on the floor next to their magazines.

He watched as Cameron walked into the safe and he could see that everything was still where he had placed it, including the box with the recordings.

Parker blinked and tried to make sense of a day that had already stretched him to breaking point. The safe had been intact when he had arrived in the house; he had opened the safe for John Cameron.

All the other man had done was get into the house without tripping the alarm. *He* had opened the safe.

John Cameron turned and took one step towards him. Parker scuttled backwards and bumped into the wall behind him.

'Don't flatter yourself,' Cameron said. The shoebox with the wiretap recordings was under his arm. 'I have what I've come for.'

Parker felt emboldened by the sheer hopelessness of his situation. 'Take off the cuffs. How can I . . .? Just take off the damned cuffs.'

Cameron regarded him with his head on one side like a curious bird. 'There's a man I will write to this time tomorrow,' he said, 'who remembers you so very well. Two years ago you identified him as a police informant to the cartel who had employed him from time to time. And by that I mean who had *forced* him to do their bidding. After you betrayed him, they cut up his face and they amputated his right hand. He was shown dozens of pictures and he identified *you* as the cop in the pocket of the cartel.'

Parker struggled against the cuffs and let out a bellow of anger, frustration and fear.

'He was a doctor,' Cameron continued. 'And he managed to survive. Now he lives in a place far away from here where what happens in this room, in this city, does not matter at all.'

Parker tried to breathe, but all the air had gone out of the room.

The last thing he remembered was John Cameron crouching by him and a needle going into his arm. When he woke up – thirsty and disoriented – fifteen minutes later, the cuffs had been snapped off and his weapons were on the floor. Parker curled up, holding his knees tight to his chest. Cameron was gone and in the open safe he could see the piles of used bills, stacked in bundles of a thousand each, three .50 BMG rifles and four clear plastic bags of cocaine.

*

John Cameron drove to Van Nuys Airport and returned his rental car. The charter plane was waiting for him and once he was on board the pilot started the Cessna Citation X take-off procedure.

Cameron slid into the seat opposite Nathan Quinn and passed him the shoebox. It was done.

The flight assistant – a young man called Rory – brought them sodas and warm, moist towelettes. 'All set? You'll get home just in time for Thanksgiving,' he added with a smile and then left them to their silence.

When John Cameron had first approached him to do this, Nathan Quinn had wondered how he would feel about it afterwards. What had he done today? He had helped Parker's family against evils they knew nothing about and he had hand-delivered a death sentence. Much of the answer to the question, though, was contained in the shoebox on the seat next to him.

The reason why Parker had not doubted for a moment that the recordings had already been taken from his safe house was that Nathan Quinn had told him. Anyone else he might have doubted, but not Quinn. Because the lawyer had come unarmed to tell a man with a gun that his life was done.

There were dozens of cherry blossoms all around the lake, Nathan Quinn thought, and in spring the grass would be covered in petals like a delicate pink snowstorm. Special Agent A. J. Parker had already seen his last spring and these final hours they had granted him were more than some of his victims had been allowed.

Cameron watched his friend and knew to let him be. He didn't wrestle with what they had done: for him it had been a good day.

Chapter 37

A time capsule. Fred Kamen's idea had taken root in Madison's mind and it was becoming the key through which she was beginning to read all of the killer's work. A time capsule.

Madison sat at her desk. Her eyes were fixed on the map – as was her habit now, whenever she was thinking. She gazed from pin to pin, as if the location of each crime was in and of itself a kind of coded message that she should be able to interpret.

This man – this repugnant accident of a human being – had created these stories that they had so easily believed. The elements for each one had been the same: a crime, a murdered victim and a scapegoat – and they were still waiting for the poor devil who would take the rap for Matthew Duncan. The details changed, the locations changed, the ages and genders of the victims changed but the storyline remained the same: on every occasion the killer had been present but never really been part of it because nothing of him was left, except by accident, at the scene. He was completely absent from his great, complex works, from these massive achievements. Except . . . except for one small act of vanity: the desire to inject himself into the narrative somehow, in a way that only he would know about but would be present, though hidden, in perpetuity.

It was the artist's signature on a painting, and he had not been able to resist.

In the box with Chris Kelly the ex-husband of the murdered woman had launched himself at the glass of the one-sided mirror and had howled in pain and fury. He wasn't being aggressive towards Kelly, he was lost and disoriented. Madison looked at the lists next to the map. She thought of the distraught man – who was being counselled by a lawyer and a medic – and she thought of Henry Karasick, at the top of the scapegoats list. A victim, just as much as Mitchell and Duncan were. *Damn.*

'Sarge . . .' she said.

Brown looked up. Madison's eyes stayed on that single name. *Henry Karasick.*

'When we investigate a murder, we start with the victim and then we find the killer, that's what we usually do, isn't it?'

It was not the time for a flippant remark and with great effort Brown waited to see where this synaptic flicker would end up.

'I don't think that's how he does it,' Madison continued. 'I don't think he looks first for a person to kill and then for a scapegoat. He does it the other way around. See, he found Karasick first and everybody who knew the two men knew they hated each other. So, he had the perfect patsy for his game – and really it could very well have been Karasick who ended up dead and Mitchell in prison.'

Brown sat back in his chair. 'Why?' he said.

'Think about it . . . it is much harder to find the perfect fall guy. That's the real challenge: to find someone who is going to fit into his narrative of murder and be totally believable. In all these cases, all of them,' Madison placed her hand on the pile on her desk, 'everybody had motive, opportunity and a weapon that could be transferred easily, together with trace evidence. He *knew* them, Sarge. He knew each one of the scapegoats he used, and from each one he inferred a victim. This was not random. He sought them out and found them. It took him months for each one of them.'

'And we couldn't see that because . . .'

'. . . because *we* start with the dead and he started with the living.'

'We didn't get anywhere looking for what the dead had in common because they don't have anything in common.'

'But the scapegoats do.'

'Karasick was the first,' Brown said.

'Yes, Karasick was the killer's way in. Once he tapped into that notion, he was home.'

Detective Sergeant Kevin Brown was the kind of man he was for many reasons. But perhaps one of the most important – and what made him a great teacher – was that he could see a brilliant idea even when it was somebody else's.

He checked his watch. 'We could catch the priest before the day is done.'

Madison nodded and in three minutes they were out and driving.

Chris Kelly wandered over to Madison's desk, picked up a pin from the plastic box and stuck it into Seattle, next to the other ones.

Father Richard O'Reilly hadn't changed much in the last seven years. His hair was a little thinner and grayer, but for the rest he was very much the man Brown remembered – short, barrel-chested and remarkably confrontational. He was in his late sixties and had small, dark eyes in a round, ruddy face.

'I wasn't a priest until I was thirty-five,' he explained to Madison. 'And before then I was a grave digger, a soldier and a boxer, which maybe gives me some understanding of the burdens people carry into my anger management support groups. Then, after the seminary, I got a degree in psychology and learnt the fancy words to go with the actual experience.'

He sat Brown and Madison around the table of his small, old-fashioned kitchen. A faint smell of vegetable soup and burnt toast still clung to the walls.

'I remember you,' he said to Brown.

Brown wanted to say *I'm getting a lot of that these days*, but he didn't.

'You knew Mr Karasick from your support group?' Madison said.

'Yes,' O'Reilly replied. 'And you didn't have to come all the way out here just to ask me what you already know. What is this about?' He spoke to Brown.

Brown looked at Madison, who shrugged. This was his party.

'What if I told you that we are looking into the Mitchell case again and that we need you to keep this to yourself, Father?'

'I'd say it was high time you did. Henry was many things, and some of those things were difficult for him to handle, but I've never thought he killed that man.'

'There are lives at stake,' Brown continued. 'Here, now, today. And what we speak about around this table can go no further.'

'I know what *confidentiality* is, Detective.'

Brown told him only as much as he absolutely had too but enough for the priest to understand the implications of finding out who knew that Karasick had a short trigger and a problem with his neighbor.

'Are you saying it could have been someone who knew him from my group?'

'Possibly, or it could have been someone in his circle of acquaintances. He had been fighting with a lot of people and the temporary restraining order his ex-wife had taken out was a serious business.'

Madison brought out the forensic artist's sketches, all adjusted for age and changes of appearance. 'What we need,' she said, 'is to have as complete a picture as possible of his social circle, because it was someone who knew him well who did this. Take a look at these.'

Father O'Reilly scanned the pictures. 'Seven years ago my group was starting out and some people – and I'm saying *people*, not exclusively *men* – only came a few times. Quite a number just came the once because it was too much for them to deal with, or maybe they weren't ready for it. Or maybe they didn't like my ugly mug and my cookies. Whatever the reasons, we had a steady stream of one-night specials. After seven years I don't remember the ones who left, only the ones who stuck it out. And I don't see any of them here.' He pointed at the pictures. 'You must understand, the idea of the group is not that I turn them magically into rosy-cheeked altar boys but that I give them the tools with which they can help themselves when they feel overcome. And because of that, they are free to say whatever they need to say in the group and they can be completely honest with each other about the things they've done – and believe me, some of those things are ugly and messy.'

'Father,' Madison said, 'you testified in court as a character reference for Henry Karasick. Do you remember any friends he might have had there, aside from his family? Did you meet any of them?'

O'Reilly shook his head. 'You should look into his other neighbors,' he said. 'Everybody in the street knew about him and Mitchell. Five minutes with Henry and you knew he was a man with issues.'

As Brown and Madison stood to leave Father O'Reilly turned to her. 'I heard about you on the news. I know which case you're working on.'

Madison met his eyes and did not confirm or deny.

'Do you believe the work of the Devil can be done by human hands?' O'Reilly said.

The words chilled her. Madison flashed to a memory of red and Gary Nolin and Eva Rudnyk on their bed.

'I don't believe in the Devil, Father,' she said.

'We should talk about it one of these days, when you can spare the time. And you, Detective Brown,' the priest's sharp eyes locked onto him. 'Any burden you need to relieve? Anything you want to get off your chest in the confessional?'

'I'm not Catholic, Father,' Brown replied.

'Nobody's perfect.'

'Billy Wilder. *Some Like it Hot*,' Madison said automatically.

'Good girl,' the priest said and a smile cracked his face in half.

'I wonder what he was like in the ring,' Madison said as they walked back to their car.

'You can ask Sarah Klein. In court, he gave her as good as he got. And she had the advantage in the end only because he couldn't say that he was with Karasick at the time of the murder.' Brown lifted up the collar of his raincoat against the chill. 'I bet that in the ring Father O'Reilly was the kind of fighter who doesn't know when the fight is done and keeps going until they carry him out on a stretcher.'

I know the kind, Madison thought, looking at Brown.

Madison's cell pinged just as she got home. She dropped a shopping bag on the floor in the hallway and kicked off her boots as she replied.

'Rachel,' she said, so glad to hear her friend's voice after a day of madness.

'Alice,' Rachel replied and Madison could see her sprawled on the old leather sofa with her feet on her grandmother's ottoman, a blanket over her legs and her husband, Neal, asleep next to her.

'Been a while,' Rachel continued. 'And I wanted to make sure I'm seeing you tomorrow.'

Rachel was cooking Thanksgiving dinner for her extended family and, as always, Madison was invited. If she'd had the day off she would have gone early in the morning and helped Rachel to cook, since there were so many guests coming that they needed two tables end-to-end to accommodate everybody. This year, though, Madison would only be able to make it there at some unspecified time of the day.

'I'll get there as soon as I can. Is Ruth making latkes?'

Rachel's mother was the kind of home cook people would cross the country for – barefoot – just for the sheer pleasure of sitting at her table.

'She's making a batch just for you.'

Madison had grabbed the bag and made her way into the kitchen. 'Thank you, Ruth,' she whispered.

'You have a shift tomorrow, right?'

'Yes, I was on duty, anyway. And after what happened today—' Madison stopped herself – in all probability Rachel didn't know about the murdered couple, and she certainly didn't know it was part of Madison's case. 'Things are pretty grim right now,' she said finally.

Madison had joined the Seattle Police Department right after college and Rachel was used to her 'cop speak'. There were things her friend would not speak of directly. However, they had found a way to talk about most things and Rachel – a psychologist – would not balk on the occasions Madison tried to evade her questions.

'On a scale of one to ten, how bad is it?' she said.

Madison sighed. 'Ten.'

'Shoot, Alice, and you're in the middle of it?'

'Smack bang in the middle.'

Rachel had read the news and she didn't need to ask what case they were talking about.

'He's not some kind of nutjob with an ax, running around killing random people. The amount of detail, of preparation, you wouldn't believe it,' Madison said.

'Do you have a suspect?'

'We're building a profile. The FBI is helping but it's taking longer than . . .' Her voice faltered. It all sounded like excuses – excuses on top of pretexts on top of rationalizations. 'I'm afraid we're just grasping at air, Rach, and he keeps on killing innocents.'

Rachel did not jump in with a reassuring cliché. Madison thanked her for it in her heart.

'And there's something else, some old trouble that's come knocking again, and I might need a good lawyer soon. Do you know any?' she continued.

'Alice Eleanor Madison,' Rachel said, 'you have never done a single thing as a cop that was not above board and good and right.'

'Rachel—'

'Let me finish. Whatever you are worried about, over and over you have put yourself between danger and the innocent.'

'Rachel, it's complicated.'

'So is life, babe, and I don't want you to get all tangled up in thoughts of lawyers when we both know you're as straight as an arrow.'

Madison started unpacking with one hand as the other held her cell to her ear. ''kay,' she muttered.

'Bad dreams?' Rachel said. Madison had told her more than she had ever confessed to any other human being, and Rachel had switched to her pro mode.

'Loads.'

'You're going back to Stanley once the case is done.' It was not a question.

It was on Madison's lips to tell her about the burglary but she didn't. 'Probably,' she conceded. 'I like the view from his office.'

'How's Aaron?' Rachel said out of the blue.

'Great. He'll be driving straight to you tomorrow and I'll meet him there.'

There had been a happy clamor in the family when it had become clear that Aaron and Alice Madison were dating. Rachel had been cheerfully supportive but she had kept her beady eye on her friend.

'We went to a wedding on Sunday,' Madison said as she put cheese in the fridge. 'Andy Dunne's. And Aaron met everybody.'

There was a moment of quiet on the line.

'Rach . . .'

'Alice,' her friend's voice came back to her then, soft and warm in the empty house. 'I'm only going to say this once, just so that you know for sure in case you've ever wondered. I have a brother, Mickey, and I have a sister, you. I love Aaron but you don't need to marry into this family to become a part of it. You already are and have been for years. You understand?'

'Oh,' Madison said, because it was all she could manage through the knot in her throat.

'Anyhoo,' Rachel continued, 'I'll see you when I see you tomorrow. And don't forget to bring Tupperware for leftovers. It's going to be epic.'

*

Madison made herself a grilled cheese sandwich. And when she fell asleep, a little later, something – perhaps Rachel's words, like embers in the hearth – kept the bad dreams away.

At least for one night.

Chapter 38

Eighteen months earlier

The wide sweep of deep blue sky above Madison's house was becoming an orange streak as the first light crept onto her lawn. It had been three weeks since she had kissed Nathan Quinn for the first time and now she watched him sleep as he lay on her sofa.

Twenty-one days. Three whole weeks. It had been odd, that sudden swell in her heart that had seemed to encompass everything in the world.

'I don't know as much about you as you know about me,' he had told her in that first week.

Madison considered her reply. 'I run,' she'd told him after a moment. 'I love running. Whatever the weather, morning or evening. I often go to Alki Beach after my shift and I run. I started doing track in high school and I sort of never stopped. I can still hear my coach, as a matter of fact, berating my stride and my – as she called it – lack of mustard.'

'What was her name?'

'Coach Lewis. I don't think she had an actual first name. She was christened Coach by discerning parents.'

'I loathe running,' Quinn said.

Madison smiled.

'But,' he continued, 'I like rowing. I used to row in college.'

'Where?'

'Harvard, but I was only a reserve and I got dropped because I couldn't bulk up.'

Madison remembered the young man with the curly hair. 'Their loss,' she said.

After their first day and night together he had returned home. And then, the following night, she'd got back to the empty house late after her shift and he'd called her.

'Would you like some company?'

Somehow, every night they had planned to spend apart they still ended up together. Most nights they made it to her bedroom – but not always.

It had been an awkward, breathtaking, miraculous process as they went about discovering the small things about each other – the important ones they had known for a long time already.

Quinn didn't like Thai food, they both loved Japanese. Madison watched classic movies before going to sleep, Quinn read Henry James and George Eliot.

They had a weekend in Vancouver: drove up in three hours, stayed at the Rosewood and had the best sushi Madison had ever tasted. Day by day she had learnt the turns of all the fine scars on his body and he had gladly let her.

One evening, after her shift, they had met at his place. He had cooked steaks and she had told him about the case she was working on: a gang-related murder which had started with a teenager wanting to join a group of older boys and had ended with the waste of two young lives. They had talked about it, about what it was like interviewing the fifteen-year-old killer, and they'd gone over the possible legal strategy the defense might use. Later, on the deck overlooking Lake Washington, Madison had realized that she had left the case inside – those words full of ache and sorrow – and that night she had slept soundly and without dreams.

Madison sat in her armchair with her feet under her and watched Nathan Quinn sleep. The previous night when they had come in she had looked at the hearth and wondered just how good it would feel to be on that sofa with Quinn and with the first autumn fire crackling in the dark room. In the end, the sofa had been enough – it had been plenty. They fell asleep and stayed there, wrapped in her blanket, until she had woken up before dawn.

It all started that morning with a simple thing. But in truth it had been there from the beginning: it was the small cloud behind every instant they had spent together, as if her joy was delivered with a bullet that was flying towards them from a very great distance.

Madison had got up to get a glass of water and Quinn's cell phone had started vibrating on the floor where he had dropped his jacket. She had picked it up because it rested against the leg of a chair and she didn't want the noise to wake him, and she had seen it: on the screen that displayed the caller ID the name *Jack* had flashed up followed by a ten-digit number. And just like that she had John Cameron's private cell phone number. The number his best friend – no, his brother – had. The number that could be used to triangulate his location, that could be used to find him anywhere at any time. And Homicide Detective Alice Madison had it. How much more information about him would she be able to gather simply spending time with Quinn? How much would she be able to understand about the alleged murderer of nine just by being close to his best friend? And what would happen on that day – and it was sure to come – when she would have to go after him, just as she had known she would from the very first time her eyes had met Cameron's on his arrest sheet?

She thought of Nathan Quinn – torn between them but unswervingly loyal – and how he would be forced to conceal things from her, to lie about meeting Cameron some night because she was pursuing him for the crimes that he was bound to commit.

Madison had dropped the cell as if it was poison but the numbers had already stuck.

She had seen this coming from a long way off and she had refused to see it for what it was. Madison had drunk a glass of water and then she'd sat in the armchair and had been watching Quinn sleep for maybe half an hour. She knew every shadow and every line of his face and still she watched him because it would have to last her a lifetime. How foolish of her not to think, not to realize that this was going to happen sooner or later, ready or not. The idea that he would feel he had to turn away from her in order to keep his friend safe was unbearable. Madison took a breath. If it was unbearable today – three weeks in – how much worse would it get with each day they were together?

Quinn shifted and opened his eyes. He saw her in the chair and his hand reached out for hers, and she took it.

'What is it?' he said.

Madison could not speak.

'What is it?'

Quinn straightened up and they were sitting with their knees touching.

If she was going to do it, Madison thought, she had to do it now and she could not waver, she could not falter.

'When you were asleep,' she said, 'a little while ago, your cell rang and I picked it up and I saw Cameron's number. I didn't mean to, but I saw it, and now I know it.'

Quinn had barely woken up and his brain was trying to compute what she was telling him.

Madison plowed on. 'The last time we spoke he said to me that he was going traveling and it would be both business and pleasure. God knows what he meant but he could have meant California. He could have meant that he was going down there to pay back the cartel, right?'

Quinn nodded, still not sure of where they were going with it.

'Do you remember,' Madison continued, 'months ago, when I needed to meet Cameron face to face for the Sinclair case and you didn't want me to? You didn't want me anywhere near him. Because even if, that day, I wasn't looking to put him behind bars, one day it was very likely that I would be.'

An idea began to take shape, an understanding, a notion with edges so sharp that Quinn didn't want to get any closer to it.

'You were right,' she said. 'The truth is that every single moment we spend together I become more of a danger to him. The more I know, the more I can use against him.'

'You're talking about a day that might never come.'

Madison didn't reply, she didn't need to. Quinn was reaching the same conclusions she had, whether he liked it or not.

'What's going to happen when I have to bring him in for something that he might or might not have done? We both know Cameron's not the type who's going to come easy. You're not his lawyer anymore, so how are you going to protect him from me? If there's a warrant out for his arrest and he calls you, would you tell me? If he's hurt and he needs you, would you tell me?'

'We can talk about this if and when we have to.'

'If he's hurt and he calls you and I'm one of the people who have to bring him in, what then?'

'We can talk about it if—'

'It will be too late by then. I will know too much.'

They were still holding hands.

'You would never forgive me if I was the one who brought him in,' she said.

'You forget I'm an officer of the court. I know who he is, what he has done. I know what he is.'

'He's your brother in every way but blood and I don't want you to feel you ever have to lie to me about it,' Madison said. 'Not about anything.'

'I never have.'

'I know.'

'And if you went after him I'd be worried about *you*.'

'I can look after myself.'

'I know that but – believe me – you're not in the same league. And I thank God for that.'

'I'm not asking you to choose. I'm saying this is how things are. You will always want to protect him and I'm one of the things you need to protect him from.'

'You saved his life.'

'And I'd do it again.'

'But you'd pursue him if you have to.'

'I would, if I could.'

'Then he would be in some serious trouble.'

Madison sighed. 'We'd just have to see how it plays out.'

Quinn stood up and Madison followed. He looked so pale in the early light and there were livid shadows under his eyes. He laid his cool hand on her cheek and they were close enough to embrace, close enough to kiss.

'I can hardly think straight,' he said and his voice was a hoarse whisper. 'I'm going to wash my face and we'll get some coffee and talk this over and sort it out. Okay?'

'Okay,' she said.

Quinn nodded and let go of Madison's hands.

She padded into the kitchen and closed her eyes. There was nothing to talk about, there was nothing to sort out. She heard the front door open and close and three seconds later the sound of Quinn's car starting. She didn't go to look; she listened as the car crunched the gravel on her driveway and then faded into the distance.

The pain was sudden and physical and lacerating. Months later, Madison could not remember the rest of that day, of that week. It had been a blur of hours when she was supposed to be asleep, but was awake, and days when she wasn't really present except during her shifts.

She had felt Brown's eyes on her but had not confided in him. She had told Rachel eight months later, when she was becoming adjusted to a life that was somewhat *less* and would always be *less*. Madison ran dozens, hundreds of miles in those months, especially on Alki Beach, and not once did she noticed the tall, dark man who would park at the end of the lot and watch her run.

Then, about one year after that day, she had bumped into Carl Doyle, Quinn's assistant from his private practice, and casually asked him about his former boss. And that's how Madison had learnt that Nathan Quinn was engaged to his college girlfriend, Erica Lowell, herself an attorney – her father had founded Greenhut Lowell. She had come back to Seattle after many years in Boston and – wouldn't you know it? – they'd run into each other six months earlier.

Madison had managed to nod and react in all the right places and had driven herself home. She'd even stuck some leftovers in the oven to warm them up for dinner. In the end, though, she had fallen asleep on the sofa with her food untouched and *Some Like It Hot* playing muted on the TV.

When Aaron had asked her out on a date three days later, Madison had said yes.

Chapter 39

John Cameron sat at the table and spread out an old *Seattle Times* on the polished wood. He unwrapped the leather straps from the shoulder holster and took out the Smith & Wesson .40. There was something very relaxing about field stripping and cleaning it.

It had always helped him to think.

John Cameron's home was a modest house in the Admiral neighborhood above Alki. It had been bought years earlier in another man's name and no other living being had been inside it since. There were no photos in frames or a scrap of paper with his name anywhere. He had made sure it would stay entirely blank – not so much a safe house, more of a doorway to non-existence. Even Nathan Quinn didn't know about it and, if John Cameron died unpredictably – either there or somewhere else – the utilities would still be paid by a competent lawyer in Tacoma who knew him as a businessman who often traveled abroad.

There was something of a dark fairy tale there, Cameron thought, because if he died suddenly his body would not be discovered for years – or possibly ever. As the house ticked over, with or without him, maybe enough time would pass for the trees and the shrubs in the wide garden to take over the house completely and reclaim the land. There would be tall grass instead of the oak floors, and branches would break through the glass panes in the windows. His body would slowly dissolve and become mulch for the roots to feed on, and nothing could ever prove that he had lived there. His weapons, of course, would not dissolve. They would remain under the leaves, the toiling insects and the damp earth – rusty but whole.

In the pool of light from an anglepoise lamp John Cameron removed the magazine from the pistol, emptied it and lined up the fifteen shells precisely on the newspaper. He checked the handgun's chamber and made sure that it was empty. Then he pulled back the slide, pushed the lock, turned the switch on the side and when he squeezed the trigger the slide came off. The man who had taught him to do it had said that ten idiots every year forget to check the chamber is empty before they do it, pull the trigger to release the slide and shoot a family member – did he want to be that idiot?

Dawn was just about skimming the tops of the skyscrapers in downtown Seattle. Cameron glanced at the glass wall and all he saw were streaks of gray and blue as the day had not decided yet which way it was going to go. He removed the spring and the barrel from the slide and sprayed some Remington oil into the lid of the can. He only used small pure cotton cloths and slim brushes which glided perfectly inside the barrel, and where they couldn't reach he used Q-tips which he dipped in the oil. First he worked on the inside and then on the outside. As he was wiping he squeezed the trigger a couple of times to see how smoothly the mechanism moved.

He was done with California for a while: he had no further interest in the people there and had reason to believe they had no further interest in him. Then again, he would just have to wait and see. Those kinds of things don't run to schedule.

John Cameron clicked the slide back and replaced the full magazine. He got up, poured himself a mug of coffee and sat in the leather chair by the glass wall. There was enough light to see the city coming to life and he never tired of that view. If he died there and then, the handgun – freshly cleaned and oiled as it was – would happily hold its own against the rain and the Pacific Northwest storms. And that, he considered, was a comforting thought.

He took a sip of coffee and wondered what kind of death Special Agent A. J. Parker would choose. The world was full of possibilities.

Alice Madison woke up on Thanksgiving and her thoughts ran to her grandmother and her usual words on that day. *Remember to give thanks for unknown blessings already on their way.* It was a Native American saying and it had stayed with Madison. *Unknown blessings.*

She hoped there was a whole load of those coming her way because she sure needed them.

Her cell pinged and she grabbed it – given how early it was, it could only be bad news. *Please no more bodies, no more victims.* She saw the caller's ID.

'Madison,' she said as she picked up.

'Just thought you'd like to start the day with a happy thought,' Nathan Quinn said.

'Haven't had many of them lately.'

'I know. I saw the news. Klein told me the two victims were *his* work.'

'Yes, he's been busy.'

'Getting worse?'

'You have no idea.'

'Who's the primary on it?'

Madison rolled her eyes. 'Chris Kelly,' she replied.

'Is he going to be able to work with you on this?'

'He has no choice. Although I don't expect he's going to share any big epiphanies he might have, he wouldn't do anything that would hurt the case – not with everyone watching.' Madison pulled herself up and rested her back against the headboard. 'I think the way forward is to look at the people the killer framed for his crimes. The most difficult part of his work would have been to find someone specifically right to set up.'

'His *work*?'

'You know what I mean. He's been doing it for so long and has put so much into it, into what he does – whatever you want to call the horrors he produces for everybody involved – that it's become his real work. What he does for money and to keep a roof over his head is entirely secondary.'

'Could be,' Quinn said. 'He hacked into the HVAC company, did he not? Could that be his day job? Not hacking, but something to do with computers?'

Madison knew in her bones that it made sense. 'Yes, if you're that good at something – and our Cybercrime section says he is – I bet that's his regular job. He's probably some kind of freelance consultant – the FBI had it in their profile.'

'How is it going with the buried tins?'

'We call them "time capsules" now: they are his calling card and how he injects himself into the whole operation. And yes, we found the first two he buried after Mitchell.'

'Two down, nine to go.'

'I'm aware of the numbers, thanks,' Madison said. 'Sorensen's people are working as fast as they can.'

There was a beat of quiet on the line and it struck Madison as truly remarkable that a single instant of silence could be simultaneously awkward and utterly comfortable.

'It might be a good time to share some useful news,' Quinn said. 'The wire-tap recordings have been, let's say, collected. They are in my possession – all of them, including your call – and I'm about to destroy them, just as I destroyed the original tape I'd made.'

Madison rested her head back against the wall.

'Madison?' Quinn said.

She had not realized how tightly that band had been strapped around her chest for days. Her voice would not come at first but then it did. 'I'm here,' she said and took a deep breath. The cartel could not come after her; she wouldn't have to go to Fynn and resign; she could stay right where she was and do what she did. 'How?' she asked.

'Cameron,' Quinn replied. 'The cartel's informant in the DEA was Parker. And he was also the one who told them where they could find Jack when they took him.'

'Agent Parker?'

'Yes.'

'Did Cameron . . .?'

'No, he has not harmed him. I'll explain in more detail another time, but Agent Parker needed to bow out gracefully and Jack let him do that.'

Madison wasn't sure what that meant – except that Agent Parker had probably learnt more about John Cameron than he had ever wished to when he was provoking her in their meetings.

'Jack's contact at OPA said that their investigation of you is still open and is very much dependent on what their informant is going to dig up. But you're not under any surveillance at present.

Apparently, they can't justify the expense of tailing and recording you.'

Madison smiled. 'Well, thank God for the cuts in departmental budgets.'

She knew that he was smiling, even though she could not see him.

It seemed that Alice Madison owed the fact of her remaining in Homicide to John Cameron. It was – as most things were in their acquaintance – surreal.

'Quinn,' she said, 'what Cameron did, it was a big help to me. It made a very big difference.'

'Jack does what he does for his own reasons,' he replied. 'But I'll tell him that you appreciated the gesture.'

Unknown blessings.

Madison and Quinn hung up without mentioning Thanksgiving or their respective plans. Those were not things they talked about.

Brown and Madison stomped their feet and tried to keep warm in the November chill. The day had decided to go for freezing and overcast, and the wind blowing in from Lake Union brought a harsh cold that reached under their clothes with icy fingers.

Henry Karasick's younger brother worked on a building site near the water and had agreed to meet them in his break. He was stocky, in his late thirties and wore a hard hat and high-visibility yellow jacket over a thick mountain coat.

Brown and Madison had debated whether she should go alone because the man might very well nurture a degree of animosity towards the cop who had put his brother in jail. But Madison had been firm: Brown had to come, it had been his investigation and he had done nothing wrong. He had to come because he had nothing to hide.

'We do have something to hide,' Brown had said in a brisk tone. 'We're not telling him it was a serial killer.'

In spite of his reservations, Madison had managed to convince him. They waited next to a hot-dog stand, by some wooden benches, in a draft of briny air and fried onions.

The younger Karasick clocked Brown and regarded him with instant wariness. Then again, he had been in court every day and he knew how solid the case against his brother had been.

'There was more to it,' Madison said and cut straight to it. 'We think there was another man involved and we need to make sure we follow that trail too.'

'Another man?'

'Yes.' Madison took out the sketches for him to see. 'Have you ever seen this guy? Maybe with your brother, in a bar, in a friend's house?'

This was not what he had expected at all. 'Seven years later you discover there might have been another guy?'

'Yes, and we're looking for the whole truth – however many years later. If this man was the reason your brother ended up in jail, wouldn't you want to know?'

'No, I have never seen this guy before,' the man said.

'Are you sure?' Madison asked. 'Try to remember all of the social situations your brother might have been in. By the way, do you know who gave him the weed he smoked on the night of the murder?'

The younger Karasick blinked a couple of times.

'I couldn't care less about the dealer. But this guy,' she pointed at the pictures, 'might have liked to know that your brother was getting high on that particular night. Please try to remember.'

The man shook his head. 'There was this place he used to go to. And sometimes, when he was worked up about something – when he was upset – well, there was a fella behind the bar who knew how to get you the weed.'

'I need the name of the bar and the name of the bartender.'

'I don't—'

'Please think. Henry must have said something to you about it . . .'

Brown stood quietly to one side. The other man stared at a speckled corner of concrete, searching for the memory of a word, of a moment. Madison knew not to interrupt. The hot-dog stand was getting busy with office workers and a steady stream of builders from the site, talking and eating as the weather got steadily worse.

'It was Kitty's Tavern in Northeast Seattle,' the man said finally with a mixture of relief and regret. 'And the guy was called Roy or Ron or something.'

'Thank you,' Madison said. 'Thank you very much.'

The wind had picked up and even the birds were quiet. The woman began and her voice filled the emptiness outside and inside.

'My name is Katherine Angela Duncan. Everyone calls me Kate. I was born in Nashville, Tennessee. I went to college at the University of Alabama in Tuscaloosa and then at UW, where I met my husband. I work in a pharmaceutical company. I enjoy running and cooking and meeting with friends. When I was little, I had a dog called Jimbo – a golden Lab, the best dog in the world . . .' Her voice caught.

They drove under the spitting rain and hoped that somebody at the tavern would remember Henry Karasick. Madison didn't want to think about how many lucky stars had to line up for it to happen: they needed someone who knew about Karasick and who could tell them about Roy or Ron or whoever the guy was. But, of course, what they needed more than anything else was someone who would recognize the man in the pictures.

Kitty's was the kind of establishment which barely changes as the decades roll on; generation after generation of drinkers and bartenders had come and gone as the red banquettes and the wooden tables had been seasoned by a few nicks and scratches.

'I think they call this *vintage*,' Madison said, looking around as they stepped inside.

'No,' Brown replied, 'it's just plain old.'

Still, it was warm and welcoming, in a scruffy sort of way, and certainly better than standing around the hot-dog stand. Madison bought them a ginger ale and a Coke and asked the bartender – a young woman who looked like she would have been in primary school seven years earlier – whether there was anybody in the tavern who was around back then.

The owner – and Madison found it hard to believe – was a woman actually called Kitty and she joined them in a booth in the corner. She was in her late fifties, a tall blonde with a voice made by cigarettes and other substances Madison couldn't fathom. Her eyes were pale green and misty and she eyed Madison with curiosity and good humor.

'I wish I could help you,' Kitty said. 'I remember Henry. He was a troubled boy but sweet – if you know what I mean. He got into fights sometimes and I had to throw him out, but he would always come back and apologize, and even bought me flowers a couple of times.'

Madison didn't dwell on what Kitty meant by *troubled* and *sweet*. She had seen Karasick's sheet and his wife's restraining order was not about flowers. Nevertheless, she nodded as if she agreed that the world had seen too many of these sweet, troubled boys.

'Did Henry have a friend here? Someone he confided in?' Brown said.

'There wasn't anybody special, just a long line of guys at the bar drinking and talking like guys do – one quarter funny, one quarter serious and half of it bull.'

'Kitty,' Madison said, 'someone sold Henry some weed. We're Homicide, we're not Vice, we don't care about a bag of pot from seven years ago. But we need to talk to the guy who sold it to him.'

Kitty examined the forensic artist's sketches spread out on the table. Her nails were a work of wonder – red and immaculate and glossy enough to see your face in. She ran her fingers over the pages and shook her head.

'I don't know who this is but I can tell you who sold Henry the weed that night and all the other nights.' Her eyes glittered. 'My son, Roy. And I wish you could ask him about it, I wish I could call him out for you to take him down to the station and put some fear into him, but he died four years ago in a car accident.'

'I'm terribly sorry,' Madison said.

'Me too,' Kitty said. 'He ran a light when he was under the influence and a truck caught him on the side. It was instant.'

Brown and Madison let her come back to them in her own time.

'Roy was not alone in the car – his best buddy, Travis, was with him.'

'Is he . . .?' Madison said.

'Yes, he's still alive, lives in a small farm out of town. Back then he was with Roy all the time and he worked here too.'

'We're going to need his address, if you have it.'

Kitty gazed at Madison with her watery eyes. 'Travis is not very good with strangers, you know, since the accident.'

'We'll have to take our chances,' Madison said.

*

Kate Duncan felt an abrupt pang of homesickness. Not for the home in southwest Seattle, no. An unexpected recollection of her father's favorite armchair in her childhood home in Nashville had given her a stabbing pain in the chest and she longed to be back there, to be back there as a child among those things that had made up her life.

She wanted her old room, the wallpaper she had chosen with her mother, and the dog who used to sleep at the end of her bed. She wanted all those things in the way someone needs air to keep going.

Every breath she took only confirmed that she was far away from that world and completely alone.

'Are we wasting our time?' Madison said as they left Kitty's Tavern. 'Is this a wild goose chase?'

'What do you mean?' Brown said.

'Jeez, Sarge, you know exactly what I mean,' Madison snapped.

'Do I?'

Madison felt the tension and the frustration of the past days coming in and flowing out like a tide. She did her best to keep her tone level and the courtesy filter switched on.

'I'm sorry. I mean about this Travis guy. Is it worth our while to go all the way out to God-knows-wheresville to speak with him when there are other friends of Karasick right here in Seattle we could talk to? I have this . . . this infernal stopwatch running in my head that keeps telling me that every phone call is going to be another dead body, another victim, another—'

They had arrived at their car but Madison needed to spend some of that pent-up energy and didn't want to get in and sit down – at least for a few minutes. The anger and the dread that had been quietly building up for days were edging to the surface, and there was nothing she could do about it.

Brown watched her.

'I need you to tell me that we're doing the right thing,' she said.

'No,' Brown said.

'No?'

'No.'

'No, we're not doing the right thing? Or no, you're not going to tell me?'

'If I told you that we were doing the right thing, how much would it be worth to you?'

'Sarge—'

'The only way this is going to work is if *you* believe in every step of what you're doing. Because when you turn around and you discover you were wrong about it, you need to know you did it for the right reasons.'

'Sarge, I—'

'Why is it important to talk to Travis?'

This was one of the times when Madison would gladly have done without the lesson. But what Brown was trying to tell her was about far more than Travis.

She sighed. 'Because he was close to Roy, and he might remember Karasick that night – and whoever else might have been there.'

'And yes, it could very well be a waste of time. But I don't have anywhere else to be, do you?'

Madison rested her elbows on the roof of the car. She thought about Dr Fellman working on the two latest victims' post-mortems. After he was done, the bodies would await their final destination in a morgue bunk next to Matthew Duncan's.

So much destruction.

'Let's go,' Madison said.

Brown nodded.

He was carrying so much, she thought, so many burdens – eleven, no, fourteen of them. And there she was, having a tantrum like a two-year-old. Madison eyed the sky over the east and it was nothing but black clouds.

Even the sun had given up on Thanksgiving.

Chapter 40

Jerry Lindquist ate his turkey sandwich and wondered how badly he would have to hurt himself to end up in the prison hospital and whether he would be safer there than in his cell.

He could always attack one of the guards, which would definitely land him in AdSeg – Administrative Segregation – also known as solitary confinement. However, that held its own perils as in his experience an assault on a guard could result in a very serious injury for the inmate and the kind of black mark on his record that would make it difficult to continue his sentence unnoticed. After all, it was what he was striving for – being completely unnoticed – as if he just happened to wake up and go to sleep in that cell but really he had nothing to do with the rest of the prison population. The correction officers had always been very decent to him and, in truth, he couldn't even begin to think about attacking one of them.

Jerry Lindquist opened and closed his left hand, watching the ligaments and the tendons move under the skin. What would it take to send him to hospital? More than a paper cut and less than an amputation.

His turkey sandwich tasted of plastic with a hint of cranberry. The Thursday bookkeeping class had been cancelled, probably because the volunteer wanted to stay home and cook and celebrate with his family.

Jerry looked at the smudge of red between the thick slices of bread. He knew exactly how it felt.

Travis's farm was past Issaquah on I-90 and close to Tiger Mountain State Forest. It was not the best day to be going visiting. But Madison knew it was a pretty valley and, if nothing else, it was a good thing to be out of the city for a couple of hours. Brown and Madison had not even considered doing their interviewing on the phone or asking a local deputy for help. This needed a face-to-face meeting. The closer they got, the more Madison wondered how much Travis had been injured in the accident. And how he felt about Roy, who had driven him straight into a close and personal encounter with a truck.

There was a whole lot of sky opening up above them as soon as they were past Bellevue and as they drove towards the mountains Madison's mood lifted a little.

Brown took a narrow turn off the main road and, after a couple of hundred yards, they saw the sign for Ridge Farm. The building, when they pulled into the uneven driveway, was neither pretty nor well kept. What the farm produced – if anything – was not clear. It was a wide wooden bungalow with a porch, attached to a garage. The dark red paint had turned to brown and was peeling off the cladding. If nothing changed the course of things, in a couple of years it would be comfortably described as a shack.

'At least we don't have the No Trespassing signs,' Madison commented.

'Sometimes it's just a state of mind,' Brown replied.

They got out of the car and looked around. There were no lights in the main building. An orange pick-up was parked by the front steps. Madison placed the flat of her hand on the hood. It was freezing cold. The inside of the pick-up was a mess of fast-food wrappers and empty beakers.

The wind picked up and roused the odor of mulch and old garbage around the clearing. Brown and Madison climbed the steps to the porch and he knocked twice on the door. The curtains had been pulled tight across the windows and it was impossible to see whether anybody was moving in the house. Although, Madison reflected, if they were moving they were doing so in the dark.

Nobody came to the door and after a minute Brown knocked again. Madison's hackles were up and she couldn't quite explain why: there was something ragged about the place, but that wasn't it. A stir of wind brought a subtle scent.

'Sarge . . .'

'I got that too,' Brown said.

Something or someone had died there recently.

'Back door,' Brown said.

They went along the side opposite the garage and saw the two windows there were as shut as the ones in the front. The back of the farm had a small clearing with an old-fashioned water pump, a shed and a washing line with no drying clothes pegged to it. There was a faint light coming through the dirty glass of the kitchen door and Brown knocked lightly. Madison's hand went to the security strip of her sidearm and unlatched it.

'Hello?' Brown said.

Madison wondered how Travis felt about the police, in general – and those who visited him at home, in particular.

There was a clatter inside – maybe a saucepan falling – and steps coming towards them.

The door opened, a narrow gap that showed the face of a man blinking at them as if he had just woken up.

Madison assessed him. *Thirty years old or so, medium height, unshaven, wearing layers of T-shirts under a thick gray woolen shirt. Hands in his pockets.*

'Hello,' the man said and waited.

'Hello,' Brown replied. 'We're looking for Travis. Can you help us?'

'I'm Travis,' the man said and Madison could hear it in his voice – a slight catch, something off in his speech.

'We're from Seattle PD,' Brown continued and took out his badge. 'We'd like to ask you a couple of questions about your friend Roy Ward.'

Travis blinked again.

'Do you remember Roy?' Brown said.

Travis opened the door a little bit more and Brown and Madison received a full blast of the awful smell.

'Of course I remember Roy,' Travis replied.

'Can we come in and talk about him for a minute?'

Why doesn't Travis come out instead? Madison thought. But they did have to go in, one way or the other, and so when Travis opened the door wide to let them pass she stepped inside and took a deep breath.

The kitchen was large enough to have a round table in the middle and the walls were covered in cabinets that would have been new in the seventies. Every surface was covered in dirty dishes, pans and piles of clothing. Travis had dark hair and Madison could see the furrowed end of a deep scar poking out from above his sideburns and running into his hairline.

'What do you need with Roy?' Travis said.

'Shall we go sit somewhere?' Brown asked him.

'No, thanks,' Travis replied. 'Here is fine.'

'Okay, Travis, do you remember when you worked at Kitty's?'

'You do know Roy's dead, right?'

'Yes, we know. Do you remember Kitty's?'

'Sure. I liked working there.'

'Good, and Roy worked there too.'

Madison's eyes scanned the room. Leftovers, laundry and more fast-food wrappers.

'Sure, it was his mom's place.'

'There was a guy who came in sometimes and talked to Roy, his name was Henry Karasick, do you remember him?' Brown brought out a picture of Karasick but Travis was quicker.

'Sure, I remember Henry . . . went to prison for murder.'

'Yes,' Brown said. 'He did.'

'What's that got to do with Roy?'

There was something touching about the sudden defensive note in his voice.

'Nothing, really, except that sometimes Henry bought weed from Roy. He bought some the night Henry killed that man.'

'That doesn't make it Roy's fault.'

'No, it doesn't.'

'And there was a big fuss about Henry – because of the murder – and the thing is, he hadn't even bought the weed that night.'

'He hadn't?'

'No, he didn't buy it. He was *given* it.'

'Roy gave it to him?'

Travis giggled. 'No, Roy didn't give it to him. Why would he *give* it to him? Another man bought it from Roy and gave some to Henry.

They made a bet, he lost and Henry went home with a bag of pot this big.'

Brown and Madison exchanged a look. 'Do you remember the man's name?'

Madison wondered briefly about the legal trail they were creating and how much Sarah Klein would love a witness with a brain injury and a history of substance abuse.

Travis gazed from one to the other. 'What do you need that for? Is it going to get Roy into trouble?'

Brown hesitated.

Travis giggled and raised a hand in apology. 'Yes, I know, Roy's dead. I forgot for a minute there.'

'Do you remember the man's name, Travis?' Brown said.

'Yeah, never saw him again after that night. His name was Joe. He was a friend of Henry's, met him in the tavern a few times.'

Joe. Madison brought out the sketches and turned around, looking for a switch. In the harsh neon lighting the room was even worse.

Travis looked at the pictures. 'This one,' he said and pointed at a sketch of the fake engineer that had been adapted for age.

'This one?' Brown said.

'Yeah, looks like him.'

'Joe, like Joseph? Did he have a family name?'

'No, just Joe. Never knew any other name.'

'You remember him after all this time?' Brown said.

Travis scratched absent-mindedly where Madison had seen the scar.

'There was a lot of talk about Henry after the murder. About Joe and the weed.' Travis leant back against a kitchen cabinet. 'I have problems with my memory after the accident but everything that happened before, that's like crystal clear.' He tapped his temple.

In the harsh neon lighting Madison's eyes traveled to the pile of clothing Travis was leaning against. Poking out, not a foot away from his hand, was the butt of a gun.

'Travis,' she said pleasantly, 'would you have a picture of Roy?'

'What?'

'Would you have a picture of Roy to show us?'

If Brown was confused by the question, he showed no sign of it. Travis seemed to mull over the issue. Madison just wanted him away from that gun.

'Sure, I think I do.' He didn't move.

'Would you show it to us?'

'Why?'

Madison knew what to say and felt like a thief about it. 'We met Kitty earlier, she told us so much about Roy, but we've never seen his picture.'

'Oh, okay,' Travis said and he ambled out of the kitchen.

Madison reached for the gun, pulled it out from under the laundry. It was a revolver – a .38 – and it hadn't been cleaned in a long time. Madison checked the chamber and saw three shells. There were sounds coming from deeper into the house, drawers being opened and shut. Brown and Madison followed the corridor to the living room.

Travis turned as they walked in. 'Here,' he said and held a photograph towards Madison.

'Thank you,' she said without taking it. 'Travis, do you have a permit for the firearm in the kitchen?'

His eyes widened for a moment and his mouth opened and closed. 'No,' he said.

'How come you have a firearm without a permit?' Madison kept it light.

She didn't expect Travis's eyes to fill with tears. 'Because I had to shoot my dog.'

'You killed your dog?'

Travis nodded.

'Why did you kill it?'

''Cause he got really old and sick and was in a lot of pain.'

'When did this happen?'

'I . . . I think about three weeks ago.'

'And where is the dog now?'

'In his bedroom.' Travis nodded towards the front of the house.

'How did you get the gun?'

'I asked a guy I know.'

'Did you tell him what it was for?'

'I did. He's going to come pick it up sometime soon.'

They drove back towards Seattle.

'There's got to be somebody who can help him with that place,' Madison said after a few miles.

They had left Travis with a couple of deputies; Brown had taken them to one side when they'd arrived and had explained the situation. He needed a social worker, not a cell.

More than anything, Madison thought, he probably needed a new dog. But she doubted he'd ever be allowed to keep one again. They had found the body of the decomposing German shepherd in one of the two bedrooms, under a sheet, surrounded by chewy toys and air fresheners.

Brown drove fast, as usual. 'We have a name,' he said.

Chapter 41

Dr Fellman looked drained and Madison was yet again pleased that they had found him writing in his office with his door open, rather than at work in his lab. It was slightly unusual to seek out the pathologist to talk about a homicide case that belonged to another detective. But as it was the same killer, Brown and Madison wanted to speak with the doctor and have the chance to ask questions about the double homicide – instead of reading his report via Chris Kelly.

The lab was winding down for the day and the only sounds were the tinkling of instruments being sterilized nearby. After Travis's farm the morgue felt chemically hygienic.

'I have done about a quarter of the autopsies of all the cases involved in this,' Fellman said. 'And I've asked for the other counties' medical examiners to send me theirs. Actually, I've just got off the phone with the Thurston County ME and I'm getting a good idea of how the killer has developed.'

'Is there an arc?' Brown said.

'In a manner of speaking,' Fellman replied. 'The killer has always used a weapon found at the crime scene or directly connected to the person he wanted to frame. That much we know. But it was quite interesting to stand back and look at how the violence against the victims has developed over seven years.'

Quite interesting. Madison thought briefly about the people gathered at Rachel's house for Thanksgiving dinner – Aaron among them – and what kind of conversations *they* were having at that precise time.

'A death by firearm or a stabbing is a completely different kind of animal from this man's work. But even between his own murders there are differences. Mitchell was the first: he incapacitated him with the first blow and then continued to hit. I'm not making any psychological assumptions on the whys and whats, by the way, I'm just comparing the different reports. Now, we can see that the pattern continued with a steadily increasing degree of violence in all the cases: first incapacitation, then different areas of the bodies targeted – hands, feet, etc. But with Matthew Duncan we have a difference.'

'He only targeted his face,' Madison said.

'That's right.'

'Is he the only one who was injured in that way?'

'Yes, he was. He was the exception.'

'Then again,' Brown said, 'the killer was working within a small window of time. He must have known that the wife would be home soon. And he did not have a lot of time to spend with the victim since he was also preparing the whole fake burglary set-up.'

'You mean that he would have progressed to inflict the same injuries we saw on the couple if he had had the time?' Madison said.

'Possibly,' Brown replied.

'Maybe so,' Fellman said. 'The damage to Mr Duncan's face was the worst up to that point. And then, with Mr Nolin and Miss Rudnyk, we have again the heightened focus on the face, but also greater damage than ever to the rest of the body.' Fellman gazed from one to the other. 'It's as if the Duncan murder reenergized him, as if it gave him a new, hellish momentum to do even more, even worse. In fact, looking at the X-rays, the blows to the latest two victims were more powerful than any before.'

It was a lot to take on because – although no one said it – they were all aware that the time between Duncan and the latest killings had been dreadfully short. And the killer was in all probability getting ready for his next project.

Joe. Joe was getting ready to go to work.

At her desk, Madison dialed the number and for a moment wondered about the timing of Mass. Were there special Masses on Thanksgiving? It rang a couple of times, then Father O'Reilly picked up and Madison was surprised at how glad she was to hear his croaky voice.

'Father, it's Detective Madison. Could I ask you another question?'

'That's all I do all day, Detective. I answer questions. So, ask away . . .'

'We think that Henry Karasick might have met the killer in a bar. It's possible that he might have come to your group once, then followed Henry to the bar where he could talk to him alone. Does the name Joe mean anything to you – Joseph, perhaps? Anyone called Joe ever come to your meetings around the time Henry was there?'

Madison could hear the man sigh and she could imagine him standing and thinking in his kitchen.

After a while he said, 'Maybe. I can give you a maybe, but I'm not sure how much that's worth to you.'

'It's something, Father. If you remember anything, please let me know.'

'I will. You take care, Detective.' His voice was deadly serious just then.

Madison hung up at the same time as Brown did.

'Just spoken to the brother,' he said. 'He definitely remembers Karasick mentioning a friend called Joe. But he's never met him.'

They had a name, they had a point of contact. They had the beginning of the whole, dark tale.

Lieutenant Fynn was on the phone with the Chief. Brown and Madison waited until he was done to brief him. Madison was well past worrying about being taken off the cresting wave of the investigation – if Fynn would rather put someone else on point, he was welcome to. She had a job to do.

'What about press releases?' Fynn said when they were done.

'I'd release the name and the sketch Travis picked,' Madison said.

'What if it gives him a hint that we're also working backwards?'

'If it does, it does. There might be more people out there who would know who Joe was seven years ago than would recognize the fake engineer today.'

'We've had no luck with those?'

'Not yet.'

'Brown?' Fynn said.

'I agree. Let's cast the net as wide as possible – we should also interview Saul Garner's clients.'

'Do you want to front the press release?' Fynn asked Madison.

It wouldn't have been her first but certainly the most well attended. 'I will if you need me to, but I'd rather keep working the phones.'

'Let's give it to Public Affairs, then – it's their job, after all.'

As they left Fynn's office Brown glanced at Madison.

'What?' she said.

'You hate doing press releases. You would rather be hanged upside down over a boiling cauldron of sheep entrails for one hour than do one five-minute press release.'

'I did say I'd do it if he needed me to.'

'And what did you wish as you mentally crossed your fingers?'

'That he wouldn't need me to.'

Brown smiled. 'You might have to do one sometime.'

Madison grimaced. Brown was right: she hated getting up and talking in front of flashing cameras and microphones. A cauldron of sheep entrails was a piece of cake in comparison.

She saw Chris Kelly walking in and decided to step over the moat that seemed to surround him at all times and speak to him before he had a chance to read her report. Whether Madison admitted it to herself or not, she was curious about Kelly, about his complicity with OPA. Would it reveal itself in how he dealt with her? How he spoke to her? How did that kind of duplicity live inside a person?

Madison approached him and his eyes hardened the instant he realized that she was going to speak to him.

'We might have a name,' she said. 'Two witnesses from the Mitchell case remember someone called Joe and that he was the guy who found a pretext to give Karasick a whole load of weed for free the night of the murder.'

Kelly grunted his assent.

'Anything new with your end of things?' Madison said.

'Things look pretty bad for the ex-husband,' Kelly admitted. 'There's a lot of witnesses ready to testify that he wanted to hurt the ex and her new man.'

'Any trace evidence picked up at the scene?'

'Have you read the report?' he countered.

'We've just got back and I'm asking you. It's called sharing information. Apparently, some people find it useful.'

'The prelims say no evidence that points to anybody but the people who lived there. They're still processing it.'

'Thank you.'

Madison returned to her desk and as she did she could feel Chris Kelly's eyes following her. His acrimony was like a low-level hum in the busy room.

Madison stepped out in the dusk without her coat and let the cold hit her. The street lights had been on for a while, but the roads were quiet. For a few minutes it had stopped raining and the sidewalks were slick and deserted because today the rush hour had played out much earlier.

She dialed Aaron's cell and he picked up on the second ring. 'Hey, are you on your way?' he said, and she could hear many voices in the background.

'No, I don't think so. I'm going to have to miss it and will have to make do with your tales of turkey wonders.'

'I'm sorry,' Aaron said. 'Everybody's here and they were hoping to see you.'

'I know, me too. Please apologize for me.'

'Can't you sneak out?' There was no reproach in his voice, just boyish disappointment.

'I'm afraid not. But could I ask you a favor?'

'Rachel's mother's latkes?'

Madison smiled. 'Yes, please.'

'They're already packed and ready to go.'

'Thank you.'

'Do you want to speak to Rachel? She's in the other room.'

'No, it's okay. You tell her. I'll call her tomorrow.'

'I'll see you later.'

It was a comforting thought that Aaron would be there – maybe awake, probably asleep – when she got home.

Madison went back into the precinct and into the detectives' room. On a television high in the corner she spotted the Public Affairs officer speaking in front of a microphone. There was a small insert in the screen with the forensic artist's sketch. Camera flashes flared hard and white on the officer's face.

Aaron found Rachel in the kitchen.

'She's not coming,' he said. 'She apologizes but . . .'

'No worries,' Rachel replied. 'It's not the first time and it won't be the last. There, pass me that plate, will you? I'm going to put half the dinner in containers for you to take her.'

Rachel watched Aaron as he sliced leftover turkey into the plastic bowl. He wasn't upset, he wasn't offended. It didn't look as if he was contemplating an at-least-on-Thanksgiving kind of row. He was simply disappointed and spooning potatoes into the bowl next to the turkey.

There was something else, though, Rachel thought. But she couldn't say what it was – or how deep it ran.

In Los Angeles Sandra Parker heard the doorbell ring and went to answer it, wiping her hands on an apron and thinking about roasting times. She had a houseful of people and A.J. was still out – which was really not helpful at all.

She opened the door and two men turned to her.

'Sandra,' Curtis Guzman said.

He was A.J.'s partner and had been to the house a number of

times. The other man was a few years older and he looked at her in a way that made the small hairs on her tanned arms stand up.

'Mrs Parker,' he said.

'A.J.'s not here,' she said, smiling as some understanding in her clicked. There was a patrol car parked in front of the house as well – and she plain refused to acknowledge it, or give it voice. 'A.J.'s still out, should be home in a minute.'

Two six-year-old boys ran through the hall chasing each other.

Curtis came in, followed by the other man.

'Sandra, something has happened. Can we talk somewhere quiet?'

She knew it was happening but it still felt unreal. They sat in A.J.'s small study off the garage.

'I don't understand,' Sandra Parker repeated.

'I'm terribly sorry,' Guzman said.

'He was shot?'

'Yes, he was.'

'What was he doing in Newton?'

'We don't know yet but we will find out. He would have gone there for a good reason.'

'Who . . . who shot him?'

'There were no witnesses. But it's an area known for gang-related crime and chances are some informant got in touch at the last minute and he went to meet him. We don't know yet.'

'But you didn't go.'

Curtis shook his head. 'I didn't know anything about it.'

'He was shot,' Sandra said and tried to keep ahead of the wave that was about to crush her. 'Did he . . . did he . . . ?'

'No, he died instantly. He didn't suffer.'

'We're here for you, Sandra, whatever you need,' the older man said.

As it turned out, he was A.J.'s boss and would make sure all the funeral arrangements were taken care of. Special Agent A. J. Parker had died in the line of duty and would go on to receive full departmental honors.

Chapter 42

Kate Duncan's Thanksgiving had begun with a hot shower. She had to get ready to go to Matthew's cousins in Bremerton to spend the day with them and Matt's brother. She would also stay the night – sharing the large attic room with their eldest daughter – instead of coming back to Annie and her family, who would have had to dampen their own family celebrations not to hurt her feelings. Fair enough, she thought – this year, talking about giving thanks seemed like an odd, exotic exercise. People who gave thanks were people for whom nothing had happened, people who had merely coasted along.

Kate Duncan felt a brittle anger at the national obsession with stupid menu plans and the fuss over home-made cranberry sauce versus store-bought. She couldn't wait to leave the house.

Kate was going to be escorted to Bremerton by a detective from the East Precinct who was a colleague of Detective Madison, and that reassured her. He was going to be visiting his own family in Bremerton, anyway, so it worked out well for both of them.

She pulled the curtain to one side – it looked like rain would be part of the day at some point. She pulled on warm woolens and boots and grabbed her wet-weather jacket. The small overnight bag was ready by the door; she stuffed her wash bag in it and left the room.

The smell of roasting turkey was already drifting up the stairs.

Detective Norton had a long blond fringe under his deerstalker hat. He wore glasses with thick frames that managed to make him look both nerdy and cool. He smiled when Annie opened the door, and nodded to his car.

'Seattle's finest car service, I'm Detective Lorenzo Norton,' he said.

He had been in touch the previous evening and Kate Duncan had been quite abrupt. 'Please describe your appearance to me, so I know it will be you at the door.'

'No problem, ma'am, I think it's a very good idea. I'm six foot one, medium build, fair hair. I'll wear a deerstalker hat and glasses.'

Once in the car, which was warm and smelled of fresh coffee, Kate Duncan turned to the detective. 'I'm sorry about last night, I think I was rude.'

He shrugged. 'You have a good head on your shoulders. It was the smart thing to do. Here,' he said and passed her a beaker, 'for the road. It's black without sugar but I've got creamer and some sachets in the glove compartment if you like.'

'Thank you, that's really kind.'

She had wanted to get away from that kitchen so quickly she hadn't even had a cup of coffee yet.

They left Montlake and drove towards downtown and the ferries.

The detective wasn't interested in conversation, which suited her just fine. Kate Duncan relaxed against the seat and sipped the coffee.

*

'My name is Katherine Angela Duncan. Kate, everyone has always called me Kate. I was born in Nashville, Tennessee. I went to college at the University of Alabama in Tuscaloosa and I did my major at UW, where I met my husband. I work in a pharmaceutical company.'

Where was she? What had happened?

She remembered traveling in the car towards the ferries. It was cloudy above and the traffic was light. And now . . .

'My name is Katherine Angela Duncan. Everyone calls me Kate. I was born in Nashville, Tennessee. I went to college at the University of Alabama in Tuscaloosa and then at UW, where I met my husband. I work in a pharmaceutical company. I enjoy running and cooking . and meeting with friends. When I was little, I had a dog called Jimbo – a golden Lab, the best dog in the world . . .' Her voice caught.

It had been hours. How many she couldn't say. Kate Duncan had woken up in the darkness of a soft blindfold and in the cool, sharp air of a place that was both inside and outside. She couldn't tell precisely. She was sitting on a hard chair and bound to it. She was confused and her mind gripped the edges of her memories, trying to get purchase, trying to get a footing.

Then the fog lifted and the dread kicked in.

Her breathing quickened and she whimpered as she remembered the voice. And this time she could think clearly, because the drug had dissolved into her system. She knew about drugs, didn't she? She worked in a pharmaceutical company, right?

The voice came back. A man's voice. He had spoken to her in those minutes or hours she had been lost to herself. And here he was now.

'Tell me about you, dear.'

Oh God. 'What do you want? Do you want money? Do you—?' She was shaking. She could feel herself shake and she knew she had to keep her mind.

'Tell me about you.' The man was calm, but the tone was terse. Kate Duncan started again.

'My name is Katherine Angela Duncan. Everyone calls me Kate. I was born in Nashville, Tennessee. I went to college at the University of Alabama in Tuscaloosa and then at UW, where I met my husband. I work in a pharmaceutical company in the legal department. I enjoy running and cooking and meeting with friends. When I was little, I had a dog called Jimbo. My parents are called Alexander and Laura and—'

'No,' the man said, and there was a streak of humor there. 'No, your parents are called Douglas and Lisa and they still live in Nashville. Start again. Tell me about you.'

There was nothing but blackness under her blindfold and Kate Duncan felt a dizzy fear, as if all her thoughts were clashing together. Her chest hurt like she'd sprinted a whole marathon. Adrenaline was a hard blow with every breath.

'Tell me about you.'

'My name is Katherine Angela Duncan. Everyone calls me Kate. I was born in Nashville, Tennessee. I went to college at the University of Alabama in Tuscaloosa and then at UW, where I met my husband. I work in a pharmaceutical company in the legal department. I enjoy running, cooking, meeting with friends. When I was little, I had a dog called Jimbo. My parents are called Douglas and Lisa and,' her voice shook, 'they still live in Nashville.'

Kate sensed, rather than heard, a whisper of agreement somewhere close. There were birds in the distance, on and off, but no sound of cars, no city hum, nothing that could reassure her that people were nearby, that someone would come for her. As the effects of the sedative wore off, her thinking became sharper. Had anyone realized that she had been taken? Where was the detective who was supposed to escort her? Matthew's brother and the cousins must have noticed that she had not arrived when she was supposed to. They must be looking for her.

There was thick silence around her like after a heavy snowfall. Kate leant forward in the chair, testing her ties and listening hard. Maybe he had gone, maybe he had left her. She listened for the rustle of his clothing and then she heard, faintly and only a few feet behind her, a gentle, steady breathing.

And the man said, 'Tell me more.'

Under the blindfold, tears of fear and anger pricked her eyes. 'What do you want from me?' she snapped.

'I have just told you what I want.'

'Why am I here? Why did you take me?'

The man sighed. 'Because,' he said, as if explaining to a child, 'I want you to tell me about you.'

'Why? What . . . what is this? Who . . . ?'

'Take a breath and start again, from the beginning.'

Kate Duncan had lost track of time. From the moment she had first woken up tied to the chair it felt like years. She had talked so much and yet it was never enough. She was hungry, freezing and her throat was raw.

'Would you like some water?' the man said.

'No,' Kate Duncan replied.

'You need to drink. Take a sip and check that it's real water.'

At first she shook her head, but then other thoughts, long

forgotten memories of television shows, intruded into her fear. He had blindfolded her. Why? Because he did not want to be recognized. Maybe because he meant to let her go. Why was he giving her water? Because he wanted to keep her alive.

He had not harmed her so far, he had not hurt her yet. *You have been kidnapped, you are being held against your will and you are blindfolded. Is this not harm?*

'I'll try the water,' she murmured.

Kate took a sip and found it was plain water. She drank as much of it as she needed.

In some obscure way it seemed to please him. 'Here,' he said, 'you should have some of this candy bar.'

This time she accepted the food. She took a small nibble first, recognized the taste and ate the bar. It was sweet and nutty and meant long runs in Lincoln Park and hikes up Mount Rainier. Hot tears – weak, cowardly tears, she thought – spilled out from under the blindfold and she swallowed with difficulty.

The night was coming, the night must be coming. Where were they?

As if he had read her mind, Kate felt the comforting weight of a heavy blanket being wrapped around her.

'Please let me go.' The words escaped her lips before she could stop herself.

Chapter 43

Alice Madison turned the key in the door and let herself in. It was just before midnight and she was exhausted. Aaron had left the light on in the kitchen and she surveyed her bounty: the table was covered in plastic containers from Rachel's Thanksgiving dinner. She noticed a small one with a piece of paper inside and opened it. It was the crayon drawing of a dinosaur – green – next to a small robot – red – and it was signed with three *X*'s and a *T*.

Tommy, Madison thought. The drawing had been wrapped around a handful of misshapen home-made chocolate-chip cookies. She ate one then found the box with the latkes, opened it, broke a piece off and replaced the lid. Too good to waste while she was asleep on her feet.

Madison showered in the guest bathroom, not to wake Aaron, and then – warm and still a little damp – she slipped under the duvet. He turned towards her and put one arm around her.

'You're home,' he mumbled.

'Yes,' she whispered, though he had already dropped off.

Madison couldn't stop thinking of Travis and his dog and Father O'Reilly's warning. She couldn't stop thinking of that one name.

After a while fatigue won over her rambling mind and she began
to fall asleep.

Joe.

Kate Duncan woke up with a start. She must have dozed off for a
few minutes and a peculiar rasping sound had startled her. There
had been more water, more food, and the blanket was still wrapped
around her, but the man had not answered her questions. He had
wandered across the darkness of her blindfold and listened to her
giving him a stilted version of her life with ever increasing details.
Nothing made sense to her anymore.

'Good, you're awake,' he said. 'One more time, tell me about
you, dear.' The words were courteous but the tone demanded her
compliance.

Was this going to be her private hell? Built and staffed specifically
for her?

The man was doing something: she could hear the rustling, scrap-
ing, splashing of something. There was purpose in what he was
doing and that simple notion filled her with dumb, animal terror.
She thought of Matthew and how he had died.

'My name is Katherine Angela Duncan. Everyone calls me Kate. I
was born in Nashville, Tennessee. I went to college at the University
of Alabama in Tuscaloosa and at UW, where I met my husband. I . . .
I work in the legal department of a pharmaceutical company. I enjoy
running, meeting with friends, I enjoy cooking. When I was little, I
had a dog called Jimbo – a golden Lab. My parents are called Douglas
and Lisa, they live in Nashville and I'm their only child.

'When I was five, I spilled strawberry soda on my father's favorite
chair and I cried about it. I used to play the violin in school and I
was a cheerleader. I b-broke my left arm once during cheerleading

practice and everybody in the class signed the cast. I kept it for years and I only lost it when I moved to my college dorm.

'My favorite film is *Toy Story*, my favorite color is blue. I tell people I'm allergic to dairy but it's not true, I just don't like it. When I first moved to Seattle I hated it, but then I met Matthew and everything changed. He . . . he . . . was killed last week. He was m-murdered in our home—' Kate stopped.

Suddenly it was impossible to speak as her teeth chattered and she trembled against the ties that bound her to the chair. She felt him come close and when the blindfold came off, the chilly air was harsh against her face and she yearned for the warmth and the protection of the fabric.

Kate Duncan blinked.

A storm lamp had been hooked onto a peg on a bare wall. She turned left and right. All the walls around her were bare brick – old and almost taken over by moss. It was a space no bigger than her walk-in closet at home and it had a dirt floor. She looked up: the ceiling was wooden planks and corrugated iron, ten feet up. The man was behind her and Kate tried to turn her head to see him. She felt him grab the chair and turn it around one hundred and eighty degrees.

She saw what he had been doing.

The man she knew as Detective Norton still wore the deerstalker hat but the glasses had come off and she noticed that he had no eyebrows. He regarded her with a half-smile, the kind you give a friend after a long and challenging ordeal you managed to get through together. Behind the man stood the fourth wall and the narrow door in it had already been more than half bricked up. His eyes reflected the light of the lamp in gold flecks.

'See what you made me do?' he said.

Chapter 44

The man was tired. There was no question about it: this had been his most ambitious project to date and it was definitely something that made him proud. Even though each venture had been chosen with enormous care and in the execution he had always paid attention to every exquisite detail – why do anything otherwise? – he knew even now, as he finished bricking up the door, that he would be looking back on this as his favorite adventure. It had paid back his attention and his diligence in ways that he couldn't even have imagined when he had begun.

The woman was crying out now, but he had stopped listening. And in a few seconds he would stop hearing her altogether as the last brick completed the wall. He had left her the lamp and the blanket. Of course, she was still tied to the chair but that set-up should give her some time. He hated the idea of her life being cut short by something as mundane as hypothermia.

The last brick slid in and the man looked around. This place was his very own private miracle.

The man walked back to the van – he had changed vehicles in an underground car park after the sedative had taken effect – and cleaned up after himself. *Be wary, be ready, be safe.* Candy-bar wrappers and bottles of water ended up in a plastic bag thrown into the back, together with anything else that might carry his fingerprints.

He had been very careful while he was in the chamber with the woman and he knew it would pay off. She had seen his face, but so what? Not even the birds could hear her and she wouldn't last long out here.

The man made sure everything had been cleaned up before he extinguished the second storm lamp and climbed into the van. Further and further behind him, a voice might have been calling out.

The drive back to Seattle would be fast at that time of night and the man cranked on the heating in the van. It had been interesting to listen to the woman, to the way she had tried to present herself to him – as if it made a difference. A little bio that hopefully would save her life: Jimbo and strawberry soda. As most people did, she had completely missed the point. Her life, he reflected, was lost the second she had stepped into his car.

No, actually, her life was already lost months ago, the first time he had seen her.

The rain had stopped a while earlier and strands of cloud were blowing east. He wound down the window to seek out a scrap of open sky and he did not see the elk in the middle of the road. It was a bull and the van caught it straight on, all three hundred and twenty kilos of it.

The van skidded on the wet road as the animal crashed through the windshield. It turned over three times before it stopped upside down in a ditch, tires rolling and steam rising.

After the screech and the grinding of metal against concrete, silence fell again on the empty road.

Chapter 45

Alice Madison was at her desk when her cell started vibrating. It was an unknown number.

'Madison,' she said as she picked up.

'It's Annie Collins, I'm Kate Duncan's friend.' The woman's voice was on the edge of panic.

'Hello, what can I—?'

'Kate left yesterday morning with your detective,' Annie said. 'I just called her cell to see what time she was coming back today and a trooper picked up and he said that Kate's cell was on the body of a man who died in a car accident late last night. I called the cousins and she had never arrived there. They told me she'd sent them a text message yesterday morning telling them that she felt sick and that she was going to stay here and sleep all day instead. Where is she, Detective? What happened to her?'

Madison had stood up in the middle of the call and her eyes went to the round clock on the wall. 'What time did she leave yesterday?' she said.

'About nine thirty in the morning.'

'Did you see the detective who picked her up? Can you describe him to me?'

'Tall, blond hair, late thirties.'

Madison checked the time. Kate Duncan had been kidnapped over twenty-fours ago. Detective Lorenzo Norton was short, stocky and dark.

'Do you remember what car the man who picked her up was driving?'

'Oh God . . . Oh God.'

'Annie, I need you to listen to me. Annie?'

Kate Duncan woke up. It didn't feel possible that she had fallen asleep, and yet she had. Coming back to consciousness was the most awful dream. The man had looked straight at her and said, 'See what you made me do.' And then he had left her there.

She turned her head as much as she could, left and right. He had left her there to die. The lamp was still going and the blanket was still around her but he had left her to die, buried alive. *Fuck him and his blanket. Fuck him.* Kate Duncan howled with fear and rage. She struggled against the ropes and rocked back and forth, trying to loosen them. She shouted for help. She shouted for anybody. She completely lost it and bounced on the chair, screaming at the top of her lungs.

'Come back here! Come back here, you bastard!'

And yet a part of her knew that she had drunk his water and eaten the food he had given her. Where was her courage then?

Her breathing came in painful rasps and she listened out. Nothing but birds – and only a few of those at that. She looked up. There were gaps and chinks of light in the ceiling. However, it was too high and she'd never reach it, even if she could stand on the chair.

She shifted and tried to stand up. If she could break the chair, then at least she would be free. One thing at a time. She had to untie herself first and then she'd work out how to get out. A reedy voice told her to take a good look around. Those were bricks, it said: they might be old and covered in green slime but they were bricks, all the way up to ten feet, and they were not going to let her out until she was dead. And maybe not even then. She was in a small hut without windows, without doors and with no way of getting to the roof.

Kate Duncan closed her eyes and started rocking and trying to stand up. The blanket fell off and she pushed hard just as something gave way and one of the chair legs broke. The chair pitched forward and Kate managed to shift to one side and catch most of the blow with her shoulder. Only most of it, though. The side of her head hit the dirt and she passed out.

'Please, Officer, tell me as much as you can about the car accident,' Madison said. Around her the room had exploded into the disciplined chaos of a kidnapping alert. There were procedures and there was training, but a hostage situation was not something that Madison ever wanted to get used to – even if she had had some experience in the past. She cleared her mind and shoved her apprehension to one side. She would be no good to Kate Duncan if she let it scramble her thinking.

'It was called in at about 3 a.m. this morning,' the trooper said. 'A driver went past and saw the van in a ditch. Didn't have to walk far to find the body. Called emergency services and we turned up. Nothing could be done, unfortunately. He was dead a few hours before we ever got there.'

'There might have been another person in the van . . .'

'No, ma'am. We searched the vehicle and all around it and the only other creature there was a bull elk that I believe caused the accident. The driver braked at the very last second – you can see the skid marks all over the road – but it was too late.'

'Are you sure?'

'It's not my first car wreck, Detective.'

'Okay, where is the vehicle? Where is the body of the driver and all he had with him?'

'What is this about?'

'The man who died,' Madison said, 'we think he had kidnapped a woman early yesterday morning and we don't know where she is or what he has done with her. I need you to treat his van like a crime scene – you cannot let anyone touch his body.'

'He's in the funeral home.'

'That's very useful, but please just wait for us to come over. We need to process the body.'

'Ma'am, we don't even know his name.'

'We're working on that too, Officer, believe me,' Madison said.

By the time Brown left an inch of tire rubber on the cement as he drove out of the precinct parking lot, Lieutenant Fynn was already on a conference call coordinating the search with the King County Sheriff Department, the State Patrol and Search and Rescue. The Hostage Rescue Team were also ready to deploy. But if the man who had died worked alone – and there was every reason to believe that he did – Kate Duncan had been left on her own too, locked up or tied up somewhere, and she needed finding more than anything else.

There was another possibility, of course: the man who had taken her had already killed her and disposed of her body and the elk met him as he was happily driving home to a cup of cocoa. Madison did not want to think about that. For her, Kate Duncan would be alive until she had seen for herself otherwise.

Lieutenant Fynn had caught his ten minutes of hell from the Chief about why the woman's security had been so shoddy.

Fynn had replied that there had been no security at all, because at no time had she been considered to be in actual peril. And if she had been, it wouldn't have been one detective on his day off who was going to escort her, would it? Norton was just doing a favor for one of Fynn's people because the woman was jumpy. Even the whole incident on the ferry a few nights earlier had turned out to be nothing. If anyone had wanted to take her, then they could have.

The Chief had reluctantly agreed and each had rung off silently berating the other.

'Madison, I don't know what to say,' Lorenzo Norton said to her. The cell phone was pressed to her ear as they flew east on the Murrow Memorial Bridge on I-90.

'Renzo, what happened?'

'I got a call at home, the night before last, this woman says that she's Kate Duncan and thanks me very much but she has decided to stay put because she doesn't feel like leaving the house. There's, like, kids and television in the background and she sounded okay. Look, the way you told me, it was just a way of making her feel comfortable and she wasn't really in any danger.'

'I know, I know.'

'So I thought, she's going to stay home, she's going to be fine.'

'I'm sorry I got you involved, Renzo, it's not your fault.'

'Damn, Madison. And this guy is dead?'

'Looks like it.'

'Who called me? Who made the call?'

'We don't know yet, but this guy was a computer whizz. He could have used voice changer software and the background noise was there to make it blend in.'

'I'm sorry.'

'No way you could have known.'

'Is there anything I can do? Shall I come in?'

'My boss has got half the state resources mobilized on it. I'll keep you posted.' Madison hit a number on speed dial. 'Sorensen,' she said, 'where are you?'

'Right behind you,' Amy Sorensen replied, and the truck behind Brown and Madison flashed its headlights.

'We need to get ALPR on board,' she said.

The Automatic License Plate Recognition technology was invaluable.

'I know – and I did – but guess what? Today the system is fighting a virus that was downloaded in the last couple of days.'

'Joe?'

'Could be.'

Madison rang off. 'He's been covering his tracks. What the hell was he doing, anyway, driving back to Seattle in the middle of the night?' she said to Brown. 'Where had he gone?'

'Fuel gage can tell us something about that.'

Madison nodded. From everything she had learnt about him, the man had been meticulous to the point of fastidiousness: if, yesterday, he had begun the day going for a long ride, the sonofabitch would have had a full tank of gas. They could check how much was left when he had the accident and try to determine the distance traveled. It was one flimsy thing and it felt meager next to the width and breadth of Washington State.

'Sarge,' Madison said as something occurred to her. 'He changed cars, right? Annie Collins couldn't remember what make it was but it was definitely a car, not a van, and it was a dark color. Now, when she got into that car Kate Duncan believed that they were going downtown to catch a ferry. So he must have switched cars before it became obvious that they were driving out of town, otherwise she would have wondered where they were going. He must have tied her up, or incapacitated her somehow, and it's easier to throw someone in the back of a van than in the boot of a car.'

There was another thought, though, and Madison tried not to dwell on it: a van is roomier, so if he was carrying tools for whatever he wanted to do with her he would have needed a van.

'A car park on the way from Montlake to downtown,' said Brown, 'and a vehicle that has been left there since yesterday morning after 9 a.m. Let's get it to patrol.'

Madison called it in to the precinct.

He might have left ID in the car, and any ID might lead them to his home address. Somewhere – somehow – he must have left them a breadcrumb trail to follow back to Kate Duncan.

The landscape was a misty blur. It was the first moment of quiet she'd had since Annie Collins had called. The first chance she'd had to consider the fact that she would not get to find the killer and arrest him, to charge him with fifteen murders and see him go to prison for the rest of his life.

If it was Joe lying on a funeral home's table, the game had changed.

Madison gazed up at the sky: she didn't know where the woman was, and couldn't make a guess at her surroundings, but she prayed for a dry, mild streak that would keep her alive until they found her.

*

Clifford's Funeral Home was white with a colonial feel to it, more of a small country club than a mortuary. A County Sheriff's deputy was stomping his feet as he waited for them. When he clocked them, he waved them in as if they were a plane coming in to land.

Brown and Madison walked in, followed by Sorensen – two of her officers had taken the Crime Scene unit's recovery truck straight to the place of the accident.

The hall was busy with visitors for one of the other current residents but the detectives were ushered through a corridor on one side and towards the back room, where the body had been laid out for them.

'I understand that this is a sensitive situation,' the funeral director said, stopping with his hand on the door handle. He wore a suit of a discreet shade of charcoal and had introduced himself as Perry, which could have been a name or a surname. Madison didn't know and, frankly, didn't care.

'Yes, it is,' Brown replied.

'You see, there's a law: we are required to either refrigerate or embalm the deceased immediately. And there cannot be a viewing without embalming.'

'This is not a viewing,' Brown said. 'The King County Medical Examiner is on his way and he'll take over as soon as he gets here. He won't be happy if he finds you've embalmed his suspect and washed away all the evidence.'

'I only thought I should mention it so we are all on the same page,' Perry said. 'Here at Clifford's we take care of all the deceased, whoever they are and however they came to be with us.'

'And we're grateful that you do,' Brown said.

It was a bright room with windows on two sides and gleaming steel all around. It felt softer than Dr Fellman's underground autopsy rooms – maybe because there was sky and trees in the windows. In the center of it, on a gurney, a body lay inside a black body bag.

Without speaking, Brown, Madison and Sorensen all took out their kits and slipped on their latex gloves.

'Here we go,' Sorensen said as she began to pull down the bag's zipper.

They had no idea how much damage the accident had made, what kind of injuries they would find. Sorensen kept the sides closed until the zipper had run its length and then very gently parted them.

Madison braced herself.

His eyes were closed and the skin on his shaved scalp was pale marble. Blood had trickled from a corner of his mouth into the collar of his thick mountain coat but that was the only visible damage. A blurred image came back to her, a yellow windbreaker.

'I've seen him before,' she said. 'He was on the ferry the other night. He walked out right in front of us.'

A bald man carrying a folding bicycle.

Madison took a photograph with the camera in her phone and mailed it to Spencer while Sorensen took pictures with her own CSU camera.

'He shaves his eyebrows too,' Madison said.

There was something unfinished in his features because of it, as if he was still in the process of becoming a complete human being.

'Less DNA evidence,' Sorensen replied.

The troopers had already checked for ID but she patted his pockets, careful not to dislodge anything from the fabric.

'Coat, shoes, hands,' Sorensen instructed Brown and Madison.

The man's coat and his jeans had been spattered with mud – the soles of his hiking boots were caked in it. Madison crouched down and examined his fingernails without touching the hands. 'They look grimy – not just dirty, really heavy-work grimy – and I can see dried mud on the fingers too.'

'Boots have one inch of it all around the sole, seems pretty fresh. He was walking around outdoors for a while. And there's strands of grass too,' Brown said.

'Look but don't touch,' the CSU investigator admonished them as she scraped some dried mud from the edge of the coat into a container.

He looked like someone who could walk through a shopping mall and no one would ever remember seeing him. Madison thought she should feel something as she stood so close to him – knowing who he was and what he had done – but there was nothing there. He was an absence now. In the slack mouth that rigor was beginning to stiffen, in the turn of the head on the table, there was nothing left there of the man.

Sorensen pushed up his eyelids. 'Not wearing contact lenses, and his eyes are not blue.'

Under the cloudiness that was starting to form, the man's eyes were hazel-gold. A bald man with tawny eyes. No wonder their sketches of the dark-haired, blue-eyed fake engineer had tanked. She texted the detail to Spencer, who acknowledged it. They had to get new photofits out to the public.

Throughout the checks a monologue was running in Madison's mind.

Is there blood on his clothing, aside from the collar? Are there any spatters of blood not his own? No, I don't see any. It doesn't mean he has not harmed her. Mud and grass could mean woods. Has he taken her somewhere isolated in the middle of a forest? Why? What happened there? Did he mean to go back to her? Has he left her there for a while but meant to return? Mud and grass. Mud and grass and no blood. Has she been left indoors or outdoors?

What was the weather report this morning? How long can she survive if she's been left injured outdoors? Are we sure there's no other blood on his clothing? Low temperatures can help keep somebody alive who's been injured, but only for a short time. Mud and grass and no blood.

'There's some kind of dark red powder smudged all over the coat . . . see?' Sorensen pointed at a few smears that were hard to see unless you were standing in the right place.

'Powder?' Brown said.

The deputy leant forward with his hands in his pockets, mindful of the invisible perimeter around Sorensen and the body. 'That's not powder, ma'am, it's brick.'

'Excuse me?' Sorensen turned.

'Happened to me last summer when I was building a wall in my garden. The bricks were old, see, they hadn't been kept as they should have been and some of them were crumbling a little. They left smears just like those.'

Sorensen dug out her cell from her bag. 'Do you have the list of every item he had in the van?' she said when she got through to her investigator. 'Look out for anything he might have stuffed in the small spaces.'

Somewhere nearby a recording of a hymn Madison didn't know had started playing as the day of the funeral home continued as normal.

The deputy seemed to be equally proud and embarrassed to have contributed something useful to the proceedings.

Madison's eyes traveled to the face of the man lying between them. Something told her he would have been pleased with the fuss, delighted by their efforts and sure that he had bested them.

Sorensen nodded. 'Thanks,' she said into the phone and rang off. 'It's not mud,' she continued, pointing at the splashes on the coat's sleeves and front. 'It's mortar. He was building a wall. There were a couple of empty bags of all-purpose, fast-setting mortar in a garbage bag in the van.' She let them take it in before she went on. 'But some good news too: a few empty bottles of water, some with lipstick traces on the rim, and candy-bar wrappers.'

He had given her water. He had kept her alive.

Kate Duncan woke up and the first impression was that everything hurt. The second was that her head, in fact, hurt more than anything else. She was lying on the ground on her side, her cheek resting against the dirt floor, and her arms – still tied to the chair – were pulled awkwardly behind her. The middle of her chest felt hot and so did the back of her neck. It was comforting, because the rest of her body was cold and stiff, even though she knew she might be getting sick.

Her eyes were gritty with sleep and tears as she blinked a couple of times. Her breath came out in a small white puff and she inhaled deeply. Nothing wrong with her breathing. Nothing broken, nothing sprained. She whimpered and a new tear rolled down her cheek as she righted herself. She had no other option: she had to break the chair because she couldn't sit on it now. And she couldn't stand, crouched as she was, for any length of time. The glow from the lamp was growing fainter and soon – she knew – all that she'd have left would be the chinks of light from the ceiling.

Looking at the broken leg it seemed that she was tied to a plain wooden kitchen chair. She took one staggering step backward and then went forward, swinging the two hind legs against the brick wall.

Once, twice, three times.

Finally, just as she was going to give up from exhaustion and the pain from her bindings, the back of the chair cracked at the same time as the legs and the pieces of wood clattered to the ground at her feet. Slowly, careful of her sore back, Kate straightened up for the first time in over twenty-four hours. She had been tied with orange climbing rope and without the tension from the chair's structure it rested limp around her shoulders and middle. She pulled it off and threw it in a corner and stood in the middle of the chamber. Without thinking she reached for the blanket and wrapped it tight around her.

What time was it? How long had passed since she had been taken? Surely by now they must know, surely they must be searching for her.

'Hello . . .' she hollered, but it came out in a strangled rasp. Even her voice was going.

A spike of anger and frustration rose out of nowhere. She grabbed one of the chair's legs and hit the brick wall. It made a satisfying crack and she clasped it with both hands and continued hitting the wall. If she couldn't use her voice she'd use anything she could find. She wasn't going to die in this shitty little hut, she was not going to give him the satisfaction.

People were looking for her. People all over the place were looking for her. And if she couldn't get out, then she'd survive long enough for them to find her.

He wasn't coming back. There was no need to be afraid, because if he had built a wall he was not coming back for her.

See what you made me do.

She had to get out of there. Every word was a hard crack against the brick wall. She had seen his face: she would send him to prison until the end of time.

There was one last flash from the lamp. And then it died.

Chapter 46

The newscasters and the reporters had jostled for the best angle and the street in the Fauntleroy neighborhood where the Duncans resided was crowded with outside broadcast trucks. The story was prime-time gold: a brutally murdered husband and a pretty wife who had been kidnapped and whose photo could be run, over and over, next to the altered picture of the man who had supposedly taken her.

The facts of the case had been repeated, assessed, examined and speculated on endlessly. Everybody was waiting for the next revelation, for the next stage of a well-established process. There might be interviews with a rescued hostage, or interviews in Nashville with the parents of a dead hostage. Reporters had packed for either scenario.

Law enforcement agencies all along I-90 had joined in the search. Troopers and deputies had been alerted to look out for building sites and abandoned structures that might have been used by the kidnapper. What nobody was saying, but everybody was thinking, was that a little shack in the middle of the woods in the middle of a mountain and forest state would be nearly impossible to find.

By the middle of the afternoon search parties had been organized. Volunteers had started walking in long lines, calling out Kate Duncan's name and shining their torches under the darkening sky.

Detective Kyle Spencer was at his desk. He badly missed his partner, who was still on his honeymoon – a six-night package to heavenly Hawaii – because he had no one to bounce his thoughts off. Kelly and Rosario were out somewhere, trying to find the killer's car, and Lieutenant Fynn was best left alone at present.

Spencer had been in charge of producing the new image of the face of the killer from the picture and the details that Madison had sent him. It had been released to the media and some responses had already started to dribble in. He was helping to sift the useful from the pointless.

He had printed a picture of the man and tacked it next to the map by Madison's desk. The picture created had been in color, though normally they were in black and white, because the man's eyes were unusual and might help to jog the memory of the notoriously unobservant public.

Spencer spoke on the phone but his attention kept wandering back to the picture.

Sorensen and Madison had fingerprinted the man in the funeral home with a mobile device. The result had been expected but disappointing: so far, he was not in the system.

Dr Fellman was about to take over. They would get back the man's clothing and personal effects once the doctor had got him in his lab in Seattle. Fellman felt the man's chest under the mountain coat. He did not often work on victims of car accidents.

'Difficult to say with rigor coming on, but he might have broken ribs – which could have punctured lungs and other organs. Internal blood loss, suffocation and shock could have killed him. Any one of those could have done it.' He examined the man's face and hands. 'No scratches, though,' he said.

No, Madison thought, it was one of the first things she had looked out for. The man had never been close enough to Kate Duncan for her to try to defend herself.

Her cell started vibrating and she picked up.

'His name is Joseph Burnette,' Spencer said. 'Joe. B-U-R-N-E-T-T-E.'

'What . . . how?'

'An old lady Andy and I spoke to last week. She recognized him from the first picture we'd had out, knew him as a boy. I checked the details she gave us and the boy was called Joseph. His driver's license did the rest.'

'Home address?'

'Lives in Queen Anne, unmarried, freelance computer consultant, no sheet. We're on our way to the house now.'

'His name,' Madison said to the others over the man lying on the table, 'is Joe Burnette.'

Madison felt conflicted: on the one hand she wanted to be geographically close to where she knew Kate Duncan must be held, on the other Joe Burnette's home was going to be the key to decoding the man's actions. She stood with Brown in the parking lot of Clifford's funeral home and watched as Sorensen and the medical examiner started on their way back to the city. The temperature was dropping and the drizzle was turning into rain.

'I think we should go back too,' she said to Brown. 'I know she's around here somewhere, but—'

'Just get in. We have to make it to his house before CSU packs it up,' Brown said as he started the engine.

The media attention had shifted to an unassuming house in Queen Anne and when Brown turned into the right street he swore under his breath as they wove around the trucks and parked inside the police perimeter.

Madison was about to dash out but Brown made her pause.

'Remember that it's not just that we don't know *where*,' he said. 'We also have no idea as to *why*.'

Brown was right. But with their prime suspect dead it was likely that some questions would never receive an answer. Madison's priority was *where* – hopefully, the rest would come later.

They made their way into the house at the same time as Lieutenant Fynn – he took one look at the crowd of uniformed officers and plain clothes inside, declared that there were way too many people walking around his crime scene, and sent everybody out except for his own detectives and the investigator from Cybercrime.

Now it starts, Madison thought: now it really starts.

This was not a house – it was a map to where Kate Duncan was kept. This was going to be a walk through the mind of a skillful and determined killer. How did that mind reveal itself through the ordinary and the everyday? A spike of adrenaline greeted Madison as she stepped inside. Where was the breadcrumb trail?

Burnette had neighbors left and right, people who lived close enough to know what he looked like, people who would have interacted with him every day and might have come inside the house. The police were not going to find anything lying around on the ground floor for some Nosy Nellie to pick up. She gave the living room and the kitchen a cursory look – tidy, modern furnishings, a couple of mass-produced prints on the wall – and she went upstairs.

The bedroom was plain and only one bedside table had anything on it. For an instant Madison mentally ran the list of the people Burnette had killed: mostly men, but there were some women too, though there had never been a sexual element to the murders. *Small mercies.*

The guest bedroom looked like it had been lifted straight from an IKEA catalogue and felt like no one had ever so much as sat on the single bed.

Madison followed the voices of the other detectives to the back bedroom. She stopped on the threshold. Books on the walls, a framed star chart, a telescope by the large window.

Here you are, Joe.

Madison tried to ignore Spencer, Kelly, Rosario and the Lieutenant, who were all discussing something over by the desk. The star chart was quite beautiful. She looked at the scattering of planets over the black velvet background. It was not that dissimilar to the murder locations map she had by her desk. Suddenly it did not seem so lovely.

There were three monitors on the desk and a number of hard drives. Madison was computer literate but it merely served her purposes – this was a different league. She scanned the shelves: there were some fiction classics, many tomes on astronomy and stargazing, a lot of titles she believed were to do with software design but couldn't really tell. A rack of magazines stood to one side. Somewhere among those pages they would find the sources of the strips in the time capsules.

With her gloved hand Madison pulled open a drawer and then a cabinet door in the bookcase. One held spare lenses for the telescope and the other business paperwork. The ordinary, the everyday, the utterly useless.

The Cybercrime techie had gone to work on the passwords. Apparently, everything was protected by so many layers of encryption that the guy must have been as paranoid as North Korea. The investigator did his hunting digitally while everyone else took a room and gloved up.

Madison crouched by a trunk behind the study door. It was locked and when she leant her weight against it, it felt heavy and packed full. It was two feet high and four feet long, and there were no obvious keys for it anywhere.

'Anyone have a penknife?'

Madison had lost hers months earlier and never replaced it – it had been her grandfather's.

'Here,' the techie said, passing her his without turning around.

It took Madison thirty-two seconds and the lock sprung open. If it was that easy, it couldn't possibly be protecting anything valuable. She lifted the lid. Clearly, she thought, there are different interpretations of 'valuable': inside the trunk Joe Burnette had stored enough top-of-the-range audio and video recording equipment to launch his own surveillance business. Then again, wasn't that what they had been saying all along? *Killing* was his business, and these were the tools.

She rested the lid against the wall – the Crime Scene unit would descend on it soon enough.

Madison shifted her attention back to the bookcase: there were no geographical or road maps that she could see. No paperwork on the desk, or notebooks, or anywhere he might have jotted down notes. But there was the star chart.

'Sarge,' she said to Brown. 'What if he took her to a place he already knew, and knew well? We've been thinking about the murder locations map, but that's not all he did for fun.' Madison pointed at the astronomy books and the telescope. 'I bet you anything he goes out to special places to look at the stars. And those are places away from city lights and, this time of the year, pretty deserted.'

'Along I-90?'

'Must be. He was driving back towards the city, so it must be east of where the accident was.'

'We don't know how long he stayed with her.'

'No, but it had to be long enough to build a wall.'

'He only needed to brick up a door.'

'True – a few hours, then.'

'We're talking about an area reached by up to two hours driving eastwards at full speed.'

'Yes.'

'Why?'

Madison knew Brown would come to that question and hoped her answer would be good enough. 'Because it would please him,' she said. 'The next time he goes off to see a meteor shower, or whatever he goes out to look at, he can think of her nearby. And she'll be there just for him.'

They found Lieutenant Fynn in the basement. It was full of boxes, some of which might even have predated Burnette.

'That's quite a way away,' he said, after Madison had explained.

'I know, but it would make sense to him. It would bring his . . . his two interests together.'

The I-90 shot out of Washington State and reached deep into Montana after cutting through Idaho, but Burnette had only had so much time to spend with Kate Duncan.

'Are you behind this?' Fynn asked Brown.

'Yes. He wouldn't have dropped her just anyplace.'

'I don't know,' Fynn continued. 'It's possible, but—'

'Sir,' Madison interrupted him, 'so far, the search has focused on the areas along the I-90 without any specific structure. But Burnette knew where he was going, and one reason he might have been there before is stargazing. Everywhere we have looked so far today is just—'

Fynn's cell rang. He picked it up and stepped away.

Madison shifted her weight from one foot to the other. 'We don't have much time,' she whispered to Brown.

'He knows.'

Fynn terminated his call and returned to them.

'ALPR has come back online. They picked up Burnette's van traveling in the early hours of this morning near Exit 63, close to Little Kachess Lake,' he said.

It took the techie five seconds on his laptop to confirm that there was a well-known spot for stargazing right on Little Kachess Lake.

Kate Duncan huddled on the ground in a corner of the shack. The damp chill coming through the dirt floor and the walls had found her in spite of the blanket that was tucked all the way over her.

She was exhausted and her head was burning hot.

She would give herself another five minutes of rest and then she'd grope in the dark for the remains of the chair and start banging on the walls again.

There had been no helicopters overhead and no sign of life, except for the odd, muted bird call. If they were looking for her, they were doing so somewhere else far, far away.

Her mind began to slow down under the make-believe warmth of the blanket as it reached for sleep – the only comfort left.

Chapter 47

Brown and Spencer traveled in Madison's Freelander, which would turn out to be more useful if they were going to end up off road. Madison drove as fast as the law would allow her in the small convoy traveling from Seattle to Little Kachess Lake in Kittitas County.

Normally it would take about one hour and eighteen minutes to cover the seventy-five miles without traffic; Madison did it in a little over one hour. She came off at Exit 63 and doubled back, heading north towards the lakeside campsite.

Around the beams of the vehicles the forest was pitch black. The lake was long and thin, surrounded by mountains and woods, and Madison wondered how many warm bodies they could count on tonight, because as sure as heck a helicopter wouldn't see anything in the midst of all that. And thermal imaging wouldn't help either – unless Joe Burnette had left Kate Duncan in a cozy, well-heated cabin.

They arrived, changed hastily into wet-weather gear and checked in at the rally point. It had gone up fast by the side of the lake and Madison was pleased to see that it was busy with State Patrol officers, rangers and local volunteers as well.

They couldn't take anything for granted, they couldn't make any assumptions. Yes, it looked like he had recently built a wall but Kate Duncan might be in a ditch somewhere around there – injured and unconscious, and exposed to the elements.

Brown, Madison and Spencer took a square of the grid that needed searching with a group of volunteers and spread out into the dark. The forest was full of sound now and sliced through by the beams of their torches. They walked, making as much noise as possible, calling out, then stopping, listening and starting over.

The air was damp and smelled of pine and Madison prayed that she had been right. She shone her torch on the ground a few feet ahead of her, swinging it back and forth, then at waist level, moving further up the trail where the ground – covered in mossy rocks, dry leaves and ferns – dipped and rose.

Brown walked a few feet from her on one side and Spencer on the other. It was not Madison's first search and rescue, but it was the first time that it had happened when she was the primary and had chosen to pacify the hostage with a placebo security detail.

The trail widened and narrowed and then fell away behind a boulder. At some point, Brown offered her some water. She declined but he told her to just drink it already and so she did.

She checked her watch: they had been walking difficult terrain for almost an hour. Her eyes caught Brown's and she wondered if she looked just as desolate and desperate as he did.

Radio crackle burst out behind them, somebody hollered for the group to stop and, just like that, it was over.

Way past the campsite, past the area people used for stargazing, a dirt road tapered into a trail and the trail tapered into nothing.

And there, built against a boulder and nearly repossessed by the forest, stood a small brick structure with a makeshift roof and a wooden door. The ranger had opened the door and found himself looking at a wall – the mortar between the bricks was still fresh and light-colored and, in the present weather conditions, it would not dry out for days.

They had called out before, and they continued to call, but there was no answer from inside. The ranger, a six-footer, stood on the shoulders of his colleague, who was half a foot taller, and carefully shifted one of the planks that covered the roof. He shone his torch inside and the beam caught a human shape curled up in a corner.

'Could have been a little kid,' he would say later to his wife. 'Could have been a little kid at the bottom of a well.'

Madison covered the distance at a dead run, barely managing not to fall or trip over the tree roots that poked out of the ground everywhere. She followed the direction in which everyone was moving, towards the growing hub of light, while it fell to other people to check for life signs, to administer aid, to call for the air ambulance to get ready.

She broke through the assembled crowd and showed her badge to get close to the hut.

'How . . . ?' she asked a trooper who was standing by a rope ladder.

'Alive, but running a temperature and dehydrated. The medic is with her. We're winching her out of there as soon as we get set up – easier and safer than breaking down the wall.'

Madison saw the rope ladder and made a move towards it.

'Excuse me, ma'am, where do you think you're going?' The trooper had stepped out and blocked her way.

'I'm climbing in there,' Madison said.

'No, you're not. You're going to wait out here with everyone else – there's barely room for the medic.'

Madison was about to reply but three Search and Rescue officers had just arrived with a stretcher and she let them pass.

It had become a show – the *Rescue Kate Duncan from the Hut Show* – and almost everyone present felt that they could relax and congratulate themselves on a job well done because the hostage had been found alive and apparently uninjured. Madison stood by holding her breath.

When the tip of the stretcher appeared out of the empty hole that had been the roof, a huge cheer went up and even Madison had to smile. Strapped in and bundled in blankets, Kate Duncan seemed tiny.

Madison made her way to her. 'Kate?'

The woman's eyes slid over the crowd, found Madison and struggled to focus on her.

'You came,' she whispered.

Madison fell into step with the men carrying the stretcher. She bent low and spoke quietly.

'He's dead,' she said. 'He died last night. It's over. You won.' She didn't want Kate to feel that Joe Burnette had any power over her, any lingering hold.

Kate Duncan smiled. 'Stay with me,' she rasped.

Madison tossed her car keys to Brown and followed the medics.

The flight was brief. However, the patient had already fallen asleep when the chopper landed at the heliport of the Harborview Medical Center in Seattle. She had been hooked to a saline IV and Madison made sure that it didn't slip off the blanket as they hunched against the wind and the rain and hurried to carry her inside.

Kate Duncan's brother-in-law and her friend Annie were already there. Madison, shaky with exhaustion, told them the bare minimum: the kidnapper was dead, Kate was safe. The rest would have to wait.

Kate Duncan lay sleeping in a private room and Madison took one last reassuring look at her heart monitor, which beeped a strong and steady rhythm, before she made her way downstairs.

When Brown walked into the precinct a little after 3 a.m. he found Madison – still covered in mud and grime – asleep at her desk with her feet balanced on an upturned waste-basket.

The graveyard shift was all out.

'What are you still doing here?' he said.

'I wanted to make sure you got back all right,' Madison said, straightening up and stretching.

'Go home, go to bed, sleep, take a shower. Maybe not in that order.'

'I might just do that.'

Madison drove with the windows rolled down. She felt numb.

She decided that it was too late and she was too tired to make a final decision on how she should feel about the day. She limited herself to a very long, hot shower and half a latke.

She crawled into her bed and fell asleep instantly.

Jerry Lindquist shifted in his cot. He did not have access to the day's news and, even if he did, he would not have connected a fatal road accident and a successful hostage rescue to the wreck that was his life.

He had managed to identify three new residents of C Wing, one of whom might be the man who was going to kill him in the near future. And that, as things stood, represented a day well spent.

Chapter 48

Alice Madison woke up and felt the tension of the previous day in the texture of soreness all over her body. She chugged a glass of milk, pulled on some sweats and left the house. As she strode up her driveway towards the main road she thought of Coach Lewis. *Biggest mistake civilians make – they stretch before they've warmed up. Don't you go and be fools now, girls.* A civilian in her world was everyone who was not a professional athlete.

The day was overcast and the air was crisp but it lacked the harsh slap of real cold. Madison started a gentle jog to get the muscles moving and the blood flowing. Joe Burnette was dead, Kate Duncan was safe. The words kept twisting and taking different shapes but it always came back to those two notions. Where would they go from there? What about the world of pain Burnette had created?

Madison ran for one hour in fast and slow segments until her lungs stung and her calves burned. Once back home she showered and found splashes of mud she had managed to miss from the night before. Her clothes from the forest ended up in the washing machine and it was a treat to spend ten minutes doing nothing more morally taxing than folding dry laundry.

When she drove over the West Seattle Bridge towards downtown, the rain started and the wind picked up.

Detective Sergeant Kevin Brown was drinking his second coffee of the day when his cell phone rang. It was Saul Garner, the lawyer from the Release Project.

'One of my clients was stabbed at breakfast today,' he said. 'His name is Lindquist, Jerry Lindquist, and he's on the list.'

There was only one list and it was the one with the names of the people that Burnette's crimes had sent to prison.

'Is he alive?'

'Yes, just about. Guards and medics got to him in time. Have you verified his case yet?'

Brown had got the message from the Crime Scene unit yesterday afternoon: all the seven cases in King County had been confirmed. Burnette's time capsules had been found in the yards of each victim's home. Including what used to be the home of Jerry and Jennifer Lindquist.

'Yes, it was confirmed yesterday.'

'Good, because we need to get him out of KCJC. He's in the hospital there, but—'

'I need to speak with him.'

'Why?'

'Because I'm the person who's going to get him out and I need to speak with him.'

'Fine, I'll see about visits.'

'The sooner, the better.'

Madison parked one block away from the Harborview Medical Center and made her way there on foot. Dr Fellman might do the autopsy on Joe Burnette today: he was going to lie on the doctor's table and still he would not give up his secrets. Madison wanted to check in on Kate Duncan before going back to Burnette's house to continue her own search. Cybercrime was still struggling against his encryption system. In the absence of their prime suspect and a confession, they would have to reconstruct each murder with whatever he had left behind.

Brown had called and told her about Lindquist. Without proper corroborative evidence all of Burnette's secondary victims – Lieutenant Fynn had come up with the name, it sounded more formal than 'scapegoats' in the press release – would stay right where they were.

Privately, Madison thought that 'scapegoats' was the right term and there was nothing secondary about what had happened to Jerry Lindquist.

Kate Duncan was sitting up in bed when Madison arrived. She looked washed out and was hooked up to an IV. An empty tray of breakfast was in front of her and on her bedside table a nurse had left a plate of home-made banana bread already sliced.

'Detective,' Kate Duncan said when she saw Madison on the threshold and extended her hand. Her voice was still a little croaky. Both hands, Madison noticed, were bandaged around the knuckles.

Madison gently squeezed the tips of her fingers. 'Did you have a good night?' she asked her.

The woman nodded. 'I woke up once but they gave me a mild sedative and I was out like a light.'

'Good,' Madison said.

In a few hours the woman might feel strong enough to give her a statement about what had happened, but right now Kate Duncan looked like she could fall asleep any moment and Madison did not want to push her.

'Someone told me that you were the one who worked out where he had taken me,' Kate Duncan said.

'Well, yes, but there was the license plate recognition technology too,' Madison replied.

'And he is dead, you have seen him?' The woman's voice had dropped to a whisper.

'I have. I saw him yesterday. He had a car accident shortly after he left you. Did he speak with you? Did he say anything that might help us to understand what he was doing?'

'He only asked me about myself. Over and over. He asked me to tell him about me, my life, what I did, my family. Over and over. He wanted details, names, stories.'

'He didn't say why?'

'No.'

'That's all?'

'Yes, that's all we talked about. And I was the only one talking.'

'And you had never seen him before?'

'Never.' The woman's eyes filled with tears and she leant back on her pillow. 'I don't know what I would have done without you.'

What this woman had gone through in the last two weeks was horrific. Madison patted her feet and stood to leave.

'It was all of us, Kate. Just get some rest. We'll deal with your statement once you feel better.'

In the corridor Madison stopped a nurse to ask what was wrong with the woman's hands.

'She wasn't going to stay locked in that awful place if she could help it,' the nurse replied. 'When she was done banging to get herself heard she just plain punched the walls. It's only superficial lacerations, don't you worry. She'll be fine in a few days.'

Madison left the hospital. She did not like at all the revelation about Burnette's questions. This was a man you did not want in your life or knowing anything at all about you. See how well it had turned out for Peter Mitchell and Henry Karasick.

Technically Madison should have had the day off, but she needed to spend more time in Burnette's house. As yet she hadn't even attempted to occupy herself with anything that was not connected to the case. Apparently, he had lived there for about five years: how much did the house know of what the man did to entertain himself?

Jerry Lindquist listened to Saul Garner and then asked him to repeat everything. Occasionally his gaze strayed to Brown, who was sitting in the other chair next to his bed, though mostly he stared at Garner.

Lindquist had a punctured lung from a stab wound to the chest, a broken arm and a number of small defensive cuts to the hands. But he was alive – at least until the inmate who had attacked him was rereleased into the general population after a period of solitary confinement. The inmate had killed two women on the outside; a broken arm and a stab wound were not going to make a dent in his sentence, and a term of isolation was probably a welcome break.

Brown showed Lindquist a few pictures of Joe Burnette – some with dark hair, one with a shaven scalp and no brows.

Lindquist examined them without speaking for a long time and then slowly, reluctantly, he shook his head.

Brown could see that he had wanted to be able to recognize the man, to give a face and a body to the ghost who had destroyed his life. However, there wasn't even the faintest glimmer of recognition.

'I've never seen this man before. And his name means nothing to me.'

'He had met one of his victims at a support group, many years ago,' Brown said. 'Did you ever go to one, even to just one meeting?'

'No, I've never been. Meetings – AA, holding hands and praying – were really not my kind of thing then.'

'And now?'

Lindquist shrugged. Everything was surreal today, starting with this cop who was telling him he knew someone else had killed his wife. 'I've been clean and sober for two years,' he said. 'If I ever get out of here, I'll just have to work out how to do without the armed guards.'

Alice Madison showed her badge to the uniformed officer at the door and walked into Joe Burnette's house. The Crime Scene unit had taken over and its officers – Sorensen, Madison noted, was not among them – were collecting, cataloguing and preserving. The computer was gone – the Cybercrime techie was continuing his offensive elsewhere – and even the telescope had a number stuck on its side ready to be packed up.

Madison looked at the bookcase, at the pattern of dust at the bottom of each shelf. It took her ten minutes to find the first book whose pages had been sheared off. It was a star atlas. She put it to one side. A cheer went up an hour later when somewhere in the basement someone found a box of empty cigar cases, ready for Burnette to fill and deliver to the next recipients.

It was odd how she felt completely justified about being there and possibly kicking a hole through the plaster and shining a torch in the space between the walls, and yet a part of her also felt like they were picking a dead man's pockets. Then again, maybe it was merely the uneasy knowledge that she was standing where he had stood, moving his books with her gloved hand, and breathing the air he had breathed.

If only they had been a little bit faster in catching on. If only they had understood more – and earlier.

After a while Madison left and went to the precinct to write reports until her eyes were ready to give up. She didn't see Brown at all and wondered how he was doing after meeting Jerry Lindquist – the secondary victim.

Madison picked up a slice of pizza from the carton and bit into it. In terms of a quick, sharp fix of temporary bliss tomatoes and anchovies did it just fine for her. Aaron had arrived with two large cartons of takeout and Madison had opened a bottle of white wine.

They had not bothered with propriety either. Instead, they'd slumped on the sofa and grasped each slice from the cardboard box, holding it over a plate. Madison poked a log in the fire and it hissed back at her.

'Is it over?' Aaron said.

'Yes and no,' she replied. 'Yes, in the sense that the man is dead. No, because there is so much we don't know about how he operated, how he chose his victims, how he got so good at what he was doing.'

'*Good?*'

'Well, yes, we didn't catch up with him for seven years, and we're not completely sure that Mitchell was the first. We think that he was, but there might have been something else that escalated Burnette's behavior and it's important that we know.'

'Why? If he's dead . . .'

Madison turned the question around in her mind. 'The more we know, the faster we can help the other victims and the better we can make sure it doesn't happen again.'

'I'm glad he's dead, the things he's done. They're . . . unspeakable.'

'I'm not glad. An elk through the windshield is not justice.'

'I'm glad he's dead. Because now you don't have to go after him.'

Madison took a sip of wine.

'And you're not glad,' Aaron continued. 'Because you wanted to – and now you can't.'

'All in all, the elk did a better job than we'd done.'

'How many people did he . . . ?'

'Killed – fifteen. Convicted for his crimes – twelve, one of whom took his life in prison.'

'Doesn't it bother you—?'

'Of course it bothers me.'

'No, I mean, doesn't it bother you to be surrounded by that . . . that . . . awfulness every day?'

Madison turned to him. In the glow of the fire he was golden and beautiful and so badly wanted her to say that, yes, the horror was too much.

'Sometimes it is – but that's when I'm not careful, when I bring it home with me. You have to deal with it like it's radioactive.'

Aaron nodded. He put down his plate and put his arm around Madison and held her.

'He had locked her in a hut near a place where he goes with his telescope to look at the stars,' she said. It was as if she was blundering forward but had to speak, whatever the cost. 'He put her there so that he could think of her when he was looking up at the heavens in all their beauty. And I knew where she was because that's what I would have done, if I were him.'

For a moment there was only the crackle of the fire. Then she felt Aaron's arm fall away from her shoulders as he stood and bent to pick up the empty cartons. 'Would you like some hot chocolate?' He smiled a little. 'I make great hot chocolate.'

'That would be lovely,' she replied, and tried not to see how sad he looked, how lost.

They went to bed soon after and Madison wondered how many weeks and how many words it would take to say what they needed to say to each other – whether five years would not be long enough, and that it was already over.

As they lay in the dark he turned to her. 'You know how when people stop seeing each other somebody always loses friends or the other person's family?'

Only Aaron's gentle heart could make those words sound consoling.

'Yes,' Madison replied.

'Well, in our case my family will keep *you* and chuck me out to the wolves. On top of which they'll tell me every day for the rest of my life that I'm an idiot.'

'I don't think you're an idiot.'

'I just . . .'

'I know.'

'I'm so sorry.'

'I know.'

They fell asleep with her hand on his cheek.

Chapter 49

Madison's cell pinged in the half-gloom of the very early morning and she automatically reached for it.

'Madison,' she said, her voice still rough with sleep.

'Good morning, Detective, the informant is meeting the OPA investigator in a couple of hours. I know where and when.'

John Cameron. Madison's brain staggered and lurched forward. 'Are you sure?'

'Would I be calling you if I wasn't?'

'Tell me where.'

'I don't think so. I'll pick you up from home in one hour.'

The line went dead.

She was going to catch him. She was going to catch Chris Kelly being the two-faced asshole that she had always known he was.

And then?

The truth was that she could not let him know that she had seen him – otherwise OPA would know that she was aware of their investigation.

Fuck it.

She needed to see Kelly in play. The rest she would work out later.

She showered, made coffee and brought a mug to Aaron in bed. He had watched her quietly. Madison leant forward and kissed him on the brow, then she reached under the bed for her shoulder holster with the Glock and the smaller one for her ankle.

John Cameron was waiting for her in a Black Chevrolet Suburban with tinted windows at the top of her driveway.

'I thought you were a Ford Explorer kind of guy,' she said.

'The meeting has been moved up, Detective. Let's skip the wry.'

Madison had not seen John Cameron in daylight for a while. He looked drawn and had the kind of tan you don't pick up in Seattle in late November. The familiar knot of ice was in its place in the pit of her stomach, as it always was when she was anywhere near him.

'Thank you for what you did in LA,' she said as they sped through her neighborhood.

The words tasted odd on her lips. Cameron did not reply.

It didn't escape her sense of the absurd that she was on her way to spy on a cop while being driven by a criminal. 'What do you know about this meeting?' she said.

'I know where and when.'

'Are you going to share that, or is it a secret?'

'OPA has been cultivating their informant for months,' Cameron said, ignoring her question, 'and they're handling the whole thing like it's made of spun glass. Do you know Lieutenant Richards?'

'Pit Bull Richards? Yes, I know him. We met years ago.'

'He's in charge of it.'

Wonderful, Madison thought. The last time they'd met she was still a probie in uniform, he's asked her to keep an eye on her training officer and she'd told him to stick it.

'Discovery Park,' Cameron said and pointed at a bag in the back.

Inside Madison found a couple of pairs of binoculars. 'I hope you can lip-read.'

The Sunday morning traffic was light and they made good time towards the promontory that stretched out towards Bainbridge Island and was cut off from Ballard by the locks and Salmon Bay.

'What happened to Agent Parker in LA?' Madison asked, and she wasn't sure whether she'd get an answer or not.

'Greed, for the most part,' Cameron replied. Then he added, 'He walked in on the wrong people and got shot for his troubles. I hear they want to give him a medal.'

Madison didn't know how to feel about his death.

'It's up to you what you do with this,' Cameron said as he drove into the park. 'And if your inclination is towards facing the inform-ant, I wouldn't hold it against you. However, you might pause for a moment and reflect on how valuable it would be for you to hold this knowledge and do nothing about it.'

Madison bristled. She was getting a strategy lecture from John Cameron.

'I haven't decided yet,' she conceded. 'There's a lot of history here. Chris Kelly has been difficult from the start. Difficult I can live with, but this . . . this is something else.'

Cameron had found a parking spot in a corner of the large lot, behind a number of people carriers. On the far side Madison spotted the metallic gray Lexus, and even without binoculars she could see Pit Bull Richards inside it. He'd gotten older, sure, but it was him all right. He had parked in the middle of an empty stretch and was reading a newspaper.

Cameron checked his watch. Something prickled Madison's scalp and suddenly she just wanted out of the car.

'Stay where you are,' Cameron said.

A burgundy Honda arrived and slid into the space next to the Lexus. Madison stiffened. Behind the tinted windows, and at that distance, she knew they were practically invisible. She leant back into her seat, her eyes fixed on the new car, and she tried to see beyond the windshield reflection. There was no need for it: as the engine and the lights cut off, the driver came out, opened the passenger door of the Lexus and sat down next to Richards.

It was not Chris Kelly.

Madison turned to Cameron. 'You knew?'

He nodded. 'Some things you have to see for yourself.'

Stacey Roberts was tanned – a week in Hawaii would do that – and her name, Madison corrected herself, was Stacey Dunne now.

'Last Sunday she got married to Andy Dunne from my unit. He's a friend,' she said. 'I've known Stacey for years.' Madison wanted to say that she'd even gone to her bachelorette party, but the words dried up.

'I know,' Cameron replied.

Had Stacey asked Andy about her, about the Salinger case, about the things Madison had told Andy and Spencer that had never made it into the official reports? What had he told her?

'Is there any question that she might be meeting Richards for another reason? Quite frankly, if they were having an affair it would be tough for Andy but it would work out a hell of a lot better for me.' It was a bad joke and she knew that Cameron wouldn't have brought her here unless his information was solid.

Madison watched in silence as Stacey spent twenty minutes with Richards and then left. He followed her out of the park one minute later.

'I know what they've talked about,' Cameron said to Madison as she stared at the spaces where the cars had been. When she didn't reply, he continued. 'He just told her that they're shutting down the investigation because they see no obvious reason to continue it.'

Madison snapped. 'Why did you bring me here? What did you—?'

'Whatcom County, Detective.'

She had saved his life in a field in Whatcom County almost two years earlier. Madison remembered a conversation with Agent Parker.

'Is he the kind of person who would consider that a debt?'

'I have no idea what kind of person John Cameron is.'

Cameron drove her back downtown and dropped her off on the corner of Stewart and 1st Avenue. Between the buildings Puget Sound looked like a sheer slate and Madison hurried towards Pike Place Market, where she had arranged to meet Brown. She had to tell him – if nothing else, because she had absolutely no idea what to do. And, given the investigation had been shut down, he was out of danger.

Madison walked into the Athenian Inn and saw Brown sitting at the bar, listening on his cell phone.

He stood when he saw her. 'Cybercrime has just cracked the encryption system.'

His car was parked nearby and as the engine came to life he passed Madison the tabloid newspaper he had folded neatly in his pocket. Kate Duncan had made the cover in a smallish square picture under the headline.

Most of the page was taken up by an image of the inside of the hut where she had been imprisoned. Madison had never seen it. The photograph must have been taken immediately after the woman had been rescued. Bright lights were shining into what looked like a brick pit nearly overrun by foliage and moss. Shards of wood on the dirt floor were broken in dozens of pieces and deep grooves had been carved out of the bricks.

Madison remembered Kate Duncan's bandaged hands and realized that some of the dark shadows on the walls must be her blood.

Alice Madison walked into the Harborview Medical Center at 10 p.m. and the bustle of visiting hours was done for the day. She waited until the nurses at the station were busy with something, then she headed for Kate Duncan's room and walked in without knocking. The lights were low and the woman was resting with her eyes closed.

Madison sat in the chair next to her. It creaked slightly and Kate Duncan opened her eyes.

She saw Madison and reached for the switch. 'Detective,' she said.

In the light Madison could see that a night and a day of rest had done her good. Her color was better and her voice had improved too. Madison, on the other hand, looked dreadful.

'Are you all right?' Kate Duncan asked her.

'No,' Madison replied and her eyes wouldn't settle on anything. She felt nauseous. 'I have some good news. We have found how Burnette chose his victims.'

'How?'

'Online. He found them online. Trawling for people who were looking for help, who needed to share their troubles with others who would understand. Instead, they found him. Alcoholics, people with addictions to drugs of all kinds, with aggression and control issues.'

Kate Duncan had paled.

'That's how he found you,' Madison continued. When the woman opened her mouth to object, she raised her hand. 'Please don't deny it. We've had your laptop since CSU processed your house, and it is not encrypted. It was easy to find your search history, your conversations on the anger management forum—'

'How dare you?' The slight woman had sat up straight and something inside her had gone rigid.

Madison could have done with a really strong drink just then. 'Joe Burnette liked you very, very much indeed. He liked how you spoke about what it felt like to be physically abusive towards Matthew, how you had been for years, and that you wanted to stop but you found it difficult. He liked how you lived in a house with a big garden around it and he thought you would be perfect for his game.'

'What game?'

'The night Matthew was killed, Joe Burnette sent you an email – you deleted it before we got there, but it wasn't hard to recover it. It was anonymous and it said that your husband was having an affair and you should check his golf bag. What was in the golf bag? Underwear from an imaginary mistress? Whatever it was, he had put it there himself when he had pretended to be an HVAC engineer.

'But you know what the kicker is? You never run with your cell – it's in the notes he made on you. You were supposed to go running, come home and find Matthew dead by his hand. Once we got there *we* would have found the email, your history of abusive behavior – two broken fingers, a broken ulna. We would have found out about your rages, your obsession with control. It would have been a strong case. But you were late and you saw the message and you confronted your husband.'

'I have no idea . . . you can't possibly believe . . .'

'I don't need to believe. We have the recording. Burnette recorded you.'

'No, it's a mistake. He must have faked it.'

'It took us the whole day to find it.'

'No.'

'It took us the whole day to find it and, once we had it, we had to listen to it.'

'No.'

'*See what you made me do.*'

Kate Duncan's mouth was a hard line.

'That's what you said after you killed him.'

The cuff went around the delicate wrist faster than the woman could move, its twin locked shut around the bar on the side of the bed. Madison stood up and read Kate Duncan her rights. The woman shrieked and lunged at her but Madison was out of her reach. The cuff rattled and banged as Kate Duncan strained to reach her.

'Confess, don't confess, I don't care,' Madison said. 'But you should know that we have the clothes you wore when you killed him and the jewelry you wanted us to believe the killer had stolen. You killed Matthew, you changed your clothes, you went running. But Burnette was very thorough: he followed you and he picked them up from the trash cans in Lincoln Park.'

The woman struggled to calm her breathing, to speak slowly and clearly, her Southern accent more pronounced now. 'You don't understand, he provoked me. It was an accident. I tried to revive him.'

Madison saw Kate Duncan in the back of the ambulance as she told them how she had found her husband's body – her voice shaking but her words surprisingly clear and sharp. She saw her in her friend's home after Joe Burnette had followed her in the gardens and she had looked terrified – she must have been, questioning if that was the person who had sent her the email and whether he'd go to the police. Madison remembered her the night of the ferry

– scared and confused because she did not understand what her stalker wanted. After a sudden bereavement people are moved by odd things: grief could be triggered by a word, a name or a memory. Kate Duncan's tears, though, had been the product of anger and fear – they had just been too blind to see it.

Madison did not know what she was looking at – what the creature on the bed pleading with her really was – and she imagined the slight woman hitting the leg of a wooden chair against the brick wall, over and over, in a wave of fury until it was nothing but splinters. *Devil's work done by human hands.* Burnette had been hiding inside that empty darkness, waiting for her.

No, not the Devil's work, Madison thought, just us and our messes.

'I think he was trying to stop,' the Cybercrime investigator had said on the speaker phone earlier in the day.

Brown had made the call as soon as they got to the detectives' room.

'What do you mean?' Brown said.

'I've been looking at his searches and all he was interested in was online support groups for anger management, alcoholism, personality disorders and every addiction possible. He spent all his time online in these forums.'

Online. Things had moved on from Father O'Reilly and his church basement.

'Was he in touch with anybody specifically?' Brown said.

'Sure, quite a few people.'

'Any names you recognize?'

'They're all anonymous. Everyone has a handle.'

'Any doctors? Anyone moderating the forums?'

'He's only been talking to the other visitors. Very supportive, actually. People poured their hearts out to him.'

'He wasn't trying to stop,' Brown said.

'He was looking for the next victim,' Madison finished the thought.

'What else did you find?' Brown asked.

'He had made documents out of the conversations with some of these people. And a lot of the hard drive's space is taken up by audio surveillance.'

'How many are we talking about?'

'Dozens. Look, I've gone into some of the conversations he had with the other people online and some of those guys had pretty serious problems. I'm going to email you some so that you can read for yourself.'

Brown called the KCJC hospital and managed to be put through to Jerry Lindquist.

'Jerry,' he said. 'I know that you told me you have never been to a support group meeting but have you ever – even once – visited a website? A forum online for people with similar problems. Even once. Did you post on it?'

There was a long stretch of quiet and then his voice came back, small and weak. 'Once. I left a message on a board. Just once. Was that how he found me?'

'It's possible.'

It was more than possible, Madison thought, it was highly probable. For someone with Joe Burnette's skills it would have been relatively easy to hack into the websites, find out which of the participants were local and follow them all the way home.

Her eyes had fallen on the newspaper.

*

Brown met Madison as she left Kate Duncan's room and walked out of the hospital with her. They left the synthetic, chemical air and emerged into a clean, freezing night.

'You're not taking this home,' Brown said, perhaps with more strength than he had himself expected. 'You're not taking this home, because it is not yours to take.'

Madison did not speak. The chill that was wrapping itself around her felt oddly welcome.

'You saved her life, and it was right that she should live,' Brown continued. 'The same stars that put her there also led you to her. And now, you leave all this here. You leave it in the precinct inside the reports. You've done right by Matthew Duncan. And that is all he could have asked of you – that and no more.'

Madison shoved her hands deep into her pockets and looked to the west, where there was no line between the water and the black sky.

'If I do, will you?' she said.

Brown shrugged. 'I'll try.'

She wanted to hug him then: he was the gold in a day of ashes.

Chapter 50

The days after Kate Duncan's arrest had their own peculiar hush, as if the whole unit was muted. Madison ran on Alki Beach after every shift, shopped at the farmer's market and cooked far too much food for one person to eat. Under the blessing of a sunny December she took out her kayak and paddled on the flat silver water between her home and Vashon Island.

By tacit agreement Aaron kept his distance and was not at Rachel's home for Hanukkah. Madison fell asleep by the fire with Tommy's head on her shoulder and a book open in her lap.

Every day she saw Andy Dunne in the detectives' room and every day she wondered what to do about Stacey. In the end, she took Brown out to the Husky Deli for a chocolate and strawberry ice cream and told him everything. As she spoke she decided that she would do nothing and say nothing to either Andy or Stacey. It would just stay in the past while the investigation stayed shut down.

Detective Sergeant Kevin Brown worked on the Burnette case for as long as it took to get every single convicted defendant out of jail and spent a lot of time with Saul Garner to that end. The day Jerry

Lindquist walked out of KCJC – with his arm in a sling and tears in his eyes – Brown met him at the gate and drove him to his sister's home in Spokane. Madison watched Brown for the scars that the Burnette case had left and knew that every hour spent helping Saul Garner was part legal process and part magical healing.

Madison saw Chris Kelly at every shift. They each did their best to avoid the other: she didn't want to think too much about either him or Stacey. They were there, they existed – like black ice and frozen mud.

Joe Burnette's notes on his past and future work were extensive. The detectives of the Homicide unit visited five homes in the Seattle area and dug up five cigar cases from their gardens. They sat with the residents in their sitting rooms and delicately explained what had almost happened to them and now never would.

Amy Sorensen carefully straightened each recovered strip of paper with her tweezers, each sliver of Joe Burnette's life: a visit to the Pacific Science Center, breakfast at The 5 Spot, groceries from Metropolitan Market. They were all that remained of his thoughts and his pleasures, what he had seen and what he had touched.

By the time she was finished, the dozens of fragments on her bench made up a huge mosaic, blank and indistinct.

Detective Kyle Spencer wanted to go home. He wanted to go home and see his wife and hug his kids. He was going to try and forget the recording they had all heard in Lieutenant Fynn's office as soon as humanly possible. If he could take a pill for it, he would. Even Andy, who had come back from Hawaii sunburnt and happy, had gone pale under the freckles.

There was one thing, though, that Spencer could do, and it would make him feel better. He rang the Cedar Grove Home for the Elderly.

He wanted Mrs Walker to know that it was her tip that had given them Joe Burnette's name and his address.

'Who's speaking?' the nurse asked.

'Detective Kyle Spencer. I visited Mrs Walker recently.'

'I remember you, Detective. I'm so sorry to have to tell you that Mrs Walker passed away on Thanksgiving.'

'But I saw her and she wasn't sick.'

'No, she wasn't. She went in her sleep after a full day with her family and her friends here.'

Spencer found himself strangely moved that there still was such a thing as passing away in one's sleep after a good, long day. He called Mrs Walker's daughter at home and explained what her mother had done and how it had saved a life.

Chapter 51

Twenty years ago and the day had been dull in the way only the days of the physically unwell can be: it had brought a combination of crushing boredom and occasional pain relieved by doctor-prescribed medicine and a single glass of wine in the evening. Edith Walker's foot was slowly improving – or so she had been told – but it was hard to tell under the cast. She had slipped on a wet spill in her own kitchen and now, at sixty-seven, she was trapped in her daughter's guestroom like a gray-haired teenager who had never left home.

Edith Walker had decided that she'd make the most of this enforced rest and learn Italian – she had always wanted to, and her French was really rather good for someone who had never left mainland USA. At school they had told her that she had a facility for languages – and so, naturally, she had disregarded them entirely and gone on to study pharmacy.

After all those years she still regretted it.

Edith did amble around the house on her crutches but mostly she sat on a stuffed, chintzy armchair near a large window that gave her an excellent view of the street. She listened to her Italian CDs, wearing headphones, read her books and watched the comings and goings of the Bellevue neighborhood.

Soon she began to see the patterns. And after the patterns she noticed the people.

There he was, the Burnette boy, with his strange gold eyes like a fox's; in the warm evenings she had often noticed the tip of a cigarette in the darkness of his open window. Mrs Walker's granddaughter liked him very much and always tried to start a conversation, but Edith was secretly glad that the boy never reciprocated. Every time something ugly happened in the street, the boy was there: an argument, the discovery of a dead cat, a broken window. There he was, watching people argue with each other, as if it were the best of times.

Edith Walker closed her eyes and listened on her headphones – she didn't understand the words yet, but she knew that one day she would.

Nel mezzo del cammin di nostra vita, mi ritrovai per una selva oscura, ché la diritta via era smarrita.

The rain had stopped a while earlier and strands of cloud were blowing east. Joe Burnette was driving fast back towards Seattle. He wound down the window, looked up into the night and did not see the elk. The accident was grinding metal and the scape of concrete.

After a few minutes, the man stirred. He found himself halfway out of the window – broken glass and blood in his mouth. He reached twice for his seat-belt lock but his hand wouldn't work. He tried to get a deep breath and failed.

There they were – his thoughts flashed – the woman in her walled prison and him, lying on the road. He coughed. She had been such a significant part of his life: the first moment he had read her words online; the first moment he had watched her run; and the shocking, exhilarating moment when he had watched her kill. He had so enjoyed taunting her and pursuing her. And now their courtship was done: now she was where she had to be because she owed him a death.

And here he was. He coughed again and his eyes did what they automatically did at night and under an open sky: he found Jupiter.

He tried to get any kind of breath and failed.

What a day he'd had, what a day.

Chapter 52

Madison drove home one evening in mid-December after running on Alki Beach and the air was so sharp it could have cut her breath in two. She toed off her trainers at the door, dropped her shopping on the kitchen table and padded to the fireplace. She was halfway through *Double Indemnity* and was planning an evening by the hearth with a glass of red and the previous day's leftovers.

Her cell pinged. She saw the caller ID and hesitated.

'Madison,' she said when she picked up.

'Would it be all right if I dropped by?' Nathan Quinn said.

'Sure,' she replied. 'When?'

'About now.'

'Okay.'

They had not spoken since the Burnette case. Madison took off the holsters and splashed cold water on her face. In terms of primping it would have to do.

She heard Quinn's car and it was a sound from other times. But, whatever he was there for that night, it was not a social visit.

She opened the door and, just as he came in, Madison realized that it was the first time they had met on their own since that day eighteen months earlier.

Quinn looked ill at ease. He had a small box in his hand and held it out to her.

'It's from Jack. He asked me to give it to you in person.'

'What is it?'

A package from John Cameron was not to be accepted lightly.

'I don't know,' Quinn said, and she believed him.

Madison took the package and placed it on her table. It was wrapped in old-fashioned brown paper and tied up with string. She undid it and revealed a cardboard box the size of a slim book. She lifted the thin lid. Inside, a line of spiky writing on a white card read: *I know you lost yours in Whatcom County.* A folding knife rested on black velvet: the handle was ebony and steel, and the blade – when Madison opened it – was simply patterned in the fashion called Damascus. It was beautiful.

There was a business card from the knife-maker's too – Ceccaldi in Paris. The knife was called Vendetta.

'He has sent me a knife and it's called Revenge,' she said.

'So it seems.'

For a moment Madison wondered whether she should accept it, and then her grandmother's teachings kicked in. 'Thank you for bringing it, it's really quite something.'

'Jack's gone.'

'Gone?'

'He left Seattle and he's not sure when he's coming back. I think he might be in Europe or in Greenland or God-knows-where.'

It occurred to Madison that she was the only person Quinn could talk to about Cameron, although that should no longer be true.

'Surely,' she said, 'he will be back for your wedding.' The words came out before she could stop them.

'Yes, he'll be back for the wedding,' Quinn said.

It shouldn't have hurt her to say it or to hear it.

'No,' Quinn sighed. 'He's not coming back for the wedding because there will not be one.'

Madison leant back against the table. She didn't want to speak, to question. She only leant back against the edge of the table and waited for Nathan Quinn's next words.

'Erica told me that she believes that some people are made for each other, that there is one person and everyone else is an adjustment. And she said that, for me, she was the adjustment. She went back to Boston the day after Thanksgiving.' Nathan Quinn's dark gaze had traveled around the room and finally came to rest on Madison. 'She was right,' he said.

John Cameron could have put the knife in the post. Hell, he could have broken into her home and left it on the table – he had done that before. Instead, he had asked Nathan Quinn to deliver it in person.

There was tension in the line of Quinn's shoulders and uncertainty in his bearing. So much time had already been wasted, the dusk and the dawn of too many days.

'Stay for dinner, Counsellor,' Madison said.

As she replaced the knife in the black velvet, the blade caught the light.

Ashes and gold.

Acknowledgments

Some of the locations in the story are fictitious because I'm reluctant to set dark deeds in a real house in a real street. Also, the various precincts and jurisdictions of the Seattle Police Department have been slightly adjusted.

I'd like to thank my partners in crime . . .

My family in Italy and my family in Atlanta for loving, reckless support.

Corinna, Francesca and Claudia Giambanco for cheerleading and prompt Spanish language assistance.

Kezia Martin and Anita Phillips, the early readers, for their enthusiasm in the face of unedited chapters, and Clair Chamberlain, for sanity and white wine.

The Berglund family in Seattle for giving Madison their home.

My mother – always.

Gerald, for all his support while I disappeared for months into the writing cave.

Stef Bierwerth, my editor, because she knows how to nurture

murder and mayhem, and the amazing team at Quercus, including Kathryn Taussig and Hannah Robinson.

Finally, there would be no book at all without Teresa Chris, my agent, who is a passionate and fearless champion.